QUEEN OF LIES
SUPERNATURALS OF DAIZLEI ACADEMY
BOOK THREE

KEL CARPENTER

Queen of Lies
Kel Carpenter

Published by Kel Carpenter
Copyright © 2018, Kel Carpenter LLC

Edited by Analisa Denny
Edited by Danielle Fine

Cover Art by Yocla

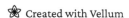 Created with Vellum

About the Author

Kel Carpenter is a master of werdz. When she's not reading or writing, she's traveling the world, lovingly pestering her co-author, and spending time with her family. She is always on the search for good tacos and the best pizza. She resides in Maryland and desperately tries to avoid the traffic.

To Matt, for showing me what a second chance is. Without you, I don't believe I could have written this.

Don't you ever tame your demons
But always keep 'em on a leash
~ Hozier

PART ONE

CHAPTER 1

THE DOOR TO THE CELLAR HUNG AT AN ODD ANGLE, THE SMELLS OF mold and musk coming from the makeshift prison I'd created. Down the steps of my dead parents' home sat Elizabeth, gagged and bound. I smiled cruelly and descended the stairway to greet her.

"It's been three days, girl. You know the drill."

I kept my tone conversational as I approached her. Dark brown hair plastered her face and neck, sticking to her skin with layers of sweat and grime. The left half of her face was smudged grey and black from the first time she'd tried to escape and I had pinned her to the floor. She hadn't tried again since, but she also sported bruised ribs the last three days, so that probably helped. Her slate grey eyes stared back at me underneath all the filth. The same hate-filled eyes that stared back at me in the mirror for over seventeen years, before Violet. I ripped the tape from her mouth and placed two fingers under her chin, tilting it up to better read her face.

"I don't have anything for you—"

3

I gripped her chin tighter. *Excuses. Excuses.*

"I don't have time for someone who is a waste of air. You came to me, darling cousin, not the other way around." I leaned forward, close enough to smell the acrid stench of body odor mingled with fear. "We are leaving today whether you give me a location or not, but your answer determines if I leave you in this basement to rot when we're gone." I curved my lips in a feral grin, relishing the small gasp that escaped her lips.

"You wouldn't..." she whispered as terror and anger fought for control over her. Elizabeth was a coward, and anger was not an emotion that won out within cowards. Her breathing began to hitch in short spurts as I grinned.

"There is nothing I wouldn't do for my revenge, cousin. It is the only reason you are still alive." I whispered the words to her, my shorn hair falling forward to frame a curtain around us. The sound of her rapid heart rate filled the silence.

"You don't even know if the Crone with the third eye can help you," she said. Her eyes pleaded like a beggar at a corner. Someone else, anyone else, might have caved and let her go by now, but not me. My mother gave her the message, and if there was anything I was confident in, it's that she wouldn't have come to Elizabeth if not to help me. Lily was with her now, and she wanted justice as much as I.

"She can, and she will. You're stalling." I switched my hold on her face, grabbing her jaw to force it open. Her eyes went wide. Her heart rate climbing in an unsteady crescendo. "You have fifteen seconds to give me new information, or we're going to play a game," I said softly.

"What kind of g-game?" Elizabeth trembled, jerking

back in an attempt to pull away, but she was tied to a chair and I held firm. She was right to be afraid. Bad things happened when I made all the rules.

"I am going to start pulling the air from your lungs, and I will keep pulling until there is nothing left to pull. After a minute, you will begin to feel lightheaded. Your throat will burn. After two minutes, your body will go unconscious. After four minutes, brain damage will start to set in, and after that you will die. Are you ready to die, Elizabeth?" My words were laced with malice, but I'd done my job too well. Elizabeth began to hyperventilate.

"Please...Selena...don't...do...this..." she panted, her oxygen level steadily rising to an unhealthy point. If she kept this up, she was going to pass out instead of suffocating like I'd told her.

"Give me a location and I won't have to," I growled. She continued to huff and puff even as she tried to speak. The words came out disoriented and garbled, until she stopped speaking all together. Her eyes rolled to the back of her head as she lost total consciousness, her body suddenly limp and unmoving.

"Damn it!" I cursed, pushing away from her. I pinched the bridge of my nose, sighing deeply while I paced for a moment.

The door above me squealed as it swung open. Johanna and Oliver waited at the top of the stairs, their faces were neutral, but I could feel the shifting energy around me.

"What happened?" Johanna asked, her eyes flicking to the fainted girl in the chair. My hair brushed my chin as I swung my head around to face them, clasping my hands behind my back.

"She panicked," I said, making a *tsk* noise.

Oliver blanched, narrowing his eyes. "Did you threaten to kill her?" The bite in his voice was unmistakable.

"What I do is none of your concern." I gave him a leveled stare. He balled his fists, opening his mouth to argue. I smirked, waiting for his reply, but Johanna touched him on the shoulder and whispered, "I'll speak with her. Go check on Scarlett?"

Scarlett was heir to House Graeme, and possibly the only Graeme left now that her brother Seb had gone missing during the attack at Daizlei. He was either dead or turned. Her parents, too, if my hunch about Anastasia was correct, but I kept those thoughts to myself. Scarlett was too emotional for my taste with the loss of her twin. Much the same as Oliver in that respect, except he was beginning to chafe at my patience. I sent a cool look in his direction as he turned and stalked off, leaving me with Johanna.

"You already know she's not lying, don't you?" she asked. Dark circles lined her red-stained eyes. She was the most put together out of the nine in that group—now six. At night though, when everyone pretended they were sleeping, I heard her, like them, crying softly for the friends she'd lost. The lives she couldn't save. It was tragic in a way that I understood but no longer felt, and we were all the better for it.

"I do."

She gaze me a quizzical stare, her cat-like eyes measuring me. "Then why continue? Why torture her?" Johanna asked. She descended the steps while I paced about, staring at the unconscious girl that I needed to give me answers.

"She needs motivation to try harder," I replied. "I'm giving her that motivation."

Johanna sighed and shook her head, pursing her lips as she did so. The older girl didn't like my methods, but hers hadn't gotten results.

"Torturing her isn't going to motivate her—"

"Your friend that died. The one you were framed for—is there anything you wouldn't do to avenge them?" I asked, stopping abruptly to face her.

Silence.

Johanna shifted uncomfortably on the stairs, but she did not deny it. As I knew she wouldn't. You don't become property of the Council and make it out alive without some level of resentment and bitterness. Johanna hid hers well, I'll give her that, but no one is that good.

I closed the space between us, looking up into her unnatural golden eyes. They reminded me of someone else, too much for my liking. She stood on the stair above mine, but we were nearly eye-to-eye as I said, "My sister meant everything to me, and I will put all of them in the grave for what they did to her. You can either help me, or get out of the way, but don't stand there feeding me some moral bullshit when you would do the same."

Ash and grit coated her hairline from where a washcloth wouldn't clean. She wore my dead mother's clothes that still smelled faintly of lilac and cinnamon. The hint of a tattoo with scales started at her hand and went as far as her neck, just below her ear. The tidbits of knowledge I'd gained from Violet told me she was not any kind of species I'd encountered before. Her kind were much older than mine, but the Supernaturals had run them nearly extinct.

7

There's no way she wouldn't go after them after what they'd done to her. I was banking on it, because she and I, we weren't so different. Johanna, like me, was a one of a kind, and she suffered for it.

It's time she took that chip off her shoulder and stopped pretending she was better than this.

Johanna gave a slow shake of her head, blowing out a cool breath. The dust drifted between us for a moment before she said, "I'll help you, Selena, but I don't want to see you lose yourself along the way."

Too late for that.

"I already have," I said, my voice devoid of emotion.

"No, you haven't." She didn't smile, and she didn't look at me like some pitiful animal she couldn't save, but the look she gave me was resigned nonetheless. "But you will if you continue down this path."

Behind me, Elizabeth's breathing steadied, and I suspected my little prisoner was waking up. If she tried that little hyperventilating trick again, I really would start with-holding air, and when she passed out, she wouldn't wake back up again.

Johanna's eyes cut to the girl behind me in a tight gaze, accepting of her fate. The burner phone in her jean pocket began to light up, sounding a basic ring tone. It only rang once before Johanna flicked it open.

"Jo," she said, by way of greeting.

"It's me. I think we found somewhere—"

"One moment," she said, holding her hand over the speaker. She glanced between me and Elizabeth, seeming to weigh whether it was worth it to say more on the subject. "This is my contact. I need to take this, but I will be back to...see how things are going."

I nodded once and turned my back to her as she left the room. Elizabeth was already trembling when I crossed my arms and deliberately raised my eyebrows, cocking my head to the side as I smirked. Her lips went white as they pinched together, her eyes wide.

This was a different reaction than the other times she'd woken up. Over the past three days, this was the fourth time this had happened, and the first that she hadn't woken up begging for her life. Something had changed.

"She came to you," I said, keeping my hands clasped behind my back so she couldn't see my fidgeting with the grey crocheted sweater I wore. It was my mother's. The same mother that came to her, would speak to her, and that I'd never see again. I stopped that train of thought. Almost like I'd forgotten it. Like I could not remember how to feel, and so I simply didn't.

"I don't—I'm not sure—I think it—"

"Spit it out. Did you get a location or not?" I demanded as she nodded her head vigorously. I motioned with my hand for her to continue.

"Go to Sin City. The Crone will find you," she rasped in broken voice. I watched her closely for lies, but all I saw was relief in her features. The sweat on her brow broke, leaving a stream of perspiration running down her nose as she smiled at the ceiling as if she really believed that was all.

"Sin City?" I asked. She nodded, swallowing hard before coughing. After being down here for three days, the dust must be getting to her. *Good. The weaker she is, the more compliant she'll be.*

The door to the upper floor swung open. Johanna stood in the doorframe alone, her face grim.

"What happened?" I asked. Her eyes scanned over Elizabeth in a cursory glance before she answered.

"My contact found us a safe house," she said.

"Then why do you look like someone else died?" I asked.

"Because it won't be easy to get to," she replied. I had this *feeling* I just knew what she was going to say. What she was going to confirm.

"Where is it?" I asked, anticipation building in my blood as my innate sense of *knowing* overcame me.

"Las Vegas. It's an eleven-hour drive. We're leaving in ten minutes," she said. My face broke into a fierce grin.

Sin City.

I didn't believe in fate because that was giving the ancients too much credit. I made my own destiny.

"We'll be ready in five," I said. Behind me, Elizabeth protested.

I pulled a Ka-bar from the knife holder hanging on my belt underneath the long sweater. Elizabeth went pale as I strode toward her, the blade gleaming in the low light.

"No!" she screamed as I slashed at the ropes binding her to the chair. I rolled my eyes and returned the knife to its holder.

"Don't be dramatic," I said as I pointed to the door where Johanna watched the exchange. Her lips were curved in the smallest of smirks.

"But—but—you said you would let me go if I found out where the Crone was!" Elizabeth stammered. I grabbed the back of her neck and started pushing her forward and up the stairs.

"I said you would get out of the basement. I never said what would happen after," I replied.

Elizabeth tried to twist as she groaned, "You can't keep me—"

"Prisoner?" I asked, clocking her on the back of the head. She blacked out, falling to the ground, limp. "Actually, I can." I said, throwing the taller, skinnier girl over my shoulder. We were going to Vegas whether she liked it or not, because I had a Crone to find and a Council to kill.

CHAPTER 2

"I'M HUNGRY," ELIZABETH COMPLAINED AS WE PULLED OFF THE highway. Aaron took a right at the corner, pulling into a rundown gas station without a name. We'd been in the car for eight hours, and all eight of them had been blissfully silent. Until now.

"Didn't I tell you not to speak unless spoken to?" I said as Aaron rolled to a stop and got out of the car.

"Oh, come on, Selena—"

"Why are you still speaking?"

"But—"

"Speaking."

"But—"

I turned in my seat fast enough I thought she was going to get whiplash from the way her eyes darted between me and the girls on either side of her. With Alexandra to her left and Blair to her right, she was trapped with nowhere to escape and no one to save her.

"Do we need to play another game?" I asked, cocking my eyebrow. Her face went white at the same instant her stomach let out a loud growl. She swallowed hard, pressing her lips together, but didn't say more. I turned around and settled back into my seat as Aaron came out of the station and began pumping gas.

"Is this the wrong time to say I'm hungry too?" Alexandra asked.

I groaned, leaning back in my seat. A food stop was not on my list of things to do. Not when we were traveling in the open and hadn't bothered to ditch the cars that they'd used in their getaway from Daizlei. It was a stupid move, but Johanna insisted we'd be safer keeping them and getting to the meeting point as quickly as possible rather than ditching them and stealing new ones. I hoped she was right.

"Blair?" I asked, a note of annoyance permeating my voice.

"I could eat."

The driver's side door opened and Aaron climbed back into the car. "I take it we're getting food," he said. Not exactly a question, so I chose not to answer as he pulled out for the McDonald's across the street. The lot was empty apart from two cars as we went through the drive-thru. Aaron ordered six meals without asking what anyone wanted and pulled up to the window.

"That will be thirty-five dollars and sixty-four cents," a girl with bright pink hair said.

Aaron handed her a fifty and winked. "Keep the change."

"Thanks..." she trailed off, leaving her question open-ended.

"Aaron," he supplied. Cotton-candy-head blushed like a

virgin at the wrong end of an innuendo. In the back-seat, Alexandra said, "Like, can we get our food?"

She looked past Aaron and locked eyes with me. Her flirty smile faltered and without a word, she turned away from the window and produced our food. Aaron thanked her, and this time she just gave a tight-lipped nod as we pulled away from the window.

I didn't say anything when a hamburger wrapped in yellow paper appeared on my lap, courtesy of the driver. I unwrapped it reluctantly, and ate with slow, deliberate bites as I ruminated on her odd reaction. It seemed a bit of a one eighty, even if she did think I was Aaron's girlfriend.

"Did her reaction seem strange to you?" I asked, swallowing a mouthful of the greasy fast food.

"Strange?" Aaron asked.

I shook my head. *Never mind.*

We pulled back onto the highway and headed south, silence ensuing within minutes.

I looked to the sun as it descended over the mountains to the west and I thought of my sister. The one who died. Who I killed. I could admit it now, with Violet here. I could admit that in my attempt to save her...I ended her life.

But did she stay dead?

That was something I didn't know.

"Until you do, it doesn't matter," Violet whispered.

I ran a hand through my blood-caked hair, pulling it back from my face. After nearly ninety-six hours without a shower, I could almost forget the battle at Daizlei. The sweat and blood and grime clung to me like a second skin, but my shorn hair was not something I could forget. My sister was not someone I could forget.

14

Use it. Own it. Let it fuel you to return every action tenfold.

I turned away from the light and glanced in my rearview mirror. To Elizabeth, who would lead me to the Crone. To Blair, who would follow me until the end. To Alexandra, who once she realized her potential, would burn the world in her rage. I made a choice to look to the future and it was filled with vengeance.

Even in my malicious meanderings, something wasn't quite adding up. The same innate feeling I had when something just wasn't right.

"How much longer?" I asked, unease prickling up my spine like a trail of knives across my skin.

"Shouldn't be too long now. The meeting point is just on the other side of the border," Aaron said.

This was all any of us were told, since Johanna wasn't being the most forthcoming about who her contact was or how exactly he planned to get us into Vegas undetected, and I was pretty damn sure walking in wasn't going to be an option. The welcome sign for Nevada appeared in the distance, shining like a beacon when the headlights reflected off it.

Something was off. Something was *wrong*.

I opened my mouth to say as much when a phone rang. Aaron pulled the burner from his pocket and flipped it open.

"Get off at the next exit," said a deep voice that reminded me too much of someone I used to know. The line went dead as soon as the words were out of Alec's mouth, and Aaron veered sharply across the highway. We crossed three lanes in a second, and took the off ramp still flying.

"He said get off, not get us killed! Don't you know how

15

to drive?" Elizabeth shouted. She broke off in a scream as he continued to accelerate the car with a curve coming up.

"What the—"

In the side view mirror, a car was eating up the distance between us and the curve. My heart began to pound as a second vehicle appeared on the other side. They were trying to box us in. We weren't going to make it.

"Floor it and don't stop until I say so," I said, gripping the door handle. Aaron didn't question it. His foot hit the gas and the engine revved. We shot forward, barely clearing the cars. I grabbed the wheel and yelled, "Now!"

The gas died instantly when I yanked the steering wheel down and sent the car skidding as it closed in on the curve. I let go of the wheel and flung my door open.

The hood of the first car wasn't even ten feet from me and the driver had a gun aimed straight for my chest.

"Now," Violet urged.

I jumped from my seat and landed in front of our pursuers.

The last thing I saw was the red of his eyes before the car hit me.

And then it cleaved in half.

Fire ignited as the two halves of the car spun wildly out of control. One drifted off into the welcome building of a rest area—the other slammed into the remaining car and sent both drivers up in flames.

I crossed my arms and stared into the fire. The smell of burnt tires and burning flesh made me grimace, but I wouldn't turn away.

I mentally reached through the flames and dragged both Vampires before me. Black blood streaked the ground, two separate trails leading to the horrid creatures at my feet. The one on the right had the gall to grin despite half his face being melted off.

The Vampire on the left averted his eyes, and there was a visible tremble about him. Why would he hunt me if he feared death? He had to know what I did to those who crossed me. I recalled what Vonlowsky had taught us about the Made. How they were forced to do the bidding of their sire.

"Who sent you?" I phrased it like a question, but I wasn't asking. I was demanding.

The one with parts of his face missing began to cackle. Black blood sprayed from his lips, coating his teeth and splattering my boots. I raised an eyebrow, daring him to speak and give me a reason to end him.

"Selena..." Blair said from behind me. I didn't need to look to know that the others had recovered and decided to join in the fun.

"Who sent you?" I repeated. I would not repeat myself a third time.

"You think you can—"

He didn't get to finish before I reached forward and grabbed a fistful of his hair. I wrapped my other hand around his half-healed shoulder and ripped his head clean off, tossing it into the blazing inferno that I'd dragged them from.

The decapitated body fell to the ground, bleeding out as I turned to his partner. I squatted down until we were eye level. His downcast eyes flicked up to meet mine and I smiled encouragingly. I didn't need to say anything. My performance was enough to make this one talk.

"Our master sent us," he said, gulping hard. The sweat on his face glistened in the sunlight and he flinched under my gaze.

"Who is your master?" I continued, my voice soft.

"Victor..." the Vampire said. His mouth opened and closed twice.

"Which one?" The voice came from behind me. I glanced over my shoulder at Johanna. She was dressed in long black sleeves and pants, despite the weather. Her lips were pursed, and her long dark hair whipped around in the breeze.

"The Dark Prince." His answer brought a spark of recognition to her eyes before she grimaced.

Good. She knew of him. It would make this so much easier.

"Why are the High Council sending their Made after us?" she asked. I stilled. *The High Council?* That can't be good.

"To arrange a meeting with Selena Foster," he whispered. His eyes were darting every which way, making me suspicious. Shadows danced in the corners of my vision. They whispered to me, telling me to kill him. To make him pay.

"You tried to kill me," I said flatly.

He gulped again and looked to the ground before he said, "Our master told us you would be resistant and to use force if necessary, but that he means you no harm."

"Why does the High Council want me?" I asked, gritting my teeth.

"My master did not share his wishes with me. My

instructions were to deliver this message and not tell his would-be queen," the Vampire whispered.

His would-be queen? One guess who that could be. It explained why Anastasia had so much control over the Vampires. What it didn't explain was why he wouldn't want her to know. Did the Vampire intend for that slip up, or if it was pure coincidence, had he given me another piece of the puzzle? He couldn't possibly be that stupid.

"Your master sent you to retrieve me, and you say he means no harm?"

The Vampire nodded. His skin was mostly healed, but still painted by his own blood. His face would have been lovely, if not for the red eyes. Too bad for him it took more than a lovely face to make me forgive lies. I may not be a truthsayer, but the helicopters in the distance probably weren't a coincidence. We didn't have more than five minutes if my instincts were right.

"I don't believe you," I snarled, plunging my hand into his chest.

His blood reeked of wrongness and that feeling intensified as I gripped his cold heart in one hand. The Vampire gasped, his eyes wide with terror.

"They're coming, Selena," Aaron ushered. I needed to end this.

Take no prisoners. Leave no messengers.

"I know," I said, leaning forward. My lips were only a hairsbreadth from the Made when I whispered, "You're stalling. I know a liar when I see one."

Vampires were the spawn of demons and my kind. Made or Born, they died the same.

Burning. Beheading. I settled for ripping his heart out

19

and leaving it on the ground next to him. That would be the only message I sent to the High Council and their queen.

I am alive. I am fighting, and one day—I am coming for you.

With that, I turned and walked away, my hand still black with his blood and dripping from the wrist down. My team stood in a loose semi-circle watching, their expressions stark. Somber. The helicopters in the distance were only minutes out and the sirens were steadily approaching.

"Where's your contact?" I asked Johanna. She stood regal despite our impending doom, should Anastasia's lackeys arrive.

"He's coming," she answered, meeting my glare with a leveled stare.

"What do you mean 'he's coming'?"

"For fuck's sake, Selena. I said he's bloody com—"

The air in front of me shimmered. Gold particles that looked like glitter shifted and merged into the form of a human. A man. Within seconds, the outlines of a face and eyes appeared. Clothes took shape. A crop of hair appeared.

The air stood still as a golden statue emerged in front of me. Then it blinked and the gold faded, revealing a young man with dark blonde hair and honey-colored eyes. *Half breed.*

Johanna stepped up to say something, but the boy didn't appear to be listening. He had his eyes glued on me.

"Eh, what is this?" he said, motioning towards me like a piece of distasteful furniture. "I specifically told you that we couldn't take her in. The alpha cannot—"

"Cade?" Aaron asked. The golden-boy turned, his anger temporarily forgotten as a smile lit his features.

"Ash?" Cade asked, disbelieving. He strode forward to clap him on the back.

Ash?

"It's Aaron now," he answered. His dark eyes flicked to me as if he were answering us both.

"Of course," Cade murmured. "I'm so sorry about—"

"Cade!" Amber yelled, ducking around Johanna to face the newcomer.

The golden-boy pulled back from Aaron, his head perking up and looking for where the yell came from. The two locked eyes and he uttered her name once.

That one word held so much, or so it seemed, as she ran at him in the blink of an eye and literally jumped on top of him. I looked away from the intimacy of the moment, only to see Aaron staring at me, a smirk on his face.

I flicked him off with my bloodied hand.

"Charming," he mouthed. I snorted and turned back to the embracing couple. Next to me, Blair tapped the toe of her white boot. We probably didn't have more than sixty seconds. This was cutting it a bit close, even by my standards.

Amber jumped down, a smile lighting her face. She tucked herself into his side as he turned back to Johanna. "Sorry about that. Back to what I was saying. I can take the rest of you, but not her. Alpha's orders."

Johanna didn't even blink as she said, "That's going to be a problem."

Cade raised an eyebrow, silently questioning. The air stirred around us as the chopping of blades descended closer. Thirty seconds. Thirty seconds and *this is what we were arguing about?*

Who were these people anyway? This *Cade* was going to have a lot of questions from me if I had to fight my way out of here and then hunt them down.

Half the group stiffened as we waited for someone to answer. Seeing as I didn't know why I'd been excluded in the first place, I didn't know what to say.

"She's my signasti," Aaron said from the other side of the circle.

Cade stiffened. "Well then. That changes things."

Nobody said a word as the trees a hundred yards away shifted in a breeze that wasn't coming from the helicopter. We were out of time, but Cade wasn't perturbed. He clapped his hands together, rubbing them while he bounced up and down on the balls of his feet. Gold dust sprinkled the air as he said, "Alright, everybody, listen up. We've got a strip club to crash."

CHAPTER 3

HAVING YOUR BODY DISINTEGRATED INTO GOLD DUST WAS NOT AS unpleasant as it sounds.

I didn't feel a thing from the moment my skin turned yellow and broke apart, until I was pieced together again under the strobe lights of what was indeed, a strip club.

Albeit, an empty one.

The lights. The girls. The bar. It was all there, just not the patrons.

"Pull it in, guys," Cade called on the other side of the room. I pushed off the bar, shaking the remaining golden flecks from my skin. The scantily clad server walking by paid me no mind as she adjusted her bra. I waded through the tables and chairs towards the back of the room where the group had gathered around a section of sofas.

"Is this it? The safe house?" I asked, a bit disbelieving. How does a strip club in Las Vegas constitute as low profile? I was pretty sure it didn't.

"Yes and no," Cade answered. "We're at the safe house, but you won't be able to enter it until we come to an understanding." He shook his finger at me like I was a bad child. "You weren't in the plans when Tam agreed to take you all in. I'm going to need to speak with him about that." He broke off as Amber stepped out of his embrace, standing in between us.

"She stays with us, Cade," the golden-eyed spitfire said. She glanced back at me, a small amount of respect and healthy amount of reproach in her gaze. "You're Aaron's signasti, and that means you are under Shifter protection whether an alpha likes it or not."

The alpha? They kept throwing that term around but still hadn't explained what he had to do with anything? And what does Aaron have to do with it? I didn't comment as she turned back to Cade, but I did wonder...

Cade nodded his head. "I know the laws as well as anyone, Amber. I'm not disputing you, but until I've spoken with Tam, she can't leave the safe house and risk anyone recognizing her."

His eyes bore into mine, searching for the truth when he said, "You good with that?"

I took five seconds to answer, measuring him up before I nodded once. I knew that he couldn't stop me from leaving if I really wanted to. Nothing could. But something told me that would make him all the more suspicious of me, so I said nothing.

If he thought I was lying, he didn't show it. A smile broke across his face as he said, "Alright then. I'll take you all up. Follow me." He turned and started walking towards the elevator behind him. There was no button on the wall to call it, and yet, the doors opened just before he ran into them.

"There's no way we'll all fit," I said, crossing my arms over my chest. The others turned, giving me curious glances.

"We'll fit," Cade said as Blair and Alexandra stepped on. One by one, the others followed until I was all that was left. Somehow, there was just as much room with fourteen people on it as there was when there were four. How was that even possible?

Magic. The thought came to me swift and sudden. There was magic at play here, and not the kind I was well acquainted with.

"You've never been to a black market, have you?" Aaron asked. Amusement lit his features as I stepped inside.

"No," I said flatly, keeping my back to the wall. The doors closed behind me, making the tightness in my chest constrict. I hated small spaces with nowhere to go, realizing that I was in some kind of magical elevator didn't help that. There were no buttons inside, or any indicator of where we were going. No one else seemed to think this was strange, so I kept my thoughts to myself.

It wasn't soon enough that the elevator dinged, and the doors slid open.

White.

Everything was startling white from the alabaster couches to the ivory end tables. The walls were just a shade softer, more of a cream than bone. Pillows adorned every seat, round and plush, shimmering with an opalescence I'd never seen on fabric. The geode table that sat in the center was the only item of color in the room as far as I could tell. The outside matched the monochromatic scheme with its pasty white exterior, but the inside revealed bright blue crystals.

"Nice place you got here," I murmured, running my clean hand along the back of the couch. The material was softer than I'd expected.

"It's yours for as long as you're here," Cade said.

"Why do I get the impression there's a caveat in that statement?" I asked. Cade gave me a lopsided grin, similar enough to Lucas that I recoiled.

"Your signasti's smart, Aaron. Snarky too. I like it," Cade said. I forced a saccharine smile and the grin fell away from his face. "I need to meet with Tam before the club opens. The lot of you need bleach taken to you. Clean up and get some sleep. I'll be back in the morning." He turned to give Amber a kiss goodbye and I wandered down the hallway to the left.

The first door had a sign on it that read: Scarlett and Liam. I looked across the hall to see another. This one read: Alexandra, Amber, and Tori. That's odd... I followed further down the hall to the last two doors. More names, and none of them were mine.

"Why do all the doors have names on them?" I asked, coming around the corner. Cade pulled himself away from Amber and said, "I forget to mention. The safe house was built on magic. It's kind of taken on a mind of its own. In your rooms, you should find clothes and anything else you might need. And a word of advice: sleep in the rooms it gives you. Strange things have happened to those that go against it. If you know what I mean." He waggled his eyebrows at Amber as he said it, and I was tempted to punch him in the solar plexus.

"No, I don't know what you mean," I muttered under my breath. Everyone stayed put as I turned down the hallway directly across from the elevator. There was a single door with my name on it. And someone else's. I could sense the eyes watching my back as I stared at the black and white sign that hung on the door.

Aaron and Selena.

I turned around and Aaron's black eyes sought me out as he approached from across the room. The others were finally starting to disperse, and I could hear Blair and Alec arguing down the other hall, but I couldn't look away. Frozen to the spot, I didn't move to block the sign as he stepped in front of me. His eyes flicked behind me, a slow grin spreading across his face.

"Looks like we're sleeping together," I said.

The scent of smoke and fire drifted over me, cracking the frozen lake that I'd built between him and I. Something like heat stirred in my chest, making my breathing slow. Warmth was the last thing I wanted—needed. I was meant to be ice. To be cold. To not feel anything except rage.

And yet his presence made me feel.

Made me *want* to feel.

"Why aren't you opening the door?" he whispered, his lips grazing the hollow of my ear. I narrowed my eyes and reached behind me for the cold handle of the bedroom door. Inside, the marble floors were black with gold veins. A canopy bed made of ebony loomed in front of me, a crackling fireplace at the foot of it. I scowled at the dark chambers. They were beautiful and far too sensual for my liking.

Approaching the long dresser, I began pulling drawers open. Plucking a shirt from one, pants from another, and

27

even a pair of underwear from the last. I didn't think about the clothes or whose they were as I slammed the drawers shut. I didn't want to think. I didn't want to analyze.

But I was not the same Selena that died either. I was not the girl that could simply escape inside my own mind. Nor did I have the emotional capacity to feel much more than icy rage and bloodlust. Yet...the embers were there. Still burning. Still waiting. I just didn't see it until now. Until I let Aaron too close.

I thought no one could hurt me, no one could touch me, but I miscalculated because he could do something I hadn't foreseen. He could make me feel.

A cough behind me made my head snap up. "Do you need something?" I tensed as he drew closer, prepared to put a shield between us before he tried anything funny.

"You've changed," he said. I let out a caustic laugh and slowly rose to my feet. You could say that.

"What would give you that impression?" I said, crossing my arms over my chest, my face a mask of apathy. Aaron stared at me, his eyes burning like the flames of hell. Dark and devilish.

"You let the other one in." He said it like I betrayed him. Like I hurt him. I shrugged callously, not denying it. Maybe if he knew I wasn't the only one in this pretty little head of mine, he might get it through his thick skull that we were nothing. I didn't have room for him in, for any of them, outside my need for revenge.

"I did what I needed to do," I replied in a monotone voice. I sounded like death, but he didn't back away. His eyes bore into mine as he stood his ground.

"No, you did what was *easy*. I was there, Selena. Hell"—

he threw his arms wide to make a point—"I saw what happened. I watched you snap and I carried you out. Don't tell me you did what you needed to do. The only person you're lying to is yourself." He took a step forward dropping his hands. "You want to be angry? Okay, be angry. You want to go after her for what she did? We'll go after her. But don't—" His voice cracked, sending another spear straight into my frozen lake. I took a step back until I was flush against the dresser. "Don't do this. Don't be this...unfeeling thing. Because you still feel. I can see it when you look at me. You are still in there, but you're choosing to feel the wrong things and eventually it will destroy you."

He took another step towards me and reached forward. His fingers stopped before they could ever touch my face, running into the invisible barrier I kept between us.

"My emotions were what made me weak. They were what got my sister killed. I will never be weak again," I said. His fingers fell to his side, closing into a fist.

"Your emotions are what keep you grounded. Without them, you'll spiral out of control until the voices consume you," he whispered. "Your rage has you by the throat, Selena, and you don't even see it."

Seconds ticked by as we stared each other down, and after nearly a minute I finally said, "I need to take a shower."

I told myself it wasn't admitting defeat as I gathered my clothes and walked away. I pretended that I was the bigger person for walking away and slamming the door in his face. I lied to myself when I said that he was wrong. He wasn't. My pain. My anger. My hurt. I had taken those things and let them fuel my desire for vengeance.

I shoved my thoughts away, glaring at the venetian bathtub. There was no shower and I would not bathe, but I couldn't just walk out of here either. Aaron would know something was up, and I was not giving him that satisfaction. Glancing across the obsidian counter, a cup appeared in front of me.

"You've got to be kidding me," I muttered. Making sure the drain wasn't plugged, I turned the cold water on full blast and settled into the tub. Over the next half hour, I washed myself with a cup. From the back of my mind, Violet said nothing as I cleaned the blood from my hair and scrubbed the black from under my nails. The dirt and the dust, and the gore of that battle went down the drain at last, but the darkness in my heart—my soul—that was something that would never leave me. Aaron may be right that my rage was going to consume me, but if I went down, I was taking the world with me. And that was something I could live with.

CHAPTER 4

COLD SHACKLES RUBBED AT MY WRISTS. I COUGHED, MY THROAT dry and burning. The air was stale with an unsettling coldness that made me shiver.

Where am I?

I pulled back, trying to get up and stand, but a sudden pounding in my head made me cry out. My knees hit the ground with a crack and the chains clanked together. I hunched over ready to vomit, but nothing would come. The dry heaves continued for another few moments before the grinding of rusty hinges had me forcing it down.

Someone was opening the door of my cell. Why I was in a cell, I still didn't understand. What had I done?

I couldn't seem to remember.

Fire illuminated a man's face as he strode toward me. I shrunk back into the wall, not wanting him to touch me. Not wanting him to burn me. But there was nothing I could do when he grabbed my chin, forcing me to look at him.

"You're not going to fight me, are you?"

This wasn't a question. It was a demand. An expectation.

*The temperature of the room decreased even further, almost...
arctic. I swallowed hard and shook my head no just the tiniest
fraction. He beamed a smile that was all teeth.*

*"Very good. It wouldn't be very smart of you to try." The
smallest of whimpers escaped me as he stroked my matted hair. I
smelled like a sewer. The air was permeating with the stench of
my fear. But that didn't deter him.*

"You're prettier than I expected."

I flinched at his words. They weren't meant to be kind.

*His hands touched the shackles and they fell away, leaving
me backed into the corner of a dirty cell with only the man and
his torch standing in front of the door. The thought of running
crossed my mind, but only for a moment. It would be stupid, and
likely anger him. I was better off going with him and biding my
time.*

They would come. They always do.

*The man stepped back, reaching out a hand. Tentatively, I
placed my dirty fingers in his, shivering when his closed around
mine. He pulled me to my feet, the pounding in my head
becoming unbearable within seconds. I put my free hand to the
wall, trying to brace myself against the overwhelming dizziness
and urge to vomit.*

*"You're hungry," he observed, pulling me towards him. I was
helpless to stop him as his arms snaked around my back and he
picked me up under the bend of my knees. "Lucky for you, your
master wants you trained."*

Master? I didn't have a master.

What happened? How had I ended up here?

*The last thing I remembered was sitting in the forest. We
were supposed to be leaving that day. I was supposed to wait, but
there was someone in the trees. I turned and—*

The cries and moans of others made me curl inward, but I said nothing. His footsteps were silent as the grave as he carried me down one dark corridor to the next. We made enough turns I got lost, but that could be because he wanted to confuse me. After all, I'd been in shackles. I don't know what kind of people would put someone in shackles without mal intent. Still, I stayed silent.

They will come for me. They always do.

I repeated it thrice before he came to a standstill. He laid me on the bed gentler than I would have expected for the type of man I could only assume him to be. A door slammed shut and panic filled my chest as I looked around.

"This is your bedroom. You will remain here until you have been trained well enough to do as you're told. That won't be a problem though, will it, pretty Made?"

Pretty...Made? No, that can't possibly be right. I shook my head as the darkness inside me unfurled. Something thick and ugly seized my throat, making me suffocate. I looked up to the man with the dark silver eyes. No...I can't be a Made. That's not possible. I can't—

"It will please your master that you are docile. So much more pliant than he was expecting." His eyes glassed over as someone entered through the door behind him. I shuffled to the side of the bed, peaking around him.

It was...a girl.

"Ahh, your dinner has arrived. Excellent."

No. No. No...

I retched, but that only made him laugh. The girl came closer, but I held a hand up for her to stay away. I didn't want her near me. I didn't want to chance that he might be right.

"You won't be able to fight it, try as you might. It's best to just relax." I couldn't tell if he meant his words to be reassuring.

They were soft, seductive, and made my skin prickle. He motioned for her to step forward and I tried to jerk back. Cold hands locked around my wrists, forcing me to stay kneeling on the bed as the girl drew near.

Her brown eyes were meek. She cast them downward as she advanced. When she was only a foot away, she stopped and slid her long brown hair over one shoulder, exposing a slender pulsing neck.

She was pale, so very pale. I distantly wondered if she ever left here. Wherever here was. But the longer she stood there, invading my space with her sweet scent, the more something in me changed. Something in me awakened.

I blinked once and my hands were no longer bound. They were pulling that pale throat closer and closer. I ran my nose over her artery, caressing her skin. The pumping in her veins absolutely transfixed me. I'd never heard anything so captivating and I couldn't tear my eyes away. I'd never wanted something so badly that I couldn't control myself. Stop myself.

I kissed her neck softly, and then I sank my teeth into her.

CHAPTER 5

I WOKE IN A COLD SWEAT WITH SOMEONE ON TOP OF ME.
Without thinking, I lashed out, my body bucking off the
bed as I psychically threw the person across the room.
Tremors shook me as shadows skated across my vision. The
whispers were already calling for blood.

I jumped to my feet, ready to strike, when the lights
turned on.

"What's going on?"

I recognized the girl before me. I'd seen her a thousand
times, and yet, I could not place the face I knew to an entity
that I cared for. I couldn't connect anything outside the
pounding in my veins that had me clenching my fists.

"Get out, Amber," said the person I had thrown. I eyed
him coldly, cocking my head to the side, examining my
prey.

"I'm not leaving you in here with her like this," the
person at the door snapped. I narrowed my eyes and
prepared to defend myself in a crouched fighting stance.

Her fear sang through the air, promising the whispers an easy kill. This one was afraid.

"Selena. I need you to come back right now," the other one whispered. The one with the black and yellow eyes. He was trying to distract me. Footsteps down the hall had me hissing. My fingers curled into claws as the whispers berated me. *Kill her. End her.*

"Leave, Amber. I can handle her," said the male.

"I'm not leaving you—"

"Why are her eyes black?" said the red-haired she-demon in the doorway. Behind her, others were lining up. *Readying to fight.*

"Selena," the male said again. The embers inside me flared, searching for something to catch fire. Something to bridge the gap.

To cross the carefully constructed void of nothingness that I'd built for myself.

"Selena," he repeated. The room stood still as the entities inside me battled for dominance. I was the monster. The killer. The whispers spoke destruction and I gave it to them.

I was the protector. The fighter. The girl who felt *too* much, only no one could see it. I needed to fight this. There was a reason I needed to fight the whispers. I need to smother the rage. I needed to cage the monster.

"He's calling her back," someone whispered.

My concentration snapped.

Phantom hands lunged for the girl at the same time a shield moved to stop them. My power slammed into an invisible force and I growled. The monster inside me lunged to the surface and swirling energy shattered the shield like glass.

"She shouldn't be able to do that," a blonde-haired demon said.

"She's a matter manipulator under strain. It's the bond madness," said the male. I could sense him creeping closer. Something *warm* brushed my mind making me stiffen. "That's right. I'm right here. I'm right—"

I lunged for him.

"No!" someone screamed. Black flames rose up around me, trapping me in. On the other side, pure golden eyes stared back, and I reached for him, but I couldn't break through. The flames licked at my skin, singeing my clothes. Fire could not hurt me, but this fire trapped me. It confined me.

I turned on the redheaded demon controlling the flames. Her eyes bled black and she stared me down. "I want Selena back. Now," she demanded. Something about her calmed the rage inside me and silenced the whispers. As sudden as my monster had taken control, it receded.

Only then did I realize I was mistaken. The she-demon —as the other me called her—was *Alexandra*. Falling to my knees, I curled in on myself, trying and failing to process what just happened.

The black flames dissipated as Alexandra came toward me. Her eyes faded back to brown as she crouched down. I didn't say anything as she wrapped her arms around me, pulling me close. I couldn't bring myself to hug her back. Over her shoulder, Amber watched me warily. She had been the one I homed in on first. The one who didn't want to leave Aaron with me, and looking at it now, I couldn't blame her.

I thought coming together with Violet had saved me. I thought I had my rage under control, but a single nightmare provoked everything inside of me and I turned savage. Unable to think or process who I was seeing. They were all a threat, and I couldn't see past that.

Blair stepped forward, her mouth set in a grim line. She sighed deeply and gave me a look like she didn't know what to do with me as she said, "We need to have a talk."

"That's an understatement," Johanna muttered.

CHAPTER 6

We gathered in the living room at three in the morning. The atmosphere was heavy, thick with tension and unspoken words. The black cotton shirt I wore was singed up to the elbow from the flames. Black flames. Flames that could trap me. I didn't know what to think of that. I didn't know what to think about a lot of things right now.

"Did you know that you are part demon?" Johanna said, getting straight to it. My eyes snapped to hers. She sat with one leg drawn up, her arm resting on her knee.

"I'm not part demon." Even as I said it, my eyes sought Alexandra. Her eyes had turned black, just like a demon.

I could deny everything. I could lie through my teeth to them. All of them.

But I saw it with my own eyes.

Could I really lie to myself?

"Oh, you are. I'm quite certain. Both of you are." Her eyes skipped between me and my redheaded sister. My mouth thinned.

"How is that even possible? You yourself said all half breeds have golden eyes," I retorted. I wanted to snarl at the accusation, rapidly realizing my emotions were not locked in tight.

"Yes, because the only children demons have are other demons or Vampires. They defy the natural order, Selena. I didn't think I needed to explain that." Johanna's voice was hard and unflinching. I don't believe she meant to be aggressive, but her abrasive tone was grating me.

"Then how do you know we're part demon? You don't have proof." I crossed my arms over my chest, looking between her and Alexandra.

"You are impervious to fire. Your eyes turned black. Your sister called upon hellfire, and now that her demon and yours have surfaced, I can see them in your auras. You are part demon, Selena, whether you like it or not. I needed to know if you knew that, because if you knew and kept this from us—"

"What would you do?" I couldn't keep the sneer out of my tone as Violet pushed forward. I snapped at my other and shoved her back. Her job was to keep us balanced, not to act as my mouthpiece. Violet shrugged coldly and settled. I would deal with her later.

Johanna still hadn't answered as she watched me. Assessing me. Studying me. I could see it on her face that she knew what just happened, and I didn't like it. Not one bit.

"You may be powerful, Selena, but you are not a god. There are not many things I have asked for, but I need your honesty if we are going to keep everyone safe." Her words were not a threat, and it was the only thing that kept me seated with my mouth shut. I nodded once to convey I understood. She let out a breath and gave me a tight nod in return.

"So, we're part demon. Question is how it happened, and who do we get it from?" Alexandra said. It didn't take me any thought at all to figure out which parent would be responsible—which one was prone to rapid, unexplainable mood swings.

"It has to be mom," I said. She nodded a few times and looked at Blair next to her.

"That means you are, too," she said to our cousin. I looked at Elizabeth standing against the wall behind Johanna. Her eyes were dark and unreadable.

"And you," I said to her. Elizabeth swallowed hard but didn't respond otherwise.

Demon. Like the very creature that carved me up. I wasn't sure how to feel about that. It did explain a bit, but... was Violet the demon? Or was it the monster?

"I am not the one you are afraid of," Violet answered.

"That's exactly what a demon would say."

"You don't have to believe me, but I strongly warn against you locking us out."

"Us? You and it talk now? What the hell is going on, Violet?" My face must have shown something because the others were beginning to stare.

"I have to use the bathroom," I excused myself. Once in the bathroom with the door securely closed, I turned to the mirror and stepped into my mind. Violet was sitting in an overstuffed arm chair, the one across from her was vacant. Waiting for me.

"What is going on?" I repeated. She looked me over once and frowned.

"You always ask the wrong questions," she said. I growled under my breath and set her with a hard stare. She sighed and said, *"Me and your demon speak, the same as you and I, because you and it are the same. It is a part of you, even more than I am. It will be here long after I am gone."*

"What are you?" I asked, no longer trusting the entity in front of me. I fell into madness and clung to her. I killed my sister and embraced her. She lied...but I didn't know what to do without her.

"I cannot answer that," she said.

"Can't or won't?" I demanded, the hairs on my neck bristled.

"Can't."

Bullshit.

"Why not? Who's stopping you?"

"I can't say that either, not that I expect you to believe me."

Damn straight I don't believe you.

"You won't tell me what you are, but you're not a figment of my imagination, or my demon. That doesn't encourage trust. Why should I not shut you out again?" I asked, vaguely aware that someone was moving in the bedroom outside the door.

"I cannot protect you if you push me away, and your demon will get out of control. If you want to live long enough to see revenge, you need to find the Crone and kill Anastasia. It is the only way." This was the most forward she has been, and it made me wonder why. Violet never did anything out of the kindness of her heart. She also never hurt anyone I cared for. I did that all on my own.

Someone knocked on the door and I knew I was out of time to chat.

"*Why do I feel again? It wasn't supposed to be this way. You told me—*"

"*I am not the one that took away your emotions, Selena. You cut yourself off from them because you were grieving. Your signasti broke the lock you held on them. Your nightmare opened the door. You can choose how much or how little you feel. That power does not lie with me,*" she said. Her words echoed over and over in my mind. Numbly, I flipped the light off and went to answer the knock. Blair gave me a hard smile.

"How are you doing?" she asked.

"Truthfully?" I asked. She nodded. "I don't know. I feel like there's a lot of stuff that doesn't add up and someone's in the background pulling the strings." She let out a breath as we walked towards the door that led back into the living room.

"Yeah, it does feel like that right now." That was all we said to each other before we sat down, but it was the most real interaction I'd had with anyone in days. It was almost...nice.

I nearly jumped out of my seat when someone touched my shoulder.

"I'm not mad at you for what happened back there. You didn't know you have a bloodthirsty, evil entity living inside you," Amber said. I think she meant it partially joking, but I wasn't laughing. Her lips quirked up and she settled back onto the couch.

"I don't suppose either of you know *how* this happened?" Johanna asked. She motioned to Alexandra and me, but we shook our heads. Behind her, Elizabeth opened her mouth. I flicked my gaze up and cocked an eyebrow, prompting an answer from her. She closed it abruptly and shook her head.

"Oh no you don't," I muttered. Mentally I dragged her forward by the throat until she kneeled in front of all of us. "You were going to say something. What was it?"

Her eyes started to water and I eased my hold on her throat. She shook her head back and forth, like that would stop me from getting what I wanted. I moved from my seat to squat down in front of her.

"What. Do. You. Know?" I asked, enunciating each letter painfully clear. It was right then that she finally understood that I had no problem hurting her here and now. I didn't care that there were people around. Johanna wouldn't stop me. Blair wouldn't stop me. No one would save her.

Her shoulders slouched forward as she whispered two little words. "My mom."

"Your mom?" I repeated. Elizabeth swallowed hard and her eyes darted to Blair. I looked to my blonde cousin who watched her sister struggle. If she felt sorry for her, she didn't show it. "Your mom knows how we became part demon?"

"If she did then she didn't tell me," Blair said.

"I don't know if she did or she didn't. She was paranoid and obsessed with the truth. She went crazy when your mom died. If anyone knew anything, it was her," Elizabeth said. Her whole body was sweating profusely. I loosened my mental grip on her even more.

"Why do you keep talking about her in past tense?"

Blair snapped. Elizabeth swallowed hard, looking at Blair with water sheening her eyes. She opened and closed her mouth three times, when Johanna spoke what Elizabeth could not say.

"Because she's dead."

CHAPTER 7

"WHAT DO YOU MEAN *SHE'S DEAD*?" I DON'T KNOW WHO ASKED the question, but between Elizabeth's shaking and Johanna's pained expression, I didn't doubt it.

"I mean she died. Her soul is...beyond here now," Johanna said slowly, weariness weighing on her slender shoulders. Blair blinked once, frozen in the moment.

"Beyond here?" I asked, raising an eyebrow. "And how would you know that?" I was more than a little defensive after the questioning I'd just received. Johanna's lips thinned as she turned her glowing gold eyes on me.

"Her soul is lingering to say goodbye," Johanna said, both by way of answering and a non-too-subtle reminder of who she was and what this meant.

"Goodbye?" Blair murmured, like it was only just sinking in.

I pressed my lips together and averted my gaze.

Not in my life had I cared for Mariana, but I never wished her dead either. With her gone, our trail ended in smoke. I knew that's what I shouldn't be thinking right now. I knew I should probably be shocked. Sad even. But there was simply no room left inside me for grief.

No room left to mourn.

No room left to...break.

Not when my own sister's death was still so fresh in my mind.

Blair let out a choked sob, collapsing on the ground in front of the couch. She wasn't loud and noisy like most people were. She was silent, in so much pain that she couldn't move. She couldn't cry. She probably couldn't think. I knew what that felt like. I remembered the day my parents died.

Johanna slowly eased herself away from the couch, coming to crouch in front of my cousin. Whatever pity she felt, it didn't show on her face. She leaned forward, offering Blair her hands. "She cannot stay for very long, Blair. It's not the way of the world, but you can see her one last time to say goodbye. Take my hands."

Blair latched her fingers around Johanna's, squeezing so tight Johanna's fingertips looked swollen, but she didn't complain.

"Mom?" she asked tentatively. She blinked twice, like she couldn't believe what she was seeing. I squinted at the spot she was staring at but saw nothing. Mariana must have said something because both girls were crying within seconds.

"I love you too, Mom. I'm sorry I didn't understand. I didn't know."

"*Didn't know what?*" Violet asked.

"*I'm not asking her right now. This is her goodbye,*" I whispered back even though it was only in my mind. The

47

moment was both so touching and utterly tragic because not a person in this room hadn't suffered. Not a single person.

"I'm so sorry, Mom. I'm sorry I didn't call. I didn't warn you—I...I thought it was better if we didn't call. I thought you would be safe. I'm so sorry, Mom. I'm so sorry." She repeated it over and over again, closing her eyes and surrendering to the tears that froze and clung to her skin. The temperature dropped a good ten degrees in seconds as Blair succumbed to grief.

Right then, I knew. I just knew that Anastasia had something to do with this. It was too convenient. Too perfect. The same day I evaded her again, the only relative we had left that wasn't with us died.

"It's almost time, Blair. She needs to cross." Johanna was gentle, guiding as she spoke. I could tell it pained her to do this, that tonight would be rough on her when this was all said and done. Like everyone else, she had lost friends, family, only days ago. The death toll was mounting by the hour, and we were helpless to stop it right now.

But not forever. We will avenge them. All of them.

"I will kill them. I will kill every last one of them. I will make them hurt as you hurt. Please," Blair pleaded. "Please don't leave." She blindly reached with one hand, and just for a second, I saw a ghost of something grab her hand.

"I will protect her. I promise. *I promise.* Just please don't leave." Blair was on her knees begging. Reaching for the ghost of her mother, but it was too late. She begged, she cried, but in the end, there was nothing she could do.

I knew the moment she was gone. The sudden

unending sadness that seemed to consume the room as my cousin cried out. The floor turned to ice as Blair screamed.

I think that was the moment my heart finally broke for her. Broke for her loss, when I thought I had nothing left to break. I got on my hands and knees and crawled across the icy floors, mentally shoving the geode table aside. Blair released Johanna's hands, and collapsed into me. She didn't shake the room with her grief, but she froze it. Ice crawled up the walls and across the ceiling. Blair and I curled together as I pulled her on my lap and rocked her back and forth.

"Shhh…" I whispered, brushing her hair aside as it bled white from the roots to her ends. Her pain…I did not know how to ease it or make it better. I knew from experience nothing I did would help. It wasn't about me, and therefore I could not fix it. I hated that. I hated myself, because just like my own sister, in the moment it mattered most, there was absolutely nothing I could do. For all my gifts and power, I could not heal anything I touched because I only knew how to destroy.

"I will kill them," Blair sobbed over and over again.

I believed it. If her mother told her who killed her, Blair would hunt them to the ends of the earth. She would use every trick I'd taught her. She would craft a punishment just for them, but in the end, it wouldn't bring Mariana back. None of us had that gift. None of us were saviors. We didn't heal. We hurt. We killed. It's what every single one of us had been trained to do, outside Elizabeth, but she was no exception.

I turned a fraction to my youngest cousin. Her dark grey eyes swirled like the clouds of a coming storm. Unlike Blair, she hadn't screamed or begged. She didn't give apologies. She didn't break. I despised her. Hated her, and yet, in that moment...she and I were the same.

Both of us feeling in the only way we knew how. I held Blair through the shudders that racked her body, but Elizabeth, she held herself. Maybe it's because she knew no one else would, or maybe it's because she finally knew she was truly alone.

I don't know how much time passed, but we stayed in the living room that night. At some point in the early morning, people started to trickle back to their rooms. But not us. Blair and I stayed on that floor through the night while Alexandra watched from her place on the couch. We banded together to grieve our losses in our own ways.

I didn't cry because I had no more tears. I wondered if I ever would again, and decided it's probably best if I didn't. I thought I lost everything when Lily died. I thought I died too. Sitting here on the icy floor in a Vegas strip club...I still had something to fight for. People needed me. Maybe I would never be the same as I was, but could I really continue down the path I was on? Could I continue to strip myself of emotion, losing more of my humanity in the process?

I had been through so much. Learned so much. To continue like this would be letting her win, letting Anastasia win. And that was something I simply could not allow.

It was a tragedy what happened at Daizlei, but I could not let it be the end of me.

Somehow.

CHAPTER 8

"What in Nyx's name happened?" Cade stood in front of the elevator, arms crossed and pissed off. I stretched languidly, popping my joints to relieve the tension within them.

Ice still coated pretty much everything, but it was beginning to melt. The cold water made my clothes cling to my arms and legs like a second skin. I groaned, pulling myself out of the slush that was the apartment living room.

"Hold that thought while we go change and wake the others," I said.

Fifteen minutes later, the group of us gathered in the magical elevator and we were on our way down.

The tension was thick, suffocating, when the doors opened.

Once again, the strip club was empty. Only this time we were meeting Tam, the alpha of the Las Vegas pack.

"Hello, lovelies."

I wasn't sure what I was expecting, but the man at the bar was not it. He was short, only an inch or two taller than me, wearing a glitter red vest and leather pants. His short black hair had spikes of blue and gold, complementing his sea-blue cat eyes. His smile was sneaky and goading, like he knew something we didn't.

"Tam," Cade said by way of greeting. Tam smirked and led us to a lounge off to the side. His hips swung as he walked, reminding me of a cat that was full of itself. He sat fluid and graceful in the only armchair, throwing one leg over the arm like he was king. *Think much of yourself?*

"Well, well. What do we have here?" he said, smacking his lips together obnoxiously. "The Wraith of London." He eyed Johanna shrewdly but was already moving on before I could ask.

"Heirs to Fortier, Graeme, and Kearney." His eyes flicked between Oliver, Scarlett, and Liam.

"The Maiden." He gave Camilla a wink before turning borderline cold.

"The right hand of Anastasia Fortescue." Alec bristled under his passive aggressive glare.

"Aaron White and his signasti, Nyx's blessed. You are quite possibly the Council's worst nightmare if the rumors are to be believed." He grinned savagely at me, either not noticing everyone's discomfort, or simply not caring.

"And you brought friends. How delightful!" He nodded to the others, making the merely uncomfortable silence downright awkward.

"Thank you for taking us in," Johanna said diplomatically. I got the distinct impression she took it upon herself to thank him because it didn't look like anybody else was going to.

"It's a pleasure to have so many interesting and highly sought-after people—"

"They need to explain what happened last night," Cade interrupted.

"What happened last night?" Tam asked.

I stayed quiet, twisting the ring on my pinky finger as Johanna gave him a recap of the night before. Blair clasped and unclasped her hands, twisting her fingers in a way that had to be uncomfortable. Her leg bounced up and down, thrumming so intensely that I doubt she knew she was doing it. I reached over and placed my hand on her knee, squeezing lightly. She stopped fidgeting instantly.

"Sorry," she murmured. I nodded once, noticing Tam out of the corner of my eye. He had moved his hands, drawn together in a steeple under his chin. His cunning cat eyes watched me with peculiarity.

"You're a demon? That is simply fascinating." His shrewd smile didn't win him any favors.

"Part. I'm part demon." His smile only widened.

"And how did that come to be?" He phrased it as a question, but it was surely rhetorical. I didn't know if he really wanted me to answer, or if his staring meant he wanted to figure out the puzzle himself.

"They don't know. And their only living relative that may have known died last night," Johanna murmured. The red tinge around her eyes had finally faded, and here to replace it was the dark circles of sleep deprivation.

Tam sat up straight, putting both legs on the ground in front of him. "Died?" he asked. Johanna nodded in confirmation. "How do you know?"

"Because she came to me," Elizabeth whispered. My

eyes snapped to the girl curled tight in a ball. The lifeless expression on her face was ghostly. Callous.

"She came to you?" he asked slowly, stroking the blue-tipped hairs on his chin. Elizabeth nodded robotically in response. "Did she say who killed her or why?" Elizabeth shrugged and turned to Blair. Even from across the room, the motion was clear.

"Yes and no," Blair said. She wasn't whispering, but there was a hoarseness when she spoke. I had a damn good idea who was responsible, but I waited for Blair's reply. "She told us someone was hunting her. That they wouldn't let her go because she knew too much. After finding out they're part demon..."—she swallowed hard, avoiding my gaze—"I can only assume it had something to do with them. It's no secret Anastasia is hunting Selena, and no one knows why. Maybe my mom did. Maybe that's why they killed her."

An uneasy sensation spread across my skin, like an itch just out of reach. There was something there, at the very corners of my mind, reaching out to me and trying to tell me something, but I didn't know what.

"Your mother had information and you think the Head of the Supernatural Council killed her for it? That's a hefty claim, but I've heard worse. You got any proof to back it up?" Cade asked, his Adam's apple bobbing.

"They saw her ghost, not her body. I don't see how you can expect proof of anything when Anastasia can slaughter a school without repercussions. If Mariana did have information, it probably died with her," I said. Around me the club music turned on, EDM and R&B melting together to induce a euphoric mood, but there was nothing euphoric about the conversation we were having.

"Unless she recorded it," Elizabeth said.

The skin on her face was drawn and tight, all semblance of the mourning daughter and pathetic prisoner wiped from her demeanor.

"You think she recorded the killing?" I asked.

"No. I think she recorded whatever she knew. My mother was a truthsayer, and it made her obsessive. She went over the edge when your mom died, thinking that people—someone—was trying to find us. If she learned something, then it's somewhere in that house," Elizabeth said. I wouldn't argue that Mariana had been paranoid, but I don't think I ever realized how deep that paranoia ran. I turned to Blair who had gone stiff.

"Do you think it's there? In the house?" I asked her. Elizabeth may not be at the top of my shit list or bound and gagged at the moment, but I didn't trust her any more than I did before. Even grieving, I had no doubt she would put her own life first and try to escape if we gave her the chance.

Blair stayed silent, her hands shifting uneasily. "If it exists, it's there," she whispered.

"Well, that settles that. We need to find a way to get to her house, like, before whatever evidence that may be there of how we came to be "—Alexandra paused, motioning between us—"is destroyed."

CHAPTER 9

WE AGREED WE NEEDED TO FIND A WAY BACK TO MICHIGAN TO search Mariana's house, but no one knew of a way how. Not that didn't risk us being attacked. Again.

"Could you take us?" Amber asked Cade, batting her eyes a little bit like that would sweeten the deal.

"No can do, babe. My powers have limits just as much as any other teleporter." He ran a hand through his honey-colored hair, seeming unruffled by it. Admitting he couldn't do something was acknowledging his own weakness by Supernatural standards. It was something most were ashamed of, embarrassed at the very least, and he didn't even seem perturbed.

Amber shrugged and looked at Tori who shook her head. "There's no way I'll be able to go that far with so many people," Tori said. I wasn't going to disagree. A few states with a couple people she could manage, but she wasn't strong enough to hop across most of the country with this many people. Especially twice, so close together.

"Hmm..." Tam said. He stroked his blue-tipped chin

hairs into an inverted triangle. "Ordinarily I wouldn't get behind this type of thing and risk angering the higher ups, but"—he tapped his fingertips together, shifting to give us his full attention—"finding out how a couple of part demons came to be is just too tempting to stop." The wicked gleam in his eye made me stiffen. "Give me twenty-four hours and I will find a way to get you there," he said.

At that, Tam jumped to his feet and gave a small nod to the group before leaving. Cade untangled himself from Amber and escorted us back to the elevator. Once again, the doors magically opened without needing to be called. It was unnerving in a way, but it had me curious.

"How does this thing work?" I asked, trailing behind the group. If you watched closely, the more people that entered it, the larger it grew.

"Magic," Cade said with a bit of flair. He clapped his hands together and gold sparks appeared in the air around him. I wasn't impressed.

"Obviously."

"The door is sentient. You think your request, and if it has access, it takes you there," Aaron answered as I sagged against the wall. The doors closed behind me. Like last time, it started moving on its own.

I scoffed. "Sentient? It's not like it's a living, breathing thing—"

"I wouldn't go around saying things you don't know are certain," Cade commented. I shot him a withering look.

"What powers the elevator then?" I asked pointedly.

"The ley lines," Johanna answered. I turned to her and raised a questioning eyebrow. "Every black market is built on ley lines and they're nearly as old as time itself," she continued. "The elevator is the only door into and out of any black market. As times change, so does the door, but no one knows how or why."

"That's why they call it sentient," Aaron said. I glanced up to see him watching me. "It opens when it's needed, and it takes you where you need to go."

"Then why don't we take it to Mariana's house?" I asked.

"It can't. It will go to any black market in the world, but that's a risk we can't take. This group showing up to the Detroit black market and then trying to get to your aunt's house would be easily noticed," Cade said.

"Alec, could you—"

"Potentially, but there are too many variables. This is a large group over a great distance. If I lost sight of anyone in the crowd, or if...one of you was in danger, I could lose my concentration and we'd all be exposed." He shot a glance at Blair for a fraction of a second before looking away.

"I guess we'll see what Tam has to offer then. So, it can go to any black market, is that right, Cade?" I asked nonchalantly. Aaron tilted his head, his eyes narrowing just the slightest as Cade nodded in response.

"The safe house isn't a black market though," I said as the doors beeped and slid open to reveal all the ice and water from Blair's meltdown to be gone. The apartment looked much the same as when we'd entered it the first time.

It was almost like...magic. Wild magic. Sentient magic.

"The safe house is special for many reasons. That's why it's safe," Cade smirked.

The wheels were already turning in my head as I stepped off the magical elevator and began to plot.

I WAITED until the others had gone to bed before I pulled on a pair of combat boots and approached the elevator. Taking a deep breath, I stared at the metal double doors. It could take me anywhere in the world, but I didn't need to leave Vegas. I wanted to enter the parts of it that were hidden from the human world by the only thing more powerful than science. Magic.

Swallowing any hesitation, I took my first step and the doors opened.

The cold metal grey wasn't a welcome sight, but it was a good sign. They hadn't lied to me. Embracing the now or never mentality, I took one look behind me at the empty apartment and stepped inside, the doors closing behind me.

Just like the other times I'd used it, there were no buttons to tell it where to go. I was supposed to trust it, but I couldn't believe in such a superfluous ideal as trust anymore. Apprehension sat like a stone in my stomach, making me grimace as the elevator began to move. I hated enclosed spaces, and elevators were the worst.

The ride was short. Abrupt. I held my breath as the doors slid open revealing a whole new world that was operating under the guise of night. I stepped out of the elevator, unsure if it really was the Las Vegas black market.

A gust of wind swept down the alley, flinging my hair away from my face. I took in the scent of mold and magic, both pungent and strong. The bricks of the alleyway were black as onyx, the grey grout gleamed in the moonlight. At the end of the empty alley, people—no, not people—paranormals flooded the street. I crept closer, peeking my head around the corner.

Either end extended farther than I could see with shops of every color. Across from me, a young Witch was running a gambling game that was roping in paranormals off the street. Next, a scarred Shifter woman was selling pelts far bigger than any animal I'd ever seen. She claimed they were Shifters that'd crossed her and this was how they paid their debt. The faint white bite marks around her neck made me disinclined to disagree with her.

I stepped out of the shadows of the alley and hooked a left down the never-ending street. Up and down either side, young men and women of all species were offering their bodies or blood. The mercenaries, or drunken fools rather, boasted their killing abilities for hire to any that could afford their rate. Even better were the fighting pits, where crowds gathered to watch two people battle it to the death. In some cases, I thought the crowd was more worked up than the fighters themselves. The paranormals went into an all-out frenzy, betting on who they thought would come out on top. It was savage and gruesome and called to me in the worst way possible.

I stayed near the outside edge of one pit, watching two particularly large Shifters swing at each other like beasts instead of men. They fought with a pure rage that resonated inside of me and made me barely able to turn my eyes away.

The larger man was a brute by any definition. He threw

his weight around like a hulking goliath, thinking he was too big to be taken down. The smaller guy, we'll call him David, he was fast and he fought with heart. Goliath could put him down, but he couldn't seem to keep him there. It was like every hit Goliath landed fueled David more, and something about that made me rage right along with him.

It didn't take long before I was pushing my way to the front of the crowd and staring down into the pit. Up close, it was clear that neither of them were small, but Goliath was a frickin monster by comparison. His mostly naked body was smudged with dirt and bleeding from the nicks that David got in on him. It didn't compare to the hits David was receiving. I wasn't sure how the guy was still standing, given the blood that coated his body.

He needed to finish it fast or he was a goner. It seemed that David realized that about the same time I did.

Faster than Goliath could react, the smaller guy swept his foot under him and sent his claws straight into the larger fighter's throat. I couldn't look away as David shredded his tendons and ligaments in half a second, and took his head clean off in the following.

The crowd went wild, high off a good fight as money swapped hands. Not I though. I watched him, David, as he struggled to bottle that rage back up. His breathing slowed as he worked to ignore the crowds, and I knew right then that he could have ended the fight sooner. But he didn't.

Because like me, something in him wasn't quite right. Something deadly and terrifying that the rest of the world was too frightened to even speak about. A rage so pure and potent that there was never any hope of taming it. The best we could do was keep that demon on a leash.

It was that moment that I understood the stranger in the pit. He looked up at me—and I realized he wasn't a stranger at all.

He was Aaron White.

And he'd just spotted me.

CHAPTER 10

I LOCKED EYES WITH HIM JUST LONG ENOUGH TO SEE THAT SPARK of recognition. His eyes shifted from black as the alleyway bricks to pure gold. Aaron was pissed. He took a step towards me, his jaw tight with tension—and I ran.

Backpedaling through the crowd, I dived down a narrow side alley, hoping to escape his notice. I had no doubt he would be hot on my trail, even after his fight, given the fury radiating off him through just a look.

I was in deep, deep shit.

Slinking down the row of tents, I could practically feel his anger pumping through my own veins. It was strong enough to make me stop short and catch my breath, reminding myself that the goddamn bond was probably acting up again. I grit my teeth against the string of curse words threatening to fly out of my mouth. Best save those for when he finds me.

I didn't even notice the jingling of wind chimes until a crooked black finger pointed at me and beckoned me closer. I paused, looking to either side. This woman seriously couldn't be talking to me, could she? The old Witch nodded her head and revealed a row of yellow teeth.

"Care to have your fortune told?" she asked. I almost said no and kept on walking, but there was something in her voice that made it sound like a test.

"Sure. What's it going to cost me?" The old woman smiled, but it wasn't reassuring.

"You've already paid," she said cryptically. Before I could respond, Aaron's anger hit me like a freight train, making my blood singe. He was getting closer.

I took a breath and stepped into the tent, feeling a bit like the idiot girl in horror movies that forgets to lock the door.

Inside her tent, a fire burned in a hearth, but it had no smoke. Next to it sat a table with two chairs and a black velvet bag. Along the edge were tables full of artifacts from all over the world, some magical, some unknown. Hanging above my head, wind chimes pealed as the tent flap fell closed behind me.

The old woman kept her hood drawn, hiding half her face in the shadows as she pointed to the table. I took the hint and sat in one of the rickety old chairs. The Witch sat across from me.

Reaching forward, she pulled on the drawstring of the velvet bag and held it up.

"Take three," she croaked. "If you dare."

I didn't hesitate as I reached inside the bag and felt for three objects. The texture was recognizable immediately.

What kind of Witch keeps a bag of bones in her shop? I meant it rhetorically, but Violet answered nonetheless.

"The kind that walks with the Three-faced Goddess."

"Those are Witch tales, Violet. The ancients left us," I said. She didn't reply.

The Witch pointed to the hearth beside us and said, "Throw them in the fire."

I did as I was told, mildly creeped out, but kind of curious. There was a popping sound as the bones shattered, turning black against the flames. That can't be good.

"Interesting..." she murmured.

"What is?" I asked, more anxious than I'd originally thought I'd be. Violet's response had me on edge, and I had no idea if this Witch could really see the future in a handful of blackened chicken bones.

"You are on a dark path looking for revenge, but you do not have all the answers. There is knowledge being withheld from you." Her voice took on that of someone who was young, but also middle-aged, and at the same time, very old. It was so contradictory. It made no sense, and the cold wind that swept through the tent had me shivering.

"Hard times are ahead of you, child. Truths will be revealed that will make you question everything you know, and your decisions will change the very foundations of this world as we know it." This fortune was oddly specific and vague at the same time, but the cold, bone-chilling tone of her voice had me questioning.

"Trust in your signasti and the darkness inside, but do not trust the one who calls to you. She is not who you think."

The chunks of bone burst into ash, and I resisted the urge to jump to my feet. This was more than I bargained for, but I wasn't running scared from an old women's tent.

The Witch let out a low chuckle and said, "You don't scare easily. That's good. You'll need it."

Her voice had fallen back into the rasp of an old woman.

"Need it for what?" I asked, hoping to get more information out of her. Whether it was true or not, she put on one hell of a show.

"Your first trial approaches," she said, falling into a coughing fit. She hacked twice and spat a wad of mucus into the fire. "Should you pass, we will meet again, and I will tell you a story. But should you fail, darkness will reign until the end of times."

"Uh huh," I said, rising to my feet. *End of times? What a crock.*

The Witch reached out, faster than I expected, and wrapped her cold, crooked fingers around my wrist. I looked up and found myself staring into eyes that changed like the shifting sands. They were red, and then yellow, but green, then blue. They were every color. "Who are you?"

"Now, Selena," she smirked. "What has Valda told you about asking the wrong questions. You already know the answer to that."

Valda? I frowned, but that's when I realized just who I was staring at.

I'd found her.

The Crone with the third eye.

I swallowed hard and blinked once, but when I opened my eyes, the scene had vanished. There was no tent, no Crone, hell, even the temperature had risen again. I blinked another ten times, looking around in every direction, but she was nowhere to be found.

It was just me and her parting words in the same side alley I'd found her in, like it never happened.

I had her. *I lost her.*

How the hell do you lose a person and an entire tent of junk?

I let out a string of curses under my breath, kicking at the air in frustration.

It took me fifteen seconds to realize I was literally just standing in the middle of a street of tents with people moving around me. Taking a deep breath, I retraced my steps back down the row, waving off the different paranormals trying to approach me for any multitude of things.

I'd just had an encounter with the Crone. The same damn Crone I had been trying to find for a week, and I didn't realize it until she was gone. I could kick myself right now, but it wouldn't appease the anger that pulsed in me.

I rounded the corner to the main street where I'd taken off from the fighting ring, and of course, that's exactly where Aaron was waiting for me. One second, I was wading through the crowd and making my way back towards the entrance, the next I had one massively pissed off Supernatural Shifter crossbreed dragging me into the gap between two tents.

"What are you doing here?" he demanded.

"I could ask you the same thing." Dirt marks covered his face and arms, but his clothes were remarkably clean for someone that had been nearly naked and fighting in the pit. A thin sheen of sweat still lined his skin, glistening in the moonlight.

"But *you* were supposed to lie low," he growled.

Like that made a difference? No one trusted me, and

while that was understandable given the situation, he was the one down here killing people in a pit fight. I crossed my arms over my chest, glaring at him.

"Why? So you could have all the fun down here ripping heads off people?" He opened his mouth, but I held up a hand for silence. "I don't see why I'm the delicate China doll being told to stay in the goddamn safe house while you're down here in a pit fight letting off steam. Does that seem fair to you? Because it doesn't seem very fair to me."

I wasn't going to mention what I felt standing outside that fight. Oh no. Just like I wasn't bringing up the Crone. Not until I sorted out what the hell I was going to do.

"Cade didn't want you to leave because Anastasia put a price on your head, Selena. Which makes you very valuable, not just to the Supes that would turn you in, but to every other paranormal wanting to get ahold of the matter manipulator that led a Vampire invasion and collapsed Daizlei." His eyes flashed with sympathy for a moment before hardening again. "I'm sorry, but they didn't want to tell you after the last few days. I was outvoted, but I think you deserve the right to know why Tam didn't want to take you in. Every paranormal in the world is looking for you right now."

That was—no—no—I mean, I did collapse the building —but—

"That's not what happened." It was all I could think to say as the cold realization hit me. "But nobody knows that...*because Anastasia and I look the same.*"

He nodded solemnly, some of the anger in his eyes seemed to have cooled, but I wasn't finished with this conversation just yet.

"I'm not staying cooped up in the safe house every day.
I can't do it." He opened his mouth to argue with me, but I
cut him a harsh glare. *I swear to Nyx if he interrupts me, I'm
going to punch him.* "Listen to me. I get it. The whole world
thinks I'm probably some kind of monster, and you know
what? I kind of am." That had him shutting up. His mouth
closed so hard his teeth clinked.

"That's exactly why I can't stay in the safe house
though, because if I'm not doing something—anything—I
will lose my mind. Ask Alexandra. Ask Blair. They will tell
you what happens when I'm forced into a box. But don't
ask me to do this when it's something not even you will
do." Aaron raised his brow and shook his head. I couldn't
tell if he was impressed or frustrated.

"What if people see you—"

"What if people see you?" I repeated back to him,
clasping my hands together and raising a brow.

"They won't."

"That's a bullshit answer," I scoffed. "You have no way
to guarantee that."

Thunder roared overhead, the declaration of an
incoming storm. We weren't done here. Not by a longshot,
and I wasn't going back to the safe house until I had some
answers.

"Actually, I do." He paused, and I motioned for him to
go on. "I can shift into anyone or any animal in the world.
Currently, I look like some random Shifter off the streets,
but it appears you can see through it *now.*"

Of course, another awfully *convenient* ability no one
tells me about until after the fact, but that wasn't what

snagged my attention. He said *now*. Like he was implying I couldn't before...

"How do you know I couldn't see through it before?" I asked sharply. His body went tense and his jaw twitched. There was something he wasn't telling me. Something that nagged at my memory like an itch I couldn't scratch, telling me not to let him off the hook. "How do you know I couldn't see through it before, but that I can now?" I asked him again.

"Because tonight is the first time I've taken someone else's form," Aaron said slowly. "And you saw through it. You saw...me." His eyes looked to the heavens and he smiled, just a little, like he thought something was funny.

"Who?"

He dropped his gaze to me and an almost painful look crossed his face. He knew what I was asking.

Whose form did he take? My heart rattled as heat rushed to my head.

I had a suspicion, but I would not say it. No...

"Don't be angry with me..."

Not the best way to start a sentence. My suspicion mounted, and I steadied myself for the truth.

"Whose form, Aaron?" I demanded for the last time. His smile turned sad and he quirked up his lips in a stupid half-smile that looked so *familiar*...

"Lucas. I used to pretend to be Lucas."

He—I—we—I didn't know what to say. But fortunately, I had Violet, and she knew how to think.

"Don't shut him out for this," she said. Her presence brushed closer to my mind and a numbing cold followed it.

It didn't take all the bite out, but enough to sort through my mess of emotions.

"He's a liar, just the same as Lucas," I snapped.

"How often?" I ground the words out, but he knew what I was asking.

"Often enough that I should be groveling right now," he replied, pinching the bridge of his nose and sweeping his hand down his face. It was a motion I did frequently. A tell when I was stressed, but much like he'd taught himself Lucas's half-smile, he also knew mine.

"Then why aren't you?"

"You know why," Violet responded.

"I didn't ask you," I snapped back at her.

"Because I'm not sorry for it and I'd be lying if I tried to grovel." He stepped a foot closer and I moved a foot back. The thick material of one of the tents brushed against my back. "I'm sorry you're pissed off by it, but I can't be sorry I did it. You wouldn't let me get close to you, and I couldn't seem to stay away."

"He cares about you," Violet grumbled. I mentally shoved her away and this time she moved willingly.

"So you thought you'd impersonate my best friend? Did Lucas know about this?" I took another step back without thinking and stumbled in the tent fabric. Aaron grabbed me by my wrist and pulled me forward. My hands landed on his chest with a thud and my head spun.

"Yes, he did," he answered. "And he allowed it because he knew what you were to me and that if he tried to stop it, I would tell you and prevent him from ever having a chance at anything with you. He entered your life and stole you from me before I was ever given an opportunity, and after you made it clear you didn't want me around, he and I came to an arrangement. So long as you were happy with him, I would stay out of your life. But I refused to keep you completely out of mine." He swept back a stray lock of hair, tucking it behind my ear. "I trained with you as him most late nights you couldn't sleep. I did the bulk of helping you study to pass our classes. I was the one that found you on the anniversary of your parents' death, and the one who tracked you down in the warehouse after you went missing."

I knew I should pull away. I knew it with everything in me, and I couldn't seem to. My body was frozen to the spot.

"So, you see, I've actually been at your side since I found you. You just never knew it." I swallowed hard as he ran his fingertips across my cheek.

Part of me could understand his reasoning. A very, very small part of me even felt bad for him, but it wasn't enough.

"You...lied to me. You—you—" I couldn't find the words to explain what he did. To tell him how it was so much worse than lying, because it was infinitely more complicated than that. He'd made me believe Lucas was someone he was not. I knew Lucas as intimately as I had ever known a person. I knew what he liked and didn't like. I knew about his parents and his family. I knew what time he woke up every morning because he couldn't sleep, and how restless he was late in the evenings...but I didn't know if that was even Lucas. Was it him, or was it Aaron? And how had I never noticed the difference?

This was wrong on so many levels. I could barely contain the anger boiling within me.

"And you've never lied to me?" he asked as his fingertips

brushed over my bottom lip. It snapped whatever trance I was in and I shoved him back.

"We need to get back." I turned on my heel to walk away and he grabbed my arm, stopping me in my tracks.

"Be angry, but please don't shut me out." He didn't plead and he didn't beg. I could give him that. But I was in no frame of mind to talk about this.

I was compromised.

He didn't know it yet, and it needed to stay that way.

I jerked my arm from his grasp and stalked off into the dead of night, wondering if every moment I had wanted Lucas, I really wanted the man who betrayed me.

CHAPTER 11

WE RETURNED WITHOUT SAYING MUCH OF ANYTHING TO EACH other and I didn't sleep. Aaron spent hours in the bathroom and I could only assume it was to try to scrub the blood from his skin so thoroughly that maybe he could pretend he wasn't that guy in the ring. Hide it just like he hid everything else.

But I knew the truth now.

And the truth is that he was just like me.

We were both liars and killers. Maybe that's why fate put us together.

Because only someone just as ugly and depraved on the inside could ever possibly be made for me. The other half of my soul.

It was sometime early the next morning that he finally came out of the bathroom. I didn't say anything, and he didn't comment as he laid on the other side of me. Our hearts beat in time with the crackling fireplace that never seemed to burn out. I felt the mattress sink as he rolled on his side, toward or away from me, I couldn't tell. I was pretending to be asleep, and for the remainder of the night, he did too.

Neither of us acknowledged our exhausted state the next morning when we rose with the dawn. I changed my clothes in an attempt to rid myself of the scent of smoke, but it clung to my skin. Snatching a new set of pants and a plain shirt, I locked myself in the bathroom and took another makeshift bath with a cup. Black particles swirled in the water as I scrubbed myself sterile with the lavender and honeysuckle soaps. Only after every hint of Aaron and the black market was down the drain did I set the cup down and turn the water off.

"Selena?" Aaron said on the other side of the door, his voice hesitant.

"What?"

"Cade and Tam are here." He didn't wait for my reply before his footsteps trailed out of the bedroom.

I dried quickly and subbed brushing my hair for shaking it like a wet dog as I dressed quickly. I was pulling my shirt down as I left the bedroom and I entered the living room to meet them. Tam quirked up an eyebrow in my direction, but I didn't respond as I took my place standing behind the couch. The sound of sizzling grease and scent of bacon drifted through the air as Amber strolled out of the kitchen holding a platter in her hand.

"Have you figured out how to get us to Michigan and back?" Blair asked, sitting next to me. Dark circles lined her eyes, and her face was drawn, but determined.

"We have actually," Tam said pleasantly, stroking his beard.

"Well, what is it?" Alexandra said impatiently. Tam

turned his eyes on my sister and gave her a mischievous grin.

"Patience, child. Good things come to those who wait." Even as the words were coming out of his mouth, the elevator chimed and the doors slid open. A tall, dark-skinned man walked forward. He was thin, but under his plaid flannel shirt I could see respectable muscles. A belt buckle twice the size of my fist reflected the light at an awkward angle.

I'd never seen a Witch dressed as a cowboy. This would be a first.

"Who are you?" I asked bluntly. The man tipped his hat to me and turned to Tam.

"This is Xellos, and he's going to open a portal for you," Tam said proudly. He gave him a feline smile and motioned him forward into the room.

"How?" Amber asked, munching away at her bacon. She plopped down on the couch and kicked her feet up. The girl liked to pretend she didn't have a care in the world, but few of us were afforded that luxury, and she wasn't one of them.

"By creating a rift in the dimension," Johanna answered, coming around the corner. My eyebrows rose in skepticism.

"A rift in the dimension?" I asked her. She sighed deeply. Tension coiled around her body like a vice, but she managed to give me a stiff nod before coming to a stop with her arms crossed over her chest. "Since when can Witches open rifts?"

"Excuse me, miss." Xellos dropped a hand to his belt as he swaggered into the living room like a good ol' southern boy, not that he had much of the accent. His cinnamon colored eyes swept over me. "But since when did the matter manipulators return?"

"Isn't that the question we'd all like answered?" I replied softly. The others all pretended to find the particles of dust in the air just fascinating. All but one.

Aaron lurked in the corner of the room, leaning against the only wall, half cast in shadow. His arms were crossed over his chest while he watched me with dark, unreadable eyes. I pushed him from my mind and turned back to the conversation at hand.

"So you're going to open a rift. How does a non-Supernatural go about something like this?" I asked, a note of my irritation creeping into my tone.

"Very carefully," Johanna muttered under her breath.

"You seem to know an awful lot about this," I noted. Johanna narrowed her eyes at me.

"The rifts in this dimension are not meant to be opened. It is a dangerous task at best, and ends with everyone killed at its worst, because it requires infinitely more energy for a Witch to do it than a gifted teleporter," she snapped back at me.

"My question stands."

"She isn't wrong," the Witch stepped forward before the silence could crack whatever semblance of peace we'd been trying to hold together. "Opening a rift is not something most Witches can or should do. The consequences are...costly."

"But you can, right?" Alexandra asked. Xellos nodded once.

"Of course he can," Tam piped up, walking forward to

loop an arm around the Witch's waist. "Xellos has many gifts," he purred.

That explains a few things.

"What's the catch?" I asked.

They turned their eyes to me and Xellos's lips settled in a wary expression. Either he was born with it, or he made himself more powerful. But there was always a catch.

"To open the rift, I will need someone who has been there to remain and act as the guide. Once the rift is open, I will need to tap the ley lines that fuel the black market. If I mess that up, the rift will do one of two things"—he paused, holding up one finger—"It will either close, killing any who are in it and trapping those who are already out on the other side."

I got the distinct impression that wasn't the worst-case scenario, and it should have scared me more than it did.

"Or?"

He glanced at Johanna whose mouth formed a thin line.

"The rift will expand until it implodes, killing everything for miles on both sides."

"And how likely is that to happen?"

Once upon a time there was a small inner voice that wouldn't have allowed me to ask that question. I would have deemed it too dangerous to attempt. Not worth the risk.

It appeared that it, too, had died that night at Daizlei.

"Difficult to say," he said and rubbed the stubble alongside his jaw. "I've done this before, but I don't make a habit of it. Probably wouldn't be here if I did."

My heart beat steady as a drum, not changing tempo in

the slightest at the possibility of a very imminent death. Thoughts about my sister swirled in the back of my mind, but I couldn't give those power here and now.

Those demons needed to stay buried for the time being.

"How soon can we do this?" I asked. Johanna went rigid as a board, and Oliver stepped forward in front of her, a blue energy swirling in his eyes, just waiting to be unleashed.

"With all due respect, Xellos—Tam, this is quite a lofty risk for us to be taking for information that may or may not be there," he said.

"Feel free to stay here, Fortier," I replied. He turned that icy gaze on me, taking a step forward.

"You would do well to remember your place in all of this," he growled.

"You mean below you? Because I'm not a royal prick born with a silver spoon, is that it?" I replied, closing half the distance towards him. I would have moved the rest of it, had Aaron not intervened. One moment he stood stoic and watching, the next he was stepping in between us, making motions like he was going to restrain me.

I stopped short, a wicked cold smile coming to my lips.

"Selena, can we please—"

I lifted my hand slowly, waiting for the flicker of fear in Aaron's eyes, but it never came. His jaw tensed as the room held its breath. His hands clenched briefly at his sides. But his eyes never flickered in fear, and I didn't like it. Not one bit.

I flicked my fingers to the side to force him to move.

My eyes dropped to that hand as I did it again.

Nothing.

Why was nothing—

"Your powers won't work on me. It's part of the bond."

I didn't let myself show how much his mention of the damn bond made me bristle. I didn't want it. I didn't need it, but yet again, the universe decided to screw me over. Not only is my soul shackled to this man, but my body, too, it appears.

He couldn't have my mind. That was blissfully untouched.

"How inconvenient," I said. My eyebrow twitched, and the couch Amber was sitting on shoved into the back of his legs. He fell backwards, clearing my path once again.

"Selena," Amber said in warning. It wasn't a warning *for* me. It was a warning *to* me. I ignored her.

"This is exactly what I'm talking about. She's out of control—"

"Stop saying that." I paused at the sound of Aaron's voice. "She's not out of control. She's grieving just like the rest of us. Her aunt died last night. Her sister died less than a week ago. She has no family outside of those here. No nothing, and to add to it, the world has gone to shit while the bond madness is setting in."

The bond madness? A chill ran through me, but I held in the shudder.

"She doesn't even want the bloody bond. It's only going to get worse," Oliver said.

"What she does or doesn't want with the bond is none of *your* business. That is between her and I, Fortier." The grave tone in Aaron's voice left little room for discussion, not that Oliver pushed it.

"Apologies for my insensitivities," he told me. "But the point still stands. Her power is part of what got us into this mess. She should not be able to break shields without effort. She should not—"

"You would think then"—I trailed my fingers along the back of the couch—"that you would believe it imperative that we find out how I came to be. If you are so threatened by my power."

Oliver scowled, cruel lines marring a more than handsome face.

"You think you're invincible because of your power and you dive into situations without having all the facts. One of these times, you're going to get someone killed." He stormed out of the room without waiting for a reply and Johanna went after him.

If I hadn't hesitated, Anastasia would be dead. Not her. Not Lily.

I would take those words to my grave before I uttered them aloud.

Xellos cleared his throat, making me painfully aware of our audience.

"Well, don't you all make a lively bunch," Xellos chuckled, unperturbed. Tam had taken a place on the white sofa with his arms spread out along the back of it, his face calculating and unreadable.

"How soon can we do this?" I repeated, already tired of dealing with them.

"Three days. There are supplies I need to get, but I should have it together by then—if you want to go through with it, that is," he said. I nodded once, ignoring the heavy feeling weighing down my chest.

"You're still breathing. Those are good enough odds for me."

I did not look to Aaron's eyes as I walked by him on my way back to the room, afraid of what I might find there if I did.

CHAPTER 12

WITH EVERY DAY THAT PASSED, I LOST A LITTLE BIT MORE OF MY mind. My sanity. The hours blended together into a meaningless void that pulled me in and refused to let go.

They hadn't come. No one had.

No one but Victor.

He came and went as he pleased. Bringing gifts of lovely young girls that tasted like heaven.

I was going to burn in hell.

I deserved to burn in hell. The things I'd done. The actions I barely held myself back from doing. I swallowed hard on the stale air, breathing in little more than dust and the scent of sweet red wine. At least that's what I preferred to call it.

Blood was such a nasty term, with moral implications.

And there was no room for such implications when you lived in a darkness where the only thing to be afraid of—was yourself.

Footsteps echoed down the hall with a steady purpose. As sure as they were silent, at least to the others. I seemed to be more sensitive to these things. Noise. Sight. Touch. They said that's *natural. It's normal. I tried not to think about it as the wooden door swung open.*

Victor.

And my meal.

Meal. My heart would have thumped in my chest at this. Under normal circumstances, I would have cringed. But there was nothing normal about dying, and then undying.

Nothing normal about drinking this girl's blood.

I was an abomination. A thing. Something that shouldn't be alive in any capacity.

I...was a Vampire.

My hands fisted in the material of my t-shirt in a vain attempt to show more control. To be better than I was. I gripped the fragile cotton and tried not to think about how long I'd been wearing this same shirt. How long had I been in here?

It was impossible to tell without windows, but I had a decent idea. I spent every second of the day counting time while it drifted by unbroken, apart from these visits.

"I've brought you dinner," Victor said, not quite cheerful, but with as much happiness as one could have in a place like this. Where even the shadows cowered in fear at what went down within these walls.

I nodded to him, going still as the girl walked forward on her own.

They dressed her like a doll in a light blue dress. Cupped sleeves stopped short of her shoulders and cut across the girl's clavicle, leaving her pretty porcelain neck bared to us monsters. She had rosy red cheeks and a mane full of chocolate curls that would have once made me jealous.

She was absolutely stunning, and just a child.

But it seemed that they had a taste for beautiful things here.

The girl reached out to me with a tentative hand, running her feather soft fingers over my cheek. I inhaled sharply, out of habit more than anything, but it was a habit that backfired.

My mouth watered at her scent. So sweet, but natural. Her blood was like a fresh plucked strawberry, just ripe with juice. Dripping with vitality. Completely and utterly alive.

I leaned into her touch, unable to control myself again.

My world faded to red the moment my teeth cut her skin.

I gripped her wrist with a bone crushing strength that I battled to control. They brought me these lovely, sweet children as a reminder. As training. They were so much more breakable than grown creatures, and all the more succulent.

Her legs began to tremble as she swayed before me, but curse me, I wanted more of these precious few moments where the dry scratchiness in my throat subsided and I felt alive. I fastened my teeth in more, trying to draw it out and make it last.

To make myself last, just long enough for them to come for me.

I told myself that three times before her eyelids fluttered closed and her body sank against me. My teeth unlatched, my lips peeling themselves away from her skin while I shifted to hold her weight. Victor snapped his fingers once and someone came forward to take her back to wherever they kept human children, like her, that they dressed up and used to train the newly transitioned.

Where the children came from, I did not know, but I did not ask either.

"That was better. You didn't break anything this time," he told me. "Your master will be pleased."

That was code for my master won't kill me. Not yet, anyways.

I chose not to respond and opted for keeping my eyes averted. He liked it when I was submissive. He was...kinder—if there was such a thing. More tolerable. Less caustic. But always callous.

"M-must I work w-with children?" I stammered, keeping my eyes downcast.

"Until you have proven yourself," Victor replied. Fancy Oxfords stepped into my vision, stopping directly in front of me. The black stood stark against the gleaming, polished white marble, drawing my attention to the droplets of blood painting the floor.

"How do I prove myself?" I asked.

It was hardly more than a breath, whispered softly into the dank air that weighed heavier on my chest with every moment I sat here. Fingertips grazed my cheek, smooth as the satin sheets I sat upon. They trailed over my jaw, securing my chin. He lifted my face to his, a silent command.

I raised my eyes obediently. Every thought. Every feeling. Every essence of me locked away, so deep that even they will not see. They will not know.

"You wish to prove yourself to your master?" he asked softly. My lips parted as I gazed into his eyes. A blue so dark they were almost black and heated with something I needed him to feel.

"Yes."

The smile he gave me would have stopped my heart, had it beat. The most beautiful man I had ever met, and he served the monster that did this to me.

I couldn't decide if it was karma or cruel, that his unwavering loyalty to this creature behind the curtain would be what earned me a smile. He had to believe it though. Believe that I wanted this.

"My dear, I thought you would never ask." He lowered

himself to his knees before me, taking my face in his hands. "I knew you were different. Your master is going to be so very pleased, my beautiful flower. So very pleased." The strength in his hands was unlike anything I'd ever felt, but I did not tremble. She *would not want that.*

I smiled back at him, small and unassuming. Timid, but hopeful.

Cunning, although he never saw it.

If I was ever going to have a chance of surviving here, this was it. My one opportunity to change the cards dealt.

They will come, *the small voice whispered inside of me.*

It was quieter with every day that passed.

CHAPTER 13

I woke with an inaudible gasp, trembling in my own cold sweat. My limbs jerked restlessly as my mind came back to the body it was trapped in. Thin sheets tangled around me, sliding over my sensitive skin with an uncomfortable softness that sent me into sensory overload. I clenched my fists around the fabric, heaving in copious amounts of oxygen, attempting to calm my rapid beating heart and the demon that stirred just below the surface.

"I didn't mean to wake you."

Without thinking, I turned my head to the voice that drew my attention. Aaron stood in the doorway of the bathroom. Firelight licked across his bare chest where condensation outlined every ridge and curvature that was him. In the dim light, his dark brown hair looked black and his onyx eyes were depthless. Gold flicked through them, like shooting stars against a moonless sky.

"You didn't wake me," I said softly. My head was in pieces and my ordinarily cold shoulder couldn't be found. I was too out of sorts for my liking. Too vulnerable to let myself occupy the same space as him and pretend that warmth didn't stir in my chest. That embers weren't beating against my iron heart, desperately trying to catch fire. All for this man.

"You look nervous," he said. His bare feet were silent against the hardwood floors as he slowly started towards me. I kicked the sheets away and swung my legs over the edge of the massive bed. It seemed that even when my head wasn't working, my instincts were.

"I'm not," I snapped. My feet touched the floor and I moved to stand on shaky legs, but Aaron moved faster. In the blink of an eye, he went from five feet away to right before me. His toes were only a hairsbreadth from mine, and my quaking limbs caused my chest to brush against his.

"Then why are you shaking?" he asked. His right hand shot forward and looped around my waist, pulling my shuddering body flush against his.

I glared daggers up at him but didn't give him the satisfaction of replying. My nightmares had a lot more to do with my body's reaction than his presence, but saying so would only open myself up to a whole new line of questioning, and the scent of smoke and savagery was already getting to me.

"Get off me." I shoved at him with both hands, but he didn't give. It was like slapping concrete. He was sturdier. Stronger. Because Aaron actually had the power to withstand me.

"Tell me what has you trembling with…" He paused. His nostrils flared as he inhaled deeply. The gold flecks in his eyes compounded together in an explosion of fireworks, turning them nearly yellow. "Fear and...desire."

Damn him. Those words brushed against my skin like a drug straight to my system.

"It's none of your business." I shoved him again and he held me tighter. His fingers wrapped around my hip, flexing against the thin t-shirt that kept my skin safe and protected from the likes of him.

From situations like this happening.

I should have worn a parka.

"You're my business," he whispered in the hollow of my ear. I shivered under his touch and it had nothing to do with my weak muscles.

"Spoken like a true asshole that thinks it's okay to impersonate people," I whispered back with bite. He chuckled darkly against my skin, his lips brushing against me. I went hot, then cold, as my body couldn't decide whether to succumb to sensation or cramp so tightly I had a heart attack.

"Spoken like someone that cares about you. I'm not an idiot. I know what you desire. What I don't know...is why you're afraid." I froze in his arms, struck by the arrogance so similar to another man I let hold me close before I had the good sense to push him away.

For all I know, they were one and the same.

"You must be mistaken. I don't feel fear." I pushed just enough impassiveness into my tone that I came across as the cold-hearted demon I was. Or at least that I had been.

"You're mistaken if you think I buy that. I don't need the bond to know you're lying. I've spent a year watching you, waiting for you." I sucked in a sharp breath and the air between my teeth hissed as I turned my face to his.

"I wouldn't hold your breath. You're waiting for something that's never going to happen. The bond isn't complete, and I have no intention of going through the claiming," I whispered. My breath fanned his face as I saw those dark eyes that I so loved to hate. It was easy for me to dislike him when he looked so like the demons that tortured me in flesh and mind. He let out the softest of growls as his eyes bled gold. Those combusting fireworks let up so much that there was not a shred of black when he looked at me, and it was this look, these eyes, that I had a much harder time with.

He was no longer reminiscent of a demon, but the most beautiful creature I had ever seen. Brimming with power I had yet to discover inside him. Sensual, yet savage. Bloodthirsty as I.

When he was like this, he was the one and only creature that could stare at me without an ounce of fear, and I hated him for it.

"You make a lot of empty threats regarding a bond you choose to know nothing about. The madness is already eating at you, and I'm the only one that can stop it. I don't need to hold my breath, little signasti. You will come to me, and we will complete it. Of that I am absolutely sure." Wind and smoke invaded my senses, drowning me in his scent. The heady combination of that scent and soap paired lovingly with the heat of the fire and warmth of his hands. My shaking legs went utterly still, pressed between him and the edge of a very large bed.

"You make a lot of promises for a man that knows

nothing about me," I replied. If only my voice was half as steady as my legs.

Aaron gripped me tighter, but it wasn't painful, as he took a haggard breath.

"I watched you with another man for a year. I tried to leave you be, to give you time, and if he could have made you happy"—his voice trailed off into heavy silence, cutting me more than I cared to admit—"I would have let you go. I would have found a way." His eyes flicked to my mouth and those embers in my chest began to grow.

"Is that why you impersonated him and never told me? Or why you strung my sister along for months?" I said harshly. It was angry and spiteful and gave him all the ammunition he needed to know that *I cared*.

I blinked once as the realization hit me. I cared. Sure, it was a dark and twisted way of it, but deep down, some part of me chafed against him dating my sister and it always had. It chafed because I cared about a man because of a bond I did not want. A bond I could only assume was the basis for everything between us, and the reason my body and soul betrayed my so very apathetic mind.

The reason I couldn't truly hate him, despite what he'd done.

"You can be pissed about me being Lucas, but don't throw Alexandra in my face, Selena. I dated her because it was the only way I felt I could be close to you. Your very soul sought me out, but *you* chose to be blind and pin it on Lucas. You *chose* to deny not only yourself, but me as well." His words were angry, furious really, and they ignited those embers into a fire that heated even iron and it had the potential to consume me.

"Get your hands off me, or else—"

"Or else what?" he asked, his face only inches from mine. I hadn't realized how close we were until it was too late. "Or else you'll continue to snap at me as a means of deflecting the truth? Or else you'll push me away because it's easier than admitting that you're attracted to me? Or, even better, you'll keep lying to yourself and choosing to see me as evil—because you can't stomach that I give a damn about you and chose to put you before everything in my life—despite knowing that you may never care enough to even look at me as a person because you fear me?"

My mouth went dry as my lips parted.

He thinks...he thinks I'm afraid of him?

If it were anyone else, I would laugh at such an obscene statement, but...it was Aaron. His heart beat as slow and steady as mine did. After a year together, I hadn't noticed until now that our hearts beat in sync. Forever locked in a dance of life and blood.

"You think I'm afraid of you?" I asked, my lips looming even closer to his.

"Yes, but not in the way you think," he replied softly.

"Oh?"

"You fear me because you know I'm the only one that will ever truly understand you."

I never told him that. Never even hinted at it...yet somehow, he was seeing what I myself was only just coming to realize. One of the many reasons, but perhaps the most important, for why I needed to stay away from him.

I realized it when I saw him fight to the death for nothing to gain but pure savage release.

We were so alike in the ways that no one else saw that it

didn't just scare me, it terrified me, because this man had a power that no other before him held.

He had the ability to change me.

Time froze as the silence slipped around us. Pressure built inside me. Climbing. Clawing. Higher and higher.

And the one thing that I clung to throughout the years...snapped.

My control broke for that moment suspended between time, as I—not him—leaned forward and closed the space between us.

My lips touched his and there was nothing soft about the scorching heat that flooded me. I kissed him with a feral need that I didn't understand but surrendered to anyway. My hands slid up his chest, my nails trailing over his bare skin as I went. Not hard enough to scratch, but enough to trigger a groan. I wrapped my arms around his neck, slipping my fingers through his still wet locks of hair.

Aaron broke the kiss abruptly, but his lips continued to pepper me with sensations as he trailed them along my jaw. He stopped at the hollow of my ear and whispered, "You have no idea what you do to me."

I opened my mouth to refute that when he nipped sharply at my earlobe. Desire clenched in my abdomen as the bite acted as a line straight to the heat between my legs.

A moan slipped out as I dug my fingers into his hair, pulling him closer. He breathed hard and heavy against the sensitive skin just below my ear. The feeling rattled me further and I didn't snap at him when he hoisted me onto the bed, placing himself between the part of my legs.

He released the tight hold he had on my waist to instead run his hands along my body. I arched into him, going against everything I believed in as I got caught up in the scent of wind and smoke. At least that's what I told myself when his fingers slipped beneath my shirt.

The shudders that racked my body were different than the muscle exhaustion that my nightmares caused. This kind of trembling was unlike anything I had ever known. Maybe it was because I never let anyone touch me. Maybe my skin really was too sensitive. Or maybe, Aaron had the power to elicit such a strong reaction because I was exhausted to the bone from fighting him.

I once told Blair that I craved touch, but that wasn't quite true.

I craved *his* touch.

As his fingers slid higher, my mind blacked out from sensation. A doorway appeared, brilliant and blinding against a world shrouded in darkness. Golden light slipped through the cracks, warming my skin without me even touching it.

It wanted me to open it. To slip my hands around the handle and just tug.

It would be so, so simple. So easy.

Had Aaron not just pulled away.

My conscience slammed into me as his hands fell to either side of me, pinning me to the bed with his strong body. His face was only inches away again, but the divide was enough to clear my senses.

"That was a mistake," I said hoarsely.

"Would you have stopped if I didn't?" he asked. The huskiness in his voice made me shiver again and he smirked.

"This changes nothing," I spat.

95

"Yet you can't answer the question." We stared at each other, locked in a battle of wills before I averted my eyes and pushed him away. This time he moved.

I practically ran from the room, only letting myself succumb to shaking once the door was closed. I stumbled to the couch as my mind tried to process what just happened and what I was feeling. He could probably hear me right now and knew how close my control came to shattering in front of him.

I curled up alone on the couch, taking deep breaths that slowed my still racing heart. As the heaviness of sleep overcame me faster than normal, I realized in that place in between—that the darkness inside didn't weigh as heavy on my broken soul right then, but I quickly forgot as the world faded black.

CHAPTER 14

THE COMFORTABLE CUSHION OF THE COUCH DISAPPEARED AS A light sensation filled me. Almost like I was floating...or falling. Flying? *That wasn't right.*

My eyes opened a second too late as that feather padded cushion was replaced by a rock-hard curvature that didn't give an inch when my shoulder blades impacted hard. My head whipped back with a thud as my arms flew out to catch myself.

My fingers brushed against soft silken material and I frowned. Groaning, I moved to pull myself up to figure out what was going on. Shadows danced at the edges of my mind, waiting to pounce when they saw the chance. In the darkest corners and recesses, a monster—no, a demon—watched intently. Violet stood at its side.

Warm arms wrapped around me, enveloping me in an all too familiar scent. It settled over me like a heavy fog I couldn't shake, calming me against my will. The shadows dissipated instantly.

"Let. Go. Of. Me," I choked out, clenching my fists in the

sheets on either side of us until they ripped. I should have recognized the gold canopy that hung far above me. I'd stared at it plenty into the sleepless hours of the night.

"Couldn't stay away, could you?" he murmured. His lips brushed my ear as he rested his cheek on my hair.

"Goddamnit—"

My cursing broke off abruptly as the door flung open. I turned my head to the copper curled spitfire that stood in the doorway. Her bleary, sleep-coated expression morphed into one of amusement as her lips tugged up into a satisfied smirk.

"I see how it is," Amber mussed, crossing her arms over her chest. Aaron growled under his breath and I tilted my head to see his face.

"Get out of here, Amber," he snapped at her. His eyes flashed between black and gold, but she didn't cower like the others did. Like Lucas did.

Lucas...his name hit me with a pang in my chest, but I wouldn't think on that now.

Vengeance would come for him soon enough once I sorted myself out.

For now, I would *let* him remain at Anastasia's side where he could see every reminder I left that I was alive and biding my time.

"Does this mean she's going to complete the bo—"

I didn't let her finish before I twisted sharply and slammed my elbow back into his jaw. Judging by the sharp pop, the bond didn't inhibit me from hurting him. Just from using my abilities on him.

Interesting...I tucked that thought away for a later time as I scrambled to get off of him and out of bed. I stumbled on the slick black marble, and without thinking, I flung out my hand to catch myself on the nightstand, accidentally taking off a chunk of wood in the process.

I straightened slowly, feeling both their eyes on me as I opened my fingers and released a handful of ebony wood dust.

"I'll take that as a no," Amber quipped. I cocked an eyebrow at her, ignoring the groaning man behind me that was creeping closer.

"Is there a reason you keep barging in here to save him?" I asked, more amused than anything.

"She has strong protection instincts. It's nothing," Aaron started to say. He halted his approach towards me, and instead slipped off the bed on the other end, giving me the much needed distance.

"Liar." His words were so smooth I wouldn't have known better, if not for the scratching along the back of my neck that rubbed me wrong. I don't know why or how, but somehow, I knew he was lying.

Amber stepped forward, all traces of humor gone. "It's not what you think," she said.

"Considering I don't know what to think, that's not a high bar," I replied dryly. The air beside me rippled as they both stepped closer, and instinctively I wanted to back away.

Distance. Distance was safe. Distance kept the emotions at bay. Distance—

"We should just tell her the truth. Daizlei's in the ground. She deserves to know," Amber said, but she wasn't speaking to me.

Aaron stayed silent. Her glare persisted.

"Asher Aaron White—"

"Asher?" I asked.

His first name was Asher? I glanced over his features, taking in the dark hair and flashing eyes. He always smelled like smoke. I suppose it was fitting that Asher was his real name.

"She doesn't even know your first name?" Amber asked. She facepalmed herself, letting out an annoyed groan.

"Well I do now."

"You seriously need to be filling her in. It's only a matter of time until your dad summons us, and she isn't going to appr—"

"*She* is standing right here," I snapped. I hated being talked about like I wasn't in the room. It transported me back to my first night at Daizlei all over again. Amber and Tori fighting, neither speaking to me like I wasn't there.

If only I knew then what I knew now. I would have... what would I have done?

The question irritated me more than I wanted to admit, because I had no idea. It seemed that every time I thought I had it all figured out, I was blindsided by the truth of how little I knew. We weren't raised in this world, but we were raised with the knowledge of it. Except even those memories weren't quite accurate. Dreamland had proved that much, although I don't know how. What had happened to my memories? Had they been altered? Changed? Or did I suppress them because they were too much?

The lies mounted on all sides, but they didn't stop there.

I came to Daizlei and thought I found a home, only to be the one to put it in the ground.

I befriended a boy I thought good and kind, and then he turned on me when I wouldn't love him.

I found a group of friends, only to be cleaved apart by the secrets we kept.

And all along, I had an unbreakable bond with the one person that I resented most in my time at Daizlei. I went from loathing him, to tolerating him, to almost acceptance, and now...I didn't know where we were or who I was.

I had emotions. I didn't feel a thing. Violet was my own insanity. Then she became the beacon of light. I was Supernatural. I was demon.

The truth was I didn't know anything.

But as much as I needed to find answers, I needed space more.

Without thinking, I walked to the other side of the room and tugged on my faded black boots. A leather jacket appeared out of thin air beside me and I pulled it on without hesitation. Behind me, their voices warbled and bled. I could hear them. I knew they were speaking, but the words themselves made no sense.

I had fallen into an ocean so treacherous that nothing could reach me. Within myself, my head slipped below the waves. It was funny, in a dark sort of way, that I could withstand the hard things without crumbling—but something so small could trigger me.

In the past, when I succumbed to such emotion, I chose limbo. Then, when my sister died, I chose Violet. Neither of those worked, so it was time to try something else.

I crossed the threshold of the room and they followed me, but they weren't fast enough to stop me from summoning an elevator.

Magic. They called it magic.

I called it freedom.

I had one foot in the metal cage and the other in my marbled prison.

Ten days. I hadn't made it eleven with this group before the need to run kicked in. Fight or flight. Sink or swim.

I descended deeper into the water than ever before. Me, my demon, and Violet.

One of them grabbed my arm and tugged hard enough it would have yanked a lesser being five feet through the air. I simply stopped in my tracks.

I couldn't hear them, but it seemed that Aaron—Asher —had other ways to communicate than words or body language.

"Don't do this. Don't run." his voice whispered across my mind like a stray wind.

"Outside," I croaked. "I need to see the sunrise."

Those were the only words I could get out before the water dragged me under again, to where even wind could not reach and smoke could not follow.

I stepped inside the elevator, barely aware of the two people that followed me in.

The doors slid shut behind us, and before any of the others knew it—the three of us were gone.

The elevator didn't go far. It didn't have to. I called upon it to take me out. To take me to the only place in this forsaken city where there were no lights. There were no humans.

And I was only a face in the crowd.

We went to the black market and no one attempted to stop me as the doors slid open again. I stepped out into the cold embrace of the early morning where twilight reigned supreme.

A sky so dark it looked black still spanned one end of the alley to the other. I raced into the streets that I had only seen once before, not paying any mind to vendors or the array of creatures that walked these streets under a moonless night.

This was a place of shadows and death. Of secrets and lies. It was where the darkest entities of this world did their dealings, and the monsters that never saw daylight lurked.

It was where I felt most at home now, as I sank to my knees.

"I'm sorry," I whispered as the light appeared on the horizon, chasing the darkest of blues. The light acted as an anchor, a signal that reached me even in the deepest parts of an ocean filled with blood. It was the blood I spilled. The pain I caused. The scars I bore. The secrets I killed for.

It was the dawn, and it beckoned me forward.

"I see the sun and still think of you. Not a day goes by that I don't wonder what really happened, and the part I played." My words were hardly more than a whisper, but I didn't doubt the ears behind me were listening intently.

Let them listen. This isn't for them. It's for me.

"I wonder if you would be proud of the monster I've become," I continued. The blinding light rose slowly but surely, and I didn't blink. Not even once. "Or would you be ashamed? I failed you, father. I couldn't keep my promise. I couldn't protect them." I took a stuttering breath, and my heart expanded and bruised as it fought with the bars of my ribcage that kept it contained.

"I don't know who or what I am anymore. Do I have you

to thank for that? For the memories I was supposed to never remember? Or is there another?" My mutterings were the words of a drowning girl, trapped by things I couldn't even comprehend.

"I never understood when I was younger. I couldn't make sense of why you pushed me, or the secrets you burdened me with that never should have seen the light of day. You taught me to fear them. To fear myself. So much so that I would die for them." The first cracks of a burning star rose above the horizon, scorching my eyes blind.

Still, I did not look away.

"But I wasn't the one who died." If I could have cried, I would have. "Did you know that? Did you know it would be her? Did you know I would lose control and end her life?" A gust of wind slapped my face, blowing my shorn hair behind me.

"I have to think you did. That you knew, somehow, the darkness that lives inside. You saw it. You fostered it. Mom thought you were breaking me, that it would destroy me, but I see it now. I see the truth, and it's a terrible thing to behold." The cold air made my throat burn and taste like blood. I licked my cracked lips, relishing the way they stung.

"You did break me, Daddy. Over and over again. But every time, I came back. And you knew then that no one else—nothing else—would ever break me the same way. For every time I broke, I healed. I am strong because you made me strong, and maybe I'm not invincible—but if I could heal from what you did, then I will heal from this. One day." My heart was an iron casket that contained the embers and ashes of a dead girl, but I was a phoenix.

And from those ashes, I would rise again.

Not as Violet. Not a demon. Not an unfeeling, rage-driven thing.

I would rise from nothing, but for the life of me—even I couldn't see what I would become.

"One day I will be whole again, because anything else means she won. And if there's anything you taught me, it's to be spiteful enough to heal."

And then I broke.

One by one the barriers in my heart and mind split apart at the seams. My chest cracked down the middle. Crashing, falling, tumbling into nothingness.

Pain racked my body, hotter than hellfire and colder than the waves that held me below. The pain edged with grief and rage consumed me so wholly that I finally broke.

I broke in the way that I wouldn't let myself for Lily.

I broke in a way that could only be described as a time bomb.

For so long I ticked away as people chipped at my heart and humanity. It's almost amusing that the thing that broke the dam within was so small. So simple.

Amber talking over me served as a reminder from a time I thought I was whole. It sent me spiraling through memories in a way I never could have predicted. It triggered an avalanche inside of me that I had withheld for so long.

But kneeling in the dirt, I made one last promise.

And then I gave into the sobs as the sun rose in the sky.

CHAPTER 15

THERE'S SOMETHING TO BE SAID FOR FEELING PAIN SO ACUTE THAT you literally black out from it, and that's exactly what I did. At some point, the sobs and shudders became too great and it was only the warmth tethered around me that kept my mind from slipping into those watery depths again. Here in my mind, only an endless darkness existed.

But I was not alone.

"Am I in limbo?" I asked them. On one side Violet stood, on the other, my demon.

"Not quite," Violet replied.

"What do you mean?" I looked from one to the other. It was a strange thing to come face-to-face with your demons. One, a glowing-eyed carbon copy that seemed to level up the more time that passed. The other, a dark-eyed version of myself that stared at me with a savageness that was all too familiar.

"You are dreaming, for now. Your signasti is already trying to pull you back, but the dragon has assisted in keeping you here." I circled them both, although there was no floor. Somehow my body stayed upright and moved just as if there was, even if I was in a place where only shadows and smoke existed. I suppose if my mind was to have a physical representation, this would be fitting.

"The dragon?" I asked. She had given me bits and pieces of information before, and there was only one person that she had ever referred to that way. "You mean Johanna?"

"They are one and the same," Violet replied. About as straightforward as it usually gets with her.

"Alright. Given how things were when I last saw her, I assume it's not out of the kindness of her heart. So why am I here?"

Violet's lips curled up into a cruel smile. "Because it's time," she said simply.

My heart stumbled in my chest as her eyes swept from me to the demon.

The other.

The very real entity I fought my entire life.

"Time for what?" I asked, leery about where she was going. She smiled again, and this time, it held an edge of sadness.

"Acceptance."

Acceptance?

I wasn't sure if I liked the direction this was headed.

"You want me to accept that *thing*, don't you?" There was a bite to my words, but not enough for what I knew Violet was asking.

"I'm not asking you to do anything you aren't ready for." Her words were resigned, staunch, and unmoving. I crossed my arms over my chest and watched them both. Violet was cold, cruel, and clinical in her assessments. It made her my greatest advisor, even if I didn't know who or what she was.

"There's more, isn't there?"

The grim resolve on her face spoke volumes. She nodded stiffly and my shoulders deflated. I didn't expect her to offer her hand, and I was hesitant to take it after last time.

"Let's take a walk, shall we?" she said softly. Something about her tone left no room for discussion. I accepted her hand and found us transported yet again.

The yellow house with a white picket fence was not what I expected. It looked the same as when I left it. Alpine Larch and all. I waded through the unkempt grass to the rock where I used to sit with my father while contemplating the universe.

"When she first died, you tried to deny. You hoped. You pleaded, and eventually you were consumed in anger. Rage." She took a seat beside me, kicking her legs out in front of her. "It led you to make a deal with me. To bargain for a revenge that has always been yours to take. I gave in and yielded to your desires because I care for you in a way I have not cared for another in a very long time."

On the other side of me, another sat. I didn't look at the demon, but I sensed her. Similar, yet entirely different from Violet.

"But when we surfaced from the veil, we were not complete. It made you even more unstable. Volatile. You turned on everyone in your life and alienated them. You fell into a depression of sorts. Grieving is what the humans call it, but you are a Supernatural *and* a demon. Grief is never so simple."

Spanning before us was the sunrise coming over the mountains. Only it was frozen, and we were suspended in time.

"And then you broke. Again, except this time you want to change. You want to heal, but there is only one way how. The dragon knows this. Your signasti knows this. They will help you, but it is you who must do the work." I dug my bare feet into the earth, flexing my toes around the bits of grass and compact dirt.

Do the work?

Why did it seem like this was only the beginning?

"Because it is," Violet replied. I wasn't even phased that she answered it. Weirder things have happened. "The last step, and the hardest one to reach, is acceptance. If you want to feel and be whole, you must look at yourself and accept it. Just as you accepted me, you must make room for the demons. For the vulnerabilities. You must *accept* that you are who you are and take your destiny into your own hands—or history will repeat itself."

"Repeat itself?" I asked. Violet nodded solemnly.

"You are not the first to come along with such great power. Your parents warned you what would happen should you stray down the road of every matter manipulator before you. They tried to fix you before you were even broken." She sighed heavily and shook her head.

"But I am broken," I said. "And I don't know how to put myself back together. But I don't want to merge with that *thing* or be angry at the world anymore." Violet made a *tsk* sound and clicked her tongue.

"That thing is part of you and it always has been," she said sternly. "You will never be whole without it. You have

109

tried for years, and for years you have failed. If you *truly* want to get better, then you need to make some sacrifices and let go of your assumptions about how the world should work, or what your demon is."

If I ever had a moment in my life where I felt like I might be speaking with a higher power, this was it. Violet was giving me the ultimatum: get myself together and let go of all the rest...or be like this forever.

Did I want to change enough to do that? Enough to be that?

Yes. Yes, I did.

To end the pain and the suffering, to give my life meaning again, to be able to continue without constantly feeling like I was jumping from one extreme to the other...I would do almost anything.

I blinked, opening my mouth to tell her my decision, but we no longer sat on a rock beside an old tree. We stood in a room with black marbled floors, streaked with gold. Beside me, a canopy bed made of ebony wood held a frail girl wrapped in golden sheets. The firelight danced across her skin, paler than it's ever been. Only once have I ever had an out of body experience like this, and it was just as trippy then.

"Is that really me?" My voice never sounded so small.

Violet nodded.

"How? How is this possible?"

"Time is passing faster than you realize. You spent more time in the darkness than before, and I could not reach you until you were ready to talk. It is only your strength and will of mind that is keeping you alive at this point." Violet walked over and brushed the hair from the fragile girl's face. She didn't respond. Didn't stir. "Eventually you will have to wake, and when you do, the choice will have to be made."

The choice.

She said it like it was that simple. Like I could just choose to be normal.

To be happy.

"It *is* a choice. You don't see that now because you're so deep in your anger and grief that you think there is nothing you can do, but all that does is take away your authority. You can choose to be better. To be *happy*." She raised her eyebrows and gave me a knowing look. "But you have to remember to choose that every day, in and out—and eventually it will come naturally." I walked toward her and the girl on the bed. She was so very pale, and her hair so very dark, that her sallow cheeks and eyes looked like bruising.

"If I choose to try and change, what will happen to me? To us?" I didn't glance at my demon, but I could feel her shifting uneasily. Did she have thoughts? Feelings of her own? It seemed like she did, but then again, I had never acknowledged her. Never let her speak. I didn't know.

"You're only going to get one shot at this, Selena. If you succeed, you will be more powerful than they ever imagined. You will change the world for the better." I didn't say anything as I stared at the girl in the bed. That couldn't be me. It's not possible. She looked like she was...dying.

I was dying.

"But if you fail, if you don't accept yourself and your future—you will doom them all. Your enemies will win, and you very well may damn yourself to an eternity of madness. Your signasti too."

"I..." My voice trailed off before I could get the words out. "I don't want to be the person I was...or *am,* but I don't know how to get better. I don't understand how to fix this, but I can't live like this." I swallowed hard.

"Then you know what to do. You've known it all along," Violet said to me. She gripped my hand in hers, giving me the strength I needed to look up. My demon stood across from us, watching me warily. She was as hesitant of me as I was of her.

I steeled myself. Straightening my spine with a resolve that had my heart hammering as it pushed blood to my head. My ears pounded with a pressure that settled on me trying to force us together.

"You have locked her away for so long that you are equally scared of each other. Neither of you are inherently evil, but you aren't good either. You're neutral beings, some of the only ones in existence." I took a tentative step towards her and Violet walked beside me. Across the room, the demon took a step towards us. Raising her hand, a question in her eyes.

"That gives you the power to choose, and your decisions will change the foundations of the world as we know it."

I'd heard those words before.

From an old lady in a tent with a bag full of chicken bones and a yellow smile.

"The Crone told me that," I said.

"If you succeed, it will not be the last time you see her," Violet replied cryptically. How could she possibly know that? How could she know any of this?

She looked at me and I stared into her hypnotic eyes.

There was something about Violet I always found unsettling, like the color of her eyes itself held secrets.

"I have no reason to believe you, but I don't know who to trust when I can't even trust myself," I said. She raised her hand to my cheek and turned my face to the other entity: the demon that waited, hand raised and arms open.

"You trust the people who have nothing to gain from you. Those who you've hurt, but that still try to help you. You look inside yourself and learn to love what you see. She is a part of you that has been waiting a very long time to be accepted." The demon took another step towards me, and I took a shallow breath. "She helps you when you need her, and you lock her away every time. You want to know where to start? Look at her."

I did. I looked long and hard, watching the way she averted her eyes. Savage she may be, but that didn't make her evil. Violet was telling the truth there. What merging with this being would do, I had no idea. It terrified me to consider it, but I had tried things my way and lost.

If my way didn't work, it was time to try another.

Slowly, but steadily, I raised my hand.

"Come," I whispered, flinching at the hope in her eyes.

Was I really so cruel not to see that before? So hopeless in myself that I didn't look elsewhere, even at the thing living inside of me?

Violet turned adjacent to me and held out her hand for the demon who took it. We stood as a married couple would, prepared to say our vows and promises. This joining would not be like any other. An unholy trinity.

A chance at something new. A reach for balance.

A gamble at what it means to be whole.

I stared at my demon and I did not feel afraid.

"You said I only get one shot," I said under my breath. "Tell me what I have to do."

We made a pact, right then and there. A union, of sorts. Sealed by a single touch.

I didn't even get the chance to pray that I wasn't a foolish idiot before my eyes cracked open.

Awake and alive, after being gone far too long.

PART TWO

CHAPTER 16

I GASPED ONCE, INHALING A BREATH OF FRESH AIR. MY BACK arched off the bed, aching and stiff. *How long had it been since I moved?* I had no idea, but I was going to find out.

Twisting my fingers in the silken bed sheets, I heaved myself up into a sitting position. My muscles protested loudly with a series of snaps and pops, but I was feeling better already. Lighter. Freer.

Just as Violet promised, my demon was with us, experiencing all of these things as if it were the first time. I suppose it was for her since she had been locked up every time before. Already my mind was relaxing as a tension I didn't know I had began to evaporate. She was content for us to move and stretch at will, not making any sudden grabs for power like before.

Tentatively, I swung my legs around and shuffled closer to the foot of the bed. The firelight licked at my skin. I basked in its warm glow as I slipped my legs over the edge of the bed and extended both hands.

The demon in me was mesmerized by the fire. It had

never seen anything so pure. It danced on the edge of destruction, depending on how you used it. A contented warmth spread in my chest, and there was nothing unnatural or extreme about it this time. It didn't burn.

I crouched down before the fire, sinking to my knees on the plush rug. The fibers tickled my overly sensitive skin and a laugh escaped my lips.

It wasn't a caustic or cruel sound. More like wind chimes.

Light and free. I had never felt so free.

Without thinking, I extended my hands towards the fire, brushing my fingers over the flames.

So warm... I could curl up inside of it. The flames didn't move for me like they had my sister, but I was impervious nonetheless. They heated my skin, but they didn't burn. They'd never burned. I guess I knew why now.

Voices carried from down the hall. It was strange how they sounded so clear but not close. It didn't make sense. I pulled back from the flames and rose to my feet. My legs were clothed in loose fitting sweatpants, and an obscenely large t-shirt bunched around my waist. If it weren't for my butt, the pants would have fallen off.

I turned away from the fire to search for clothes. The magic drawers ought to have something. I reached for the one that usually contained tops and pulled out the first thing I saw. Except...it was too big.

That can't be right.

I placed it back in the drawer and pulled open another. Sweats. All the wrong size. Then I went to another. Jeans. Still far too large.

Okay, looks like the magic safe house was broken

because this was all meant for Aaron. Still, I dug through the drawers and the closet, and while all of it was men's clothing, a few pieces looked like they might fit me. I swapped out the baggy t-shirt for one that I found in the back of the closet with The Beatles printed on it. It was still loose, but not so loose I was swimming in material.

Pants were a bit trickier. I debated going in the boy short underwear, but I found a pair of male boxers that looked about the right length for actual shorts. After rolling them a couple of times, they fell to mid-thigh and fit me almost perfectly.

I stepped out of the closet and looked to the door again. If I concentrated, I could hear a lot more than voices down the hall. Grunts and growls sounded further away, followed by a—was that howling?

Must be the strip club, I supplied easily enough. That was a perfectly logical conclusion.

My feet were silent as I padded across the cool marble floors. They didn't feel as cold as they used to. Come to think of it, everything was warmer.

That was a little odd, but maybe it was just me. I had no idea what effects my body would feel from merging with my demon. Whereas Violet by herself turned me cold, and I alone had been burning, this combination seemed to be the most comfortable.

It was definitely the easiest on my mind.

I hadn't needed to focus on so many barriers now.

It was refreshing.

My fingers brushed over the door handle and I lightly opened it.

But the safe house wasn't what awaited me.

While the bedroom was an exact copy of the one from the safe house, this living room was not. A crackling fireplace burned in the center with black leather couches positioned around it. The room was small. Cozy. It only had a single door apart from the one I stood in, and that one was framed by bookshelves on either side, and an abbreviated bookshelf sat snugly over the doorframe. They ran from the floor to the ceiling, roughly twelve feet above.

So. Whoever lived here liked to read. I've heard of stranger things.

What also surprised me was that it was entirely empty. I could have sworn I heard voices...my gaze went to the other door. The sounds were slightly more pronounced now, but still muffled. Whoever it was must be on the other side of that door.

I crossed the living space, ignoring the tremble in my veins. My fingers closed around the handle as I took a deep breath. Somehow, the air tasted cleaner here.

Well, that definitely can't be right. There's no way we could have left Las Vegas without me knowing.

Or so I thought.

It didn't open to a room. It opened into a hallway. I popped my head out, and once again, no one was there. Only beige walls with fancy lighting. This door sat at the very end of the hallway, with six more doors on either side before it opened at the very end.

I couldn't tell anything more about it from here, except that it had an oddly familiar metal railing that shined in the startling light. I swallowed hard, cringing at the scratchiness of my throat. I needed something to drink when I found someone.

My feet carried me down the hallway on their own accord. I hadn't even realized I'd moved until I was standing at the very end looking over the railing. It opened into a large room that looked almost like a ballroom, just smaller. This landing was three floors up and it appeared the room had a semicircular shape. Down below, an opulent staircase led from the first to the second floor, but this floor didn't have a connecting staircase. A simple elevator with one button was placed where the staircase was below.

If I had to bet, that elevator was my magic elevator, but still left me with the question of where the hell am I?

I eyed the drop from here to the floor below. It looked to be less than forty feet. Surely I could jump that? I'd jumped twice as far before, and while that was out of necessity, my demon was quite curious about the actual confines of my body now that all three of us were here.

I didn't think as I hooked my hand around the railing and swung myself over it. I was falling before it even occurred to me, and landing on the balls of my feet when a girl's scream pierced my ears. I clapped my hands over them, flinching away from the noise.

"Ohmigawd—are you alright—what just happened—who are you?"

Her questions assaulted my senses, putting an end to my blissfully peaceful return to the world of the living. I eyed her cautiously, my demon both wary of another being so near us, and curious about the other living creature.

She had beautiful dark brown locks of hair swept back into a French braid with a few loose strands framed around her face. Suddenly, her panicked reaction made sense. She couldn't have been older than twelve or thirteen—and she certainly wasn't like Milla, whose personality was quiet and reserved.

"Do you need a doctor? That was like, an insane jump. Only a couple of Shifters I know could even make it, and no offense, but you're looking a little *wild,* if you know what I mean." The girl babbled on, completely oblivious to my lack of a response.

"Where am I?" I rasped. It was nearly a croak, given how dry my throat was. I swallowed again, hoping to clear it.

"Just outside Carson City, of course. This is the main residence," she boasted proudly. A shadow of a girl I once knew shone in her face, but that was a different time. A life before monsters and demons, where the only thing we had to worry about was getting her through history.

"Carson City?" She nodded. "As in Nevada?"

Her nose scrunched as her eyebrows drew together. "Are you sure you're alright from that fall?"

"It wasn't a fall. I jumped." That didn't seem to make her think any differently.

"Right," she drawled out. "Who did you say you were again?"

I eyed her, weighing my suspicions back and forth.

"Lena." The young teenager clicked her tongue and motioned for me to follow her back up the staircase.

"So, what brings you here, *Lena*?" she asked, clearly not buying my name. I trailed next to her, damn silent by comparison. She stomped like a herd of buffalo, and her voice hit an octave that made me wince when she spoke. Did she have to be so loud?

Fortunately for her, the demon found her fascinating. I studied her while we walked, taking note of her lithe frame and honey-colored eyes. Half breed.

"I'm not sure, really," I replied, detailing the many hallways we passed by. It would be easy to get lost in this place without her, even with my sense of smell.

"You don't know why you're here? Oh man..." She stopped and regarded me a bit more shrewdly. "I got an idea."

"Do you now?" I asked, a little amused. She beckoned me on, turning into a bigger hallway. This one followed into a very large room where several people were clustered about. I took in the broad stature and height of the men as they looked up. None of them were familiar, and that didn't sit well with me, or my demon. She regarded them as a threat.

The younger girl didn't seem to skip a beat as she went up to them, asking if they knew me. Every single one shook their heads and before she could ask any further questions, a shout echoed from the balcony outside. I crossed the foyer, stepping around the strange men entirely, and emerged on a white marbled terrace.

And what I saw went beyond my wildest dreams.

I want to call it a yard, but a green space this large couldn't be considered that. It was easily the length of three football fields, and just as wide. Out in the very center, a contraption of some sort rose above everything else, even towering over the house.

The base was like a giant corkboard that wrapped around like a cylinder. Stacked a good twenty feet above it shifted to solid wood, or really, wood that was more akin to

Swiss cheese. Giant spikes poked out of holes in it, almost impaling a man attempting to climb it. I grimaced at the realization that it was an obstacle course, not all that different from the simulator at Daizlei. The next level started at least forty feet above the ground and I had no words for it. The hall of spinning knives came to mind as I stared at the inner workings of several layers of pendulums. The metal glinted in the sunlight as they swung ready to strike.

Not that anyone seemed to get that far.

Beyond the device that drew my attention, hundreds of men and women sparred in the field. Some fought with weapons, others their hands and feet. Even more odd were the animals that attacked each other. Massive grizzlies that stood over ten feet tall. Wolves of every size and color. Birds of prey with wing spans twenty feet wide. Hell, there was even a hippo tromping through as it let out an angry roar and proceeded to sit and roll, causing the three large cats trying to pounce on it to run for their lives.

I'd run, too, if an almost two ton herbivore tried to roll over me.

The girl's words came back to me.

Shifters. These were Shifters.

My gaze swept the grass looking for a recognizable face, but I didn't have to wait long. The brown-haired beauty put two fingers to her lips and whistled sharply.

I snarled at her without thinking as I clapped both hands over my ears.

The entire yard came to a complete halt and looked to the girl.

All but one.

He was farther away from the house, sparring with five people: three men, two women. One of which had unmistakable red hair. The other, so blonde that dye could not achieve that color, and if that didn't give her away, the sword of ice would have.

My heart surged in my chest as the demon instinctively reached for them, and by extension, I did as well. I swung my legs over the balcony, ignoring the shouts from below as I landed silently. The people—Shifters—parted before me. As a quiet hush fell over the yard, I paid them no mind, relishing the cracking of twigs and slick grass beneath my feet. They carried me far and fast across nearly two football fields. The girl followed behind me, although her tramping was beginning to get on my nerves. The demon found her utterly charming when she wasn't loud as shit.

How lucky for her.

That thought died away as I stepped past the last of the Shifters that stood waiting. Watching.

Just as quickly as I reached the people I sought, a wall of men appeared before me, brandishing swords.

I stopped instantly, knowing there were more at my back.

The hair on my arms rose at the perceived threat. None of us— me, Violet, or the demon—were going to tolerate that.

"Who are you?" one of them asked. I wondered why I was getting asked that so much. Surely if my sister and cousin were out here, they would have some idea who I was?

Yet it seemed no one did.

"Move."

It was a single word, and the only command I would give before parting them myself. The air held still as I raised my eyes to the man directly in front of me. He was easily twice my weight, and there were a good twenty of them surrounding me.

But they were the ones who should be afraid.

No one keeps me from what's mine.

"Who are you?" he asked again. Behind him, the clash of swords clanged again before halting.

I hadn't used my power since coming back. Just as I heard all that was around me, I felt it too. There was a shift in the air as someone drew a bowstring. It was easily a hundred yards away, but I heard it as if it were right beside me. I tasted the change in the wind.

"I wouldn't do that if I were you," I whispered. The Shifter in front of me frowned, his eyes drifting from me to what I knew to be the archer far behind. His eyes narrowed just the slightest when the arrow released, and I spun on my heel bringing my hand up to catch it only two inches from my face.

First, there was an audible intake of breath. It seemed the crowd only then realized that something very different walked amongst them. Then there was a cry to stop as I threw the arrow with pinpoint accuracy—back at the archer. It sailed straight and true, landing with a thunk in the wooden post just above his head, nestled between his curly hair.

"Selena?"

One single word shouldn't hold so much anguish, but my name did, and I knew the voice as well as I knew my own. I sighed softly as I turned back to the wall of men. They had parted, and there, before me, was Aaron.

I didn't even know what I was supposed to call him now. I had only just found out his name when everything happened. It was odd. Awkward.

"Selena!" another voice nearly yelled. I flinched at the volume but resisted covering my ears again. Since when did everyone speak so loudly?

"Anyone care to tell me where we are?" I asked, searching the faces behind him. There were so many people here. Too many. It set me and my demon on edge. Was it strange that I didn't view us separately like I did Violet? I wasn't certain. Maybe that was part of it.

Footsteps trampled grass, almost as quiet as my own. My sister and cousin ran for me, but it was not them who swept me into a tight embrace.

It was Aaron.

His arms wrapped around me, cradling me close. I always thought his scent was understated while clinging to everything, but I realized it now invaded every particle of air. Smoke wasn't a strong enough word for it. It was a smoldering fire. Crackling flames and just the briefest hint of something I couldn't name.

I allowed it, for a moment. The last memories I had of being awake were gut wrenching and terrible. I had collapsed in the middle of the black market, but he held me together. He didn't pull me away from the sunrise until the screaming started. Screaming that I knew without asking was my own.

Another twig snapped, and the man that had his arms

wrapped around me bristled. Instantly, the demon went on the offensive too. But not for my sake.

Oh no.

She viewed them as a threat to *him*.

Goddamnit. I wondered what the consequences would be. When they would hit me.

I suppose they could have been worse, or at least that's what I shrugged it off as while I twisted in his arms.

A statuesque blonde with bright blue eyes watched us, two male Shifters at her side. It wasn't really me she was watching, but him.

"Who is this?" she asked sharply.

My fingers curled and uncurled as I pinned her with a level stare. Her eyes flicked to my hands and narrowed.

"And why is she wearing your clothes?" the girl continued.

Of course, Aaron decides right here that now is the moment to make my big introduction. If only he could have done it with less snarling.

"This is my signasti. Selena."

I pulled back from him, batting away his clinging arms. With this many people around, I wasn't comfortable being close to anyone. It made me restless.

"Signasti?" the girl asked slowly, like she misunderstood.

I ignored her and instead turned to my sister and Blair.

Now that I had parted from Aaron, they didn't seem to have any qualms with running forward and throwing their arms around me. The comfortable warmth from earlier spread throughout my limbs. They were alive and well.

But something had clearly happened here.

"We were worried about you. Don't ever scare us like that again," Blair whispered against me.

"What are you talking about?"

They both froze and a sense of dread settled in my stomach. It wasn't as hard not to succumb as before, but the darkness still edged my emotions. At least the darker ones.

"I don't know how to tell you this..." Blair said as she pulled back a little.

"Just spit it out." That came out harsher than I intended.

"You've been asleep for a long time," Blair supplied, glancing to Alexandra for help. My sister's lips pressed together as she cupped my face.

"How long is a long time?" I asked.

"Two and a half months. It's mid-November."

I think the world dropped out from under me.

My feet lost their balance as I stumbled back, fighting for control of shaky legs. No one made to move towards me as I stared between the three of them bewildered.

I was asleep for over two months? November? I'm eighteen now?

What had happened? How was that even possible?

For every question I had, another followed it.

I searched desperately for something—someone—that could make sense of it all.

No one wanted to get near me. Not even Amber, who I had spotted just off to the side of the crowd. They were... scared of me. All but Aaron. He fearlessly approached me, hands held up in a posture of surrender.

"Why don't we go inside and talk?" His voice soothed me and I nodded slowly.

"I would like that."

They had shocked me, and I wasn't freaking out.

Yet.

I was...trying. Just as Violet told me. It wasn't a lot, but it was a start.

Let's see how long it lasts.

CHAPTER 17

WE DIDN'T RETURN TO THE ROOM I HAD WOKEN UP IN. THIS ONE had bookcases mounted along two walls, mismatched furniture, and a large weathered rug. A globe sat on one end table, ancient and peeling. The polish on the bookcases had clearly seen better days, and while the furniture was nice, it was also broken in. On the far wall, two French doors were slightly ajar, letting in a soft breeze that sent the billowing white curtains dancing.

I walked to them, lifting my hand to catch the sheer material between my fingers. If a material could be creamy, that was the only way to describe the sensation. Somehow the thin curtains were supple, yet delicate.

"I never thought I would be able to take joy in such small things. I woke up and the world feels different. I feel different," I murmured.

"We didn't know if you were going to wake up," Alexandra said. There was so much pain in her voice. So much hurt. And I had unintentionally put it there.

"I always do."

"How much do you remember of what happened?" Blair asked me. She stepped forward and I turned to face her. To face them. Alexandra and Blair, two young women that hated each other and now found themselves standing on the same side. Amber and...Aaron. The two who saw my downfall. Strangely enough, no others had followed, though I was positive that they must be here.

There was a time that I would have answered, *enough*, and made them accept it.

But that answer wouldn't do. Not anymore.

"Bits and pieces. It's hard to say really..." I swallowed hard, moving around them to take my seat in the only chair. They followed my lead, seating themselves.

They thought I was going to run, I realized.

"You always have before. It will take time for them to see," Violet whispered.

Time. Yes. The one thing we never seemed to have enough of.

"You collapsed in the street and started talking to yourself. Then you started screaming. Do you know what happened after that?" Amber cut in. Her voice wasn't gentle or coddling like the others were trying to be. I appreciated it. The last thing I wanted was to be coddled.

"Amber," Alexandra snapped.

"Don't," she snapped back. There was more bite than I expected. "You didn't see what I did. She *leveled* the market, Alexandra, and that's not even—"

"What? What did you just say?"

I didn't speak with anger or demands. It was small, like the broken person I was. A person only holding on by the tiniest of threads. I came back to do better. To be better.

132

I hadn't considered the mess I left behind.

"You didn't even realize, did you?" Alexandra asked, but it wasn't really a question. She knew I didn't. I could see it in her eyes. She was my sister, after all. If anyone here knew the madness that plagued me, it was her.

I shook my head, averting my eyes to my lap.

"Tell me everything," I whispered.

"You caused an earthquake," Amber replied.

Okay...at least she gave it to me straight.

"How bad?"

"It would have only been the black market, but somehow you tapped the ley line. The tremors reached as far as San Diego. Over two thousand people died," Amber continued.

Two thousand...?

Just like that, and I didn't even remember.

My lips parted as the first inkling of ice ran through me. I shied away from it, pulling myself back to the present. The shadows danced but the demon banished them. It seemed that together we could do what I could not.

If only that had been two and a half months ago.

"How did you stop me?" I asked, my gaze darted to Alexandra, but she didn't provide the answers.

"We didn't," Amber replied. "He did."

My eyes shifted from her to Aaron, another pang filling my chest as I took him in.

His cheeks were hollower than I remembered. His skin paler and almost...clammy? He looked damp, but not from sweat. His dark brown hair flopped across his forehead into his eyes. It was him, but he was not well.

"How'd you do it?"

"I spoke to you."

It could have only been the two of us in that moment for all I knew. If I was broken and he was the other half of my soul, did that also make him broken? Or was he the stronger half—the half that would make me whole? Our entire relationship was so messed up.

It was hot and cold, filled with a passion that strayed so close to hate. I suppose they were two sides of the same coin. I couldn't feel nothing for him, but I didn't know what I was supposed to feel either.

My demon wanted to reach for him. To soothe the crinkles in his brow, but I would not do that here. Not in front of all of them. There were things that needed to be said, but those words were private.

"We should talk," I settled on eventually. His expression stayed guarded, but he gave me a tight nod. It was a start. I was trying.

"That's long overdue," Amber retorted.

"What happens between her and I is none of your bus—"

"I know," I said.

Aaron's eyes flashed a question. So hopeful but scared to hope. Could I blame him? I'd done this to us, to him, to everyone. At the end of the day, it was my fault in every sense of the word. I needed to own up to that and be honest.

The cold chip on her shoulder melted a little as Amber sighed.

"You're different," she said. I cracked the first inklings of a smile.

"I know that too."

Another breeze swept through the study and I lifted my face to greet it, relishing the coolness against my skin. I flicked my fingers and the doors slowly opened further, allowing a tidal wave to blow against my skin. It carried the voices from down below with it, melding with every beating heart and breath that my friends took. A lullaby meant only for my ears.

The moment was surreal in every sense of the word.

"I've done a lot of bad things, and I will probably do more before this war is over...but I'm sorry. I'm sorry for everything I've done that has led us here. And I'm sorry for missing our birthday, Alexandra. You shouldn't have been alone," I said, my voice came out rasping and harsh. Then again, I think anyone's would have.

We descended into a comfortable silence and for once it wasn't taut with some kind of pressure just waiting to break. There was no rush of power or heavy tension. Only the sound of breathing.

I wouldn't call myself a changed woman. Not yet—but one day—one day I would be. For now, I had reparations to make. Answers to find.

Listen and learn. The words settled over me. Violet's words.

I once said that the greatest revenge came from knowing your enemy so intimately that you pitied them, but that wasn't quite right. It came from knowing your enemy, understanding them, watching, until you had no choice but to love them—and in doing so, you had the power to break them.

You can't love someone if you can't see outside yourself, and so my job was to listen, to learn, and to try.

It was so simple, but the hardest things in life often are.

"After the tremors died away"—Alexandra swallowed—"we told ourselves we would stay at the safe house for three days. Surely you would come back...but you never did. After five days, Aaron declared that he was leaving and taking you with.

"We didn't know what was wrong or how to help you. Your eyes were open, but no one was home. He could calm you, but he couldn't pull you back to us. We were running out of options, and I wasn't letting him take you anywhere without me." Her eyes glistened with tears I wished she wouldn't shed. Certainly not for my sake. "So we came with. Most of us. Elizabeth disappeared again in all of the commotion, and by the time someone realized...she was already gone."

"What about Cade and Tam?" I asked.

"They stayed behind with Xellos for...damage control," Alexandra said. I nodded. It made sense. "And Milla is staying with them to receive proper training."

"Training?"

"She's a Witch, and a very powerful one at that. Johanna thought it might be best if she could begin learning about her people with Xellos," Aaron supplied. I nodded in agreement. She was only a child, not even thirteen. If sending her to Xellos would let her learn and keep her out of this war, I wouldn't argue.

Speaking of Xellos...

"What about Michigan? Did you ever return to find out more about—"

"The house was already burned down by the time we could leave to go," Alexandra answered. Blair stiffened at the mention of her childhood home and the place her mother had likely died, but she didn't speak.

"I see..."

Alexandra reached across the empty space and placed her hand on my bare leg.

"We'll figure out what happened, but it's going to take time," she said. I nodded again and her hand slipped away from my knee leaving me somewhat empty as the chill of the air settled inside.

It always came back to time.

I turned to Aaron and asked, "Why did you choose Carson City?"

"It's my father's main residence."

Main residence...

The main Shifter residence.

And it belonged to his father.

Which made him the...

"Your father is the Alpha."

"Yes."

I nodded, more for them than for myself. They needed to know I was here. I was present, and I wasn't freaking out. Yet.

"And what does he think of all this?" I motioned to Alexandra, Blair, Amber, and myself. If we were here, then the others were as well.

"My father has been working with the rebellion for some time now. Provided there is no danger to our people, he sees no problem with them being here," Aaron supplied with a tight turn of his lips. It suddenly made a lot of sense how so many Shifters had tried to come between me and him. I probably looked like a crazy woman if I'd been asleep so long.

"And me?"

"You're my signasti. You will always be welcome, no matter the circumstances."

That was an awfully altruistic view. Just goes to show how different Shifters and Supes really were.

"Is there anything else I should know?" I asked.

"My father and his guards have known you were here, but today is the first day the rest of the world learned of your existence." He paused, his eyes flicking towards the heavens as he took a deep breath. "Most of my people will accept you as my signasti, but they are going to question you. A lot. That's the Shifter way, but it's nothing you can't handle."

His unyielding faith scared the shit out of me, and for the first time since waking up, ice settled over me. It turned my fingers and bare feet cold, spreading from the outside in.

Deep breaths, I reminded myself.

In.

Out.

In.

Out.

You can do this. You are making a choice.

A knock on the door came and Blair jumped to her feet to get it.

"Please," I whispered. She stilled halfway to the door. "I'm not ready to see anyone else yet. I need—" My voice cracked, and I swallowed the lump inside my throat that tried to silence me. "I need more time."

Blair nodded, and I had to avert my eyes to stop myself from lashing out at the pity I found in hers. I didn't want pity from anyone, and that part of me would never change.

I rose to my feet and walked to the balcony, trying to block out her voice as she whispered for them to leave. Whoever it was, they didn't speak, but their footsteps echoed in my ears as they walked away.

I had let myself break. The ocean pulled me under, and only the light of dawn drew me out. Then I slept. I slept for weeks. Months. Depression claimed me until I had no other choice but to come back to this world of the living and feel everything all over again.

Last time, the sunrise broke me, but this time...I would look to the dusk.

To the setting sun.

"One day," I whispered. It was my promise to myself.

I swore it before the dawn, and now again before a dying day.

There would be many, many days that I would falter and fail, but just as the sun always rose, again did it fall. I would not be the moon that eclipsed the world. I would be the sun.

And one day I will rise, but for now...for now I must fall.

CHAPTER 18

I STAYED ON THE BALCONY FOR A LONG TIME. LONG AFTER AMBER excused herself and Blair followed. Even Alexandra gave me space now that she was sure I wasn't going to have a repeat.

No one said it, but I could feel it in the air. Their pain. Their tension. The resigned sense of disappointment that I was back but somehow lacking. I was different, but not whole. I don't think they recognized the girl that came back from the darkness, and maybe that was because they could not see me. They did not know what took place in my mind, or just how different I was. But the crippling sense that they somehow saw me as *less* stung.

How do you fix that?

The question echoed within me long after the skies turned from blue to black. Brilliant orbs of fire lit the night. Stars young and old, burning. Always burning. My father once told me that the stars were the last remnants of the ancients.

That somewhere up there Nyx was locked in a burning prison.

I always wondered if she was waiting for something, someone, that could set her free. After all, wouldn't you want to be free from that kind of eternal hell? My father never answered me, but part of me now wondered if she did it to herself. If she couldn't stand what she saw when she looked at the world, and so she locked herself away.

Forever burning from what became of her children.

Did she even try to fix us? Could she? And did I have any chance of freeing myself if even a Goddess preferred her prison to the world she created?

The energy around me stirred as he walked out onto the balcony beside me.

Silent footsteps. Slow beating heart. Steady, even breaths.

"Penny for your thoughts?" he asked. His voice was deep, dark, and lovely.

"I'm contemplating the secrets of the universe," I replied, honest with him for the first time.

"Let me know if you discover anything," he said lightly. I wasn't fooled by the nonchalance, but it was better than talking about heavier things.

"I should probably figure out how to fix myself before I look at the rest of the world. With my track record, I'm more likely to break it," I said, cringing once the words were out of my mouth. There was honesty, and then there was brutal self-loathing. I made a point to never show anyone how deep that streak ran, but my demon didn't want to hide from him. I would have to be wary of that.

"Or you could let him see it all," Violet suggested, piping up from her corner. I could feel how much my demon eagerly agreed and I grimaced to keep from telling Violet to buzz off.

"You have been through a lot and I don't think anyone can blame you for struggling. It is not an easy transition for anyone, Supernatural or Shifter, when we come into the age of maturity. Yours has been made even more difficult," he said. Was that...understanding in his voice? Was he trying to empathize with me?

I glanced sideways, but his eyes were not on me. He looked to the night sky.

"You're only saying that because of who I am."

"You mean the first matter manipulator of the new age? Or a girl that lost her sister while trying to stay afloat?" My lips thinned into an even line. "I know what you're referring to, Selena, but I am not blind to your faults because you are my signasti. I have never seen you as anything but what you are."

Unlike how I see you? I thought bitterly. Luckily this time, my thoughts stayed in my mind and didn't come blurting out of my mouth.

"Answer me this," I said. "How can you stand to look at me—to save me—after what I did? How are you not afraid like the rest of them?"

And the truth comes out. He nodded like he was expecting it. Maybe he was. Violet always found my questions quite predictable. I must be losing my touch.

"Because I know the madness you walk in. I see your shadows, as you call them. I know how afraid you are of yourself, but most importantly, I see how much you want to change." He paused, taking a deep breath. "And I know that if you can find it in yourself to be better, then so can I. You give me hope."

Hope.

Such a sentimental feeling. Yet it was the only thing that stood between me and utter destruction. Hope that I could get better. Be better.

"You're quite the smooth talker when you want to be," I said, pushing aside the light fluttering in my chest. He chuckled.

"You would dismiss anything I said that didn't line up with your own views of yourself," he replied. I pursed my lips just a little as I considered it.

"Perhaps." It was the only acknowledgement I would give of just how close to the truth that statement was.

We stood there well into the night, like two people getting to know each other for the first time.

I DIDN'T REMEMBER FALLING asleep but woke to light filtering through the dark curtains of Aaron's room. It was the same one I'd woken in the first time, and just as empty. Beside me sat a folded note.

WENT FOR A RUN. —A.

A RUN SOUNDED blissful right about now. Nothing better to clear my head than the pumping of blood and muscle exhaustion. I hopped out of bed, raring to go. Not that I

could actually do anything without real clothes, or shoes...
come to think of it...when was the last time I showered?

Footsteps approached the door, heavy and lumbering,
but familiar. I opened the bedroom and crossed the small
living space. My stomach rumbled as the smell of bacon
and eggs hit me, and the smell of—was that coffee?

I grasped the door handle and pulled it open. A wicked
snap filled the air. The blood drained from my face as I took
in the door dangling from my hand.

"Ohmigawd—did you just take the door off—that's
like, the coolest thing ever!"

I cringed, dropping the door to clap my hands over my
ears as I jumped away from the obnoxious child.

"Do you have to be so loud?" I snapped. That seemed to
shut her up. She cocked an eyebrow, not even phased by my
reprimand.

"You really are his signasti, aren't you?" I rolled my eyes
at the smile on her face and motioned to the tray of food in
her arms.

"Is that for me?" I asked, jutting my chin towards her,
still not willing to lower my hands until she could prove to
speak in a reasonable tone.

"Yup."

"You can leave it on the coffee table," I said dismissively.
Not that she paid any mind. She dropped the tray on the
table and plonked her ass on the fluffy leather couch.

"You seem kinda grouchy to be his signasti. I mean,
don't get me wrong, he's no basket of sunshine either, but I
just thought you were supposed to be the better half of
him—"

Does this girl ever shut up? I wanted to snap again, but

my demon had other ideas. I settled for taking the chair across from her and sipping the coffee.

"You seem to know a lot about me. Have any idea where I can find some clothes?" I asked her. She flicked her eyes across my makeshift outfit and wiggled her eyebrows. Good god, she was like a younger version of Amber—that somehow the demonic beast inside me found adorable.

"He hasn't gotten you any clothes yet? Typical. He probably wanted you to smell like him to ward off any other males. He's a bit territorial like that. Gets it from our father, my aunt says, but you didn't hear that from me." She plucked a piece of bacon off my tray, completely oblivious to the little nugget she just gave me.

"Your father?" I asked. At this point I would probably learn more just to let her keep talking. She didn't seem to have any sort of filter on her. How lucky for me.

"Oh yeah, he's just like dad. Not that he sees it. If anything, he hovers even worse. Aunt Sarah says it's an Alpha thing, but she's an Alpha and you don't see her going all growly over shit," she said and then quickly cupped her hand over her mouth, her face going a little red. "Oops. Pretend you didn't hear that. They don't like it when I cuss."

Despite my initial urge to throttle her, I found myself smirking instead.

"Don't worry. I don't care if you curse. It'll be our little secret," I said very seriously. You would think I hung the moon with the smile that broke across her face.

"You know, I'm starting to see what he likes about you, Lena. I'm Keyla." She half waved at me while taking another piece of bacon. I took a piece for myself, savoring the salty crunch. Yesterday I was too overwhelmed to eat, so food was another first for my demon, and it made me appreciate my first meal back a little more.

"My name's actually Selena," I said, pausing to swallow. "I just don't make a point of giving it out when I wake up in strange places."

"I know your name *now*, but I like Lena better. Plus, it'll piss him off that I already have a nickname for you." She cackled wickedly and I suddenly saw a glimpse of why my demon found her so endearing.

Taking a bite of eggs, I continued. "Speaking of pissing him off...I'm feeling cooped up. I want to go on a run. You think you could help me find some clothes?" Maybe it was sneaky to manipulate a kid, but she wasn't *that* much younger than me—and it's not like she was entirely innocent.

"That depends. Can I go running with you?"

My eyes swept across her face. It was such an innocent question, but given what I woke up to yesterday, I hesitated, and only for a fraction of a second.

"What? Think you're too good for me?" she asked, a bit defensive.

Why on earth would she assume that?

"Not at all," I replied. "I'm just surprised that you're not afraid of me." It was the honest truth and it would have been completely awkward had she not thrown her head back and laughed.

"I'm not afraid of anyone. My dad's *the* Shifter Alpha. You don't get far being afraid of people," she replied.

"No," I agreed. "You don't."

"So, can I come with you?" she asked again.

"Sure," I nodded to her. "If you can keep up."

Her eyes sparkled at the challenge. "I'm the third fastest in our pack, second only to my cousin and brother. I can do better than keep up."

I smiled faintly at the confidence she exuded. My demon found her absolutely charming, and I guess I could kind of see it. She did bring me food after all.

"Your cousin? They must be pretty fast if they outrun Aaron," I mused, piling the last of my eggs onto a slice of toast.

"You could say that. Amber's next in line to be the alpha over the cats, and she's got a *gift* for speed." She snatched the last piece of bacon off my tray, completely oblivious to my pause.

"Amber is pretty fast," I agreed, chewing slowly. *Amber? Amber was his cousin?*

That made so much sense, but why didn't he say anything? I would have to ask...

"You know her?" Keyla asked excitedly. "You must have gone to Daizlei with her before—"

She broke off sharply, as if it only just registered with her that Daizlei was gone. I wonder if she would have gone there, had it not been wiped off the map. Clearly, she didn't know the part I had to play in that.

"Yeah, we were roommates at Daizlei," I said softly, not thinking about all the people that have died since that night. Thinking on it did no one any good. "I didn't know she and Aaron were related at the time though."

We sat in a slightly awkward but comfortable silence while I finished off my breakfast with haste and drained the coffee in large gulps.

"Ready?" I asked her, getting to my feet. She jumped up next to me and led the way out, only sparing the door a brief glance.

"We're about the same height, don't you think?" she asked, plowing down the hallway. It was a wonder she didn't wake anyone else with how loud she was.

"Yeah, about. Why?" I asked, coming up beside her as she stopped at a door at the very end of the hall overlooking the three floors drop I'd jumped yesterday.

"Because if my brother sees you wearing the community clothes he'll bitch at me for it later," she answered, opening the door. Inside it was what could only be described as a preteen's bedroom. Lime green walls assaulted my eyes almost as much as the smell that was coming from the door at the back. Clothes littered the floor, draped over the couches, a bra hanging off the lamp by her bed.

It was the complete opposite from the room I was staying in, but again, it reminded me of a certain copper-haired roommate of mine that I'd shared space with for a year. Now I knew why.

"Here, try these on." She thrust a wad of material towards me and I hoped she didn't have an aversion to nakedness because that bathroom smelled seriously rank. I stripped right then and there, refusing to go another foot closer to what smelled suspiciously like a clogged toilet and rotten eggs.

I slipped on the itty-bitty shorts she handed me. They were a near exact match to the spandex ones I wore for years, only a tad tighter. The plain black sports bra wasn't quite as good a fit. She wasn't nearly as chesty as me, but her rib cage was similar. I ended up with a good amount of cleavage, but my boobs pressed smack against my chest. It wasn't perfect, but it'd do.

"I think I should look for a t-shirt for you. My brother—"

"Isn't my keeper," I said sharply. Normally I wouldn't care all that much, but by no means was I letting him and his Alpha shit run my life. He'd seen me dress much the same and spar with many men over the last year. This wouldn't be any different.

"If you say so," Keyla grinned. She changed into a matching set of workout clothes and passed me some fancy shoes. My sneakers before had been so old and used they nearly contoured to my feet, but these were almost new and light as a feather. I appreciated the snugness of how they fit, as perfect as you could get without breaking in. At least our shoe size was the same.

"Alrighty, so we got a couple of options for running. We can either hit the gym and jump on some treadmills"—she paused at the purse of my lips—"Or we go outside and I'll show you some gnarly trails around the residence."

"Trails," I said.

"A girl after my own heart," she agreed. We exited through the elevator and went down to the first floor. While I had no qualms about jumping off buildings, it seemed the young half Shifter, half Supernatural had other ideas of a good time. Although, it did give me the chance to confirm that it was, indeed, the magic elevator. Which means we were either on a ley line, or a black market was around here somewhere. Possibly both.

I followed beside her silently until I saw the double

doors ahead that led out into a wide green space. Stopping dead in my tracks, I grabbed the younger girl's wrist. I meant just to give her pause, but she snapped back to my chest like a rubber band, her head only missing mine because I thought to dodge it.

"Whoa," she said and blinked her eyes five times. "You got some serious strength, but why don't you save the manhandling for my bro—unless you want to train in other ways. I'm damn good with a mace—"

"Can we not go this way?" I asked, skipping straight over whatever other ideas she seemed to have about what her brother and I did.

"Cutting through the training area is the fastest way to the trails," she said, almost whining.

"I'm not in the mood to meet anyone else new. Find another route," I replied.

She gave me an appraising sweep of her eyes before grumbling, "Fine." She wrapped her hand around my elbow and started pulling me down a hallway. There were still Shifters and they paused to look, but there were less of them, so I took it as a win. The fewer people I had to see and answer to, the better for now.

"There's no way to avoid everyone entirely, but this way we should be going around the training yard instead of through it. Happy?" she asked, kicking open a door with an emergency exit sign over it.

"Peachy." She chuckled under her breath, the feminine version of Aaron if I ever heard it.

In front of us, miles of woods covered the landscape, rising up to form mountains as far as the eye could see.

"This way," she grunted. I turned to follow her down

the narrow strip of grass. The echoes and shouts were putting me on edge, but the clang of weapons had my palms sweating as we rounded the edge of the house. As she said, we wouldn't be going through the yard, but around it. Not that it stopped people from staring as I went. I kept my head down and eyes averted, opting to stare at the young girl's shoes instead.

"What are you doing?" Keyla asked. We were only halfway across and the group of tigers next to us looked over almost...cautiously? Reserved?

"Walking. What am I supposed to be doing?" I replied. She came to stand beside me instead of in front of me.

"I'm not talking about your feet. I'm talking about your eyes. You're staring at the ground like a weak Shifter," she said, obviously upset.

"I don't care what they think and neither should you," I replied. Clearly the girl still had more to learn.

"But you should care," she butted in, not willing to let it drop. "How do you expect to—"

"Keyla. I don't give a damn. I just want to go on a run. You can either drop it and come with me, or I'll go by myself," I said. She narrowed her eyes at me.

"You wouldn't dare," she challenged.

"Next time you see him, ask your brother what happens when people tell me that," I replied, smirking at the memories. We'd passed through the majority of the yard and while I could feel eyes on my back as we walked, I paid them no mind.

"You're kind of spiteful, you know that?" she said.

"You have no idea."

We didn't even make it all the way across the training

area before she broke into a run and I took off after her. My feet barely touched the ground as I quickly gained on her and had to slow myself just to not pass her.

"Is that the best you've got?" I asked, heaving in crisp mountain air. My lungs tasted of blood and ice, but I relished in the pain. That sadistic part of me still fed on it.

"Not even close," she called back over the wind. She picked up her speed, but it wasn't enough to outrun me. Not even close. We neared the edge of the training yard and I floored it. We hooked right, following a jagged trail that led off into the woods.

Out here, I was one with the world. One with nature. This is what I was good at. Every part of me was blissfully at ease once we were away from the others. It was my demon's first run, and the first thing that I found myself cherishing just as much as she.

"Damn, you're fast!" Keyla squawked from several yards behind me. I was impressed she even kept up this far.

"Try to keep up!" I called over my shoulder and then I let loose. All inhibitions left me as I raced up and down hills, across a valley, and even jumping over a small river. I ran until I couldn't, and not because I was tired, but because the trail disappeared.

In front of me, a massive lake glistened in the early afternoon sun.

I would think it was beautiful, if not for the flashing images of the hydra. It was doubtful that something that deadly lived out here, but that didn't make the squirming in my chest any better.

Endure it. Embrace it. Then you can control it.

Another command of Violet's. Another ultimatum, lest I bring about my own end.

Enduring the slithering sensation across my chest was not the easiest. Not by a long shot. I inhaled slowly and focused on making my exhales twice as long. It helped to a certain extent, but after five minutes, the shadows started to creep into my vision and I knew it was my cue to go.

"One day," I whispered over the water.

It was becoming my mantra to myself. My reminder of what I was fighting for.

I retreated into the woods with one last look over my shoulder.

I started my run back at a leisurely pace, wondering how long it would take Keyla to catch up. She wasn't slow by anyone's standards, but she wasn't part demon either. To expect her to keep pace the whole way would have been unrealistic.

My feet carried me swift and near silent through the woods. If not for my breathing and heartbeat, I would be a ghost. As it was, I moved fast enough that animals didn't even notice something was in their midst until I was gone.

It was freeing, in a way. To exist but not be seen.

A shout, far in the distance, pulled me back. At the same moment, a stray wind carried a scent to me. Keyla. She wasn't far.

I picked up my speed down the trail, coming to a stop right in front of her.

She didn't seem to have noticed me at all until I appeared right before her. Her long legs skidded in the dirt, kicking up a cloud of dust and debris. Her large golden eyes flew wide as she put up both hands to try to stop herself from running into me.

I smirked, sidestepping her but wrapping my fingers around her bicep to pull her to a complete stop.

"How far did you go?" she demanded.

"To the lake." Her mouth popped open and closed three times before she found her voice.

"The lake is ten miles from here. How is that even—"

"Do you hear that?" I held up my hand for silence.

There it was again. A shout. A cry. Was that...*a roar?*

What the hell was going on back at the mansion?

"I don't hear anything," Keyla said quickly and shrugged.

"Just stay close to me."

We left the conversation at that as we took off back towards the residence. While I could tell that the younger girl was brimming with questions, she seemed to have the good sense to keep her mouth shut when apprehension edged at me. Inside, my demon paced. She didn't like this. Not one bit.

The shouts grew more pronounced as we neared the training yard. Roughly a mile out, I began to make out some words.

"WHERE is she?"

Oh shit. That was Aaron. And he was in Hulk mode from the sound of it.

"She took off with Keyla. We don't know—"

"I'm sure they're fine, baby. Your sister's probably running circles around her as we speak."

Baby? Something dark and ugly unfurled in my chest.

I flexed my fingers but controlled my urges. *Better.* I'm

supposed to focus on getting better. Not bashing someone's face in. That was the opposite of Zen.

"Check yourself, Jessa. He's not your anything," a brisk voice retorted, cold as ice. *Blair*.

As much as me and my demon appreciated her saying something, why wasn't Aaron?

You know what? It doesn't matter.

Better. Focus on *better*.

I repeated it three times in my mind before the trees drew near. Beside me, Keyla started to slow to a crawl, but I reached out and curled my fingers around her wrist. She looked up at me as I dragged her several feet before she got the hint and started to pick up the speed again. A wicked smirk crossed her lips.

"Don't look at them. Just keep running," I murmured, pulling my hand away. As soon as I spoke, we burst from the trees and saw the party gathered around the edge waiting for us.

Keyla didn't spare them a second glance, falling in line next to me as I cranked up the speed and started to hightail it down the spray-painted line of grass that marked the edge of the training yard.

"Selena! Keyla!" The voices began shouting.

"Goddamn. Bunch of nosy pricks that can't—" I stopped swearing the moment Keyla threw her head back and burst out laughing. Not paying attention to her own two feet, she accidentally knocked into me. Her right foot twisted around mine, throwing us both off balance.

Reacting without thinking, I braced her fall as we went tumbling into the grass and she laughed the entire way down. Something about the sound eased my aggressive nature and I found myself laughing too.

It started as low chuckles of amusement, but with her laughing beside me, my heart relaxed just enough for me to feel the first inkling of true happiness in this new body and life.

I threw my head back against the grass and clutched my stomach, laughing so hard tears brimmed my eyes. I couldn't remember the last time I felt so at ease.

So free.

Maybe there was something to what Violet had been telling me all along. Maybe I did need to accept every part of me to understand any semblance of peace and happiness.

Or maybe the kid beside me had something to do with it.

I didn't really care. I just never wanted it to stop.

CHAPTER 19

Aaron spared me the introductions with the Shifters and instead excused himself for the day. It was a polite dismissal, but a dismissal nonetheless. Even my friends and family remained on the training field as he and I walked away.

"Wait!" Keyla called. I looked over my shoulder at her to see her smile spread from one dimpled cheek to the other. "Go running with me tomorrow?" she asked, her voice carrying a good fifty yards.

Half the Shifters in the field turned to me, awaiting my response for the daughter of the Shifter Alpha. Something told me she did it that way intentionally. She certainly was manipulative enough to attempt it.

I took a deep breath and quirked an eyebrow. "You think you'll be able to keep up better tomorrow?" I asked her, putting just a smidge of swagger and arrogance into it.

"I know I will," she called back.

"I'll hold you to that."

Aaron didn't say anything as we walked back inside, but he somehow knew to take the long way around and not cut through the crowd. We walked side by side through the mansion. With just him and no Keyla, friends, or family, it was a very different mood than when we were surrounded by hordes of Shifters.

"She likes you," he said as the elevator doors opened on the third floor.

"You sound surprised by that."

"Keyla never likes anyone," he said as we came to the room. It occurred to me then why he might have been in a panic trying to find me on the training field—given the ebony door I had accidentally taken off its hinges and tossed aside without regard.

"Well, I guess that makes two of us. My demon finds her absolutely fascinating. I didn't get it at first, but she kind of grows on you once you get past how loud she is..." I trailed off, when I realized what I'd said and how he froze.

I brushed a hand over my jaw and through my hair, tugging on the tangles to break them apart. Ordinarily I hated it when people fidgeted, so I couldn't understand why I found my tangled locks so interesting right at that moment.

"I should probably go," I surmised, averting my eyes.
Idiot. How could you possibly think that—

"Don't do that." He stepped in front of me to stop me from walking out on him. "I didn't mean to upset you. I've just never heard you talk about it...I assumed you were still processing and didn't want to."

My lips parted before I remembered myself and hastily closed them.

"I had a lot of time to think while I was...sleeping," I replied. It was awkward at best, but at least it was an honest response. Aaron raked a hand through his own hair, and I got the idea that he was completely out of his element with this.

"Would you like to talk about it?" he asked. I blinked once and cocked my head.

"Would you?" I asked. He sighed deeply and moved from the doorway to the couch—leaving the offer open for me to walk out right now—or take a seat.

"I won't lie, I'm curious. But I haven't pushed because I respect your privacy." He seated himself on the long black couch completely facing away from me, towards the crackling fire.

"You've pushed on plenty of *other* things." He let out a dark chuckle.

"Take a seat or don't, Selena. I've always given you the choice."

Choice. That word rattled around in my brain, evoking memories of stolen touches and scorching kisses. Late nights staring at a golden canopy while the fire crackled at our feet. Angry words and hurtful truths brought forth by rage and desperation on both sides.

Being around him—near him, with him—was so very different than Lucas.

Lucas always pushed to know more. He always sought for a way inside my mind. He judged me for the bad but craved me for the good. He lied to try and keep me for himself, because he was too scared to give me the choice.

In the end, his actions are what brought about an end to our friendship, letting the bond push me toward Aaron.

Funny how little actions and choices lead to things in life that go beyond our wildest dreams.

I took a seat at the other end of the long leather couch.

"My demon is not evil like I thought she was. She's a part of me, with urges and thoughts and feelings that are mine...but not." His eyes watched me with a startling intensity that no one in my life knew how to exude quite like him. "I probably sound crazy, don't I?"

"I've heard crazier."

We didn't talk anymore after that, but the quiet that sat between us was no longer awkward or uncomfortable. It was a gentle, tentative acceptance that shook me to my core, but I never spoke a word of it.

A STACK of woman's workout clothes sat on the edge of the bed the next morning.

And the next.

And the next.

Three days passed where the only two people I really saw were Aaron and Keyla. He was gone every morning before I woke and Keyla would bring me breakfast. We would run together and no one bothered us. Not a soul.

The living room door had been magically fixed, and I took great care with my strength not to break it again, but Aaron never asked what happened. The same as I never asked about the others. I never asked about the bond. I never asked about much of anything.

But slowly, excruciatingly slow, my heart was beginning to thaw.

I was not fixed or whole by any means, but after only three days of watching, I was beginning to see what Violet was talking about. So, I stayed quiet. I waited. I watched.

Every afternoon, Aaron came back alone. Every night, we would eat dinner, and for three days we didn't speak.

Until today.

"I was thinking it might be nice to eat dinner with the team tonight. They've been asking about you, you know..." he trailed off.

I looked up from the fireplace, finding it difficult to drag my eyes away from the flames.

"Dinner?" I asked faintly.

"In the mess hall," he clarified. "All of the team sits at the same table. I thought it might be nice," he continued. My lack of an immediate reply had him taking a deep breath and turning back towards the bedroom.

"I would like that," I said quickly. He paused in the doorframe and I could have sworn I felt a surge of emotion in my chest that didn't come from me.

"I'll go find you some clothes then," he said. I used his absence to retreat to the bathroom and start a bath. It wasn't really a bath because I wouldn't leave the stopper in, but it was close enough. With only the hot water nozzle turned up and steam clouding the air, I stepped into the tub and began to wash myself.

It certainly wasn't my first bath since I'd come back, but I took more time with it. I savored the blistering heat that couldn't burn but came close. Just like the fire, it straddled the line of an invisible limit that would never be crossed, but I liked to dance on it.

I washed my hair clean with the same citrus smelling

shampoo I'd been using for the last few days, taking care to try and untangle the knots in my growing hair. Before it had been shorn at my jaw, and already it was to my shoulders.

I finished my bath and stood to wring out my hair, twisting it in a tight swirl. Droplets of water fell, echoing across the bathroom walls. I flicked my fingers to flip the switch for the fan while simultaneously reaching for a fluffy black towel. The mass of soft material settled around me like a cloud, pulling all remaining moisture from my skin before I patted my hair dry.

Every movement was quiet. Deliberate. I was preparing myself in a sense for what came next.

Without delaying any more, I set the towel aside and turned my eyes to the mirror before me.

My lungs constricted for a moment and I fought the urge to look away.

It's not like I could unsee the face before me. Or the eyes.

Nor could I change it.

All that was really left was to accept it.

Hesitantly, I lifted my hand to the glass, resting it there beside my reflection.

Two eyes with two pupils ringed in three circles of color.

The closest to the pupil was my own eye color. Grey as slate. Turbulent as a coming storm. Familiar enough that my heart squeezed in my chest.

The next ring was violet, purer in hue than any color my eyes had been before. The glow from behind them wasn't as unsettling as I would have expected.

Then came the onyx. This band was a true darkness, so devoid of light that it did not glint or shine. It was the darkness that I always saw when I looked at Aaron, but only now realized that even he couldn't quite get right. My own brand of darkness. My demon.

I stared at the proof of what I'd done—what we'd done —and I couldn't find it in me to feel afraid. Not anymore.

A series of knocks ricocheted across the small space.

"I'm leaving your clothes on the bed," Aaron said.

I didn't hear him retreat but knew when he was gone. The emptiness sat in my chest almost as heavily as the surge of belonging my demon felt when I looked in the mirror. I didn't really want to think about either, so I exited the bathroom and focused on dressing.

The dark grey cargo pants hung low on my hips, lower than I was used to wearing, but I didn't complain. Clothes were clothes, and anything beat walking around in *his* clothes, even if the t-shirt he gave me was an exact replica of The Beatles one I'd worn my first day here. I smirked to myself and slipped it on, sauntering out into the living room feeling a little bit more like myself.

"Ready?" I asked.

Aaron looked up from the book he was holding and snapped it closed instantly. His eyes roved from the hair of my head to the combat boots he'd brought me to replace the ones that we abandoned in the earthquake.

"Let's go," he said softly. We walked to the elevator, quiet as always, and I found it uncanny how easily we had fallen into this routine.

"Will Keyla be there?" I asked absentmindedly.

"She will, but she'll be sitting at another table." I

ignored the spark of disappointment my demon felt and settled into an impassive state.

The elevator dinged as the doors opened.

"Will the others be as distrusting of me as Amber?" I asked, stepping out into the empty hallway. Aaron stiffened, but quickly recovered and followed after.

"It's not that Amber distrusts you. She doesn't understand what you're going through, but she's starting to. The rest of the team is a mixed bag, but they all asked to see you." He led us down a wide corridor with off-white walls and polished hardwood floors. The sounds of people talking, and clinking plates drifted from down the hall.

"And you?" I asked. "You understand what I'm going through?"

The snark in my voice sounded hollow, even to me. Genuine curiosity was creeping through and I wondered if he heard it too.

"You are not the only one the bond madness affects. In many ways, it's worse for me because I can actually feel it. Being Supernatural, you can't sense the depth with which it runs, but maybe that's for the best."

My heart shuddered in my chest. *Is that what he thought?* If so, I didn't understand how he could even say it without a shred of resentment.

My steps slowed just outside two massive double doors where the dull roar was coming from. I glanced up at him, my breath coming in short, shallow bursts.

"Tell him," Violet chided at me. *"Go ahead. Do it."*

I inhaled once and held my breath.

"I feel more than you realize." It was the smallest of

confessions, but I knew it reached his ears the moment I stepped in front of the doorway. He inhaled sharply beside me. His only tell that my words affected him. We strolled into the room side by side with ambivalent faces and a building tension.

No one knew it; no one but us.

The roar seemed to quiet as more people looked up from their tables at us and began whispering. They thought I couldn't hear it when they leaned over to their neighbors across the oak tables. That because they were Shifters, and I a Supernatural, that I didn't possess the same level of hearing.

Oh, but I did.

I heard every single one of them and it took everything in me not to turn and run because there were too many. Too many voices. Too many people. If it weren't for the sheer size of the hall and dim lighting, my instincts very well may have carried me away.

"Tolerance," Violet told me. *"Endurance."* I urged my feet to keep moving. *"Listen and learn."* I came to a stop at the table in the very center where faces I hadn't seen in too long watched me.

The air was still, the anticipation mounting.

Maybe it wasn't such a good idea—

"Pay up," Alexandra declared.

"Damnit, how was I supposed to know he'd be able to convince her," Amber whined. She dug a twenty out of her pocket and Alexandra grinned into her salad. It was almost like old times.

"You were betting on whether I'd come down?" I asked.

My voice was quieter than the others, but it seemed I still had that magical ability to silence a room with only words.

"They were," Blair cut in. "I was smart enough to not even attempt at guessing what you would decide."

I smiled at that and my heart thawed a little more.

"She's my sister. If anyone can predict that mind of hers, it's me," Alexandra boasted. It was such a one-eighty from the last time I'd seen them, that all I could do was stare.

And then, going against everything I was and abandoning all pretenses of how this dinner would go—I laughed. It wasn't a strong boisterous laugh, and certainly not the snorts that Keyla seemed to be able to draw from me, but it was something.

"When I don't surprise you anymore, you've known me too long," I said. Half the table went very still. The half that lived with me. That boxed with me. That grew up with me.

It was the first thing I said since coming back that was reminiscent of the old me.

"Welcome back, sister," Alexandra said, breaking the silence.

The corners of my mouth tugged up in a small smile.

"It's good to be back," I said quietly.

"You know, we did come down here to actually eat," Aaron broke in beside me. Instantly, two seats appeared, one between Alexandra and Amber, the other between Blair and—

"Scarlett?"

"Aye, in the flesh," the girl in front of me murmured. I took my seat between her and Blair, letting Aaron sit across from me.

"I hadn't realized you were back as well." I took the plate that was passed to me from down the table.

"Earthquakes are good at making you get yourself together," she replied lightly. Her voice still rang with a hint of sorrow, but she was here. Functioning. Liam sat on the other side of her, their hands intertwined beneath the table.

"At least something good came of it."

I meant it. The knowledge of what I'd done was still a bitter pill to swallow.

Scarlett didn't say much after that, so I took to listening while I ate. Catching up with the rest of the team by following their body language and conversations.

Next to Alexandra sat Tori, of all people. I hadn't spoken to her in so long, I didn't know what we were anymore. During my rampage, I refused to even acknowledge her existence because of who her brother was, but here she was, months later, laughing and smiling beside my sister.

Good for her. At least they had each other all this time, even if I never saw it.

Moving down the table, past Aaron and Amber, sat Oliver. He whispered back and forth across the table with Johanna, who sat on the other side of Liam. It was nothing nefarious or cunning, but still irked me.

Who was I kidding? He irked me. Period.

"Have you seen her eyes?" he asked, very carefully avoiding my gaze. Johanna nodded.

"She has changed," the golden beauty said.

"Yes, but how?"

"I can only assume, given her aura, but I think it's for the better. Something happened while she was sleeping, and she is not the same person she was," Johanna murmured.

Well, she was right about that. I had changed, but something told me she wouldn't think it was for the better if she knew the truth.

There was only one other at the table that looked like he felt as out of place as I did.

Alec sat on the opposite end from Blair, and given their history, I didn't wonder why. A lot may have changed while I'd been asleep, but some things never would. Blair's cold, hard, unyielding nature was one of those things.

She was loyal to a fault, but when you betrayed her... there was no earning her back.

It was one of the things I'd always appreciated about my cousin; appreciated enough to train her. To befriend her. I wondered how she was after all this time, but I suppose sitting on the end by yourself is telling, isn't it?

We always were loners. Two people that never quite fit in. I kept my mouth shut and averted my eyes to the pork chop on my plate.

"You're very quiet for someone who's been gone," Blair whispered beside me, pulling me from my musings.

"You learn a lot more listening than asking questions," I said softly. She nodded, sipping her water.

"Do you ever think it will be like it was before?" Her lips barely moved, but her question struck true. I took a bite of my dinner and chewed slowly, thinking about how to respond.

"No," I settled on. "I think we can be better."

She wasn't expecting that answer. I could tell by the tilt of her head and shrewd gaze.

"It really is you," she said.

"I never left. I just needed to figure out my own shit," I said honestly.

"And have you?"

I looked up at the candlelight coming from the golden chandeliers. The tiny flickering flames called to me.

"No, but I will."

CHAPTER 20

I WAS GETTING READY FOR DINNER THE NEXT EVENING WHEN KEYLA barged into the bedroom. The door bounced off the wall leaving a small dent where the lock turned in the center of the handle. Her eyes flashed from the wall to me, her cheeks flaming.

"Shit—I mean—I didn't mean to do that—you know..." she trailed off, smiling in a kind of awkward apology while scratching the back of her head. I rolled my eyes, tugging my shirt down over my stomach.

"Not like I have room to talk." I shrugged and my wet hair brushed my shoulders, transferring tiny droplets of water I hadn't been able to shake free. Keyla chuckled and slowly pushed the door flush against the wall.

"We'll just keep that between us, right?" There was a mischievous glint in her eye. "And if my brother asked, it was you," she added.

I snorted. "Why would I tell him it was me?"

Keyla grabbed my arm to start pulling me through the

apartment. While she still hadn't said what she came here for, her manhandling was a clue.

"Because he won't get mad at you," she insisted as she pulled me out the door.

"Fair enough. Mind telling me where we're going?" Keyla dropped my arm like she only just realized what she had been doing.

"Dinner. Duh," she said and motioned for me to follow like I was the slow one here. I shook my head, chuckling under my breath.

"That doesn't explain why you're dragging me to it," I said. We stepped into the elevator and she hummed impatiently, shifting side to side.

"Because I have to arrive with you *before* my brother gets there or he's going to make me sit at the kids' table," she whispered conspiratorially.

"What's so bad about the kids' table?"

"They're all butt nuggets and nose pickers," Keyla griped. I snorted to myself in mild disbelief and utter amusement as the elevator doors opened. Keyla straightened up and motioned for me to go first, following closely behind.

There were so many people in the hallways it was impossible to walk side by side. Must be because we were early. Not all the Shifters had gone to the dining hall yet.

We rounded the corner and my steps fell short on what I saw.

Aaron had beat us to dinner, but instead of sitting at our usual table, he was hanging with the rest of *his* kind around the doorway...and Jessa was hanging on him. She leaned in close, wrapping an arm around his waist as she did so. Her rose-colored lips angled upwards as she moved to whisper in his ear.

"This is how it should be, Aaron," she said huskily. Her long, lithe body pressed against his and Aaron went very still. He looked past her to see...and saw *me*.

I cocked my head and raised an eyebrow but turned to go to dinner without him.

"Selena, wait!" he called out, much louder than needed, but I wasn't sticking around for this. I told Keyla I'd eat dinner with her so she didn't have to sit at the kids' table, and that's exactly what I'd do.

"Ohmigawd—I never liked her—Jessa's being a total skank—" Keyla said loudly behind me. The dining hall went quiet and I just knew.

I took a deep breath, stopping directly beneath the massive chandelier that lit the entire hall. Keyla was only a few feet behind me, and behind her was Aaron; behind him, an obviously pissed off Jessa.

"You'd rather a *Supernatural* be our next female Alpha, Keyla?" she asked in a high-pitched voice. I rolled my eyes at the dramatics of it.

"I'd pick Selena over you any day," Keyla piped off. "Not that any of our opinions matter because she's *my brother's* signasti. Aren't you, Selena?"

Aw, hell. Why did she have to do that? Drag me into this? The last thing I wanted was to risk getting pissed in the dining hall and leveling it.

I stared at Aaron who stood with Jessa at his side. Her arm was no longer wrapped around him, but she stood close enough it didn't matter. My demon wanted to smite her from this world, but that wasn't my call to make. Not for something as insignificant as this.

If he wanted to screw around with Shifter girls, then that was his prerogative. *Clearly, he hadn't changed that much.*

As soon as the thought had formed, there was another presence pressing against my mind, looking for a way in. Except unlike Lucas, I had no idea how to block this one.

"It's not what you think," his voice whispered in my mind.

I mentally lashed out at him, sending a wall of straight power between us. He inhaled sharply as I shrugged my shoulders to the rest of the room. Not confirming or denying. I knew it would piss him off, his control was wearing thin, but I didn't really care so long as I kept mine. The Shifters could think what they wanted. I grabbed Keyla's wrist and started to forcibly drag her to the table.

"What are you doing?" Keyla protested loudly. "You can't just let her talk about you like that. It's not the Shifter way—"

"I'm not a Shifter, Keyla," I snapped. *And it's not like this is the first time I've seen him wrapped around other girls. Guess I know who kept him company while I was gone.*

Hurt flared down the tethered bond between us as he took in my actions. An acute anger followed...rage. *Hell.* I had a feeling I was going to get a front row seat at what it meant to be the Shifter Heir.

"See how she cowers from a challenge?" Jessa projected, clearly not sensing the building storm inside of Aaron. "See how she *disrespects* our Alpha? She's no signasti, she's—"

"Silence!" Aaron commanded.

Jessa broke off mid-sentence, but I wouldn't turn. I wouldn't give him that satisfaction.

"Selena."

He said my name like a *command*. As if the same power he possessed over the Shifters would somehow stop me as well. I kept walking.

"*Selena*," he repeated. Harder this time. My demon whimpered, wanting to go to him, but even she wouldn't fight me on this. I kept walking.

"Selena." Someone grabbed my arm, and with the tension in me coiled tight, it took all of my self-control not to jump and lash out. I tried to walk, but he held tight, somehow every bit as strong. I schooled my face in a neutral mask. "Don't walk away from me."

Don't walk away? That's what he had to say?

"You sound like Lucas," I replied. The grip on my arm tightened, but not to the point of hurting. Bruising. Where Lucas had no problem manhandling me in anger, it seemed that Aaron drew the line there.

"Why would you compare me to him?" he asked softly, his breath fanning my ear. The hurt in his voice made my own chest squeeze.

"Because he said the same thing and it didn't stop me then either."

His grip dropped from my arm and I started for the table again. My heart hammered out of control, like a train going too fast, I was worried I might derail.

"I will be different," Aaron called out. The Shifters in the room held their breath and they weren't the only ones. "I may not be the first to go after you, Selena Foster, but I vow here before my people that I will be the last."

Warmth ignited in my chest, but I wouldn't smile. I wouldn't let him off that easily...but I wouldn't leave it there either.

I paused at the table and glanced over my shoulder. He stood there by himself, beneath the chandelier. His eyes golden and hopeful.

"We'll see," I answered.

When I took my seat, Keyla was grinning like a fool and Amber waggled her eyebrows.

"Is it always that hot between you two?" Amber whispered across the table.

"Yes," Violet said smugly.

"Put a sock in it," I said back.

No one said anything about my lack of a response as dinner was served.

CHAPTER 21

WITH THE END OF THE WEEK CAME ANOTHER TEMPERATURE DROP as we rolled into late November. Wind swept across the residence like a vengeful spirit, howling well into the night. The panes of glass rattled viciously in their sockets, waiting for a gust to come along that was just strong enough to shatter them into oblivion.

Sometimes I felt like these windows, just waiting for something to happen. Someone to come along and destroy the progress I have made. Something that can send me right over the cliff where I teetered back and forth. The climb out may have been hell, but it was *staying* out that proved ever more difficult.

But every day I talked myself away from the ledge one more inch.

It was enough. For now.

Overlooking the lake, I found it easiest to let my thoughts wander and not focus too much on the rippling surface of the icy waters. Anything was better than that.

The sky. The wind. The whispering of leaves behind me and howls in the far off distance.

These things were my arsenal. They were the tools I used to build a tolerance, and after standing in the same spot for twenty-one minutes and thirteen seconds—the longest I had to date—the edges of my vision began to drift and curl inward.

I turned my back on the shore without any delay. While coming here was helping, it was best not to push it. Once the shadows appeared, voices were never far behind them, and Keyla didn't need to see that. No one did.

My feet carried me far and fast down the winding trail through the forest. When I focused, I could hear as far back as camp, but out here was as close to quiet as it ever got, until I ran into Keyla that was. Slowly but surely, she'd been making it farther down the trail as I built up a tolerance to the lake.

"Ah man! Why do you have to be so fast? Huh? You couldn't let me make it there once?" she griped as soon as I came into sight.

"Look at it this way, when you finally do make it to the lake, you'll know I didn't go easy on you," I said. She rolled her eyes and scoffed.

"Oh puh-lease, I just want to know how you're so fast. Supes are never as fast as Shifters, but I bet you could outrun Aaron without trying."

Because I'm not just a Supernatural, I wanted to say. But how do you tell a thirteen-year-old that you're a demon? You don't.

"Your brother is my signasti. It stands to reason that I

am above average," I said. My breath came slow and steady while my heart thundered in my chest.

"You never talk about him," Keyla started. "Not that he talks about you...but you guys are weird. Like, he clearly cares and you kind of do, but you're not like any of the other signasti couples I've met."

Did Keyla know she was astute? Did she realize she hit a nerve that I so carefully tried to hide from the rest of the world?

I glanced sideways at her flush cheeks and bright eyes. Sneaky as she liked to be, I don't think she really saw or understood how strange my relationship with Aaron was.

"Your brother and I...we had a rough start at things. I didn't know who he was, and he didn't tell me for a long time. It's complicated," I said carefully. There was a fine line to straddle in what I told Keyla. On one hand, she wasn't *that* much younger than me, but clearly more sheltered. On the other hand, Aaron and I were in a strange place right now. I still didn't know how I felt about the bond or whether I wanted to complete it, and something told me she wouldn't understand if I told her that.

"Yeah, but it's not like you're the first Shifter-Supe pairing. My parents started off worse than you and Aaron, and clearly they got over it or I wouldn't be here to grace you with my beautiful face," Keyla said. I snorted, elbowing her in the ribs.

"You sound like my sister," I groaned.

She really did. Some strange mix between Amber and Alexandra, with twice the confidence of either.

"I mean, we kind of are like sisters, aren't we? If you think about it, the signasti bond is deeper than marriage.

You guys are literally soul mates, and if you got married, I'd be your sister-in-law at the very least..." she trailed off, glancing sideways at me. "Why do you look like that?" she asked defensively.

"Like what?" I swallowed, my breathing coming out much heavier and it had nothing to do with our pace.

"Like you're going to run," she whispered, coming to a stop. I slowed down in front of her a few feet away.

"In case you hadn't noticed, we were running."

It was a poor attempt at a joke, and Keyla didn't seem to buy it. The younger girl stood steady with her arms folded over her chest. The fire in her gold eyes was nearly tangible and just as intense as the gaze her brother leveled me with.

"Are you planning on leaving? Because if you are, I need to know right—"

"I'm not leaving, Keyla. At least not anytime soon," I replied in a grave voice. She stared at me with her mouth half-open before recovering.

"Well then, what is it? Do you not want me as a sister? I mean, I get that I'm kinda loud and the other Shifters don't care for me very much, but you don't like them, so I didn't think it would matter—"

"It's not you, Keyla."

"Then what is it? Did something happen with Aaron? I'll kick his ass if it did—"

As much as I wanted to laugh at that, a stone had settled in me, weighing me down with the heavy burden of truth.

"Alexandra and I were...*are* triplets," I said, cutting her off. She paused, her jaw falling open as a slow realization crept up on her. "We had another sister. Her name"—I broke off at the choking sound that threatened to escape from me—"her name was...Lily."

The dam in my chest threatened to shatter, but the shadows hadn't arrived yet. I took that as a good sign and continued.

"She was very dear to me, but when the Vampires came...I couldn't protect her." I took a couple of deep breaths, trying to break apart the lump that formed in my throat. "You don't want to be my sister, Keyla. Bad things happen to those I care about."

Keyla approached me with slow, steady steps and wrapped her arms around me.

"I don't want to be protected. I just want you to stay," she said in what was probably the closest to a whisper this girl could ever get. "Stay here with me and Aaron. Please."

"I'm not planning on leaving."

"Good." She ended the hug abruptly and sprinted down the trail yelling, "Race you back!" I cocked an eyebrow at her rapidly disappearing back.

Seriously? And they thought *I* had mood swings?

I shook my head and took off after her, letting her get a good bit ahead before I ate up the distance right at the end. We crossed the tree line within six inches of each other, but instead of rubbing it in my face as I expected, she whirled around on me.

"You let me win!" she accused, jabbing a finger into my chest. A wry smirk painted itself on my lips while I stared at her.

"Let you win? Didn't I just tell you I was going to make you earn it?" I asked, stepping around her.

"Lies!" she declared. I cringed but resisted my urge to

cover my ears. "You're a liar. I'm calling it here and now. Liar, liar, pants on—"

"Where is everyone?" I asked, stopping short on the edge of the training field. I'm not sure how I hadn't noticed earlier, or maybe they'd left since then, but only a very small fraction were out practicing today—and that small fraction primarily consisted of my team.

"Off getting ready for the full moon party, of course," Keyla said.

"Full moon party?" I asked.

"You've never been to one?" Keyla asked, gripping my arm with a steadfast strength. Goddamnit. I knew exactly where this was going. I should have kept my mouth shut.

"I just don't get why you would have a full moon party when you don't need the moon to shift," I replied tersely, trying to avoid the question on her tongue.

"Ohmigawd, Lena—you have never been to a full moon party—we must correct this!" she declared, doing that thing where she started to speak very loudly and changing thought mid-sentence, letting her words run together.

"Oh no, I think I will be quite fine. Thanks for offering," I said, trying to weasel my way around her. She used the one hand she had locked around my arm to start dragging me across the field and used the other to put two fingers to her lips, letting out a shrill whistle.

Every Shifter and Supe stopped in their tracks looking to the young girl who may not have the power of an Alpha behind her, but damn did she have the personality.

"Brother! O' Brother! Where art thou?" she started yelling at the top of her lungs. I put my foot down, literally, stomping once and it planted six inches through the dirt.

My body went ramrod straight, refusing to yield while Keyla continued tugging on me.

"What the—"

"Come to train with us, Selena?" Aaron asked, strolling up. He was shirtless in the early afternoon sun and glistening with sweat.

"Uh—no. Thanks, but no thanks," I said, declining his offer for the third time this week. Keyla wheeled on me.

"Wait a second—you can fight?" she squeaked. I clapped my hands over my ears as both my demon and I winced in pain.

"She can do a lot more than just fight," Alexandra scoffed, coming up beside Aaron. The other Shifters in the yard perked their heads up toward us and I bristled instantly, sending glares at both of them.

"Keyla and I were just leaving," I said, sending a lethal look her way. Not that it perturbed her in the slightest.

"Oh, no we aren't. I want to see you in action," she pushed. It wasn't a whine, but I knew it would continue that way if this kept up.

"Too bad. I'm not in the mood," I snapped at her. She glared shrewdly at me.

"What? Are you too scared? Afraid my brother might kick your ass?" she goaded.

Oh child. If only she were doing it half as good as she hoped. My demon thought her just as amusing, more like a hissing kitten than a grown lioness.

I tossed my head back and let out a quick caustic laugh.

"Keyla, I don't think you realize the number of times I've kicked your brother's ass," I said and chuckled to myself. Behind her, Aaron's eyes flashed gold, a not so subtle reminder to me that there was more to him than what I always saw.

"Then prove it," Kayla argued. "I'll even make you a deal," she continued. Her eyes took on that bronze fire they did when she got excited.

"Oh, will you now?" I asked, smirking at her.

"If you fight him and win, I won't make you go to the full moon party." Her face lit up like a thousand-watt bulb. She was weighing my dislike of people against what she thought was a slight pacifistic tendency. *If only that were true.*

"I'm not seeing how there's a win in this for me. Either way, you get me to fight when I can just decline to do either." I shrugged at her, stepping out of the hole I'd created. They all must have only just noticed it because their eyes flicked down simultaneously to where my foot had been as I walked away.

"Lena!" she wailed. Not crying, but so fucking loud she knew I would stop.

"Don't even go there. I don't appreciate you trying to manipulate me." She lowered her eyes, taking all of one second to at least look ashamed.

"You're right. I'm sorry," she said. "Will you go to the full moon party with me? We don't have to stay forever, I just don't want to go alone."

Her golden eyes pleaded with me and my demon tugged at my heart strings. She wanted to go with the girl and was more than curious about the party. This was all so new to us together.

"Fine. But I get to leave when I want to leave and no whining about it," I said.

"Deal."

She flashed me a Cheshire smile and winked, sauntering past me towards the residence.

Why did it feel like I'd just been played?

"Because you were," Violet snorted. I rolled my eyes and continued on, pretending to be completely unaffected by the Shifter Heir I knew was watching me.

CHAPTER 22

The chill of twilight swept over me. With the skies painted a dark indigo and the last speck of sunlight disappearing on the horizon, the wind went from cold to downright frigid. I tugged my leather jacket closer, digging my hands into the faux-fur lined pockets.

"Hurry up, Lena. We're almost there," Keyla yelled. She grabbed my hand to pull me past the tree line where a bonfire raged. The glowing red-gold embers drew my attention immediately. "I'm going to find drinks. I'll be right back!" Keyla called, quite literally abandoning me to the wolves while she disappeared into the crowd.

I took a few mesmerized steps towards the fire. My demon was completely enthralled. The flames danced and swayed in the unforgiving winds. Fluid but graceful. Beautiful in the most lethal of ways. If a single ember traveled too far, too fast, the entire forest would be set ablaze. Of course, that wasn't possible with Alexandra here.

My sister sat on the log closest to the fire. In one hand, she clutched a Styrofoam cup filled with a steaming liquid.

Her other moved effortlessly as she twisted and twirled her fingers. The fire followed her command, forming flaming women. Dancers that sashayed and twirled, one even leapt from the fire onto her palm.

The display wasn't for me, and it wasn't for the other Shifters. It was for the girl sitting beside her. Tori's golden hair was longer than I'd ever seen it, blowing behind her in wild strands. A bright smile lit her face as she looked at my sister and the truth of it hit me.

Does Alexandra return her affections? Does she see the way Tori looks at her?

It wasn't my business, but I found myself wondering.

"They're quite the pair, aren't they?"

I jumped at the sudden sound of Blair's voice beside me. Her pale skin was tinged pink from where the wind whipped against it, but not a single strand of her braid was out of place.

"Yes, they are."

"Amber and I have a running bet on who will realize it first," she mused. I chuckled under my breath.

"Alexandra will, but she won't act first."

From this angle, I couldn't see my sister's face clearly, but I knew her well enough to guess that she already knew. You didn't live with sisters for eighteen years and not learn to read body language. You didn't date a boy who couldn't love you, never having him look at you the way you longed for, and then be blind to the way that Tori looked at her every day. Yeah, she knew.

"What makes you say that?" Blair asked.

"She's more perceptive than anyone gives her credit for, but she also worries too much about what people think.

Tori doesn't give a damn. Men. Women. She loves who she loves," I said, running a hand through my windblown hair.

"You sound like you envy them," Blair replied.

If it were anyone else, I think that statement would have sounded judgmental. I had a signasti, after all, and if you listened to Keyla, you would think that's some kind of fabled love that could overcome anything. Blair said it with the same tone that she used to talk about the weather.

"I don't envy them for love. All I ever wanted was for Alexandra to find happiness..." I trailed off, wondering if I should really put words to the truth that bothered me more than I let anyone know. "I envy their ability to choose."

My cousin didn't act surprised in the slightest. She only nodded and looked to the sky. Like it held answers that neither she nor I could see.

"I used to feel the same," she started. "In the beginning. I thought I would never get him out of my mind. That I would always remember our time together and think that because he was bound to my soul, that meant he owned my heart too. But that wasn't the case. It took me seeing him again to realize it."

I frowned, playing that over in my mind a second time, and then a third. Was she saying what I think she was saying...

"You have a signasti?" I asked. It was hardly more than a whisper.

"I do," she nodded. Her eyes were lost. Wistful. "We met when I was a freshman at Daizlei, and he was a senior. I didn't know who he was, only that I was drawn to him in a way I wasn't with anyone before and haven't been with anyone since. At the time, I thought it was normal. I was barely fifteen, after all." She paused, smiling to herself at a memory, but that smile fell and I knew without asking that her love at first sight went sour.

"What happened?" I asked softly. She laughed, and it was a cold, emotionless sound that didn't belong on her lips.

"What always happens. Anastasia."

My mouth fell open as a terrifying realization swept over me.

"*Alec* is your signasti?" I asked, being careful not to utter it any louder than a whisper. The wind and fire may rage, but that same wind could sweep my words to unwanted ears.

"He is."

"How do you know? How is that even—"

"Possible?" she asked, a small smile coming back to her lips. "When Anastasia came, I already thought I was in love, and he certainly acted like it. Everything was perfect. We were perfect. But he's the first born of his family and she had come to collect." My heart stuttered in my chest as I replayed every interaction between the two of them that I had ever seen.

She hated him from the moment I met him. Despised him. Hell, I told her I would take him out if I had to, but she had declined.

"In the Supernatural world, when a firstborn child turns eighteen the ruling families have a claiming of sorts. In return for the protection and schooling that they provide for all families, they take the first child during their last year of school and *enlist* them."

She said the last word with a scathing harshness that left little question.

"They're slaves. Paid slaves, but slaves. They have no choice. Alec is powerful, and the Fortescues took an interest in him well before his birthday. He knew she was going to take him, and he was okay with it. If he went, then it meant Lucas and Tori could have a future they chose. He hadn't planned on meeting me," she said, her last words filled with so much regret. So much hurt and pain. It was only the sound of her voice that told me how much this memory hurt.

"But he did, and when she came for him there was no hiding it. Even to this day, I don't understand what possessed her to give the order she did, but after what happened at Daizlei, I can only assume she's insane. No person in their right mind would have told him to do what he did next."

She didn't laugh and she didn't smile. The wind whipped at us and Keyla was still nowhere to be seen, but Blair and I existed within a moment that I would remember for the rest of my life. No matter how long or short that may be.

"What did he do to you?" I whispered, fearing the truth that had already settled in the back of my mind.

"I knew something was wrong the night it happened. I could *feel* it inside of him. His terror. His revulsion. At the time, I didn't know half the things I do now, but that night I knew something was wrong when he led me out into the woods." Her eyes fluttered closed, and when they opened they were glacial.

"He raped me," she whispered. "Or at least he wanted me to *think* he did."

My breath caught in my throat, so swift and sudden that I almost didn't notice the clench of my hands and the sudden shift of the winds. They swooped and curved every which way around us, howling in my ears but keeping this conversation between us.

"At the time, I couldn't understand or think through the terror when I saw him split in two. One second he had been kissing me, and the next he stood over me and started pleading for the ancients to strike him dead." A strange calm settled over her as she turned and looked to the fire. "An illusion with his face pushed me down, made me think he was undressing me. My clothes never left my body, but at the time I was overwhelmed. I saw what he wanted me to see, but it was watered down, per se. Only in the coming weeks did I start to put together what I really saw. The books on Supernatural and signasti bonds are quite limited at Daizlei. During a trip to the black market, I did some inquiring on my own into how his powers didn't work on me. Why. There was only one explanation."

I wanted to murder him. I didn't care that he hadn't really done it, or who made him. If anything, it fueled the anger more. He deserved to pay for this.

"Selena," Blair said lightly, wrapping ice-cold fingers around my wrist. "Don't. I've made peace with myself, and I didn't tell you this so you would rip his throat out. I told you this so that you understand being Aaron's signasti doesn't make you love him."

I stopped and let the tension drain out of me. My muscles uncoiled under her touch, but the rage didn't fade.

Rage towards Alec for what he'd done. Rage towards Anastasia for the lives she'd ruined. Rage towards the world for being so dark and cruel.

"How do you do it?" I asked her. "How can you stand to sleep under the same roof as him? Train with him? Hell, you saved him in the simulator when the bomb went off. How do you do it?" I turned to look her in the face and she watched me with slate grey eyes. Her fingers dropped to hold both my hands between hers.

"I forgave him." She smiled when I cocked my head, my lips parting. "Forgiveness isn't for the person who hurts you, Selena. It's for yourself. Without it, I would have become bitter and succumbed to the bond madness long ago."

It seemed that Blair had more lessons to teach me than I realized. Of course, I always knew she had a strong mind and will. She never would have survived training with me if she hadn't. Now the tables were turned.

"Does he know? That you know he's your signasti? If you guys never completed the bond—"

"No. As far as he knew, I was a Supernatural, and most Supernaturals don't realize who their signasti is until they complete the bond—which we never did. Signastis can't use their powers to harm each other once the bond begins to form. That's how I figured it out after he was gone."

I recalled the number of times I'd hurt Aaron in my year at Daizlei. The glass that I threw him through during our time in the simulator. Yet, only a few months ago, I couldn't even push him aside. I had to move a couch to get him out of my way.

He'd told me then that it was because of our bond. I'd never thought much on it until this moment.

"And now?" I asked. "How are you defeating the bond madness now if clearly the bond had started to form?" She gave me a look like she knew what I was getting at.

Did you find a way to break it?

It was the question on my lips, but for some reason, I couldn't bring myself to ask it.

"There's no way to break the bond." Her eyes flashed with what looked like a warning. "But when neither person wants the bond, and enough distance is put between them, it goes into a stasis of sorts. We still experience the madness, but it creeps in much slower. It's like...freezing it. Eventually it will get to us, but it hasn't yet, and it probably won't for years to come."

I released her hands and pinched the bridge of my nose as my eyes fell shut. I turned, pacing in place for a minute, and then two, before I finally said what I was thinking.

"If all it takes is neither of us wanting it, why hasn't mine stopped?" I asked her. She swallowed and gave me a level look.

"You already know why." She flicked her gaze past the bonfire to where Aaron stood messing around with Keyla fifty yards away. It looked like she was mouthing off—shocker—and he picked her up, slinging her over his massive shoulder. She screamed and squawked like a bird, wiggling in his grip.

"He can't possibly want to be bonded to me," I whispered.

"If you think that then you're a fool," she replied sharply. I whipped my face around to glare at her. "You think I don't see how you look at each other? How you tense up whenever Jessa goes near him? You wear a good mask, Selena, but I know your tells. He's not the only one that wants this bond, and you're lying to both of us if you tell me otherwise."

She lifted both her eyebrows, waiting for me to say something. To refute it.

"How do I know that anything I feel isn't just the damn bond? You said yourself, you thought you were in love before and I don't think I'm in love, but I don't know what I am. He knows just how to get under my skin, but then calms me when no one else can." I threw my hands up and the winds followed. Blair smirked, looking around us as cups flew towards the trees and the fire shot up twenty feet in the air. I took a deep breath, releasing the wind and dropping my hands to my sides while I was at it.

"I can't tell you what you are or aren't feeling. That's not my place. What I can say, is that whatever feeling you have is entirely your own. The bond makes it easy to love them, and almost impossible to leave. I thought I was going to have to rip my heart out when I rejected Alec, but I'm alive and smiling to this day." She quirked up her lips looking at something over my shoulder. A familiar tug in my chest told me *exactly* who was coming our way.

Blair reached across and squeezed my shoulder before disappearing into the crowd.

CHAPTER 23

"WHAT WERE YOU AND BLAIR TALKING ABOUT THAT HAD YOU SO UP in arms?" a rough voice asked behind me. I turned to see Aaron still holding Keyla over his shoulder.

"Nothing important," I said smoothly.

"Put me down, Aaron! You—you imbecile! Ha! Yeah, I said it—whatcha going to do—agh!" she screamed as he flung her in the air fifteen feet or so, then caught her with ease. "I should murder you," she hissed as he set her back on the ground with a gentleness I rarely saw in him.

"I don't think you want that. Who's going to convince them to let you be the stag if I'm dead?" Keyla's eyes lit up like twin yellow moons and she threw her arms around him.

"The stag?" I asked.

"For the wild hunt," Keyla answered. "The stag goes to hide in the forest and then the Shifters are let loose. The first one to find the stag wins."

The blood drained from my face as I looked between the

two of them. Kayla beamed up at me with an innocent smile and shadows began to creep into my vision.

Goddamnit. Not now.

"Are you okay?" Keyla asked, moving to hug me. Aaron reached forward and snatched her fingers away just before she touched me.

Good. At least he had some sense.

"What are you thinking sending her into the forest right now?" I snapped at him. "After what happened at Daizlei, how could you possibly think it's safe?" My voice rose to an almost hysteria. Aaron pushed Keyla to the side and stepped towards me. Into the very space he stopped his sister from crossing.

"It is safe. For nearly fifty miles in every direction, this is Shifter territory. Keyla knows the rules and she won't stray beyond that," he said softly. I didn't realize when his fingers wrapped around my upper arms, lightly massaging circles into them.

"I don't care. It's not safe for her," I growled. That seemed to perk up some ears. Several bodies moved closer to us, but I had no idea who.

"Who are you to speak to *our* future Alpha that way?" a sharp voice scolded. I froze beneath Aaron's fingertips, the shadows once again pushing their way to forefront.

No. Not here. The last thing I needed was to take ten steps back by killing a Shifter on their territory.

That would send me right over the ledge.

I took a deep breath, and then another.

"She is *my* signasti, Jessa, and *you* would do well to remember it," Aaron snapped at her. If only she had the good sense to stay quiet.

"I'm having a hard time believing that with the way she cowers. No true signasti of an Alpha would hide behind her partner," Jessa argued.

I wanted to cover my ears. To stop the talking. This was exactly why I didn't raise my fist today. Why I wouldn't train. The urge to hurt something was rearing its ugly head the longer that went by. How could I possibly chance it after everything I'd done? The people I'd killed...

How could I justify that?

The answer was simple.

I couldn't.

I wouldn't.

"What? No answer? Color me shocked," she continued. "You call her your signasti, but all we see is a broken piece of Supernatural trash—"

Fire drowned out her reply as it broke out across the clearing, swift and sudden. I shoved Aaron aside as I turned on my heel to face the direction where Jessa had been and to where Alexandra now stood. She scalded the earth with vengeful steps as she approached the now silent blonde.

"You do not speak to her like that," Alexandra said. The voice that spoke was not my sister. It was her demon.

Fucking hell.

Without thinking, I crossed the stretch of burning grass. Faster than lightening. Silent as the dead. I stepped between the demon that was my sister and the girl that did not deserve my protection. The eyes that stared back at me were not warm brown, but an endless darkness that sucked in all light that dared shine on them.

I should have been terrified, but the creature before me was no different than myself.

And if there's anything I knew, it's how to control the entity within.

"I want Alexandra back. Right now," I barked. My voice was every bit as cold and callous. The creature cocked her head slowly and fire pressed in around us.

"The Shhhifter overstepped herssself," the demon hissed out of my sister's mouth. The flames surged against my skin, burning at my clothes.

She was testing me. Seeing how far I was willing to go, but the demon should already know that answer.

For my sisters, I would do *anything*.

"She's ignorant and jealous. That doesn't justify death," I replied just as cold, letting my own demon surface entirely. I used my own power to thicken the air and take control of the flames.

That got her attention.

She took a step back, but I advanced on her.

Alexandra may be powerful, but she and her demon both knew I could put her in her place. She knew what I could do if push came to shove, and even her demon, who came to my defense, did not want to test that. I curled my fingers and sucked the flames inward, towards us and away from the Shifters that lurked on the sidelines.

Watching a battle between two sisters.

Two demons.

"Alexandra. Now. I will not ask again," I commanded in a snarl, redirecting the flames at her with a snap. They poured down like sky fire, relentless in their assault.

The demon stared through the flames and gave a slight bow of its head.

Alexandra dropped to her knees in the dirt, and I extinguished the fire immediately, leaving only the bonfire burning like nothing had ever happened.

"I'm sorry," Alexandra whispered hoarsely. She still hadn't opened her eyes, but the voice of the girl before me wasn't lifeless or cold.

"I know." I went to her, crouching down on my knees over the charred earth.

I reached inside myself to call my own demon back, and for the first time, she went without question.

We were equal now, in every way, but my sister and her other self were not.

"I didn't mean for that to happen, I just got so *angry* when I heard her talking to you like that. She has no idea what we've been through, what you have..." Alexandra said roughly. I slipped two fingers under her chin and lifted her face.

"Listen to me," I said. "You have another being inside of you. One that is going to get angry sometimes. It's going to want to scratch and claw, even kill, but that doesn't make you a bad person. It's what you do with that power that matters. Do you understand me?" My voice was strong, softened from the icy tone I used to command the dark entity down. This was the role I'd played for her enough of my life that I knew it like the back of my hand. Hard enough to give her reassurance, pliant enough that I wasn't overbearing.

Alexandra drew her eyes up from the ground slowly, and only when she searched over every visible part of my skin that the fire had burned clothes from did she nod.

I sighed deeply, exhausted to the bone, and lifted my head to the crowd.

"Where's Tori?" I asked. The ground shifted as someone slowly came toward us. I didn't have to look to know it was the girl in question.

"Here," she said behind me.

"Do you feel comfortable enough to take her back to the residence and stay with her tonight?"

Under normal circumstances, I wouldn't have been so blunt with her, but I had two reasons. The first is that I already knew what she would say, and she was probably one of only three people that would. The second is that I wanted my sister to see it and hear it, because the second someone called her a monster it was all over.

She needed to believe that she wasn't a bad person, and that started with Tori's response.

"Of course," she said without hesitation. I released a breath and stood to my full height, pulling my red-headed sister up with me. All I had to do was step to the side and Tori filled the void where I had been. She wrapped her arms around Alexandra, and in the blink of an eye, they were gone.

I turned to the crowd gathered around the ashen circle and raised my chin defiantly. They all needed to hear this, but one person in particular. I crossed the ten yards at the same speed Tori used to teleport out. Appearing directly in front of a very tall blond who's normally lovely skin looked rather pale at the sight of me standing before her.

"Let me make myself very clear," I said, using small threads of power to project my voice over the hundreds of Shifters gathered. "I saved your life tonight. I could have just as easily let her *burn* you alive—and she would have—because unlike me, you are not fireproof." She stumbled back, and the group parted. No one caught her, and no one stopped me as I took another step.

"So this is what's going to happen. You are going to repay me in the only way I deem acceptable: by keeping your mouth shut. You will not continue to challenge me. You will not test my patience again, and you damn sure will not say a single fucking word to her."

She stumbled back again, tripping over a tree root in her haste. She landed on her ass, looking up at me with large blue eyes. I parted my lips and breathed in the scent of her fear, but I wouldn't revel in it. That was where I drew the line.

"Do I make myself crystal clear? Because I will not give you a second warning. Next time you try something, I am going to challenge you to a duel, and I will make burning alive look like child's play. By the time I walk out of the ring you will wish I killed you. You will beg me for death. Do you understand?" My voice was not my demon's, nor was it the one I talked Alexandra down with. It was my voice, filled with resolute determination and anger. It spoke of the darkness inside me. It was all that I was, am, and ever will be.

It was the voice of the leader and the assassin.

Three beings, drawn together in the most unholy of ways, but somehow completed each other.

"Y-yes," she stuttered, nodding her head so hard her teeth chattered.

"Excellent." I turned my back on her and started towards Aaron and Keyla, but paused halfway. "If it happens again, I will come between her and the rest of you, but the moment one of you calls her a monster, that deal is over. It may be a dog eat dog world, but fire burns everything. Take that as you will."

My heart hammered as I crossed the remaining space towards Aaron and Keyla. I half expected her to be hiding behind him after that, but she stood tall and faced me with the biggest smile I had ever seen on her face.

"Alright guys, listen up!" Aaron shouted, waving his hands to call people in. "Given all the excitement, I'm postponing the hunt until the next full moon."

Several Shifters gave an audible groan, namely Keyla who went from looking at me with something akin to hero worship—to glaring daggers.

"Don't worry, little sis. You'll still get to be the stag." He mussed his hand in her hair, and she swatted at him with annoyance. "And," he drawled, "you'll get an extra month to run with Selena and have a better shot of outrunning her."

She perked up at that idea and sent me a wicked smile. Ordinarily, I would have snapped at Aaron for volunteering me to participate, but it was a good idea. I could catch her faster than anyone and drag her back here. She won't have the chance to get further than twenty miles.

Problem solved.

"I think I can safely call this a night," I said, motioning to the tattered remains of my leather jacket and almost entirely bare legs. My toes squished into the ash and dirt as a frigid breeze swept the dead land, making me shiver. I started towards the residence without waiting for a reply.

"Can I join you?" Aaron asked. My feet halted mid-step, my heart thumping a little harder. Blair's conversation by the fire came back to me and I didn't let myself think too long or hard before I blurted out my response.

"I would like that."

I almost missed the stutter in his own chest when Keyla shouted, "I'm coming too!"

Almost, but not quite. Neither of us were as unaffected as we liked to pretend.

And in the midnight hour where no one could see, I smiled to myself.

CHAPTER 24

I KNOCKED LIGHTLY ON THE STAINED POPLAR DOOR. THE SCENT OF cedar and peppermint drifted through the space underneath. Footsteps crossed the space coming to a stop directly on the other side. Metal scraped metal as someone turned the lock.

The door cracked open.

A single evergreen eye peered through the sliver. Tori breathed a heavy sigh and swung the door open for me. I crossed into the small living room where Blair sat in an overstuffed armchair with her ankles crossed. Her grey eyes were like fractured ice on a dark road. She stared at Alexandra's reclined figure, her expression unreadable, but her posture was that of someone watching their ward.

She's guarding her, I realized. Not from me, but everyone else. Anyone who might think to come to this door and trigger the only other known demon in their midst.

The Shifters had no idea what we really were before. Aaron had explained that last night, the vague details they'd given to those at the residence months ago when we arrived.

Refugees, he'd called us. Survivors, from what happened at Daizlei and from the earthquake that killed thousands. *The earthquake I caused...*

Yeah. No way in hell was anyone going to buy the sad Supernatural story now, but that wasn't my problem.

"How is she doing?" I whispered under my breath. Tori grimaced, locking the door behind us.

"Y'all are remarkably similar when you get like this," she murmured. Blair said nothing, and maybe that was the most telling of all.

Last night I'd been thrown off guard when Alexandra's demon came out swinging in my defense. I had assumed they'd made peace and that my sister had control over hers, given that she never struggled the same way I had.

Apparently, I was wrong.

Once again, I was the early bird and now the only one left that could train her.

"Alexandra." I approached her on the cream-colored couch. Her brilliant red hair spilled across a fluffy beige pillow as she laid almost catatonic, watching the flames in the fireplace.

I dropped to my knees in front of her. "I want to talk to you about last night," I continued lightly. She didn't even twitch. "About your demon." A heavy pause punctuated the air as her eyes slowly slid from the fire blazing behind me, to my face.

Her normally warm brown eyes were a shade darker than normal, turning them a flickering amber filled with shadows and fire.

"My demon," she said dryly. It wasn't a question, but I responded nonetheless.

"Yes."

"I knew I had one, in theory..." she trailed off momentarily as her eyes shifted back to the fire. "But I've never felt it like that."

I leaned back, resting on the heels of my feet. Four heartbeats and a crackling fire filled the room with an intimate silence. "Felt it like what?"

"Vengeance," she whispered. "And rage. So much rage. It was like..." she paused, her eyes flicking to the corner of her vision. "Like I could have sent it all up in flames. Just to burn her down with it."

I nodded sadly. I felt empathy, because for the first time I think she truly understood me, and I wish she didn't.

I wish that this terrible gene that made me what I am had skipped her entirely. That I could bear that burden of loneliness and isolation on my own—for the rest of my life —if it spared her.

But that wasn't the world we lived in, and thinking on the should have, could have, would have...it made no difference. All we could do was move forward with the here and now, where my sister was every bit of demon as I, and possibly Blair too.

"For me, the rage was the hardest to handle. I was angry about anything. Everything..." I took a deep breath, wanting to say more, but finding honesty and vulnerability to be the most difficult admission. "It gets better—more manageable—when you learn to accept it," I eventually said.

Her gaze narrowed by a hairsbreadth. So little that I

wouldn't have noticed if I hadn't been watching for it. Her jaw clenched with a subtle tension that could have been written off as any number of things, were we talking about anything else.

"Accept it?" she asked, a challenge masked as an innocent question. "*That's* what you did? You-you *accepted* this monster? This *thing*—"

"Yes, you accept it, and before you go calling your demon a thing, understand the only person you're going to hurt is yourself. I've made peace with mine and I'm better for it."

Alexandra shifted from laying down to standing in the blink of an eye, her demon riding her hard. Her eyes darted around for a second before settling on me.

"You really have lost it if you think I'm going to give that thing any kind of power over me and what I do. It would burn the world down!" She paused as hysteria began creeping in. "Don't you get that? Don't you see? Like, you may be fireproof, but they're not!"

She glanced at Tori, an anguished sorrow permeating her features. She clenched her fists at her side and the fire died down. Behind her, Blair watched the scene play out between the two of us. Her cool features revealed nothing.

"That's why you need to train with it. If you think that burning the clearing is the worst thing you can do, then you're mistaken. Hellfire was able to confine me. If you could control it at will—"

"I don't want to train with it!" she snapped. "I want nothing to do with it."

I felt the fireplace explode outwards. Heat lapped at the rug beneath me, traveling to my heels like the hounds of hell. Alexandra's control wavered back and forth, her eyes flickering from amber to onyx as they darted towards the corners of her vision.

Blair chose that moment to act, twisting her hand sharply to let out a geyser of snow that settled over the burning fire. Within seconds, the only thing left was a puddle of water that slowly seeped its way into my jeans. I rocked forward then back, using my momentum to push myself upward in a standing position.

"You don't have to want it. You don't even have to like it—but you need to do it unless you want to end up exactly like I was three months ago," I said. Her chest rose and fell as she tried to slow her racing heart. Despite her best efforts, it continued erratically thumping, out of control.

"You don't know that. There's no way of knowing if I'll be like you. Like, maybe I can—"

"Do you see shadows in the corners of your eyes?" I asked briskly. Harsh, but to the point.

Alexandra didn't answer, but then again, I didn't need her to. The signs were there.

"What about the whispers? Have those started yet?" I continued. Alexandra swallowed hard and her eyes bled brown. The last remnants of her other gone, for the moment.

"Last night was the first time I heard them," she whispered. Tori came around the back of the couch and wrapped her arms around my sister's waist. The top of her head only came to Alexandra's jaw.

"You're lucky then. I've heard them for years, and if I can get better, that means you can too." I glanced over to

207

Blair who sat as still as an ice sculpture. "Have you shown any signs?"

"No," she said and shook her head. Her features appeared absolutely glacial in the absence of light. Only two muted rays of sunlight broke through the opaque curtains on both sides of the fireplace.

"Then you both need to train with the assumption that you are, until proven otherwise." Blair nodded once in acknowledgement.

"What if I hurt someone?" Alexandra asked. She stood on shaky legs, but Tori's arms kept her grounded and standing.

"You won't. You'll be working with Blair and I'll stand on the sidelines to make sure the fire never gets out of control," I replied. An uncomfortable twisting settled in my stomach, knowing where this was going to go.

"That's bullshit," Alexandra quipped back. "You slept for months and came back different. You haven't practiced with any of us even once, and now you expect me to do as you say? What the hell, Selena? That's complete bullshit."

She released Tori to cross her arms over her chest, giving me *the look*. The fearless stare that she reserved for moments when she wasn't backing down, and there would be no reasoning with her.

"I understand you're upset—"

"No. Don't pull that with me." Alexandra shook her head in disbelief. "Don't you *dare* pull that with me. Not if you expect me to believe anything you say." She stalked across the charred mush remains of the rug, coming to a stop directly in front of me. "You said you're different. That you've changed, and you don't want to live in lies anymore.

Prove it. Tell me why you won't train with us. Give me one good reason why I should do what you're saying, and not expect the same in return."

I grimaced but gave her the truth. "When I lift my hands, people die. When I get upset, people die. When I use my ability, people die. It's only since I woke up that I'm even able to hold it together. How can I gamble with everyone's lives on the chance that I've healed enough to not kill anyone?" I lifted my hands, as if to examine them. These cold, killer hands meant for ruthless acts. Strange how they weren't particularly large or rough. They really looked quite ordinary.

Until I splayed my fingers and turned them over. Those scars never lied. The twin pentagrams that adorned my palms, put there by demons. Much like her and I.

Alexandra reached out a sun-kissed hand and closed her fingers over my own.

"Because you're not alone." She wrapped her other arm around my shoulders, pulling me close. "Fire can kill just as many as an earthquake. Nyx knows what hellfire really does. It could be worse. You may be a matter manipulator, but if we're both demons, then we work together. As equals."

"Equals?" I repeated.

Huh. After over eighteen years and only eight minutes apart, it dawned on me that we really were equals in everything now. She no longer needed my protection, but truth be told, she hasn't needed that for years. She didn't need a guardian. She didn't need a parent.

She needed a sister and an equal. Nothing more, nothing less.

"Equals," Blair affirmed, coming to stand beside us. I couldn't dispute Alexandra any more than I did Blair, my cousin turned apprentice.

Maybe I should learn to treat them all like equals, even Tori—the sister of my sister's killer. The roommate turned friend, once upon a time. The young woman that stands beside my sister with her head held high.

I sighed deeply, knowing they were right despite how at odds I was with myself.

"If I train with you, do you promise to work on it with your demon?" I asked Alexandra. She didn't look any happier about it now than she did when I first brought it up, but the steel in her spine was resolute. I wouldn't be the only one making compromises today.

"Yeah, but only if you help me. I don't want to accidentally burn the residence down." She flipped her mass of red hair over a slim shoulder. "Also, I don't think Aaron would be very happy with us if I did. I mean, he'd deal, but let's not."

She diffused the tension with a wink, but I couldn't help wondering how long it would last. How long would we get to be like this? Together, not quite happy, but alive. If there's anything Lily's death taught me, it's that the only thing that is guaranteed in life is change.

And every one of our lives could change in the blink of an eye.

Or just one training session gone wrong.

CHAPTER 25

I ONCE READ THAT SOONER OR LATER, EVERYONE SITS DOWN TO A banquet of consequences.

I couldn't help but wonder if this was mine.

I was a failure. First as a daughter. Then as a sister. As a Supernatural. Now as a Vampire.

I had been Made for the sole purpose of serving a master I'd never met. I was supposed to be stronger and faster than the other Vampires. I should have retained my ability and become unstoppable.

But instead, I had failed in that too.

And after three months of playing the game, it was getting clear that Victor's patience was tiring. His beautifully high hopes crashed and burned because instead of getting stronger, I was weaker with every day that passed, and blood wasn't helping me.

So here I was, locked inside a dusty, old room and starving. No one had come in over three days. No beautiful children dressed like dolls. No leering guards that made no mistake about what they wanted from me.

And no Victor.

I once regarded him as the most beautiful creature I'd ever seen, despite his cruelty. I'd hoped that his lovely smile meant he liked me, favored me enough that I could earn a single sliver of freedom. That he would find my submissive nature so endearing that he would let down his guard.

I see now that I was a fool.

Victor didn't have time for Made that couldn't do as they were told, and certainly not weak, pathetic creatures like me.

I tossed back my head and let out a terrible laugh, pushing the disgusting blankets away from me. The scents of mold and mildew caked my body like dried mud. My throat burned from a fire that only blood could sate, however brief that relief may be.

A sharp knock pierced my ears before the heavy door opened.

"Hello, flower," the guard said, his red eyes harsh and cruel.

I chose not to reply and instead averted my eyes to the bag of crimson liquid in his hand. Hoping he would mistake my clawing hunger for submission. They were big on that around here. Downcast eyes. Closed lips. Heads tilted forward just enough that it was almost a bow.

This guard was no different. He closed the door behind him and stalked towards me like the predator he was. It didn't even occur to me that I should be afraid.

No one closed the door except Victor, but he wasn't here anymore.

"Your master wants you fed. Thinks it might make his pretty little Made more compliant," the guard continued. His black boots stopped directly in front of me. Close enough that if I knew how to feel fear and I had a beating heart, it would have pounded in my chest.

But I couldn't feel anything beyond the thirst that enslaved my body and mind.

I lifted my chin just a fraction, my eyes traveling back to the blood bag in his hand.

Dinner. The first I'd have in three days.

"Please," I croaked. The hoarse whisper scraped against my dry throat like sandpaper.

"Please what?" the guard coerced. I lifted my head so he could see my pleading eyes, hoping it would spare me from using more words. "Oh, this?" he asked mockingly. I nodded my head despite the demeaning nature of his words.

My lips parted in anticipation as I waited for him to place the bag just close enough to my face that I could bite into it. He did.

The sharp points of my fangs punctured the plastic and a sweet aroma filled the air. I was too far gone to feel guilt for where the blood came from or disgust with myself for drinking it. Not when the cracks in my throat instantly mended.

The guard didn't shy away as I drank greedily, too starved to even register the way his tongue darted out to wet his bottom lip. I was only halfway through the bag when he ripped it from my mouth.

"That's enough," he snapped, tilting back his head to drink the rest. Dribbles of blood spilled over his lips as he smiled maliciously. I glared up at him, hating him, hating myself and this new body with its foreign urges. I didn't understand my anger. It was not logical and defied everything I knew.

Then again, so had my depression. And so had the darkness. Was this really so different?

A rough snarl escaped my lips, making the guard narrow his

eyes. My mind told me I should be afraid, that I saw the way this guard looked at me...but my body said different.

A cold hunger had me in its grasp and I lunged for his throat.

The guard reacted faster, striking me down with a backhand to the face for my insolence. I spat at him, making his already red eyes turn hot as flame. It reminded me of someone. My sister. Alexandra. I held onto that thought of her when his hand came down on me again.

The flesh didn't not sting as much this time, but the crack was still jarring. I'd never been hit like that in my life. The thought sent my anger spiraling. Reaching. The darkness in me opened and for the first time in months, I felt alive.

The feeling was short lived when he turned away. I grit my teeth but couldn't stop myself from calling out, "Is that the best you've got?"

The guard stopped, but his chest didn't heave at the insult. He didn't have a beating heart or need lungs to breathe. When he turned back towards me, his eyes narrowed as another cruel smile skirted his lips.

"You want more?" he asked, his voice oozing with vulgar satisfaction. It should have disgusted me, but it didn't. I stared back at him as he stalked towards me. The air in my room was stale, but the hardness of his hand when he struck me again made it seem fresh. Crisp.

I drifted for a moment. Almost content.

Until he began unzipping his pants.

"What are you doing?" I croaked, averting my eyes when he removed them entirely. I wasn't playing submissive this time. I'd never seen a man naked, and I didn't want to. Not here. Not like this.

"You asked for more. I want a taste of you, flower."

The words chilled me, and I tried to pull away when he crawled onto the bed.

No. No. No. This can't be happening.

I kicked at him, attempting to mimic the way my sister would use her legs to crush a man's skull, but he was stronger, and my body was not what it once was. I bucked off the bed, punching him in the face. He swiped my arms out of the air and pinned me down with one hand.

The darkness in my chest rose up—like bile in my throat.

"Don't touch me!" I commanded in a hoarse, broken cry. You would think that it wouldn't have taken three months for me to find my voice. My fight. But it did, and it seems that it happened too late.

I screamed again, a guttural sound more akin to that of a wild animal.

The images of my death flashed back to me. The moment when I was overpowered. The second I died. They could not save me then, why did I think they would now?

My panic heightened to an unbearable crescendo as he reached to rip my shirt open. I moved to avoid it and he laughed harshly, making my insides begin to burn and harden, like tempered metal forged into a weapon. In my rage and desperation, something cracked inside of me, lashing out.

Dark shadows appeared over my skin. Swirling. Writhing. They latched onto his moving hands and began traveling up his arms—not even making it to his elbows before the screaming started.

With every second he hollered, I grew stronger, drawing in more to feed my darkness. To feed myself. I twisted sharply without breaking contact and grabbed the dying man by his hair. His screams had already begun to fade into the silence. He wasn't long for this world.

I pulled myself up to a sitting position and held his head between both hands. The shadows still danced across my skin. I wondered what it would be like to crush his skull, here and now. Would he die from it? Would he even feel it? The splash of black on his lips caught my attention.

Blood. Vampire blood.

He'd bit his lip and now the scent of the sickly-sweet ichor was calling to me. I inhaled deeply but resisted the thought. A Vampire drinking a Vampire's blood?

Was that possible? I'd never heard of it. Then again, I had only awoken three months ago, and before that, I knew nothing beyond the textbooks at Daizlei. My resolve floundered at the thought of ripping his throat out and killing him.

I did not want to be a monster, but a certain dark thrill took hold at the realization that I'd finally done what Victor wanted. I had my powers and I was stronger.

"Is-is that the b-best you've g-g-got?" he coughed out, black blood spraying from his lips. I stiffened as the flecks splattered my skin, calling to the hunger within.

I wasn't a monster. I was defending myself—from when he comes back to fight another day. I was ensuring that they wouldn't starve me and my master wouldn't kill me. I had to make sure Victor wasn't swayed by whatever the Vampire would tell him.

It was only self-defense.

Yes, that's it.

I repeated it thrice in my mind.

"I'm not a monster," I whispered—before I ripped his throat out.

His blood ran free through my fingers as I pulled the last of his essence from the body. Vampire or not—he was dead. Truly dead. My hands didn't even shake when I stood and dumped his body on the floor, waiting for the horror of what I'd done to hit me.

But it never came.

Whatever heaviness that should have weighed on my heart died along with my morality and did not return when I drank his blood like a glutton. I guess that made us even.

The whispers in my mind applauded as I positioned myself daintily on the ornate chair in the corner of my room.

It was self-defense. I had no choice.

That's exactly what I would tell Victor. It's what I chose to believe.

Even if I did kill a man—and liked it.

CHAPTER 26

I BOLTED UPRIGHT IN BED, THE THIN SATIN SHEET POOLING AROUND my waist. My breath came in hot, heavy gasps as I tried to breathe again. To breathe at all.

My burning throat cracked under the sharp inhales. The fissures were imaginary, as were the dank musk and mold clinging to the inside of my chest, but they felt real. So very real.

It wasn't my body that was undergoing such horrors. Not my skin that was defiled. Not my thirst for blood, human or Vampire. Not my power that lashed out and drained the undead dry.

A cold settled over me like a blanket. It seeped into my flesh, and blood, and bones. A chill that could not be banished by the heat of the fire, or a warm summer air.

Because deep in those bones of mine, I wondered, and I wept.

There had to be some kind of explanation for these dreams.

Was it her ghost haunting me?

Was it my subconscious trying to punish me?

Or maybe it was something else entirely.

Something far darker that I wouldn't dare put the name to. Couldn't.

I pushed the sheets aside, only then noticing the empty space beside me. Aaron was gone again. His side of the bed rumpled, but cold to the touch. I wasn't sure what to think of that. Why he was gone at this time of night.

Why he was gone when I—

I stopped myself before I finished the thought. It was an idea almost as insurmountable as the truth behind my dreams, and just like them, I wasn't in the headspace to handle it alone in the middle of the night craving the most unholy of things.

Both Violet and my demon pressed against me, oddly comforting and reassuring. I took a long, deep breath, fully expanding my lungs with oxygen until they hurt. The muscles constricted sharply as I blew it back out and slid off the obsidian sheets.

The marble was cool against my bare feet, but not cold. The fireplace at the end of the bed kept it warm enough to ward off a chill, but not so warm it suffocated. I blew the fire out with a wave of my hand as I crossed the empty space and grabbed a sweatshirt by the door. The material on the inside was downright rough compared to the sheets, but it would keep me warm on my walk.

The living room was empty, as I expected. Not a trace of Aaron. Not a hint of smoke.

I left the apartment to wander the halls of the residence. At this hour, very few Shifters were awake. The ones that were kept to themselves, which suited me just fine.

They weren't the reason I was lurking in the halls before the crack of dawn on shaking legs with a cold sweat dripping down my back. I took the elevator two floors down and let my feet carry me through the beige halls.

The exit was just around the corner...or not.

I came to another set of taupe walls that led down another maze-like hallway. Glancing over my shoulder, I debated the merits of backtracking and simply jumping over the balcony from the third floor, but I dismissed it. Taking an unsteady breath, I started down the unknown corridor. Surely one of these would lead outside.

Wouldn't it?

After the fourth turn leading nowhere, I stopped and ran a hand through my sleep-knotted hair. You would think that after so many wrong turns I'd either end up where I started or have found my way outside, but no. It seemed that this place was built like a maze. The walls were all the same ugly shade of off-white, not quite brown or grey. The trim was dark mahogany, polished to perfection without a speck of dust in site.

If it weren't for my sense of smell I might have gotten confused and assumed I had already gone this way, but the orange and freesia was new. I followed the scents down a long corridor to a pair of cracked walnut double doors.

I lifted my hand to the hardwood and tapped the door open another six inches, stepping through without a sound. My breath caught in my throat at what I saw.

Bookshelves lined every inch of the circular room, climbing straight to the ceiling over twenty feet above. A ceiling made of stained glass that swirled to form shapes that changed and moved. Splotches of color bled from rose red to cobalt blue with swatches of gold and evergreen in between.

I stood transfixed to the spot. This can't be real. Could it?

That was a dangerous question for me because I often asked it when I already knew the answer.

"It's beautiful, isn't it?"

I dropped my head, moving my gaze from the ceiling to the man sitting in a dark red chair.

"Yes," I agreed. "Are the shapes really changing?"

"They are," he nodded. "Would you like to know its story?"

He inclined his head forward, motioning to the second chair across from him. His dark brown hair hung lank against his sullen skin. His cheekbones were more prominent than was considered healthy, but he didn't smell of sickness or death. He smelled like oranges and freesia.

I could have left it at that and backed out of the door without a second thought. Run off to find a quiet place outside where I could talk to the rising sun and get lost in old memories that were better left alone. Pray to some ancient that never gave a damn while I deconstructed my nightmare a thousand times over until I convinced myself that the impossible was possible. That she was alive. Changed.

But my nightmares were just that.

Fiction created by my own psyche.

Fears generated by grief and a deep-seated hatred of the creatures that killed her.

False visions from a dead girl I killed.

The old Selena would have walked away to wallow in

self-pity, but I couldn't be that girl anymore. Just as I couldn't be the unfeeling wretch I was after she died, but instead, the girl I saw on the horizon.

I tilted my head forward knowing the moment of silence had already swung past a polite pause and was soaring to downright awkward. Still, I took a seat across from him and rested my shaking hands on my lap where he couldn't see them beneath the small circular table.

"So, what's the story?" I asked, looking back to the stained glass masterpiece.

"Well, like all great stories, it started with a beautiful young woman," he said. I resisted the urge to roll my eyes and waited for him to continue. "A slave, to be exact, although the Supernaturals would never call her that. She was sent to the Shifter Alpha as a ward shortly after he took office. A present, if you will." The older man uncrossed his ankles and got to his feet.

"That's some present," I muttered coolly. The older man chuckled under his breath, an old, earthy sound. He's probably heard that before.

"It's customary for the Court to send wards between the Councils, but yes, in her case she was treated no better than a slave. In many ways, sending her to the Alpha was a kindness that the Supernaturals didn't see. You see, she was his signasti." The old man paused, glancing up at the ceiling and then again to the books around us.

"But she didn't know it because she was a Supernatural?" It came out like a question, but I already knew the answer.

"Yes, and because of that he had to earn her love." He motioned to the room around us. "He built her this library and commissioned a Witch to work with an architect to create the stained glass ceiling."

I stared at the whirling splotches of color; so vivid, but fleeting. They swirled almost like...*smoke*. The metal shapes moved like mercury.

"Why stained glass?" I asked, never taking my eyes off the ceiling. It was magnificent, but it's not the kind of thing that is usually gifted.

"Katherina Branislav was from Bulgaria and spent a great deal of time in cathedrals as a child," he answered. "Playing spy from the rafters on all the wealthy landholders and government higher ups. She fell in love with the stained glass windows there and as his wedding gift to her, the Alpha had this one built to be greater than any that came before it."

Ah, that made more sense, but it still left one question...

"Branislav. That's a ruling family," I said. "I've never heard of ruling families sending their own children as wards." *Only them poaching children from other families*, I added silently.

"The families on the Supernatural Council will give many things, including their children, if they think it will better help them keep their power," he replied. There was an edge of underlying resentment that hadn't been there before.

"I don't see how giving away one girl—"

"Katherina was a forfeit," he interjected. Not harsh or cold, but straight to the point.

"A forfeit?" I repeated, unable to hide the chill that ran down my spine. He must have read the surprise on my face and known that I wasn't asking for an explanation when he only nodded.

A forfeit.

The polite term for the rare Supernatural born without powers. Instead, any magic that lies within them is passed onto their child at birth, making for children that are powerful beyond compare.

They are called forfeits because they don't only give their power to that one child, but it costs them their life. Except...

"Keyla?"

He smiled grimly. "Katherina was stronger than any forfeit I've known. She survived the birth of her son, but not her daughter," he said softly. Above us, the stained glass shone brighter as the dawn crept over the horizon.

"How do you know so much about her?" I asked. The older man took his seat beside me again and rested his elbows on his knees, bringing his hands together in a steeple while keeping his eyes to the sky.

"It's the job of every Shifter to know their Alpha and protect them, just as it's the Alpha's job to make the best decision for the pack. Katherina may not have been born a Shifter, but she had the heart of one."

He whispered her name with such reverence that I had to wonder. What kind of woman, born without power and given as a slave, could be every bit the Alpha as the natural born heir?

The kind of woman I could aspire to be.

Now that was a dangerous thought, considering I was the current heir's signasti and a highly sought-after fugitive hiding from the Supernatural Council. But if I wasn't...yes,

Katherina Branislav would be the type of woman I could aspire to be.

I rose to my feet, making my way towards the door without a single tremor. The nerves that shackled me on my way here seemed to have eased their restraint. I lifted my hand to the door and turned halfway back to the stranger.

"I forgot to ask your name." He smiled and swept his dark hair from his eyes. From several feet away in a half-lit room, they were a combination of dark umber and cedar brown.

"Nate," he said after a slight hesitation.

"Thanks for the story, Nate. I'll see you around." I tipped my chin in a small nod and closed the library door firmly behind me, breathing a little easier than when I walked in.

CHAPTER 27

THE AIR SMELLED CRISP AND CLEAN WHEN I WALKED ONTO THE training field later that morning. Overnight a snowstorm had blown through leaving several inches of snow that was already melting in the morning sunlight.

"They're staring," Keyla stage whispered. She strutted her way across the field beside me like a Goddess whose mere presence was a blessing.

"You love it," I replied. She threw her head back and laughed, loud and boisterous. I'd never known someone that could laugh so free and without a care. I envied it, but was happy for her all the same.

"You're right. I do. This is the most attention they've paid me in ages," she giggled.

I snorted, rolling my eyes. "Sure, we'll go with that."

Our easy banter fell into a silent anticipation as we approached the training ring I had Aaron set aside for my sister, cousin, and I. *Ring* wasn't quite the right word to describe it. The twenty-yard-wide dip in the ground was closer to a hole than anything.

I walked right to the edge and stopped, peering down at the Shifter made arena. Flat stone walls ten-feet tall and a dirt floor covered by snow. In the center, Blair and Alexandra were already fighting, but it only took me a moment to realize their sparring lacked any real fierceness.

Blair was on the offensive, slowly backing her towards the stone wall. Her movements were quick. Precise. So were Alexandra's blocks, but my cousin had something that my sister didn't.

Absolute concentration.

I called it three moves before it happened.

Blair went for a pop to the head and Alexandra ducked straight into the blonde girl's waiting knee. She brought it up hard into her chest, simultaneously pulling a dagger from her waist and pressing it into my sister's exposed neck as she pushed her into the wall the last two feet.

"Pinned," a Shifter called from across the ring, only inches from the lip of the arena. Several others had gathered around, including Aaron and Johanna. They stood by silently, either watching for trouble or waiting to see what I would do.

I didn't ask.

"Break her hold," I commanded quietly. Alexandra's eyes flicked up instantly. Trepidation and warning filled her gaze as she stared silently. I toed the edge of the arena and raised a condescending eyebrow. "Break it," I repeated.

"I can't," she spat.

"Bullshit," I scoffed, fanning the flames that started in her eyes. She was close to snapping, but the second she turned her gaze to the girl holding her in place, that inner-fire all but fizzled out.

She didn't want to hurt Blair.

Luckily for us, I knew all the right buttons to push and force it.

Unfortunately for me, I had to hold up my end of the deal.

"You can do it," Violet whispered. *"You are ready."*

Without letting myself overthink it and trusting my own inner demon, I stepped over the ridge and landed deftly on my feet.

"What is she doing?"

"She doesn't even have a weapon."

"She got lucky during the full moon—"

"Silence," Aaron commanded. The whispering died out instantly. The Alpha's order was law.

The snow crunched under my boots as I stalked across the clearing—every bit the predator both inside and out. Alexandra's attention didn't leave me for even a second as I slowly approached behind Blair.

"Blair, please step aside." She dropped her hand back to her waist immediately and exited the makeshift arena.

Alexandra eyed me warily as she darted away from the wall, crossing to the other side in the blink of an eye. I don't even think she realized she was already moving with demon speed, even if it was just to put distance between us.

The whip she kept coiled around her wrist slowly unwound as she spread her feet in an aggressive stance. Like a cornered animal.

There was something oddly intimate about the whole situation. Me finding myself back in the ring because we are the only few of our kind. That we know of. I let that thought fall to the wayside as I crossed my arms over my chest and smirked with just a touch too much of self-satisfaction. It would piss her off, her demon even more.

"You haven't trained in months. What makes you think that—"

I moved while she was still talking. Using the same speed she had already mastered with ease, I crossed the clearing and placed myself behind her.

"I run forty miles a day and exercise my mind even more than my body," I said.

She jumped, then whirled around already moving her whip to catch me, but I caught her off guard when I moved into her attack instead of away.

I brought my hand down on her wrist, twisting it sharp enough to cause pain but not so much to break. She dropped the whip, her eyes darkening as she moved her gaze from my hand to my face.

"How did you—"

"Lesson one," I twisted my grip again and forced her to lean into me. "Expect the unexpected."

I relinquished her wrist and slammed my other hand into her chest, putting just enough of my power into it to send her flying across the clearing.

She let out a gasp as her body hit the frozen ground only inches from the stone wall she could have landed against. My demon stirred restlessly, wanting to come out. Wanting to play.

I hesitated for a fraction of a second before silently letting her forward.

Trust. The only way we'll both survive is a foundation built on trust.

She shivered in delight and rubbed her presence against

me reassuringly. I eased into it, ignoring the gasps from higher above as my eyes turned black and blotted out the white entirely. They didn't understand, but just like Alexandra, they would. Being part demon didn't make me inherently evil.

If anything, my demon side was a hell of a lot more benevolent most of the time.

This was not one of those times.

Alexandra rocked her legs back and arched her body as she shot her momentum forward, jumping to her feet. Obsidian ashes swirled in her eyes as her demon vied for power. She flicked her glance to the corners of her vision, taking her eyes off me for a second too long.

I capitalized on her crippling mistake, jumping the distance between us. I clasped my hand around her throat and pushed her back into the stone wall.

"Lesson two," my demon and I said. "Trust yourself. Trust your demon. Without you, she is dead, and without her, you are weak." I tightened my grip, pushing the pads of my fingers into the soft, *burning* flesh of her throat.

She was getting close.

"Lesson three," I whispered, leaning close. "Let go. Fearing yourself will not change what you are, but it will get you killed."

She flinched under my inscrutable gaze and I shook my head, releasing her to step back. I had to mentally prepare myself for how far I might have to push her and make sure I didn't get lost in the madness while I was at it.

"Do you remember," I started slowly, "how father trained us?" I heard her breath catch in her throat when I held out my hand and the whip shot straight towards it. I caught it in mid-air and stroked the handle thoughtfully.

"S-Selena," she whispered.

I think she meant to admonish me for even considering this, but the strain behind her voice told me that I'd hit it on the mark. If I couldn't goad her into it, maybe an overwhelming combination of anger and fear would set it free.

It is, after all, what worked for me.

Only she doesn't know that I won't do it.

Oh, but I could make her believe I would. Me, the queen of lies. I resigned myself to my faults, because even liars and thieves have their place in this world. Right now, mine was provoking that demon out of her. Making it come to her aid.

Forcing her to protect herself in the only way she can from another demon.

"So, you do remember?" I poked. Prodded.

"We were children. He was only trying to do what was best for us," she snapped. Those midnight shadows in her eyes swirled more as her demon hammered away at her defenses.

I laughed cruelly, a dark chuckle that had the hairs on her arms standing at attention.

"If you think so highly of his methods, why don't we revisit them," I murmured.

In the back of my mind, I was aware that I was dancing perilously close to the edge of where my control sat. Alexandra was only a hairpin away from losing it, and I was prepared to pull the trigger.

Above us, the apprehension thickened with every second I let this charade go on. One wrong move and someone would spring. I mentally placed a barrier over the lip of the ring, pre-emptively preventing any of them from entering and any fire from escaping.

I angled my body toward Alexandra, stiffening my spine with resolve. My heart beat slow and sure as I began stalking towards her.

The moment my hand lifted, the tension snapped.

Her eyes blackened instantly as her demon sprang forward and sent the snow covered ground up in flames. Heat washed over my skin as the fire consumed me.

I tossed the whip away and into the fire, glancing up to ensure my shield held.

It did.

Until the flames turned black. She homed in on me like a lion with its prey and locked me in a cage made of dark fire. I lifted my hands to the onyx flames, but these didn't burn. They trapped me.

I focused my energy on pushing the flames out. Extinguishing the entire arena, but the tables had turned, and this was her playground now. My demon snarled at her through the wall that separated us, but she only smiled.

"It's not nice being trapped, is it?" she goaded in an empty voice.

I shifted my aim from controlling the fire to controlling her. Alexandra's eyes widened as I wrapped an invisible hand around her throat and brought her to her knees.

She may be able to lock me in here, but she couldn't hurt me. I may not be able to control her flames, but I could still do far worse.

"Who's at whose mercy now, sister?" my demon and I said softly. She narrowed her shadowed eyes.

"Release me," she demanded.

I smiled lazily and crossed my arms over my chest, ignoring the cries of outrage from those outside the arena. My head pounded as heat imploded inside it and a splicing sensation ripped down my chest. It wasn't my actual body, my reactions, or my emotions that fueled it—but I felt it all the same. Aaron was growing more agitated and angry by the second.

I needed to speed this up before he did something rash.

"Show me you can be trusted," I replied. "Show *her* you can be trusted."

She continued to stare at me with a blank apathy, but beneath her emotionless façade, I was not fooled. I think her demon knew what I was doing, and as much as it was pissed at me for going about it this way, it recognized the importance of this moment.

My sister would know everything she said and did. Alexandra would understand her reasoning, her thoughts, her feelings. She would be forced, at the very least, to acknowledge this other part of herself.

Acknowledge that it had the chance to act out and burn the residence to the ground, but it chose not to. Selfish reasons or not, it was a choice.

A very small pucker formed between her eyebrows, the first emotion outside of an impassive rage that she let herself display. That slight pucker drew her eyebrows together in an almost thoughtful way—were her eyes not black and emotionless.

The flame prison that held me at bay dissipated without a trace, and every flicker of black flame in the clearing followed it. The once snow-covered ground was now hard and baked from the prolonged heat. The stone walls of the arena covered by dark ash marks. Above them, the crowd had grown, but not even one looked burned or had singed clothes.

All in all, I'd mark this as a success.

Now I just had to talk her demon down.

"I'm impressed," I told her. "You have more control than I did." I wasn't lying. For this being the third time that she's called forth her demon...color me green. She was going to be just fine.

My dark-eyed sister watched reproachfully as I walked to her and dropped down on one knee. I relinquished the phantom hands that held her, the same as she had done the flames. She didn't jump away or make any move to fight me, as I suspected. I took it as a sign of good faith to raise one hand and extend it towards her. Another gesture of trust to bridge the gap between my sister and her other half, as well as the rest of us.

She frowned at my hand, staring at it like she didn't understand. A minute passed. Then another. Silence spread across the residence. Only a howling wind and the rustling of dead leaves made any sound.

She raised a steady, burning hand to mine—and two demons formed an unspoken trust founded on an understanding that hadn't been there before.

CHAPTER 28

"Ohmigawd—you're a demon! Like a full-blown, badass—"

"Language," Aaron scolded.

"—demon." Keyla paused to look sheepish for about a second before continuing. "How did I not see this? It's *sooo* obvious." She reached across me to snatch another hulking slab of ham, dumping half the contents of the gravy boat on top of it.

"First of all, I'm only part demon. Not full. So don't go around spreading rumors," I corrected her with no small amount of snark. She rolled her eyes to the heavens and Scarlett muttered a complaint about her behavior for the third time since we'd sat down for dinner. "Second, you didn't see it because part demons have never existed before to anyone's knowledge. We're a bunch of special fucking snowflakes." That seemed to crack grins around the table and pull some chuckles from a few.

"Right," Keyla drawled. "*Part* demon. How's that even possible? Does it mean you have like, two sides? Do you demon-out on people?" She tapped her chin thoughtfully with the fork before digging into her second plate of pineapple glazed ham and mashed potatoes.

"No, I don't 'demon-out' on people, as you say," I pursed my lips taking a drink of water. Several ears at the table perked up at the turn in conversation, particularly Johanna and Oliver. Whatever I answered right now was going to set a precedent in the future. "My demon and I are the same, but like two sides of the same coin. Think about what happens if you try to destroy one side."

The table went dead silent the moment the words were out of my mouth, but Keyla was oblivious. I had counted on it.

"You can't. Not without destroying the other...*oh*." Her mouth popped open giving Scarlett and Liam an eyeful of her mashed-up food as they were sitting across from her. "So, you can't exist without each other?" she asked without judgement, only innocent curiosity.

"No, we can't." My gaze swept up without thinking to gauge Alexandra's reaction. She wasn't looking my way, but the concentration with which she stared at her food was telling. "My demon half is *me*, just a bit more...savage."

I paused at the way Amber choked on her water. She shot a suggestive grin between me and Aaron. He flipped her off and gave her a stern *don't fucking say it* kind of look.

"Savage?" Keyla asked. "You want to kill people?"

"No." *Not kill, per se, but occasionally maim. Or torture.* "It means that part of me thinks a bit more black and white. My instincts can rule me at times, but sometimes those urges are for things other than just violence." I shifted on the uncomfortable bench, accidentally brushing my arm against Aaron. He stiffened beside me, but Keyla didn't seem to notice my reaction.

"Like sex?" she asked. It was my turn to choke on my water and Amber busted out laughing.

"More like you. My demon decided that she was fond of you before I did," I replied, avoiding her question entirely.

But she wasn't wrong. The goosebumps that broke out across my skin at the slight brush of his skin had little to do with the cold and more to do with the craving for intimacy.

It started months ago and I thought it was because my powers were coming back, or the confused feelings about Lucas. Now with my demon and I merged in a holistic unit, I've come to realize that's her. She craves intimacy in all forms, more than I ever did before.

I never considered myself a hugger, but if she had her way, I would be.

"She has her own thoughts?" Keyla continued.

"Err," I paused to think. "It's kind of hard to explain. It's less her own thoughts than it is instincts." I toyed with how much to tell them because I didn't know how they would respond. But if we were ever going to get over the past, to learn to trust, the truth seemed like the best way to go. "She's still very new to being able to experience things with me, and that makes her less cynical at times. More open to...everything."

My throat locked up at the uncomfortable vulnerability of the moment. It wasn't a lot by most people's standards, but for me, I may as well have bared my soul to the world. My gut reaction was to shut down, but that wouldn't help anyone. Certainly not Alexandra, who was learning through my conversation with Keyla.

"Hmm," Keyla hummed to herself. "It sounds like what Shifters say about their inner animal." She mused around bites of food making Scarlett glare death at her.

"What's having an inner animal like?" I leaned across the table to reach for the bowl of mango salad only half paying attention because I was focusing on not accidentally getting touchy with Aaron again.

"I wouldn't know."

I frowned, and without thinking, the bowl leapt from the table to my hand. Some of the Shifters cast me wary looks, but that wasn't anything new. Being a Supe in Shifter territory tends to draw attention, matter manipulator or not. The weird part is that I wasn't the only one they were looking at this time.

"What do you mean?" It wasn't like her to be shady about stuff. She was normally running her mouth a million miles an hour.

"I don't have one."

Don't have one?

"What do you mean you don't have one?" I asked, a pit of dread settling in my stomach when she didn't answer right away. From the other side of me, Aaron had gone very still.

"Keyla was born as what we Shifters call latent," he answered quietly.

"Latent? What does—"

"She's a Shifter that can't shift."

Oh. Suddenly, a lot of Keyla's behavior made sense.

She was the Alpha's daughter, but without the ability to shift.

Shit.

I could do one of two things in that moment. The first was apologize and tell her I didn't know. Something told me that would only make it worse for her. Keyla didn't want my pity. She didn't want anyone's pity. She never said anything before, and I could only guess as to why.

Which left me with the second option, and that was to let her know I didn't care. She was still Keyla, with or without the ability to shift. Just like I was still Selena, demon or no demon.

"Well then," I said, a lot more boisterous than I felt, "I guess that makes us both special snowflakes." I waited two long seconds hoping I didn't guess wrong. Peopling and feelings weren't exactly my forte, but then again, they weren't Keyla's either.

She looked over at me and cracked a slight smile, her lips quirking up despite her solemn eyes. Those deep, soulful amber eyes seemed to tell me more than words could have, and we continued our dinner without another word of it.

EARLY THE NEXT AFTERNOON, I walked up to the edge of the arena to stand beside Aaron.

"Where is Alexandra?"

"Tori said she wasn't feeling well. *That time of month*," he quoted, rolling his eyes.

I snorted. Time of the month, my ass. We stayed up the night before watching reruns of Charmed, but if I could get my ass up in time for training, so could she.

"Wars don't stop for that time of the month," I replied,

crossing my arms over my chest. "Keyla, can you go get her?" On the other side of me, Keyla groaned but nodded before marching back towards the mansion. "Bring a jug of water with you in case she does anything rude!" I called as an afterthought. Keyla let out a sharp laugh and picked up her pace.

"She's going to throw water on her now," Aaron sighed.

"I'm counting on it."

He let out a dark chuckle before turning his eyes to the scene below where Blair and Oliver were sparring—an odd pairing if there ever was one. Blair was short by anyone's standards, and while her whip-fast blade skills weren't something to be underestimated, her real skill lay with her ability: ice.

Oliver Fortier came from a long line of force field manipulators. His own particular skills lay in physical shields, making him nearly untouchable to everyone here with the exception of two people. The first being Johanna, whose Heinz57 blood made her a woman of many talents and one of the deadliest people in the entire residence. The second was me. I had the ability to shatter his shields, as my demon had already proven.

Knowing this, I wasn't surprised when he enclosed her in a shield, instantly rendering her knives useless. She let out a curse and sheathed her blades, taking deep even breaths. From up here, the clang of swords and animal roars made it difficult to pinpoint subtle noises, but in the eerie still space where I stood, almost like I was outside of time itself...I heard her heartbeat.

Low but quick, and rapidly increasing.

I tilted my head, studying her for all of three seconds

before the electric blue shield surrounding her broke apart and dissipated like it was never there at all.

"What are you doing?" I asked Oliver as he moved towards her.

"Checking to see if she's alright—"

"You're coddling her," I replied swiftly before he could get the words out. Oliver stopped mid-stride and his lips thinned.

"She was surrounded. What would you have me do?" he replied tersely, crossing his arms over his chest.

"Challenge her." I swept my gaze from him to my cousin, hunched defensively where he'd left her .

It was so out of place for her, so...her eyes twitched to the side and a cold realization descended upon me. Making a snap decision and wasting no time, I stepped over the edge and into the arena. Snow plumed a foot or two off the ground as I hit it with a soft thud. The ice itself seemed to crackle with the otherworldliness of something more.

Or someone.

"You're looking a little pale, cousin. Are you feeling alright?" I asked casually as I took slow, exaggerated steps around her. She narrowed her stormy grey eyes, watching every move I made.

"Fine," she replied stiffly. There was something else to it, a hint of roughness beneath her tone that wasn't just her. I cocked an eyebrow.

"You sure about that?" I asked nonchalantly. In my gut I knew what it was. I just needed to lure her out a little bit more...

"For fuck's sake, what are you doing?" Oliver said angrily, stomping over towards her. For someone that was supposedly skilled in politics, you would think he could read body language well enough to know something was up.

"I wouldn't do that if I were you."

Blair's breathing quickened as he crossed the space towards her and cupped a hand behind her elbow, almost... tenderly. I tucked that away for another time as I waited for her snap.

I wasn't disappointed.

From the sideline, Johanna screamed for Oliver right as Blair's eyes darkened to pits as black as hell.

Bingo.

Blair twisted in his grip and I anticipated her move just before it happened. She reached out to gouge his jugular, but I mentally pulled him away from her and tossed him over the lip of the arena. A spray of blood showered the air and I grimaced.

She was faster than I anticipated. Faster, maybe, than even me.

This was going to suck.

CHAPTER 29

I HOPED HE WASN'T DEAD, BUT IT WASN'T LIKE I HAD THE TIME TO check. Blair was already moving. I ducked just in time as a dagger came flying at me and I grabbed the second between two flat palms as she hurled them at me in quick succession.

Both were aimed for my eyes.

"You're very angry," I said, keeping my voice at a conversational tone and pace. For one, yelling would probably only piss her off more. Two, her senses might be heightened. If they were, then she was probably already going into sensory overload. "Want to tell me why?"

Blair's demon glared at me distrustfully, only flicking her eyes up to the ridge for the briefest of moments. "He's not my signasti," the demon replied.

Shit. I had two choices here, and both of them had unwanted consequences.

I could talk her down and let everyone know who her signasti was—and that she's known this entire time. Or I could try to subdue her—which may result in a very real fight between demons.

Goddamnit.

"Oliver?" I asked, playing dumb. Blair gave me a pissy look and nodded. She knew that I already knew. Which meant her demon was privy to that as well. Crap.

I wrangled the two options back and forth in my head needing to buy time and see if I could coax Blair out. There was no way she wasn't fighting for control right now.

"Okay." I started edging my way around the circle. "What's that have to do with anything?"

Blair wasn't having any of it. She walked opposite of me, never letting me get any closer than the farthest point from her.

"He doesn't touch me," she snarled.

Okay then. I was beginning to wonder how much of the bond madness had set in for her as well and she just couldn't see it.

Maybe with distance between them it was easier, but they'd stretched it much further than Aaron and I. And now they were in close proximity again. They'd also endured worse stress to it, but a string between two people can only be pulled so far before it either snaps or they are drawn back together.

"How does Blair feel about that?" I asked, distinctly trying to avoid *who* her signasti was. Her demon growled.

"She's being dense," it replied vaguely. I cocked my head. That was an awfully thought out answer for a being that only just surfaced. Different than Alexandra and hers, but clearly not united like me and mine. Somewhere in-between.

We were going to have a talk if—when this was over.

"Mhmm." I forced myself not to look up over her head where Alec was standing over her. Out of the corners of my vision, I could tell he was trying to make sense of the scene in front of him. "Blair is a lot of things, but I wouldn't call her dense, and I don't think this is going to earn you any favors *when* she takes back over."

She stared back impassively, giving absolutely nothing away.

"That's an *if,* not a when," she replied coolly.

Alright then, I guess it's going to be like that. Snow started falling lightly into the wind. But the forecast didn't call for snow. I briefly considered the possibility that it was Blair, but that kind of power...well, it would rival very few in the world.

And that realization instantly made me wary, because if there were any who could control the weather...it would be Blair, whose very last name was Stormer.

A chill went down my spine and the demon smiled knowingly.

"Worried, cousin, that you won't be able to force me back?" She flicked her eyes to the sky and smiled a bit more as the snow really started to come down. I bit my cheek, mentally cursing, but smiled lazily on the outside.

"Not at all," I replied as a mass of gleaming red hair appeared over the arena. I lifted my eyes from my cousin to my sister, pleased to see hers held a steely resolve before bleeding black. Not a trace of white in sight.

"What are you—" The words were only partially out of her mouth when she turned and froze.

Alexandra chose that moment to step over the lip of the arena and join us, casting a barrier of black fire over the pit.

Blair paled, but did not cower or try to run. I didn't expect her to, and I would have been disappointed if she tried.

"This is how it's going to be?" she asked, almost like she was giving us a warning. A chance to turn back now. I wondered what card she had up her sleeve that made her so confident, or if she was just bluffing.

"It doesn't have to be any way," I replied. She shot me a scathing look and I shrugged. "You're Blair's demon. She needs you just as much as you need her, but if you go off vying for control and trying to kill people, she's going to lock you away." I held up my hand and Alexandra, currently merged with her demon, copied the sentiment.

"You can't possibly *know* that's what she'll do," the demon replied with a glance at our outstretched hands. I smiled, completely genuine, but took no pleasure in what would come next if she didn't cooperate.

"Oh, believe me, I do." I nodded, motioning to myself. "I locked my own other half away for years, as I'm certain she has been doing with you." I took three steps toward her and she took one step back. "And she will continue to if you show her you can't be trusted. So, your choices here are this: join with us as an equal so that we can help you, or fight us and find out how strong your other half really is."

I continued walking toward her with Alexandra until her back was completely against the wall, and our hands were only feet away. She had nowhere to go and no way out, and I didn't for a second think she would stop fighting if she didn't take the offer.

Blair's demon glanced between us and slowly extended her hand.

But I wasn't born yesterday.

The wicked gleam in her eyes did not trust us. It didn't trust anyone. I wasn't surprised when her other hand went for a blade, but she caught me off guard when a flood of water came out of nowhere and condensed around me, forming a globe around my head.

The images before me distorted through the liquid. One moment I was standing with my hand out in good faith, and the next I fell to my knees, gripping my stomach as a slicing pain ripped through me.

I gasped, accidentally opening my mouth and the water pushed its way past my lips and down my throat. I choked on the lack of air, a sudden panic filling me.

She's trying to drown me.

No. Her demon half was trying to drown me.

But she underestimated one thing: I was a matter manipulator, and no one played games quite like me.

I mentally reached for my connection to this world and space around us, while my own demon pushed forward more. The water distorted my vision but the unseen strings around us flashed from black to white. I blew outward, mentally forcing the water out and away from me.

It dropped like rain, falling on the fresh layer of snow.

To my side, Alexandra and Blair were battling it out, but the shield that previously separated us from the training field had fallen. Patches of fire and ice dotted the arena in between sludgy piles of mud. I tore my eyes from the two viciously battling girls to the pain coming from my stomach.

"You've gotta be fucking kidding me," I growled. The bloodied handle of a dagger protruded from my stomach where I can only assume Blair had stabbed me.

She owed me after this. Big time.

I grit my teeth as I wrapped my hand around the hilt, prepared to pull the sucker out and hope I healed fast.

"Need some help?"

I looked up to where Aaron had suddenly appeared. He kneeled in front of me, his face edged with concern. I pursed my lips against the snarky reply that wanted to come out. This wasn't the time.

"Sure," I replied tersely, releasing the handle to be able to grasp my stomach and staunch the bleeding when he pulled it out. Aaron placed one hand on my shoulder and one on the dagger.

"On three," he said. I nodded.

"Three."

"Two."

He pulled.

"Mother—" I swallowed the rest of my insult as my body rocked forward into his.

"Shhhh," he murmured, wrapping his bloodied hand with the dagger around me. We didn't move or speak for almost a minute while my cousin and sister fought behind me. I half expected to get stabbed in the back, but Aaron didn't leave my side.

"Can you help me up? I'm almost healed, but I need to end this so I can go lay down." I kept a hand pressed firm against my stomach and wrapped the other arm around his shoulders, inhaling the scent of smoke and the wilderness while he lifted me.

By the time I was standing, the blood had clotted and the wound in my stomach was healing, but it would probably be a few hours before I could move without pain. As it was, I had to bite the inside of my cheek to swallow my groan when I stepped away from Aaron.

Blair and I were going to have some choice words very, very soon.

"Alright, cousin. I'm royally pissed, so let's—"

My words broke off when I saw both Alexandra and Johanna fighting to subdue Blair. Together you would think it was a quick dispatch, but Johanna wasn't fireproof like the rest of us and that made Alexandra have to hold back, giving Blair the upper hand.

My cousin deftly blocked Alexandra's punch and sent a kick into her stomach while casting a jet of water at Johanna to slow her down. In some ways it was impressive, how she managed them both while simultaneously staying one step ahead.

In other ways, it was a vision and a nightmare of what she'd become if she never merged with her demon.

She wouldn't merely be a force to be reckoned with. She would be a force that the world would come to fear, should she ever fall as deep as I.

You won't let her.

I swore it to myself, and then I brought her to her knees.

Phantom hands wrapped around her, forcing her down. Her will thrashed against mine, causing the snowstorm to turn downright treacherous. Chunks of hail the size of coke bottles rained down on us, and I had to mentally umbrella the arena so no one was killed. The slush around our feet swirled together as if to prepare for another attack, but I was done playing this game.

"Listen to me, cousin, and listen loud and clear," I commanded without moving. I would fall to my knees if I tried and that wouldn't look very intimidating. "You will merge because you have no other choice. Without each other, you will go insane and die, and I have lost too many people to let that happen." I swallowed hard but didn't take my gaze away from hers. This was a challenge like any other, and I would not lose. "If I have to do this every day with you, I will. Give me back my cousin."

Her demon stared at me like it didn't have a care in the world, and part of me wondered if it really didn't. The rest of me knew there was no point in wasting time to keep this up.

She spat at the ground, making her decisions abundantly clear.

I sighed and nodded to Johanna.

She struck her temple once and Blair collapsed like dead weight.

Her beautiful blonde hair turning grey and muddy in the wake of the already dispersing storm.

Alexandra walked over to me, her obsidian eyes already fading to rusted brown. She wore a grim expression on her face and sported several shallow but already healing cuts of her own.

"Well, I guess that confirms which parent this comes from."

Alexandra and I shared a look, but she didn't reply. She didn't need to.

If all three of us were demons, then *both* our mothers were as well, which means it was someone further back that caused it. The question is who?

And even more importantly, how?

CHAPTER 30

I WAS KNEELING BY THE EDGE OF BLAIR'S BED WHEN HER EYES
fluttered open. Grey—not black. I breathed a sigh of relief
and brushed a hand over my newly healed stomach.
Thankfully, I'd taken the time to bathe and change clothes.
The clean cotton t-shirt was as much for my benefit as
hers.

The last thing she needed to see when she woke was my
blood from her hands.

"How are you feeling?" I asked. She rubbed her head,
cringing when she touched the spot where Jo had hit her.
After Blair took a chunk out of Oliver, I don't think she had
bothered to be gentle.

"How do I look?" Blair groaned. She moved to push
herself up and I gave her the space, ignoring both
Alexandra and Aaron's slightly jumpy reactions from the
doorway. They'd insisted on being here. Just in case she
woke more akin to Lily...than me.

"Like shit," I shrugged. It was a given. We hadn't bothered with her slightly dirty clothes or muddied hair. I

thought she might appreciate the chance to hide, and taking a shower was a great way to do that.

"Sounds about how I feel." I nodded while she stretched her arms to their breaking point before relaxing back. "I think it's safe to assume you're here because we need to talk," she continued. Blair scooted over on the bed to make room for me and shifted to sit cross-legged. "Well, you may as well take a seat." She motioned to the bed. "All of you."

I rose to my feet and situated myself on the edge. Alexandra came around to sit on her other side, but Aaron remained standing. Stoic.

"I'm sorry, but someone needs to remain vigilant until we know more," he told her, apologetically, but firm. His eyes flicked to me, my stomach, before moving back to settle on her.

"I get it," Blair said softly. She was struggling more than she wanted to let on, but she was also being compliant. There's a lot to be said for that when I was very aware of her still too-fast beating heart and reflexes. She was using her speed without realizing. Which meant her demon wasn't far.

"It's nothing personal," Aaron said, trying to assure her. She waved him off.

"Please," she said. "Don't coddle me. I'm lucky it's only you three and not chains in the dungeon after this morning, so spare me the pity. You have no reason to feel guilty." She picked at a stray thread in the expensive sheets, trailing a short fingernail across it.

"After everything that's happened, do you really think we'd throw you in the dungeons?" I asked her. "I caused an earthquake and you guys didn't do it to me." I thought maybe if I appealed to her logical side she wouldn't feel quite as bad, but Blair was a realist. She reached out and placed a hand to my stomach.

"First, you're the Shifter Heir's signasti. Second, I stabbed you. In their culture, that's more than enough reason to be executed," she said without emotion. There wasn't a trace of fear in her when she looked expectantly at Aaron. He sighed deeply but nodded his head in agreement. "So yes, I am lucky this was the reception I woke to."

Right at that moment, a heavy pounding and a roar more animal than human echoed from the other side of the door. "Blair!" Alec yelled.

Damnit. I told Johanna to keep him out of here...

"Is that..." Blair's face paled as her voice trailed off. She knew who it was. I didn't need to tell her. Still, I nodded. She swallowed hard. "I don't want to talk to him."

"I know," I said. Behind Aaron, the door rattled and then came a loud thump. On the other side, I could hear Jo speaking under her breath in another language, probably cursing to herself.

"Do you know who he is?" Alexandra asked.

"Yes," Blair said without hesitation.

"But you never told him you knew?" There was a hint of judgement in her tone. Her eyes flashed between Blair and I, like she blamed us somehow. Like it was our fault we didn't jump for joy that we had found our soul-shackled partners.

I bit my cheek and kept my thoughts to myself.

"Yes," Blair repeated. There was a harder edge to her tone, daring Alexandra to say what she clearly thought when she didn't know the half of it.

"How?" Aaron asked from behind us. I suppose it was natural for him to wonder, given our situation. But this wasn't about us, and her problems with Alec weren't the thing we were here to discuss.

"I don't really think this is our business, and we have slightly more pressing matters," I interjected, ignoring the brief flash of Aaron's eyes.

"But if the bond madness is causing—" I cut Alexandra off with a sharp glare of my own.

"Don't talk about things you don't understand," I said, harsher than I probably should have. Alexandra's mouth closed with a sharp clink of her teeth.

"She's not wrong," Aaron pushed, refusing to let it drop. I couldn't use the same argument with him because he *did* understand it. Possibly better than I.

"I've known what Alec was for almost two years," Blair said, placing a hand on my shoulder. "I don't think this is the bond madness," she continued. "My demon has been around for a little while now, but I didn't realize what or who she was until Selena's came forward months ago. It scared me, and I tried to hide it."

On one hand, I appreciated her being honest and straightforward, on the other hand—she lied to me—and this could have been prevented if she hadn't.

"I asked you less than forty-eight hours ago and you lied to my face." She looked at me with remorse and a sad smile.

"Yes, I did, and I'm not going to make excuses for it."

I breathed a steady sigh of frustration, trying to calm the slicing sensation through my chest that stung of betrayal and made my own savage half go into a frenzy.

"So," I started, choosing to focus on what mattered here. "You think this is entirely your demon instead of strain from not completing the bond?" Blair's hand dropped away from my shoulder and back into her lap.

"Yeah, I do."

And despite her lying to my face, I believed her. At least believed that she really thought that. I sighed deeply and rose to my feet, pacing around the empty room. Unlike my sister, Tori, and Amber—Blair had kept her room practically untouched. Sparse. The faint smell of her clung to the sheets, but there was no other indication that she'd been staying here for months. I had to wonder if that was part of this. If she instinctually separated herself, even from her living space, because of the conflict inside of her.

"Okay, where do we go from here?" I asked, weighing our options back and forth.

"I'm not cool with practicing here. There's too many things that can go wrong," Alexandra said, crossing her arms over her chest.

"My father has also expressed a preference for you to practice elsewhere," Aaron sighed, clearly bothered by this. "The Shifters are already uneasy with us harboring known fugitives from the Supernatural Council. We don't need a civil war on our hands, which is what will happen if they think he's choosing your safety over his own people."

"Then the residence is out of the question," I murmured. "That complicates things."

"We could not practice at all," Alexandra suggested. "You could just teach us whatever you did while you were sleeping?" I snorted.

"First, that's not going to work for either of you."

Because I had help from Violet, and I'd yet to figure out *who* or *what* she really was. "Second, Blair's other half is more vicious than yours. I don't think she can hold it off for months."

"I can't," Blair agreed. "I'm not sure if I'll be able to hold off for more than a day at a time right now. We'd be living with a hair trigger, and with Anastasia out there and the Vampires biding their time—ignoring this won't be an option." She brushed a handful of her white blonde hair from her face. "I'm going to need to practice so I can get ahold of these new aspects of my ability, and my demon. She's not as neutral as yours," Blair said to me. "Or as trusting as yours," she said to Alexandra. "And with all of her urges riding me and the shadows whispering...I don't give it more than twelve hours before I try to kill someone."

Well, that settles that then.

"We need to find somewhere they can let it out without worrying about getting hurt," I murmured, more to myself than anything.

"Or even better, somewhere where people go to satiate their own bloodlust," Aaron suggested. It was the spark of epiphany in his voice that had my head snapping up. A memory and a place from not long ago came to mind, and I knew we were thinking the same thing.

"What are you talking about?" Alexandra sighed, clearly frustrated to not get it without being told.

"The black market," Aaron and I said in unison.

It was perfect. We could train without fear of hurting the Shifter community—although we would need to be vigilant about making sure the fight stayed contained. While most of the paranormals who worked in the black market were shady, that didn't mean they deserved to die. I'd already leveled it once, and while it had been rebuilt...I would need to be very careful in how we proceeded. Still, this could be my chance to find the Crone again and see if she has anymore answers.

Alexandra's mouth popped open and she said, "You've got to be kidding me. Please tell me you're like, joking." I smiled like a mad woman.

"They're not," Blair said. There was a weary resignation in the way she said it.

"That's a terrible idea," Alexandra blustered. "Anastasia's still out looking for you." She pointed at me, jumping to her feet in indignation. "Not to mention all the paranormals that want to kill you because they think you were the cause of Daizlei. Can you honestly tell me that you think you're ready to fight off that many people and not accidentally cause another earthquake?"

She had a point, but so did I.

"I know she's still looking for me, just as I know the average paranormal can't tell the difference between me and her." Her mouth pressed into a thin line. "When word reaches her that she's been slumming it in the black market, she's going to be pissed, and that will make her desperate. So while you two are sorting your stuff out, Aaron and I can try to track her down." I was well aware I was avoiding her last question. Was I ready? I had no idea, but there was only one way to find out. "Her working with the Vampires may be a grab for more power, but I don't think that's why she's trying to kill me—and what better way to find out than luring out Anastasia herself."

"Sometimes I don't know whether you're crazy or brilliant," Alexandra said, placing her hands on her hips.

"I'm starting to think a bit of both," Blair replied. The troubled look in her eyes was still there, but it was the best plan we had.

I just hoped we didn't come to regret it.

CHAPTER 31

IT WAS NEARLY MIDNIGHT WHEN THE SIX OF US STEPPED INTO THE magical elevator. Alexandra, Blair, and I wore dark clothes with weapons strapped in hidden places. Aaron carried the backpack of extra clothing so that we wouldn't draw any attention when sneaking back into the residence. Johanna and Tori came as back up, but if all went as planned we would be out of the Las Vegas black market before sunrise.

After meeting up with the rest of the team over dinner, we decided to test the waters with a small group of people; an in and out job.

The idea was that if tonight was a success, then we could access black markets all over the world and attempt to track down Anastasia while learning to harness our abilities, and in my case—find the Crone.

I'd yet to tell anyone about that encounter months ago, and after so much time passing, it seemed inconsequential to bring it up now. So much had happened. So much had changed. At least that's what I told myself as the doors slid open, revealing the same alleyway from months ago.

I stepped onto the compounded dirt and the scents of magic and mold hit me. A gust of wind tunneled down the alley and slapped my face with a brisk freshness that had me wide-eyed and alert. I faced the market, once again falling down the rabbit hole that was my own fascination.

Months had passed since I'd caused an earthquake, but you wouldn't know it. Tents of all shapes and sizes lined the never-ending street like nothing ever happened. The stall set up across from the alley showcased a selection of fancy looking glass bottles that the salesman was claiming were love potions. I found that hard to believe given that the man could have used moonscreen. Only Witches could make potions, and he certainly didn't look like one with his pasty white skin.

I shook my head as Blair grabbed my arm and said, "Come on."

The street was crowded tonight as we made our way towards the pits. This was so different than the times before. I was different. While the same wonder and fascination filled me, I was no longer drawn here by a need to escape.

The thought kept me grounded as we approached the crowd. They cheered with a thunderous roar that had me cringing as we walked around the edge. Most had their backs to us, but every now and then I spotted someone paying a little too much attention to us for my liking.

"Wait here," Aaron said, taking off through the crowd. I frowned, slipping out of Blair's grip to follow him. Some might say I was being paranoid, but for someone that was concerned about safety down here, splitting off didn't seem like the smartest idea. Call it a hunch, but something wasn't right.

Aaron weaved through the crowd with expert skill, but he was bigger and bulkier than me and that left a trail in his wake. I made sure to stay far enough back he couldn't see me, but close enough I could track his scent through the crowd.

At first, it seemed like he was going straight for the pit, but then he veered left, cutting back towards the street we had just come from. I stumbled out of the crowd after him, suffering from sensory overload. This many sounds were overwhelming, but when the scent of smoke and wind drifted by, I picked it up like a hound on a trail.

I tracked it fifty yards away to a dark red tent with gold trim. Outside, two burly looking guards stood by with their hands crossed behind their backs and feet wide. The door was just flapping closed as I caught sight of it.

What are you doing, Aaron?

I shied away from the thought immediately because it sounded too close to home. Too intimate. And there was too much between us still unsaid.

I kept telling myself one of these days we'd get around to it, but somehow the time never seemed right.

I slinked closer to the tent, stretching my hearing as far as it would go...

The world flashed and instantly everything changed.

I was no longer walking by the tent, but sitting in a leather cushioned chair looking at...*was that Tam?*

What the actual fuck. The cat-eyed alpha grinned viciously, stroking the triangle of blue tinted hair on his chin. He had both feet kicked up on a desk that sat between us and a fluffy white cat on his lap.

"Will it be the usual, Alpha?" Tam asked me.

Me? I frowned internally but my lips wouldn't move.

"No." The word came out of my mouth, but not on my command. "I'm not here for me tonight."

Was that...*I knew that voice.* And it wasn't mine.

"Oh?" Tam asked in mock delight. "I've heard whispers of your signasti and her growing bloodlust...am I to suppose the rumors are true?" Tam asked lightly, petting the cat on his lap. He wore three gold rings, two glinted with red.

What the hell was actually going on here?

"Selena is getting better. Tonight isn't for her." Aaron paused to readjust himself, sighing deeply. "It's Alexandra and Blair. I need two inmates for them. Paranormals with heinous crimes that they won't feel bad for executing."

Inmates? Executing?

I opened my mouth to shout at him and the world flashed again. Instead of the blood red tent walls and Tam, I was facing the open market and standing rock still like a crazy person staring into nothing. I shook my head and stormed towards the tent, not slowing my steps as two paranormals—*Shifters*—stepped in my way.

"Excuse me, miss—"

"We're under direct orders to—"

I stopped two feet from them and crossed my arms over my chest. The looks they were giving me made me think they knew exactly who I was. Perfect.

"Aaron!" I snapped, raising my voice. "I know you're in there and if you don't call off the guards, I *will* come in, with or without your permission." From within the tent there was a shuffling before the flap opened.

"Selena, darling!" Tam gushed. "It's so lovely to see you—"

"Cut the crap, Tam."

His mouth snapped shut and he pursed his lips, giving me a mildly amused inspection before saying, "Fair enough. Come in."

I stepped past the guards and beyond the velvet red curtain. Not two feet in front of me sat Aaron, stiff as a rod, in front of the same desk from my vision. The fluffy white cat perched on the edge, her fur tinted red from where Tam had been petting her.

"You don't look terribly surprised to see me," Tam mused as he plunked his ass down in the massive oak chair across from us, resting his elbows on the desk to steeple his fingers.

"Do you run the market or just the fights?" I asked, my voice deathly quiet. Tam didn't seem bothered by this, but Aaron had the good sense to look worried. He cast me a wary glance like he was trying to decipher how much I knew.

"Well that depends on your definition of *run*," Tam said. "If you mean handle all of the ins and outs of the market, as well as the betting pool, then yes. Yes, I do." His glittery red vest sparkled under the chandelier.

"And the inmates? You want to tell me about those?"

Tams eyebrows rose. He wasn't expecting that.

"How exactly did you—"

"Answer the question or we can revisit how blood-thirsty I am feeling," I replied. Aaron's gaze nearly burned

264

holes into my skin as a slow realization seemed to dawn on him.

"I handle all of the fights that go down in the Las Vegas black market. That includes picking the opponents. Most are predators that I keep locked up and choose to have executed by a fight to the death. Some people"—Tam flicked his gaze to Aaron—"choose to engage in these fights."

"And by 'some people,' you mean Aaron," I surmised. Tam shrugged in a non-committal gesture, but Aaron was well aware of the hole that was deepening. His grave.

"It's not what you think," Aaron said.

"Oh?" I cocked an eyebrow, waiting for the excuse. This better be good.

His jaw tensed, and in the candlelight coming from the chandelier, he had a faint five o'clock shadow. His normally onyx eyes glinted with a hint of gold.

My heart skipped a beat in my chest, pounding like a drum.

"I've been coming here to let off steam the past few months," Aaron started. "Like you, I have some...*tendencies* that aren't easy for people to always accept, and the bond madness has been making it worse. Tam has been assisting me in keeping it under control."

I stared blankly, my lips parted, and my thoughts jumbled as I tried to come up with a response to that. A cold kind of clarity came over me about the grey area on which we were treading.

An area that I was all too at home with.

"You called them predators?" I asked slowly, shifting my attention to Tam. I ran my fingers across the mahogany desk, tapping my nails on the varnish. "Is it safe to assume these are people the world is better off without?"

A short silence. "Yes," Tam supplied. I nodded.

"And what will your silence cost?"

Tam grinned like a fool.

"For you and your family, nothing. It would be my honor"—his eyes slid sideways—"as a service to the one-day *Alphas*." I stiffened but didn't comment on his choice of words. I was well aware the kind of game I was playing. It was one my father taught me well.

"Very well." I paused. "I need you to find me monsters that my cousin can rip apart without thinking. Her demon is vicious; it will want a challenge. Vampires and demons are preferred."

Tam flashed a Cheshire smile. "Duly noted. Demons are hard to hold, but I've got several Made on standby as we speak."

"That will do," I said, playing with a speck of dust on the desk. The tent was relatively small, and Tam's chair and desk took up most of the room, leaving only a small place for the rickety chair Aaron sat in and a lone barstool.

"And your sister? Does she have any specific *tastes*?" he inquired. I knew it was entirely morbid curiosity that brought on his line of questioning, but anything that made it easier for them would help.

"Feisty," I replied. "The ones that run their mouth will piss her off. Vampires are preferred but prioritize behavior over species." I rattled off her specifics without thinking. After training with them for so long, it didn't take much to know what would be triggers. The undead that killed my

sister and Blair's mother were the first and most obvious
go-tos.

"And what about *your* preferences?" he asked, his sly
smile never slipping.

"The worst of the worst, of course." I didn't hesitate. "I
want the monsters that are so messed up they even give
you nightmares. The ones that are dangerous enough you
usually have them killed on the spot because letting them
live is too big a risk. Those are the predators that *I* prey on."

Tam's cat eyes gleamed with something almost like
pride as he said, "I can see how fate chose you for him. You
will make a great Alpha one day."

I shrugged. "The way I see it, I'm not a good person, but
I'm not bad either. I'm somewhere in-between, and that
puts me in a place where I can do this world some good by
eliminating those that are very bad. Good people don't have
it in them to kill, but I do."

Tam thought on this for a moment before saying, "My
comment still stands."

I clicked my tongue. "Are we done here?"

He nodded. "I'll have your cousin's fight scheduled to
start in half an hour. Your sister will go after. Does this
work?"

"Yes, thank you." Aaron stood and I took that as our cue
to leave.

What's the worst that could happen in half an hour?

CHAPTER 32

BLAIR'S BODY SHUDDERED AND HER DEMON SURFACED THE moment she stepped into the pit.

The crowd noticed the change instantly and grew fevered in their cheers. They laid down wagers left and right, exchanging money, favors, and unspeakable deeds like it was all nothing more than just business. I suppose out here, for some people, that may be quite true.

Beside me to my right, two young women hung on the arms of a very tall blonde-haired man with a scar running down his face where his left eye should have been. He had a fur cloak wrapped around his shoulders with a pattern I'd never seen. His hands were large and meaty.

The giant grinned vilely at me. "Would you like to join us?"

"Piss off," I muttered, turning back to pit. I knew better than to stare but I couldn't seem to help it down here. The man let out a boisterous laugh and leaned over to whisper something in one of the girl's ear. She giggled like a bimbo and I was all but forgotten.

Turning my attention to my cousin below, I toed the edge of the pit uneasily. A guard came through a hidden door escorting a red-eyed Vampire. The Made leered at Blair with pointed, pearly white teeth and a vulpine grin. His skin was unearthly pale, and even under the moonlight I could see the tell-tale black veins of starvation that pulsed when he looked at her. She met his stare unafraid, with death in her eyes and his funeral march in her heart.

"Let the games begin," I whispered while a charismatic Shifter with a booming voice listed off Blair's alias and then that of the criminal they put down there with her. The crowd didn't seem to give a shit that one of the people before us was rapist and a murderer. If anything, it excited them more to see tiny little Blair. It made the betting more fun, they said. Unaware that this was not a true fight, but a staged execution that Tam used for monetary profit and we were using for far more nefarious purposes.

I kept my mouth shut, my eyes glued to the larger guard that was unlocking the creature's shackles. He stepped away, releasing the Vampire, and disappeared through the door from which he came.

Silence and tension wrapped together in a combustible ammunition that exploded the moment the Made attempted to move. I wasn't sure what I should focus on more, the crowd around me that was shifting uneasily, the cousin below me that moved twenty feet between one heartbeat and the next, or the sudden sense that I was being watched.

Across from me, Alexandra stood at the exact opposite end, while Aaron and Jo found spots in between us. We surrounded Blair on every side. It was as much for her protection as our own, and Tori acted as a guard.

So why do I suddenly feel like I've walked into a trap?

"Hello, Selena," an old woman's voice whispered across the back of my neck, making my hairs stand on end. I spun around to find...nothing.

"Wha—"

"Looking for me?" she cackled, choking on her own spit. Her laughing turned hoarse as she trailed off in a fit of coughs. I followed the sound to my right, and lo and behold, there she was.

"The Crone with the third eye," I muttered to myself. "Come to tell my 'fortune' again?"

She tipped back her hood and smiled a row of yellow teeth. Her umber skin was aged and cracked, combined with the gleam in her eyes made her look like she was constantly grinning. Then again, maybe she was.

"I could, but your fate has not changed, only your focus," she said, her voice coarse and dry. I eyed her warily.

"My focus?"

"You passed your first test and are no longer on the path to revenge, but instead, healing. You are growing into a young woman that would have made Valda proud," she rasped. Her deep purple cloak swayed in a gentle breeze. "And that's why it's time."

"Time? Time for what?" I asked, more than a little dismayed. I took a step back, bumping into someone. I turned, halfway expecting a jeer or to be punched on the spot, but neither happened. The person stood silent as a statue, still watching the fight.

The fight that I was also supposed to be watching.

I ran to the edge of the ring and froze.

Not a single person was moving. Not my cousin. Not the Made. Not Aaron, or Johanna, or Alexandra who were also watching them. No one, but me and the Crone.

Somehow, some way, she had stopped time.

"How is this possible?" I asked in a shaky breath, looking back over my shoulder to the ancient Witch. She smiled knowingly and pointed a single crooked finger at me, bending it to beckon me forward.

"Let us take a walk, you and I," she said.

I suppose it was a given that I would follow her because she didn't wait for my reply. We stepped through the crowd, weaving between the catatonic paranormals that had no idea what had happened, and probably never would.

When we reached the edge of the street where the clumps of people thinned and we could walk side by side without jostling anyone, the old woman finally spoke.

"I am going to tell you a story about two young women whose bad decisions changed the fate of the world for over a thousand years," she started. My skin broke out in goose-bumps, a combination of the chilled air and the mystery in her words.

"Valda?" I asked, hardly a whisper. She nodded, her silver hair reflecting in the moonlight.

"And me," she said.

I shuddered. *A thousand years?* The old Witch smiled, her kaleidoscope eyes changing from a deep purple to a wistful blue.

"A thousand years is only a blink in the life of our ancients, but it is longer than either of us were meant to stay." It was only then that I realized she was talking about her—Valda—in the present. A sickly sharp feeling pressed against my mind, but I didn't let myself think anything of it. Not until I heard what the Witch had to say.

"I have gone by many names across my time. Back then, I was known as Livina—it meant friend. Beloved. As Valda's personal servant, I was named by my mistress herself because I was also her friend, and in many ways, her only one." She paused, her eyes changing color again—to a rosy pink hue.

"Valda was a Konig, and heir to the strongest Supernatural house of the age. Their power was unrivaled by any because they were Nyx's Blessed. The matter manipulators that your world now considers legend—apart from you." My heart pattered on the precipice of a knowledge that would redefine me once again, should I believe this old Witch's tale.

"I've never heard of her house," I said and the Witch chuckled.

"History is written by the winners, or have you already forgotten what the current Fortescue has done in your name?" I bristled but didn't reply. She was right, and while it grated me, it served as a reminder that I had a lot more to learn.

I ducked my head and motioned with my hand for her to keep talking.

"She was just like you, you know?" the Witch continued. "Headstrong, opinionated, and loyal to a fault. She loved her people and wanted to rule, but her spirit was wild. Untamed. It shouldn't surprise you then that she was madly in love with a servant boy, but betrothed to a Fortescue, unbeknownst to her." Her face soured at the very mention of the current ruling family. People always said they'd been ruling for a thousand years, like that meant they'd always been ruling and would continue to.

Suddenly, it didn't seem so cut in stone.

"I can't imagine that went over well."

"It didn't," she said. Her eyes darkened to a crimson red with flecks of yellow and orange. "The day she went to tell her parents the truth, they told her she was betrothed—and executed her lover on the stairs beneath their thrones as a lesson to her." The Witch's face went grim, her purple cloak stirring in the breeze.

"That seems a bit harsh," I commented. The Crone shrugged.

"It was the times we lived in. As the Konig heir, Valda knew the risks and she chose to take them anyway, just as she chose to put her people first and go through with her parents arranged marriage—until she met him." She paused, her steps falling still as she looked to sky. "Cirian Fortescue was everything Valda would have loved in a life partner, had her parents not killed the one she loved. That alone wasn't enough to make her hate him. Cirian was Valda's signasti animam. Her soul-bonded partner. His mere existence made her love for the servant seem inconsequential, but the bond wasn't so consuming that it made her love him either. Instead, it took away her only love and made her feel hopelessly lonely—and desperate."

"Valda came to me the very night she met him and asked me to break the bond. She said that she would marry him, but only if I could break the bond. She needed to know that the choice was hers." The Crone paused, shaking her head in...regret? "Signasti bonds were considered sacred. It was banned for Witches to try to tamper with them, but Valda was my friend and I couldn't say no."

"I was only fifteen when I devised the spell that was meant to break Valda's bond. It was old magic that I had no business messing with, but I did, and it *cost us everything*." She blinked away any emotion from her face and replaced it with an impassive mask. "When I cast the spell, Valda and Cirian's bond changed. It didn't break, but weakened so much it drove them both mad. Valda already struggled with her sanity, and being the strongest matter manipulator ever born, she ended up trying to take her own life, but her body healed so fast she couldn't. I had to do something."

A slow creeping sensation ran through me at the eerie similarities between Valda and I. Was it coincidence? Maybe a younger version of me would have assumed so, but I didn't believe in coincidences anymore.

"I created a spell that was supposed to fill the void left by what I did to their bond. Something that would replace what was lost and make her whole, but something in the spell went wrong, and when she opened her eyes I realized what I'd done. I made her and Cirian demons, the first to ever be created—and the last.

"Not all demons are evil, but after suffering like they had, Valda and Cirian were ruthless. Without their humanity—and only memories of the darkness I'd put them in—Cirian became obsessed with Valda and wanting to claim her." She sighed, and it was a sound that was leaden by a thousand years' worth of grief and sorrow. "But Valda, without her emotions, she was not herself. She laid destruction on the world like it had never seen and hasn't since. Cities were decimated. Earthquakes followed wherever she went. She killed her own parents in a rage, and when Cirian came for her, she killed him too. The world was plunged into a dark age."

I could see it so clearly—the shadows that haunted her —the visions of destruction that ravaged the world. This was the reason that matter manipulators were feared beyond measure.

Earthquakes. Tsunamis. Wind storms. A single matter manipulator can change the world, but not for the better. Our gift was destruction.

"I prayed to the Three-faced Goddess for guidance and the ancients responded. Angered by my actions, they gave a single way out that would right the balance. A spell to bind her immortal soul to mine, so that when I sacrificed myself, we would both die. That was how it was supposed to be, but I was young...and a coward."

The Witch fell quiet for a moment, but I was at a loss for words. What exactly do you say to this? Clearly, she didn't sacrifice herself because she was standing before me. So, what happened?

"I thought that I could outwit the ancients. That I could still have everything. That Valda and I could both live, but the balance always has a way of righting itself." Still looking at the moon, she paused and turned her gaze to my face, and I could have sworn it wasn't me she was looking at, but someone that should be long gone. "I went to kill her, and instead found her in childbirth. As it turned out, she was pregnant from the lover her parents had killed months prior. I helped her deliver the baby, and while she was recovering in those minutes after, I stabbed her in the heart. I killed her hoping to kill the demon, but not myself, and in those moments after her death, I knew Valda was still there. She died in my arms while the baby slept not ten feet from us, and then I bound her soul in the way the Three-faced Goddess had taught me. For the third time, I defied the natural order of things. In attempting to bind her soul, I brought her back from the dead—and the ancients punished us for it. Valda's soul came back, but it did not bind to me. Instead, her soul clung to the only thing that still had meaning. Her child."

An unsettling calm fell over me as the sound of my heart beat heavily. Blood pumped through my veins, rushing to my head. I swallowed hard, trying to make sense of everything she was saying. To remember every word, because there was only one place this could be headed.

"And because Valda was soul-bonded, Cirian also came back. Unlike her, he did not have a child, but he had a younger brother he had once adored. Cirian's soul attached itself to his brother and Valda attached herself to the babe in my arms. I knew the moment it happened, and the consequences that ensued because of it."

My skin prickled as an unknown energy washed over me, but it was somehow familiar—exotic and powerful. It reminded me of damp woods and compact earth. Running through forests late at night. A nightmare I used to dream.

It reminded me of—

"Cirian, influencing his brother, persecuted the remaining Konigs. He laid waste to Valda's family and then removed every trace of them from history. After a hundred years, the name was no more than a legend, and after a thousand, the world has all but forgotten the matter manipulators that once ruled it."

"And Valda?" I asked. "What happened to her?"

Was I ready for this? To know this?

"Why don't you ask her," the Witch replied.

If I could have, I would have fractured on the spot.

"I don't know what you mean—"

"Valda's soul has traveled from mother to daughter for the last thousand years. It was her *curse*. The price she paid to Nyx for deaths she caused."

Suddenly, that familiar but strange energy inside of me was easy to pinpoint.

"Valda?" I asked, both fearing and already knowing who would answer.

"It's been a long time since I've heard that name. I must say, I do prefer Violet."

I shuddered, nearly falling to my knees in the dirt at the truth that now weighed on me. A thousand years. She watched her daughter, and her daughter's daughter, and so on and so forth— die—for a thousand years. I couldn't comprehend it.

There had to be more.

"And you? What price did you pay?" I asked, already fearing the answer.

"To bring two souls back, two had to die. I was the Maiden once, like your friend Milla is now. But in trying to save Valda, I killed the women who were then known as the Mother and the Crone—the two that embodied the Three-faced Goddess the most—and broke the cycle. I disobeyed the ancients. The Three-faced Goddess punished me by seeing to it that I would live as long as Valda and Cirian were bound to this earth, and because I was elevated to Crone—that is what I have remained. Just as Valda"—she paused and pointed a crooked finger at me—"became the Mother. The Witches know the cycle is broken, and they still tell their children of it, but the truth of what happened was lost in time." I frowned, thinking back. There were clues all along, but not enough that I had any hope of seeing them until now.

"This doesn't make sense. You said that everything has a balance. Cirian slaughtered the Konigs. What happened to him? What price did he pay?" I asked, outraged as much with myself for never asking as I was with them for what they'd done. The Crone smiled, but it was not a kind smile. It was strained.

"Just as Nyx cursed Valda, she cursed him. His soul has traveled from firstborn to firstborn down the Fortescue line and wrought unspeakable things in their name."

Without realizing it, we'd walked all the way to the end of the line and back. In front of me was the same crimson tent from earlier, where Tam conducted business. To the right of it, several yards off the beaten path, was the pit where Blair was fighting.

"For a thousand years, the Fortescues have held the rest of the world under their thumb, and you mean to tell me it is because of Cirian—because you couldn't accept the consequences of your actions?" My head felt hot and my body feverish as the anger made me sizzle with rage.

Still, all the Crone had to say was, "Yes."

"Why couldn't Valda tell me any of this?" I asked, throwing my hand out, wind followed its command blowing into the crowd of people and knocking them over.

Easy. Reign it in.

"Valda wasn't permitted to tell anyone who she was unless they already knew. The same as Cirian," she replied. She snapped her fingers once and a staff with a large glowing blue orb appeared in her hand.

"And you? You're the one that caused all of this," I said to her in a harsh voice. Angry on both Valda and Cirian's behalf. "Why haven't you found a way to end it? *What's your excuse?*"

The older woman didn't get angry. She didn't scream or yell. She didn't narrow her eyes. The Witch, the Crone, Livina, took a very deep breath and whispered hoarsely, "We've known since the beginning how to end our punishment. I'm staring at it."

My mouth fell open, but in between the tremble that took me and the questions that rattled in my mind—no words came out. I stumbled back.

When she had first appeared, there was a mischievous glint in her eye, but after her tale that glint was long gone. Only a bitter resentment, weary resignation, and staunch resolution remained. And perhaps, more than a little guilt.

But tears didn't glisten in her eyes when she said, "I'm sorry."

And before I could respond, she lifted her staff and brought it down onto the cold, hard dirt.

A bright blue light flared from the orb, blinding me temporarily. I blinked once, and she was gone. Every person in the paranormal market was a witness to the power this old woman yielded, but as I looked around—befuddled, pissed off, and without the answers I needed—I realized I was the only one who knew it.

CHAPTER 33

DEEDS THAT SHOULD HAVE NEVER BEEN DONE WEIGHED ON MY chest like an anchor did a ship.

Secrets that were now my burden to bear.

Lies that were now mine to tell.

I came back to this world swearing that things would be different. That I would be different. But stepping into the elevator after their fights that night, I didn't know how I was going to tell them the truth.

But I had to. I had to find a way.

The elevator pinged before the doors slid open to reveal the still quiet and sleepy Shifter residence. Through the arched windowpanes of glass, a steady stream of low light illuminated the third floor of the residence. Dawn. It was already a new day.

I said my goodbyes to everyone and walked back to my room with the sound of footsteps and Aaron's heartbeat following me. He sighed deeply, catching the living room door as it started to swing shut behind me.

"I know you're angry I didn't tell you."

Were we going to do this tonight? Have this conversation? I wasn't so sure I wanted that anymore. Not when I could barely think, let alone process everything the Crone told me. I shrugged, unzipping my leather jacket and tossing it over the back of the couch.

"I'm sure you had your reasons."

I kneeled down to undo the strings on my boots, peeling off my socks in the process. The hardwood floors were cold as stone against my bare feet. I walked around the loveseat to stand before the fireplace.

"What's that supposed to mean?"

I squatted down and reached into the fireplace with my bare hands to rearrange the logs. Hot embers flared, tickling my skin with their heat. I savored the warmth of the flame. Hoping it would keep the cold cruelty I was so accustomed to from creeping in and ruining everything.

"Nothing." I shrugged again. "It means exactly what I said. I'm sure you had your reasons."

"Really, Selena?" Aaron asked as his harsh voice cracked at my shields. "Are we really back to this bullshit?"

"I don't know what you're talking about," I said slowly, withdrawing my hands from the flame.

I didn't hear him move. I didn't sense the shift in matter soon enough.

But the scents of smoke and an untamed wind never lied.

Aaron carried an err of caution everywhere he went. A warning that very few could sense. He was not all that he seemed, but something more. Yes, he was the Shifter Heir. He was an Alpha and a Supernatural. But he was also my signasti.

And the signasti of a matter manipulator, as I was coming to learn, was not someone you should underestimate.

Not even if you were that matter manipulator.

"Don't lie to me," he snapped. "You were pissed off when you found out about me going down to the black market without you. Be angry. Yell at me. Curse. Whatever. But don't go back to this."

I should have known that out of everything I could have said or done, it was the nonchalance that would bother him most. He could probably hear the indifference in my voice as easily as I heard the barely contained fury behind his.

"What do you want me to say, Aaron?" I stood up and turned to face him, expecting him to be a few feet away and not inches from my face. The lines of his jaw were drawn. Hard.

"I don't care," he murmured. "I just want you to say something *real* because I've been worried out of my mind for the last four hours that I screwed up the progress we've made." He paused, swallowing hard. "That I've lost you again."

I didn't know how to respond to that. To tell him that yes, I was pissed, but I get it. I get it more than anyone. How hard it is to tell the people you care about that sometimes you feel a little crazy. Sometimes you need to do bad things for good reasons.

And sometimes...there was no easy way to tell the truth. So, you don't. You lie by omission and pray they never find out how truly twisted and dark your heart is.

I didn't know how to say those words.

But maybe I didn't need to.

Without overthinking it or what it meant, I leaned forward and closed the distance between us. Aaron froze when my lips first brushed his, but I didn't pull away. Slowly, achingly slow, I reached out and placed my hands on either side of his face, deliberately twining my fingers in his hair. I tugged sharply, pulling him closer.

And after the months of tension and build up, something snapped.

Aaron let out a masculine growl, full of longing, possession, and something wild. I clung to that. Clung to him, kissing him harder. His lips parted in invitation as he grasped my hips and picked me up.

I wrapped my legs around his waist, locking my feet behind him. He groaned in approval, his tongue sweeping forward to taste mine. I welcomed it. Hell, I embraced it. I encouraged it. I wanted it—wanted this. He'd stood by me when I despised him, hated him, tried to kill him, and rejected him. He defended me when no one else in their mind would.

He...loved me when I didn't know how to love myself.

How could I possibly not want him?

Even if he drove me absolutely crazy—and he did—quite often.

A doorway lined in gold appeared before me, and this time, I did not shy away.

Not when my back hit the bed or when I pulled Aaron onto it with me.

Not when I flipped our positions so that I was straddling him.

Not when he kissed me so thoroughly that my head spun.

I clung to him as the doorway loomed in my mind, beckoning me closer with every brush of skin. Every taste of ecstasy. Every touch that made my heart pound and my core throb.

Gods above, I *wanted* him.

Arching my back to draw myself up, my fingers skated down my sides to grasp the hem of my shirt. Aaron's smoldering gaze watched every movement with an unreadable expression. His hand reach out to hold mine and stop me.

"What are you doing?" I breathed, cocking my head.

"Making sure you know what you're doing *before* any clothes come off," he answered, husky and seductive. I leaned forward, resting my forearm just above his shoulder as I ground into him. The air hissed between his teeth as he inhaled sharply. "Selena..."

"The claiming," I replied breathlessly. "What does it entail?"

For a second, he stopped breathing and only stared.

And when he lifted his free hand to my hip to grab hold of me, there was a resolution in him. He flipped our positions again, using his strength to hold me underneath him because his weight wasn't enough. I smirked as he ground into me in return, tempting me in the most delicious of punishments for teasing him.

"Aaron," I moaned. It was a sound that no one had ever been able to bring from my lips. No one but him. He lifted a finger to silence me and trace my bottom lip's outline simultaneously.

"Ash," he corrected. "Call me Ash, please."

"Ash," I whispered. He nodded, staring at me like I was the sun and the moon and everything in between.

"If you're seriously considering this, then I want to do it right. I've been waiting too long to want it any other way," he whispered. Using his free arm, he ran his hand down my side and up the curvature of my leg wrapped around his waist—pulling me taut against him.

"Then tell me," I pushed. "Tell me what will happen if *I claim you.*" The words were a plea and a growl, warped by my own frustration at wanting more than the bits he was giving me.

"If we take each other this way, it will complete the bond." He lowered his head to the crook in my neck, brushing his lips against my pulse. "You will be my partner, my equal..." he paused to bite me softly and I gasped. "*My mate.*"

"Is that what you want?" I asked him. Aaron—Ash, lifted his head to look me in the eyes.

"Of course," he whispered without hesitation. My heart stuttered, unable to hold the emotion overwhelming it. "I don't just want to be your signasti. That's not enough for me. I want to be your best friend, your boyfriend, your lover, and *your mate.* I want to be everything that you will let me be."

That lingering ember inside my cold, lonely heart drifted in the scent of wind and smoke—catching fire. Could I hope? Did I dare?

"I want to love you every day for the rest of our lives, no matter how far apart this war may carry us. And I want you to know that even if every single person you have ever known fails you—I won't. I want to give you everything I have to offer," he said, and I knew what was coming next.

"But the real question is, will you let me? Do you want that too?"

My chest was a blazing inferno, waiting to unleash hell and havoc on this world.

But in that moment, I believed that if it did, he would stay and burn with me.

He wouldn't leave me like others had before him.

And he wouldn't force me to stay.

Somehow, Ash knew just how much to give and how much to take. In some ways, it was like he was made for me.

An ebony doorway loomed in front of me with golden light spewing from the edge around it.

I grasped the handle, shivering against the flash of warmth that rolled through me.

Our combined future sat on the precipice of my answer.

"Yes," I whispered. "I want *everything*. All of it."

Ash's lips crashed into mine as he rocked my body back and forth, one hand still gripping my thigh and the other kneading into my hair. I wrapped my arms around his neck, unable to stop myself from grabbing fistfuls of his shirt. My heart pounded as the door began shaking. At first, it was only a tremor.

But it grew to a quake.

And as the metaphorical door shook in my mind, my grip tightened. I tore his shirt off him, trying to hold in the power I could feel building inside of me.

"Ash," I groaned, breaking our kiss. While his slow sensual teasing heated me to my core, I didn't know how much I could take before an accident happened.

"Shhh..." he whispered, trailing his lips along my jaw. Patience wasn't my forte. I raked my nails along his back, letting him *feel* my need for him. He cursed and groaned under his breath, pressing into me harder.

"You're driving me crazy," I murmured as he moved his hands to the hem of my shirt. His fingertips brushed my skin just beneath the fabric and my breath hitched. He chuckled.

"Now you know how I feel," he quipped, tugging at the shirt. I arched my back off the bed for him to lift it over my head. He flung it aside, proceeding to kiss a path straight down my chest. "That's better," he whispered between my breasts. I angled my hips and he obliged by dipping his fingers into the waistband and his thumb flicked over the button of my jeans.

"You're sure about this?" he asked again, pulling back to slowly unzip my pants.

"Yes," I said without hesitation. He nodded, completely and utterly sure of himself as he started to peel my jeans away from my legs. I only wore plain cotton underwear and a bra, but he looked at me like it was the sexiest thing in the world.

I sat up, leaning back on my hands as I arched an eyebrow at him. "Your turn."

He grinned, sliding off the bed to remove his jeans and boxer briefs in the same fluid motion, and then produced a foil packet from the drawer in the nightstand.

"How long have those been in there?" I asked, more curious than anything. He stalked towards me, his eyes smoldering.

"Since we started sleeping in the same room."

Well then...

Ash climbed on the bed and came to rest between my

legs. With me sitting at an angle and him on his knees with a hand on the bed to either side of me, it was an oddly intimate position. Odd in that I didn't feel the need to run.

I reached up with one hand and grabbed him by the back of the neck, pulling him forward so I could kiss him. My body was a live wire and only his touch would ground it and shatter me wholly.

Ash groaned, pulling me to him and rolling simultaneously so that he was on his back while I straddled his torso. With him completely naked beneath me, I felt like I was wearing too many clothes.

I reached around myself and unhooked my bra with a sweep of my thumb. The straps fell limp from my shoulders, hanging in the crooks of my elbows. I pulled one arm out and it slid free off the other, falling to the floor.

"You're perfect," he whispered as I leaned forward and captured his bottom lip between my teeth.

"Don't go getting sappy on me now," I growled.

"I wouldn't dream of it." He chuckled, slipping his thumbs into the waistband of my panties. I shuddered at the hardness of him beneath me. I rocked back and forth twice before his patience finally exhausted itself and he tore the thin piece of fabric right off me.

I was so worked up I didn't complain and instead held out my hand for the foil packet. He passed it silently. I ripped the top open with my teeth and pulled out the condom, frowning when it didn't slip right on the first time and it occurred to me that I didn't have a clue what I was doing.

"Let me," he said. I handed it to him, ignoring the sly grin on his face. He pinched the tip and rolled it on smoothly. Then his hands dropped to the side as he let me make the final move.

I inched forward on his lap, wrapping my hand around his rigid length to hold him at my entrance. My body was shaking hard with need and desire, the pent-up frustration making his entrance slick and painless. My lips parted in an 'O' at the fullness of having him inside me.

He groaned, lifting his own shaking hands to my hips as he guided me up and down at a steady but relentless pace. I moaned deeply, losing control of my limbs as the tension built. The doorway in my mind was only seconds from blowing open if I didn't open it myself.

When my shaking became too violent, Ash rolled without missing a beat. He alternated between hard and fast, and slow, sensual teasing—somehow knowing when I was approaching the brink, and how to keep me from going over the edge. I ground my heels into the bed on either side of him, fighting against the pressure that was building inside of me. It was too much, too soon. It gathered so fast I didn't know how to diffuse it, but I couldn't stop.

I wouldn't stop.

The last thing I saw before I turned the handle with Ash's face.

And then my world shattered.

Golden light filled every corner of my vision as my very soul itself reached blindly into the void beyond the door—reaching for Ash. His soul was ready and waiting. It brushed against mine, just a single touch and everything clicked into place.

I didn't know where he started and I stopped. His

emotions were mine. Mine were his. We'd all but lost our form as the bond settled into place.

It was the flicker of pain laced with pleasure in my periphery that drew me back.

I cracked an eyelid open, vaguely aware that he was still inside of me and that pain, whatever it was, was already fading.

"I'm sorry. I didn't know whether that bite would happen or not," Ash murmured against my neck. I blinked my eyes, trying to think past how great I felt.

"What are you talking about?"

He lifted his head just enough I could see his lips. Was that blood?

"Did you bite me?" I deadpanned, no screaming or cursing. It would explain the brief pain. Ash grinned sheepishly, reaching a hand around to scratch the back of his head.

"Technically it's called marking," he said. "When a Shifter claims a mate, some of us have urges to 'mark' them. There's not a lot of choice involved on my part..." Ash pulled away from me and strut towards the bathroom. I noticed then the way every dresser drawer and fixture hung at odd angles. Clothes littered the floor. Three different lamps shattered.

"Did I do all of this?" I asked, brushing a hand against the tender flesh at my neck. It was already healing. There were some perks to being part demon. Being a matter manipulator? Less so, I was coming to find out. I still hadn't told him about the Crone.

Later, I told myself. *I'll tell him later.*

"I can only assume so. Considering how powerful we both are, I think this is pretty minimal damage." He appeared in the doorway of the bathroom donning a pair of loose fitting sweatpants.

"I suppose that's true..." I trailed off upon seeing the thin golden thread tethering us. I swept my hand through it, but nothing happened. "I guess we're bonded now," I said, letting my hand fall back to my side.

"Yes."

"It's not what I expected..."

"What did you think it would be like?" he asked, getting back into bed.

"I don't know. More intrusive, I guess." I shrugged, not bothering to get dressed or cover up. Ash laid on his side, watching me closely.

"That's because the only experience you seemed to have was when we were mentally communicating, or when you forced your presence into my mind. While those are things that we can do, and are easier now, I don't think it will be like that most of the time. The bond is different between every couple though, so it's hard to say for certain."

I frowned.

"Can you feel it? When I'm in your head?" I asked him. He sighed, seeming to consider how to answer that.

"Not really, no. I wouldn't have even known you could do it, had you not walked in on my meeting with Tam earlier," he said. He snaked an arm around my naked stomach, pulling me closer. My demon and I preferred it this way. The strain...god, I didn't realize how bad it was until it was gone.

"How do you know I didn't just hear you talking?"

"You may be a matter manipulator and part demon, but

your reflexes still aren't as good as mine." He chuckled and pressed a light kiss into my hair. "Also, Xellos put spells over that tent himself so that it was completely soundproof. There was only one way you could have known what we said."

"I see." I nodded, yawning loudly. As much as I wanted to talk, sleep was overcoming me faster than the events of the day. Tomorrow I could mull over everything and come clean, but tonight I was content just to sleep and know that Ash was there. Right where he said he'd be.

It didn't even occur to me what nightmares I would face in my dreams.

CHAPTER 34

He locked me away. He starved me when I couldn't perform.

He left me to die at the hands of one of his guards.

And now he wanted to sit before me like nothing had changed. Like he was still Victor, my rescuer from the dungeons. Like I was his perfect flower, the Supernatural turned Made that wanted to serve my 'master'.

I hated him.

Hated all of them.

They stole my life from me just when I was learning to live. Turned me into this monster—this thing—this horrible soulless, undead creature that preyed on children and the weak.

And now he wanted to sit before me like I should be kissing the ground he walked on?

I took a stuttering breath and averted my eyes like he preferred. Not because I gave a damn about pleasing them anymore, but because if I didn't...then they might see that I am not the fragile flower they'd like me to be.

They might see how deep my hatred runs. How much I loathe them.

They might see that there is darkness in my heart and they have fostered it. Fed it. Groomed it.

And now it has festered into this living, breathing thing inside of me—that one day very soon—was going to slaughter them all.

But I kept my head down and my mouth closed so that they didn't see it. After living in my sister's shadow for so many years, I was acutely aware of how much blind arrogance predators had. They saw the world in shades of black and white. Weak and strong.

They never stopped to think about those they placed beneath them.

Never bothered to analyze how strong us lessers truly were.

I wore downcast eyes and a timid demeanor the same way my sister wore her scars.

And Victor—cavalier, condescending Victor—he wore a cruel smile not realizing that I saw through it.

"I am happy to see you being so useful, flower. Your master is quite pleased." Victor's words were crisp, as planned and pressed as the white button-down shirt he wore. He drummed his fingers on the aged wooden table, leaning back in his fancy chair.

Everything here was so lavish. Expensive. You could stuff as many nice pieces of furniture in here as you wanted and it wouldn't change the stale air. It wouldn't fix the scent of mold and mildew that clung to me.

"Have I proven myself yet?" I asked him, crossing my ankles very ladylike. They were big on that here—women being submissive. At least with me.

"Proven yourself?" He asked it like a question, but I knew

better than to answer. I kept my eyes down, my back straight. "Do you think you have proven yourself my dear?"

I weighed my answer for only a brief moment because any longer would be seen as a hesitation, and he didn't like that. Hesitating meant you were thinking. That you were questioning your place in this world. Which was below them. The Born.

"I have only proven myself if you think I have. If not, I must try harder," I replied, careful to keep my voice somewhere between apathetic and pleasant. They didn't like obvious groveling. It was weak. True apathy was not good either, it meant you couldn't be easily controlled. Easily mind washed.

And they only wanted the best of puppets.

Those that lay somewhere in between and had a healthy amount of respect and obedience, but were competent enough to do what they wanted without question. It was a fine balance to strike, but where I did not possess sheer power, I possessed intellect and a will to survive.

And I would survive this, even if I had to kill every last one of them to do it.

"You know, Lily..." Victor paused. He leaned forward, resting an elbow on the table. "You somehow always know just what to say to please me. I was so worried that you would be difficult, given the Supernatural family you stem from, but you have been a surprising treasure to behold."

This was high praise from a Born to a Made. He was testing me to see how I'd react.

"Thank you, Victor," I regurgitated, adding a touch of false sincerity to make it sound believable.

"You're very welcome, flower," he murmured almost affectionately. Darkness crept through my veins, waiting for its next victim. "I am so pleased by the progress you have made and your *willingness to embrace your new life, that I am going to offer you a deal."*

Behind me, the door opened, but I did not look. A sound like the pattering of wings filled my ears, and with it came the scent of something sweeter. Something more potent than wine.

I inhaled deeply, red glinting the corners of my vision instantly.

Victor motioned with his hand for whoever stood there to come forward. The footsteps were so slight, so...I had to mentally force myself not to flinch when I saw the red-haired child. She was younger than the others they'd brought to me. No more than six or seven.

Her porcelain skin and warm brown eyes...

She was meant to look like Alexandra.

And she'd achieved it.

"I have one last test to ask of you, flower."

Victor reached for the girl, cupping his palm around her cheek. She didn't flinch, but I'd long since learned they trained them not to. They didn't like their dinner stinking of fear. I stared into her hauntingly familiar eyes.

"Anything," I replied without emotion.

"Save her."

Wha—

He slit her throat using the edge of his fingernail. Before I could school my reaction, scarlet spilled down her puffy white dress, the scent of blood everywhere.

It covered her clothes and the floor and the table between us.

Red droplets stained my hands. They flecked my powdered blue shirt. Clung to my skin, bathing me in the very substance that held me prisoner in my own body.

Save her. That's what he'd commanded me to do.

He didn't think I could. That either my ability or my hunger would fail me.

Oh, how wrong he was.

Victor didn't realize that I had developed a taste for not just blood, but Vampire's blood, and after being starved, I would not break so easily again.

Only a fraction of a second had passed. Inhaling a tight breath, I reached out with a single hand and wrapped it around the girl's slender throat. She scratched at my fingers. Clawed at my wrist. Her child's strength was useless when held at the mercy of a monster like me.

The darkness leapt forward. A seductively sinister power slithered across my skin like a living, writhing thing. I pushed the energy outwards, forcing it into her skin. Searching deeper than her flesh or bones, to the source of her life force—her energy —and melded my own with her.

Masking my own power within her so that her body did not recognize it as a foreign force when I pushed the broken and hurting parts back together.

Pushed—until there was nothing beneath my fingers but smeared blood against unblemished skin and a steady pulse.

I dropped my hand away, sitting back against my ornate chair like the obedient Made that Victor wished me to be. I hoped this would be enough of a show for him. That he wouldn't demand more of me, more of my soul, in return for a chance at escape.

But fate had never been kind to those of us that had to work for our place in life.

"Well done, my flower," he murmured leaning back. "Well done indeed."

He rose swiftly from his chair to stand behind the young

child, resting his palms on her shoulders. Her eyes fell closed as she leaned against him for support. Ordinarily, the children knew better, but the exhaustion of almost dying wiped it out of her and Victor allowed it.

"Thank you. I have learned a great deal of control so that I may be more useful." *My voice had a pleasantly bored tone. We could have been talking about the weather. Here, there wasn't a lot of difference.*

"You've proven you have both the restraint not to lose yourself around blood and the control to use your ability without pressure..."

His eyes darkened at the mention of my near rape. Victor had been quite pleased at the rather gruesome end his guard had found. He didn't like others touching me. Handling me. His possessiveness should have frightened me, but it only served my purposes further.

"But I do have one last thing to ask of you," *he continued. If I had a heart it would have dropped, but I was already dead and trying to survive in a land of horrors.*

I raised my eyes to his, unflinching from what I knew was coming.

"Kill her."

And there it was.

The order that would either haunt me or define me for the rest of my days.

I had to choose.

Freedom or chains.

Murder now or murder later.

Survive or risk something worse than death...

When you are alone in a strange place with no one but yourself and your own thoughts to judge you, the line between right and wrong blurs quite easily. When killed, enslaved against your own will, starved and tortured...there is no line.

No one came for me. No one is coming.

There is only me and my freedom. Everything that stands between it are consequences that I will have to pay.

The ends will justify the means.

Because I've lived through too much not to survive this too.

I reached for the child and the darkness grew. She looked so much like Alexandra. That should have bothered me.

It should have.

But it didn't.

I WOKE, drenched in a cold sweat. Shaking. Screaming. My fingers clawed at the soft expensive sheets, shredding through them like an animal.

I tried to jump to my feet, but the weight holding me down trapped me, pushing me into the mattress. I let out another animalistic scream in fury and pain.

Footsteps. I heard footsteps running, racing, as the bed creaked beside me. Every sound was a battering ram to my brain. Chaotic. Angry. Disorienting.

My head swam with the thoughts, feelings, and sensations of someone else. Someone that was supposed to be dead. Logic and reason told me it was nothing.

Just a nightmare.

Just a dream.

I'd long since learned that not everything that was real could be logically explained, and somehow, someway, I just knew.

And it utterly destroyed me.

The bedroom door came flying off its hinges, and before I could register the whos or whats, I acted. My palm thrust outward, fingers curled inward as I slashed at the person holding me down. They held firm and terror seized me. Like a puppet on a string, I couldn't stop myself from what came next as I launched a full-frontal assault.

The canopy above broke apart into infinitesimal pieces of the lush gold fabric it once was. They swirled round and round like a sandstorm that came out of nowhere. The wooden bed posts broke off and went flying. All four of them circled the bed like a pack of dogs waiting for the kill. Drawers opened and closed so hard the wood began to crack and splinter like the pieces of my soul.

And amidst it all, was me, trembling so hard that I couldn't make sense of the scene before me.

I screamed with the pain and anguish of that night.

I screamed for a sister that was supposed to be dead.

I screamed because deep down I knew, and I hadn't come for her.

I screamed...because it was too late.

And when my voice broke, the wind itself responded.

Howling and screaming in my stead.

"SELENA!"

That voice. I knew that voice.

He repeated my name again and again and again. No quieter than the first time. Hands touched my shoulders, my face, my chest. It wasn't a sexual touch, but a soothing one. He was rubbing at the black and purple tendrils swirling across my skin.

"Breathe with me." He spoke firm. Controlled. Not a

trace of fear within him as he breathed in and out beside me, coaching me down from this ledge that I had placed us all on.

The winds outside quieted as my breathing slowed and my heart followed with it, but from inside—inside the residence—people were screaming.

"Talk to me. Tell me what's going on inside your head."

I stilled, breathing slow and steady as I listened to screams and footsteps below.

"She's alive," I rasped. Ash looked at me like I'd grown another head.

Of course, that was the moment that people would come barging into our room. Not that the hole in the wall where I'd taken the door off provided much privacy.

"For fuck's sake—you better have a good excuse for this, Selena."

CHAPTER 35

"I'M NOT SURE IF I SHOULD ASK ABOUT HER LACK OF CLOTHES FIRST or why every window in the residence was just blown out..." Amber stalled, her eyes flicking over the rumpled sheets and Ash's missing shirt. A wide inappropriate smile lit her face. "No fucking way. You guys—"

"They're bonded," Johanna finished for her.

Awkward silence ensued where I mentally forced the bed posts to drop in their circling and pulled the sheet close, folding and fashioning it to cover my naked body. The end product was a gold toga styled dress, and while it wasn't the most practical of garments, it certainly beat wearing the sheet like some kind of blushing virgin.

Bonded or not, I was not letting them give me shit.

"Are we supposed to congratulate them or somethin'?" Tori asked, wrapping an arm around Alexandra's waist. My sister said nothing, her face an unreadable mask as she flicked her eyes between Ash and me.

"That depends," Johanna replied tersely. "Was your

shift in power caused by this"—she waved her hand between us, wrinkling her nose—"or something else?"

Amber started cackling like a fucking hyena.

"Dude, if you guys literally broke the mansion fuc—"

Tori leaned away from Alexandra to stomp on Amber's foot. She yelped and snapped her mouth shut, her eyes slitting to cat irises as she glared at Tori who proceeded to ignore her.

"Something else," I said quickly, not just wanting to steer the conversation away from Ash and I, but needing to focus on the problem at hand: telling them my sister wasn't dead and coming up with a way to get her back.

"What happened?" Blair asked, cutting straight to the point. She stood separate from the group, her arms crossed over her chest. Not terribly surprising given that Alec had stationed himself just beyond the gaping hole in the wall.

"She..." I started and stopped three times. Unsure how to say it. Unsure where to start.

Telling lies are easy, but the truth...the truth is hard.

Telling your friends and family that you'd been having nightmares of your dead sister for months? Few things were harder.

Telling them that you believed she was alive—after months of being called mad—well, that was worse.

I pushed away from Ash, climbing off what was left of our bed. Fabric bits and wood chips clung to the simple dress as I slid over the edge. My legs were remarkably steady for the pounding in my chest. Heat flushed my skin, making my head throb and my neck burn.

I faced the fireplace at the foot of bed, looking at none

of them as I tried to say the words that were going to change everything.

"She's alive."

Silence, from all but one.

The one I should have told from the very beginning.

After all, she was her sister too.

"Who's alive?" Alexandra asked. Emotion thickened her voice with a barely contained—fury? Pain? I couldn't tell, but I knew by the way she asked that Alexandra knew exactly who I was talking about. Still, she was going to make me say it.

"Lily."

A harsh intake of breath. A gasp. Gritted teeth. Exasperated sighs. None of their responses were unexpected. I myself hadn't wanted to admit it. For months, I'd tiptoed around my dreams. Acknowledging them as nightmares, but not wanting to admit to myself what I was seeing. Lily, my dead sister, was somehow alive. Not breathing. But not dead.

"Selena..." Alexandra started. Her voice shook. From my periphery, I could see her hands trembling as she took a step towards me. "That's not...possible. I was there. I saw her die. I, like, *saw* the building collapse—"

"She was bitten. She was bitten *so many times*." My voice almost broke, but it didn't. "How likely is it that it was only the Made? That she wasn't bitten by the Born and transitioned?"

I twisted my fingers together, trying to sort through this mess of emotions and find reason. An explanation for how I was seeing what I was. Ash placed his hand over mine. I looked up right as he spoke.

"Even if she did—how could you know? She hasn't contacted you. There's been no trace of her since that night." He wasn't wrong, but that didn't make him right either.

"I have nightmares—about her. About when she woke and what they did to her. How they trained her. She's been so smart, so brave..." My voice cracked like panes of glass, but I could not break again. I couldn't afford to break. Not when my sister was out there somewhere. Waiting for me.

I took a stuttering breath, squatting down. I rocked forward onto my knees to sit in front of the fire. It comforted me—melting the shard of ice in my chest that hurt so bad it was difficult to speak.

I couldn't choke up now.

"Breathe," Violet whispered. *"I'm with you."*

As odd as it was, her being a soul and all, I found comfort in that.

Enough so that my chest loosened and I began to speak, recalling those days after Daizlei's collapse. The nightmares that plagued me. I talked about Lily and Victor. How he pulled her from a dungeon just to chain her in other ways. How the Vampires used children to train her—to break her. How they starved her, and beat her, and would have done worse—had she not defended herself. I talked about the ticks and tells that she'd unwittingly told me of Vampire society. I spilled her private thoughts and fears and dreams with them.

And by the end of it, a single tear had escaped my watering eyes, silently sliding down my cheek. But I had told them the truth—almost all of it.

All except the darkness that had long been settling in.

"Those are nightmares, girl. They're not rea—" Oliver started to say. I clenched my hands into fists, digging my nails into my palms. I wouldn't plead or beg him or anyone to understand, but I wasn't yielding either.

"She's telling the truth."

It wasn't Ash that spoke, or even Alexandra.

It was Johanna.

"You can't possibly believe her, Jo—"

"I can, and I do," she replied sternly. "You should know by now not to discredit something just because you don't understand it. As Jayma would say, we live in an impossibly possible world." Oliver flinched like he'd been slapped. Whoever Jayma was, I got the impression she wasn't around anymore.

"Be that as it may," Alec interjected, "how do you know this isn't just in her head? She may believe what she's saying, but that doesn't make it true."

Given that his abilities lie in making people see something that's not actually there, I couldn't be terribly offended by his questioning.

"My sister is alive," I murmured hoarsely in response. "*Lily is alive.* And you have no reason to believe me. I have no proof, no evidence whatsoever, only what I see when I'm sleeping. But I know..." I paused to swallow the lump in my throat. "I *know* she is alive."

I didn't look at them. Any of them. Not Ash. Not Alexandra. Not Blair.

Because if I had to see one more person look at me like I'm crazy *after* I had completed the bond—I really would snap.

"I believe her," Blair spoke up. I wasn't sure if it was in

direct correlation to Alec's questioning, but Blair never sided with anyone without considering the facts. "Just because we can't explain it doesn't mean it's in her head. We are part demon, and yet no one knows how that is possible. Lily was also part demon. We have no idea how her powers could have grown if she was changed."

No one could deny Blair's reasoning as much as I could tell they wanted to. Because if that was true, if Lily truly was a Made now—she would be strong enough to make our world tremble in her wake. In her rage.

"Can a Supernatural-part-demon even become a Made?" Ash asked. No one had the answer.

"We possess at least some of the same DNA as a Born Vampire. Who is to say that we don't become something else entirely? That she hasn't become something else..." I couldn't let myself finish that. No matter my nightmares. No matter the evidence before me.

She was Lily. My Lily.

And I would not give up on her. Alive. Dead. Undead.

"Don't do that to yourself. Even if she did survive, somehow changed, she never possessed any form of telepathy and she'd be communicating over hundreds of miles, if not thousands. Not even demons can do that."

"No," Johanna agreed. "Demons cannot, but the Mother can."

The Mother...

How had I not even considered that? The Crone herself told me that Valda was the Mother. In my ignorance, I hadn't thought to really ask her what that meant. I hadn't even considered that being a possibility. Instead, I assumed, like Ash and Blair, that whatever happening was coming from Lily. Not me.

Certainly not Valda.

"The Mother lost to time," I breathed, recalling a memory from those first moments after I'd woken after Daizlei. Isn't that what Johanna called me?

"Yes," Johanna nodded.

"I'm sorry, but are we really considering old Witch tales?" Alexandra asked. Her feet tapped restlessly as she looked at the ceiling. "The Mother? She's like...as much a legend as the Crone and the Three-faced Goddess." She pulled away from Tori and began to pace.

"Now, yes," Johanna said. "But it hasn't always been that way. And if the legends are true..." Johanna's golden-eyed gaze swept my way, eyeing me with curiosity and no small amount of certainty. "Then we are on the cusp of a new age. Selena carries the soul of the Mother."

Alexandra frowned, and she wasn't the only one.

This was my moment. My chance to come clean all the way.

Tell them about the Crone.

Tell them the story she told me.

Tell them about Valda.

I opened my mouth to speak and—

Silence.

I tried again, but no words would come out. My vocal cords would not work.

Something was wrong—something was—

"I am sorry you must share this burden, my daughter. I'm so sorry," Violet whispered. I blinked and the world swayed.

"No. No. This can't be happening. I have to tell them—"

"They do not know; therefore, you cannot tell them. That is our curse."

Our curse? No. That was her curse. Her and the Crone and Cirian. They were the ones that messed up the world. They were the ones that caused this.

If Ash learned that I knew...if Alexandra found out somehow...if Johanna thought I lied to them...

I swallowed hard and stilled myself. A hand touched my back and I turned to Ash. "Are you alright?" he asked, drawing me back to them. In my mind, Violet hung her head in sadness, and while I was angry with her, this was not her fault. Not really.

"I will be," I said quietly to him before focusing on the conversation. I had to focus. I had to keep going.

"But that's not *possible*—" Blair said.

"We live in an impossibly possible world," came Oliver's reply. She ghosted him with a chilly sweeping glance that almost made me want to snicker.

"How do you know?" Amber asked, speaking up louder than the others. I stayed silent.

"Witch blood runs in my veins, and while I've never been able to master their magic, the Three-faced Goddess has accepted me as her child. Which means"—she paused, her eyes flashing bright as molten gold—"I, just like any other Witch, can recognize the Goddess's chosen vessels."

"But I'm not the Mother," I said slowly, testing how far this invisible boundary would go. "I just carry the soul of her. What does that mean?" I was dancing a fine line between drawing information out of Johanna and incriminating myself by asking questions I shouldn't know to ask.

Not that Johanna seemed to notice. She cupped a hand

to the side of her neck, making her long sleeve shirt fall an inch short of her wrist, giving the briefest hint of scales curled around it. I tilted my head to get a better look and she dropped her hand, crossing it behind her back *almost* nonchalantly.

"That depends on whether you believe 'old Witch tales' or if you think the 'other' you talk to is a hallucination, now doesn't it?"

I couldn't say for certain, but there was a dry snark in the way she said it. Almost like she was angry or amused, maybe a bit of both.

I tucked my toes under, rocking my weight back to stand on my own two feet. Moving to stand beside Ash, I became hyper-aware of the eyes that followed my every move.

"I think that when you can control matter itself, nothing is impossible. I know that my sister is alive, but I have no proof to explain how. If you do, then I'm all ears." I crossed my arms over my chest and nodded for her to continue.

"Every paranormal has a deity they look to in times of need. For the Witches, that is the Three-faced Goddess. Maiden. Mother. Crone. Past. Present. Future. She is balance in all things. A neutral entity, unlike most other ancients."

I don't know if she meant to project her voice so that it wove magic into every word, but as she spoke, the air itself seemed to quiver and listen.

"Just as Nyx had her blessed," Johanna motioned to me, "and the Consort had his heirs," she looked to Ash, "the Goddess had her vessels. Young women—Witches—born of immense power. This vessel would grow from a child to that of a woman, and when the Crone died, and the Mother took her place, so would the Maiden take the Mother's, and a new Maiden would be born. This was the way of the Goddess. Birth. Life. And ultimately, death." As she spoke, pieces of what the current Crone—Livina—told me, began to fall into place.

"To be born as the next Maiden was considered the greatest honor, and the greatest sacrifice. These Witches can harness an immense amount of power, but all magic has a cost. The vessels of the Goddess were born with the magic to save lives or end them, but to do so would cost them their own life."

A sickly sort of creeping began to make its way up my spine. Almost like déjà vu, but worse. It was the sense of knowing what was coming, knowing it, but not admitting it.

The balance...

"Yes," Johanna agreed. I must have spoken it out loud. "The balance. This is what separates Witches and the Three-faced Goddess from the other ancients of old. Nyx chose to favor power. The Consort chose might. The dragon chose honor. But the Three-faced Goddess chose balance. She gave her vessels power to protect the Witches should there ever come a time, but with a cost. This was to prevent Witches from growing too bold and forgetting their roots. Forgetting the balance."

Like Livina did when she brought back Valda and Cirian.

But I couldn't say that.

"A thousand years ago, a young Witch walked the earth

as the Maiden. Even for a vessel of the Goddess, she was born with exceptional power. Some might say too exceptional, and that the balance was broken when she was born. Others will tell you it was her choices that broke the balance and doomed the Witches—and the world—to a thousand years of darkness."

That was one hell of an understatement. Bad choices?

She tried to break a signasti bond, then create a replacement, and proceeded not to heed an ancient's warning—oh, and let's not forget the bringing back the dead part.

But once again, I couldn't say anything.

"What did she do that broke *the balance*?" Alexandra asked with no small amount of sarcasm, but perhaps a little curiosity. She may not believe Johanna just yet, but she wasn't outright discrediting her.

"She created a monster and the Three-faced Goddess demanded that she slay the beast and take her own life as payment. She didn't listen, but that itself wasn't what broke the balance. It was when the Supernatural families of the time killed the beast, and she not only brought it back from the dead, but its child as well."

Wait a fucking minute—a monster? That's what they thought?

She didn't just create a monster—she created a demon. That's skipping over all the fun bits about how she fucked Valda and Cirian over, meanwhile saving herself.

But the baby? That part was new. Livina told me that it was bringing back Valda and Cirian's *soul* that caused the punishment. She never said the baby died.

Did that mean she brought three people back? Or two?

Is this just the version that has been passed to Jo, but the Crone told me the truth?

"This young Witch had taken the steps to save herself and bring back two from the dead, not accounting for the balance, but all magic has a cost. When someone kills a vessel of the Goddess, she exacts her revenge sevenfold, but what do you think happens when the Maiden—a vessel of the Goddess—uses magic that takes the lives of both the Mother and Crone?" Johanna paused to let that sink in. "The Three-faced Goddess was so infuriated that she punished not just this girl, but the Witches as well. The legends say that she sentenced the Maiden—now the Crone—to walk until the end of days, allowing only the Maiden to be reborn as a reminder to her children that they still have a future that is bright, should the Mother ever return to set the present right."

I wasn't sure if the story Johanna told was kinder or not. Both of them made the Three-faced Goddess out to be a bit of a...well, Witch.

"You say set the present right," Blair said slowly. "What does that mean?" Her stormy grey gaze flicked to me. I couldn't tell whether she believed all of this or not.

"For her to restore that balance, she would have to push the darkness back. Not destroy it entirely, but right the scales. To do that, the Three-faced Goddess said it would be this descendant that would slay the children of the monster her vessel created and return what was lost."

My heart stopped beating.

My head spun.

I staggered back a step, wanting to run, to hide. To

unhear what I just heard, because she had to be wrong. Johanna had to have her story mixed up.

If what she said was true, and I had to kill the descendants of Valda's...

I was going to be sick.

My feet moved on their own accord, lurching forward towards the bathroom. My arms batted at the hands that tried to stop me. My shoulders pushed them aside as my bare feet ran. I hit my knees hard on the tile floor, hunching over the toilet.

Warm hands pulled my hair away and secured it behind my head. As it was, shudders racked my body. My palms sweat. My head pounded. My stomach heaved, but nothing came up.

Fear, real and sharp as I was strong, ate at me.

If what Johanna said was true, if I was destined to kill Valda's descendants, then...

I was destined to kill my sisters and myself.

And I couldn't speak a word of it.

Strong hands kneaded my shoulders. Ash was sweet. Kind. He gave me the benefit of the doubt when I didn't deserve it, and never asked why. Even now he didn't ask. He simply sat with me without demanding a single goddamn answer.

Voices drifted from outside the door. "—clearly it's not just some story if Selena's in the bathroom throwing up—" That was Blair. Always the observant one.

"Maybe not, but what does this have to do with her knowing Lily is alive?" Alexandra asked. I rested my cheek against the edge of the bathtub. Wanting to scream and shout but knowing it would do no good. Now was not the time to get angry about ancient prophecies that may or may not be true.

"The Mother was the seer of all things present. The guardian of time as it was happening. It is not unreasonable to assume Selena is seeing what your sister is going through while she is sleeping. When Milla was younger, she used to dream things before they happened. I think Selena is experiencing the same." That was Johanna again. I curled my fingers around the bathroom tub, bracing myself as I sat up, pushing against the smooth surface to haul myself to my feet.

Lily needed me. Ancient prophecy or not.

I could handle the processing of this later, after I've spoken with the Crone again.

If my gut was right, and it always was, last night would not be the last I saw of her.

"—what now?"

"How do we go about finding her?"

"If she was bitten and turned, she will be with her sire—"

"What was his name again?"

All eyes turned to me, as I stood in the doorway between the bathroom and disastrous bedroom. The tile floor felt like ice against my bare feet. I crossed my arms, barely containing a shiver from the cold that threatened to hold tight and not let go.

But I couldn't let that happen.

They would just think I was losing it again and Lily would die in that hellhole.

"She was never told who her master was. Victor wanted her to prove herself first."

Johanna nodded grimly. "That's not uncommon for Made that are brought over by Born who are higher up in the pecking order. She'd have to have a sire that's powerful enough to control her, maybe even someone on the High Council..." She did that thing again where she cupped her neck, her brows furrowing.

"How on earth would we go about finding her—" Amber started.

"Maybe we don't have to," I said abruptly. All eyes turned to me. "Maybe we just need to lure one person out."

"Why do I get the feeling I'm not going to like who this person is?" Amber groaned.

"If it's who I think she's thinking—you won't," Blair sighed.

"You want to lure out Anastasia," Alexandra said. Not quite accusing, but she certainly wasn't happy.

"I do." She shook her head, looking away. Blair looked at the floor, weariness tugging at her. We were in an impossible situation, but to a matter manipulator, anything was possible with enough motivation.

My sister was out there somewhere. That was all the motivation I needed. This prophecy shit could wait for another day.

"And how do you plan on going about that?" Oliver asked, clearly not understanding mind games the way I did.

Anastasia took everything from me. My freedom. My life. My sister.

She impersonated me and let the world blame me for something she did.

She wore my face as a mask and a shield.

And now, I was going to return some of that.

I was going to take the only thing she had left. The only thing I knew would lure her out from whatever hole she crawled into these past few months. Because I needed her for answers and as a trade. It would be my pleasure to watch all of her carefully crafted lies come apart around her as I took away her greatest prize and let it become her downfall.

Her reputation.

"How fast can you get me a box of blue contacts?"

CHAPTER 36

Standing in the center of the pit was a strange and familiar experience.

I could almost pretend I was boxing. That this was just another match. That Lucas would be coming right around the corner any moment now. That Ash was just the boy from the gym that saw too much. That Lily would be in the crowd with Alexandra, cheering for me.

But none of those things were true anymore, and they certainly weren't true this night.

The dirt still stank of fear and wrongdoings. Blood and bits of Vampires covered the walls, the floor—leftover from Blair's *fight*. But who was I to criticize?

Who was I to say what was right or wrong when my hands were so unclean that I didn't remember what they looked like without blood on them?

No one. That was who. And if I had my way, that's who I would fight as.

"You ready for this?" Ash asked from the edge of the pit above me. To anyone else he would probably look like he was talking to himself. They certainly wouldn't hear my reply.

"Yes." It was instantaneous and without hesitation. I meant it.

"Don't lose yourself," he murmured. The door to my left opened. I felt it. Whoever they brought out, the crowd went wild. Their cheers were thunderous. Wild. Savage. I took a deep steadying breath, clenching and unclenching my fists.

Blood. Sweat. Tears.

This is where I was made.

"You'll pull me back," I muttered. It was the last thing I said to him as I turned to meet my opponent. Alexandra's flaming red hair caught the corner of my eye, but I didn't stare too long. I couldn't. Not when I had a game of cat and mouse to play.

His eyes were dark, unbelievably dark. Not black like Ash often turned his, but instead the darkest shade of green. His skin was pale in the bright moonlight, reflecting like the surface of a pearl, complementing his silver hair.

It made the smudge of black around his lips stand out even more.

Blood. Vampire's blood.

The very blood that ran in my sister's veins.

The blood I was going to spill as a sacrifice to whatever dark god would listen.

"Gregory Kamarov," a Shifter said over us, outside the pit. Unlike all the other fights I'd seen, Gregory had two guards escorting him and neither of them were the ones speaking. "Born Vampire and cousin to Ivan the Cruel," the dark-haired Shifter above said before pausing. Was that fear in his eyes?

No wonder the Born looked so fucking smug. He had immunity for all intents and purposes—except this one. I suppose no one took the time to tell him that it wasn't the Supes or the Shifters that apprehended him—but the flaming gay mob alpha of the Las Vegas pack.

Who operated only in business that was strictly off the books.

Like conducting an unofficial execution.

"Gracing us with her presence in a special turn of events —" The announcer paused for dramatic effect. With my blue film covered eyes and cold sneer, I wore the perfect mask. Staring up at the paranormals surrounding the pit like they were somehow beneath me. Unworthy of my attention. No one would ever know. No one but her, that is. "Council Member, Anastasia Fortescue!"

The Born Vampire blinked and narrowed his eyes. "Wait a minute—"

"Supernaturals. *Subjects*," I pronounced clear and precise. My voice rang with the same condescending clarity Anastasia liked to use. "I am standing here before you because I have been away too long. In my absence, certain *species* have felt they could get away with anything. That they are invincible. Untouchable."

Murmurs broke out above me and inside a fissure of hope sprung. A crack in my chest...because it was working. They really believed me. They believed I was Anastasia.

She's going to be furious.

"It'll make her that much more desperate to rush into something. We'll be ready," Valda assured me. The breath hissed between my teeth as I sneered at the Vampire before me. He

tried to open his mouth again to object, but I telekinetically kept it shut.

Panic clouded his vision. Feeding me. Feeding the show.

"Let me remind you that *I* am the only invincible being on the face of this planet, and as such, it is my *divine duty* to uphold the natural order of things." I motioned for the guards to release him. They undid his shackles and removed the collar from his neck. Meanwhile, the Vampire didn't say a word. He physically couldn't.

"Gregory Kamarov, you conspired in the plot to overthrow a Supernatural Institution and that offense will *not* go unnoticed."

"Did he go before the Council?"

"Does the High Council know?"

"Since when do Supernaturals exact punishments on other species?"

The rumors circled round and round, building traction. Building momentum.

By the end of the night, every paranormal in the market would know what happened here.

And by tomorrow, Anastasia would know.

I am alive. I am fighting.

I am coming for my sister.

She can only hide so long before the damage is irreparable.

"As such, you can die with honor, or fight me—as futile as that will be." The Vampire's eyes flicked to the crowd. He was going to run.

Excellent. This was going according to plan.

"Choose," I commanded. He flashed me a wicked smile, moving as he did so.

Vampires were considered the fastest paranormals out there, apart from demons, that is. Knowing that, I moved with exaggerated slowness to dodge him. He took the bait, doubling behind to backhand me. I ducked under his arm, stepping into his chest.

The Born blinked in surprise but recovered quickly.

His right hand shot out to grab me, but I kneed him in the groin and shoved him away, giving myself enough room to step back so I could redouble with a roundhouse kick to the head. He narrowly escaped, allowing me to clip him just hard enough so he had the opportunity to rethink fighting me.

As it was, I had to slow myself down and fumble on attacks so I didn't *accidentally* kill him.

As lovely as that would be, he served a greater purpose alive.

The Born backed away hissing, his nose wrinkling in disgust.

"We had a deal," he breathed. A warning, hardly more than a whisper. I didn't know what the exact deal she struck with them was, but he didn't seem to know that.

"Deals can change," I replied. I spoke just loud enough that my voice carried on the wind. More murmurs traveled through the crowd as our small exchange caught on like wildfire.

"I'll be sure to let Ivan know that's how you *feel*," he sneered back coldly.

"What—" I asked dumbly, internally applauding my own performance. Not only did the crowd believe I was her, but so did this bloke.

Was it too much to think that luck may be on my side for once?

I pretended to be slow, then stunned when he turned and jumped for the gap that just magically appeared in the crowd. Shouts of outrage. Cries of dismay. The black market took only a moment to explode into complete and utter chaos. Tam's Shifters had been carefully placed further from the ring than normal—because Anastasia requested it. She wanted to deal with the Vampire on her own, of course. This both protected the Shifters and made for the perfect getaway. If my gut was right, it wouldn't take him more than a minute to lose them. No more than five to be a scent on the wind.

I leapt from the pit, landing beside Ash, hoping and trusting that with all the commotion Alec would fulfill his job to disguise me from the masses.

"Do you think I pulled it off?" I murmured, hoping he could hear me above the madness.

"Look around."

People were already turning and looking for Anastasia. Whispering about the weak Head of Council that couldn't defend her people and let a Vampire go, while simultaneously calling her a hypocrite for trying to execute a Born Vampire that was practically royalty.

This didn't sit well with the paranormals of the black market, but it was nothing compared to the shitshow that would be starting up all over the world once people heard the news.

Paranormals looked every which way for me—for Anastasia—for the Supernatural Head of Council, but no one saw me standing there among them. Not when Alec had made me just another face in the crowd. They saw what he wanted them to see, and the powerful, invincible, untouchable Anastasia Fortescue was long gone.

Finally showing the rest of the world the coward she really was.

CHAPTER 37

Ten minutes.

That's how long it took me to realize that I was different than the other Made as Victor walked me out of my room, arm-in-arm. For me to notice the quiet looks of envy. They were my first inclination something wasn't quite right.

Two hours.

That's how long it took for me to put together that Victor was more powerful than I'd originally thought. He wasn't simply an errand boy to a higher Born. He was a higher Born.

Five hours.

That's how long it took me to realize that him walking me around the fief was not necessarily a good sign. That his tender hold of my arm was meant to manipulate me into believing it was. That his gentle probing of my life before was not pure curiosity.

Twelve hours.

That's how long it took me to figure out the truth. That Victor was not all he claimed to be.

But something more.

It started as an itch I couldn't scratch and blossomed into a well of anxiety the darkness stroked. Feeding my irrationalities and paranoia. Telling me something wasn't right.

The problem was I couldn't see how the pieces fit together. Shards of truth and lies. Slivers of unspoken understandings. Scraps of black and white secondhand information I thought I'd never use.

Twenty-four hours.

That's how long I got to enjoy my freedom before a Vampire stepped through an elevator, shouting about a deal and a devil.

History teachers in America talk about the Revolutionary War and the shot heard around the world. I'd never understood it quite like I did in that moment.

I was walking in the garden with Victor—pretending to marvel at all the things that no longer brought me joy. How could they? The lilies that should be dead this time of year, that shouldn't grow on land this cold and hard, that Victor just loved showing me—shouldn't be alive and thriving. They should be as cold and withered as I am. And yet, they weren't.

Victor plucked one from its stalk with deft, bone-white fingers, offering it to me. It took all of my willpower to reach out and accept the flower without strangling him instead.

"I had these brought here for you, you know," he said. As if that made him some type of saint. Like he was the good guy in this story. Like he deserved my thanks. My praise.

Still, I tilted my head submissively and murmured, "Thank you."

"You know, flower, I have found your obedience to be quite refreshing. Enough so that..." He paused. In the distance at the far edges of where my hearing could reach, a man was shouting. I frowned.

No one ever raised their voice here. For one, the Born did not tolerate it.

For two, it wasn't needed.

Yet someone was shouting.

"What is that?"

He scowled. I tried not to grimace about what that might mean for me, given what happened last time he was displeased. The darkness pulsed just beneath my skin, I tried to pull it tight, but it was too late. He tilted his head, examining me closely.

"Something wrong, flower?"

I shook my head slowly, thankful for the lack of a beating heart and rushing blood. It's amazing how much less fear one can feel when your biological urges are no longer riding you.

"No, I just..." I stumbled for the briefest of seconds and had to close my mouth and bow my head. It was that or let him see how little he frightened me. "My apologies, sir."

"There is no need, my beautiful flower. I think I see what's going on here." I stayed silent. "You're concerned for my well-being, aren't you?"

I pressed my lips together at how laughable that idea was. Not that he could know that.

Not until I knew for certain if I was right. Until it was time.

I raised my face, widening my eyes so they appeared larger. Innocent, despite the blood on my hands. The blood I so easily spilled for this man. For my freedom.

"Yes," I murmured, speaking softly so he took my lie for sincerity.

Victor raised a hand to my cheek, cupping it.

"You are perfect, Lily. Simply perfect." He dropped his hand away, holding it out for me to take. Victor was not a gentle man. He wasn't a man at all. He was a cold-blooded killer.

327

A murderer. A Vampire.

But I suppose we were no different in that way.

I placed my hand in his.

"Come. You are ready."

We walked hand in hand through a garden that flourished on blood and bones and death. A garden where lilies grew, no matter how harsh the conditions.

And maybe unnatural magic kept them alive.

But unnatural magic was also what kept me alive.

And like these lilies, I was going to survive.

No matter how many lies I had to tell. People I had to kill. Pieces of my soul I had to sell.

I would survive.

And with the sunrise behind me and my enemy leading me, I turned my back on the light. Embracing the darkness.

The shouting grew louder. More fevered. Desperate. I straightened my spine as Victor led me down a hallway lined with Vampires. Made. Except unlike me, they were not walking with a Born Vampire towards the double doors at the end of the hall. They were standing outside them.

Red eyes watched me. Cautious. Jealous. Creepy. Everything in-between. I did not spare even a glance in their direction. Maybe that's what separated us.

They were too busy fighting over scraps with each other. I was smart enough to know where the real power was, and strong enough to reach for it.

Victor didn't stop his stride. He walked with purpose. No one questioned him when a pair of lower Born opened those double doors and he ushered us in.

I let my eyes flick up to take a snap shot of the room that my memory would process later. Lowering them again, before anyone, especially Victor, could read the curiosity on my face.

I'd never seen a room as stark white as this one. Pure marble made up every foot, every inch, every crack. It was carved and crafted into ornate walls that rose sixty feet. From where we stood, the floor descended inward. An amphitheater...but with an elevator?

I clenched my jaw, trying to keep my face tight. Impassive.

An elevator in here didn't make sense. This building was old. Really old. Not to mention Vampires didn't seem too fond on most technology, and it wasn't like any of them would need it to get around. We moved faster than an elevator could.

So why did they have it?

A man stood in the center of the floor down below, glaring up at us with hateful eyes. His silver hair and light skin was streaked with mud and grit.

"Gregory Kamarov. We haven't heard from you in a time. What brings you home to the Motherland?"

Victor was the first and only one of the congregated Vampires to speak, drawing their gaze to us. Dozens and dozens of some of the most ruthless predators in the world looked to Victor with respect, and then their eyes dropped to me.

"You bring a Made into the Council, Victor," a Born woman two platforms below said. Her voice cut sharp, like metal meeting metal. "Have you no propriety?"

"What I do is none of your concern, Nikita," Victor replied, his tone pleasant but his words sharp. I didn't move a muscle.

"This is not the time for dinner or pleasantries, Victor. Surely even you can see reason here as to why the lessers are not welcome?" the woman prompted.

A muscle in Victor's jaw twitched.

"What she means to say, Son," said another voice, though I couldn't tell where it came from, "is why have you brought a Made into our sacred space? Surely she could wait outside with the others."

Where was that voice coming from? And why did it sound so old?

Yes, most of them gathered here had to be hundreds, maybe even thousands of years old, but they never sounded like it. This voice did.

"Lily is not like the others, Father. She is special."

How was it that he could pay me a compliment and still make it sound condescending

"Special how?" the same ancient voice spoke, deep and dark, brimming with power.

As the Made in question, I was unsure how I was supposed to respond. How Victor wanted me to respond. When he saw the darkness swirl beneath my skin—what he assumed was for him, his safety—he declared me ready. For what? I wasn't entirely sure.

I had been weak and docile in his mind for months. Hardly worth his time of day until I showed my hand. My power. Which meant he didn't want weak, but he also preferred my obedience. He didn't want me to turn from the violence of this world but I was to be a dog on a chain.

Victor wanted me to straddle a razor edge, where either side ended in my destruction.

Oh, what precarious positions he liked to put me in.

Victor squeezed my hand sharply, but not quite painful. I turned my face to his, asking without saying a word. Asking him what he wanted me to do.

He looked to my hands and jutted his chin toward the female Vampire. Nikita.

Did he mean—was he asking—was I supposed to kill her?

I dropped Victor's hand and took a step towards the edge of the marbled floor. With him, my eyes were to be averted, but with them—with them I would show no mercy. If Victor wanted me to be his guard dog—his pet—unknowingly feeding me while at it...then why not?

I took another step. And then another. And when I reached the edge of the platform, I stepped off and dropped the three feet to the first level in the amphitheater without losing my step.

I walked towards the sneering, belittling woman who would rather see me dead. And when I stood before her, almost a foot shorter, surrounded by other Born who might attack, prepared to have to defend myself, I did not ask Victor what he wanted. I wrapped my small, slender fingers halfway around her hand.

She frowned. "What is the meaning of this—"

I beckoned the darkness forward. Then the screaming started.

"Stop her," the ancient voice commanded. Oh, what a mistake that was.

Any who dared touch me fell to the darkness within as it sought them out in return. They, too, screamed.

Plumes of black danced across my body like moving tattoos, traveling to those who tried to stop me. I held the screaming woman with nothing more than a light grip on her hand. My power invaded their senses, funneling deeper and harder than I had with the child. Aiming to cause pain while I simultaneously harvested their own energy.

"Victor, what is the meaning of this?" the ancient one asked

as darkness began to thicken in the very air, reaching its tendrils to those that weren't even touching me.

Her knees collapsed, hitting the marble floors with a crack.

One by one, those around me began to fall, but they couldn't break their grip. No one could. No one but me.

More, the darkness urged. Take more. Take everything. Leave them as nothing but hollowed-out h—

"Enough," Victor commanded.

The darkness growled, not liking how he spoke to us. Not liking how he thought he could control us. I should make him—

A sharp tug inside made me stop. It was not light or dark, but something else.

I stared down at my chest, following the thin red line that ran between Victor and myself.

What was that—

It tugged again and I dropped the Born Vampire's hand. Her screaming cut short, warbling in her throat like a whimper before falling silent. I stepped away, breaking contact with my other victims, and it wasn't entirely of my own accord.

The darkness in me snarled at the grave insult to our power.

Victor was a Born. He didn't have any power outside that of his bite...unless he had already bit me.

All of those little bits and pieces came crashing together.

Victor's demands. His persona. The way the others looked to him, Made and Born. The way the Made looked to me. It all made sense. Every little bit, if he were my master.

If he could control me.

I raised my eyes to his, the darkness still riding me hard, urging me to rip his throat out. That lying bastard. All this time he'd made me believe my master was someone else. Some other

Vampire that had forced me to undergo the transition, but all this time it was him.

And yet—could I really be surprised?

I didn't think I could. I'd been suspecting it for a few days. Now there was more to him. To us, than he'd led me to believe.

Who was I to know if all I could remember were dark green eyes...

I pulled the darkness inward, hiding it from the Council and from him. Hiding my strength. My knowledge. My power.

Then I climbed the steps and came to stand right at his side like I'd never left. Without making him ask again. That was important. If he brought me here as a demonstration, I needed to play my part perfectly. Make him think he could trust me. Should trust me.

That I was so wholly devoted to my master, to him, that I couldn't possibly be planning to plant a dagger in his heart.

A feather-light touch brushed across the small of my back as he rested his hand there, an almost purr rumbling in his chest. I'd pleased him. Good.

"As I said before, who I bring is no one else's concern. Lily is mine. She will do as I command her, won't you, flower?" *His strong fingers brushed up and down my back in slow, rhythmic circles.*

"Of course."

"Excellent," *he said, almost affectionately. His hand slid lower, curving around my side.* "Now, where were we?"

No one said a word, but all eyes turned to the man standing in the center of the amphitheater.

Gregory Kamarov, that was his name, wasn't it? I filed that away for later.

"I believe, my prince, that your betrothed has taken you for a fool."

A pen could have dropped a mile away and we would have heard it.

"Is that so?" Victor asked, a vengeful edge entering his tone. Unforgiving.

I didn't know who his betrothed was, but something just told me that I may end up being ordered to kill her.

And the prospect didn't bother me as much as it should have.

In fact, it didn't bother me at all.

ONE DAY. Isn't that what I swore?

That one day things would be different.

It was a promise I made to myself on this very balcony beneath the stars during an autumn night standing next to Ash. Here we were. Today was that day, but I didn't quite imagine it like this.

I didn't imagine that when the sun rose for me again, finally, that it might also be the last one Lily ever saw. That even in death, she would never stop fighting to survive—no matter what that turned her into.

"I will get you back. One way or another," I whispered out into the open air.

No one answered me as the sun went down. As it set, I knew that come dawn tomorrow everything was going to change.

CHAPTER 38

IT WAS JUST BEFORE MIDNIGHT WHEN WE ENTERED THE BLACK market.

The scent of sweat, clay, and blood tainted the air. Beneath it, subtler tones laced the breeze. Brutal northern winds, smoke and ash, pine trees from the south, honeysuckle, and sage. No stench of rot and I took that as a good sign.

We beat them here.

Clouds blotted out the sliver of moon, allowing the lights of Vegas to reflect, giving the sky a purple-maroon hue. The wind blew bitter and coarse, cutting me to the core. I tugged my leather jacket tight, stuffing my hands in my pockets as I hurried down the alley and out into the busy street, my footsteps sure and silent. Ordinarily, I would take my time looking at the booths and listening to the vendors as I walked by, but tonight wasn't the night for that. I kept my head down and my pace steady as I approached the pits.

A series of snaps, thuds, and grunts told me a 'match'

was going on below. I wouldn't have thought it with so few people hanging around the edge. The crowd was abnormally small for this time of night. Typically, there were hundreds hovering around the pits, trying to place bets or just get in on the action.

Tonight, there were only seven.

Out of the entire black market that was swarming with paranormals, only seven were standing at the pits. Something wasn't right here...

An uncomfortable scraping brushed against my neck, telling me that not all was what it seemed. I took a step back, stumbling when I bumped into someone.

"Sorry," I muttered, not even turning to look.

I needed to get the hell out of here.

Cold fingers wrapped around my wrist, bringing me to a standstill. Very slowly, I turned to face whoever thought to stop me, blinking twice when I saw who it was.

My mind had to be playing tricks on me. It couldn't possibly be...

"Elizabeth?"

"In the flesh," my youngest cousin quipped. Her chocolate waves had been chopped short and died purple. She sported two nose rings and a bruised cheek. Her clothes were black and disheveled, but mostly fitting. A swipe of black colored her collarbone beneath her crew neck shirt. A tattoo maybe?

"Where have you been?" I asked, not concerned per se, more curious as to what had happened over the past few months for the drastic change in the girl I saw before me. She shrugged coolly, dropping her hand from my wrist.

"Here and there. It's not safe to stay put for too long.

You should consider yourself lucky I made the trip all the way out here for you," she said. I rose both eyebrows. To say she'd changed was an understatement.

"How did you find me?" Apparently, that was a dumb question to her. She cocked an eyebrow and tilted her head forward.

"Really, Selena?" she asked in a hushed voice. "Anastasia is a lot of things, but I find it awfully convenient that after being gone for months she comes back to the same black market I last saw you in and declares a war on Vampires. You sent a message to the world. I hope you're prepared to back it up."

"What's that supposed to mean?" I leaned away, crossing my arms over my chest, trying not to bristle at the implications. There were a lot of ways to interpret her last sentence. None of them boded well for me.

Elizabeth unzipped her jacket and pulled out a manila folder. "You wanted to know why Anastasia was after you. I think I found the reason." She extended it to me and my fingertips tingled where I touched the envelope. A heavy feeling settled into my stomach.

"How? Blair said the mansion had been burned down..."

"I burned it down."

I blinked rapidly, playing that over in my head to make sure I heard it right.

"Did you just say—"

"Yes. I burned the mansion down," she repeated. "After you went batshit, I snuck out of the apartment and took the elevator to the black market in Detroit. It was easy since it was just me. From there, I hitched a ride with some elderly pixies in a biker gang"—she paused when my mouth fell open—"and made it back to the mansion. Took me nearly two days to find my mom's secret office, but I did. This," she tapped on the envelope in my hand, "is everything I found. Make sure you open it alone."

I narrowed my eyes in confusion. My spine prickled in apprehension. "Why?"

Elizabeth hesitated, biting her lip in indecision before saying, "Because what's inside that folder changes everything, and I don't know if you're going to want to change."

My muscles tensed, my fingers itching to open this here and now, but if what she said was true...I unzipped my jacket and slipped it inside.

"Why are you doing this? I've been nothing but awful to you after last spring. I'm not apologizing because I thought you deserved it, but why help me?" I asked. My fingers trembled with the zipper as I closed it.

"I..." Elizabeth paused, sighing to herself. "I'm a lot of things. A coward included. I honestly don't know why I'm helping you. I wasn't planning to until I realized what it all meant." She paused again, shifting from foot to foot as if weighing something back and forth in her mind. "I don't like you. I don't think you're a good person, but I don't think you're bad either. I think...you're somewhere in-between, and right now the world needs an in-between. Someone that can do bad things for the right reasons. That folder has the power to change the world, but only you can do it. You and Alexandra."

I gaped at her, completely and utterly stunned.

I'd said almost the same exact thing not forty-eight hours prior. Funny how it seemed like so much time had passed. When in reality, it wasn't all that long at all.

Elizabeth backed away, slowly slinking toward the crowd. I made no move to stop her.

Instead, I whispered, "Thank you."

She nodded and then disappeared into the crowd like she'd never been here in the first place. It took a moment for me to collect myself and my thoughts. By the time I'd sorted through enough to leave it for later, I became distinctly aware that someone was watching me.

The scent of pine and forests hit me. Familiar, but not recently so...

I whirled around, my fists tightening, ready for a fight.

"Hello, Selena."

Well, if it was none other than my piece-of-shit ex-boxing partner that got my sister killed.

What an unpleasant surprise.

Tori would be arriving with the others very soon, and it was going to make her and Alexandra's relationship awkward when I killed him.

CHAPTER 39

"Lucas," I breathed. A slicing sensation ran down my chest, opening the void of memories that I never wanted to recall.

It burned like vodka, but that was betrayal for you.

"You're looking well," he commented. I could easily have returned the statement, but to even speak to him...I prided myself on my self-control, but seeing his face— perfect, tan, healthy, *alive*—I didn't know how long I could hold it in.

The resentment. The anger. The hate.

His raven black hair, just as dark as mine, was trimmed as if not a day had gone by. He wore a suit, black and white. All it was missing was the red.

I bit my lip, the copper taste clearing my mind. Reminding me that if he was here, so was Anastasia. This is what we wanted. This is what I worked for.

And still, it was only the bitter truth that escaped my lips.

"You killed my sister," I spat. Instinctively, I took a step towards him and he grinned that all too familiar lopsided smile. His eyes, once emerald green, were nearly black.

"No. I found your sister and carried her to the ballroom. *You* killed your sister because you couldn't control your power. So, you see, Selena, we're both monsters." His paper white teeth glinted in the low light, making his smile look sharper. Feral.

Blood rushed to my head.

Did he really just say that?

"I would be very careful with your words, Lucas, because I could kill you with a thought. A. Single. Thought. Can you even comprehend that? The kind of power I hold? Because very soon, that power is going to be the death of you."

The wind picked up, howling in my ears like a wounded animal still grieving the loss I felt so acutely. Dead or undead, Lily had suffered immeasurably so, and it was the only reason Lucas was still alive. He needed to suffer too.

"So bloodthirsty. I'm happy to see that time with the animals hasn't changed you," he grinned. I grit my teeth.

"Why are you here, Lucas?" I asked him sharply. He laughed, and it was nothing like the way he used to and I was grateful for that. Before, it would be a quiet, thoughtful chuckle. Now, it was loud, boisterous, and obnoxious.

"For you, of course."

Of course. Like that was a given. A guarantee.

My head grew hot and my heart beat erratically, trying to keep up with the growing fire inside of me. I couldn't let that power out. Not yet.

"For me?" I asked, my voice dripping with condescension. "How on earth do you think that you'd ever have a shot with me after everything you've done?" The grin on his face froze and slowly started to fall. "You lied to me for *over a year* about Aaron and made me feel bad for not telling you my secrets—even though mine had *nothing* to do with you and could have gotten me killed if the wrong people found out. That alone is inexcusable." His eyes tightened as he clenched his jaw. "But kidnapping my sister? Killing my sister? Lucas, I don't know what la-la-land you've been living in, but I am going to take great pleasure in killing you."

His tan skin flushed as his breathing sped up. Clearly, not as unaffected as he would like to seem.

"You keep saying that, yet you haven't tried to kill me once." He touted this, like it was infallible proof of my devotion. I threw my head back and laughed, just as cold, callous, and cruel as he had been to me.

"You think," I started, having to pause for another bout of mocking laughter, "that because I haven't killed you *yet*, that means I *won't*?" I lifted my head to look him in the eye and let him see the truth in my words. "You poor, pathetic fool. I haven't killed you because I want to draw it out."

His head jerked back as if I'd slapped him, but I hadn't taken a single step.

"You can't mean that..." he stumbled for the first time, struggling with his words.

"Oh, I can, and I do," I assured him, not hesitating in the slightest. His eyes darkened to a true black that I would have mistaken for demonic had I not known that it wasn't possible for other demons to be created. Still, it was unnatural. A sign of Anastasia's influence over him.

"Then it appears I will just have to change your mind,"

he replied, his face going impassive. I narrowed my eyes at him.

"What is that supposed to mean?" I snarled, not liking the implied threat behind his warning. He smiled again, but there was nothing sincere about it.

"Anastasia promised you to me, and I will have you. Even if I have to kill the other half of your soul to do it," he replied.

He couldn't possibly be insinuating...

Behind him, coming from the pit, an animal roared.

No. Not an animal...

"Selena!"

I ran past Lucas, as fast as my feet would carry me, pushing two blokes out of the way so I could stare down over the edge of the pit.

No. No. No. No. No.

This cannot possibly be happening.

Not again.

Ash sat slumped over in a wooden chair. Bound, but not gagged. His skin blurred, as if he was trying to shift...but couldn't. Beside him stood none other than Anastasia.

Holding a knife to his throat.

"I got your message. I thought you might like one of my own," she sneered. Her lovely, beautiful face contorting into something ugly and dark. It was only at that exact second that I noticed something off about her.

Her eyes. They were no longer blue, but black.

Demon black.

Inside me, Valda sighed as if she already knew the answer I was only just coming to.

"*Hello, Cirian,*" she whispered softly.

No fucking way.

Behind me, people began shouting. I couldn't hear them and maybe that was because I didn't care. In that brief fraction of a second that I took to come to realization of what—who— Anastasia truly was, she slit his throat.

Scarlett flowed like a crimson tide, straight out of a holy book.

My chest throbbed painfully tight and my throat constricted. I couldn't think. I couldn't breathe. All I knew was that my heart should have stopped.

I loved my sister. I loved her dearly.

But I can honestly say I'd never felt pain like I did in that moment.

It was like...my soul being ripped in half.

I didn't even have time to see red. To anguish.

All I knew was how to act.

The world flashed from black to white, like an optical illusion that no one but me could see. It was everything and nothing simultaneously.

It was matter.

And it was mine to control.

Using nothing more than my thoughts, I pulled the injured pieces of Ash's throat back together. Forcing the arteries and muscles and veins to fuse, forcing the skin to reconnect and repair.

It shouldn't have been possible, not for a simple telekinetic.

But for a matter manipulator, *nothing* was impossible.

I could break and remake.

Hurt and heal.

Fixing Ash was no more than putting a shattered window back together again.

It was the opening of that kind of power, the creaking of the valve that suddenly thickened the air.

In a blink so fast that even time may have missed it, Ash went from bleeding—dying— to healed entirely, but unconscious.

I moved from the edge of the pit to the center down below.

And Anastasia...disappeared.

When time caught up, I did not feel it resume, but the shouts that had been following me were now suddenly much clearer, and the incoming storm louder.

Thunder rolled as lightning cracked across the sky. It had gone from a slightly cloudy night to a nasty combination of rain and snow. That had to be Blair, but I couldn't afford to focus on that just yet. Not with Ash unconscious and bound to a chair.

Mentally I unraveled the ropes. They disintegrated into a pile of mush beneath him, mixing with the dirt and blood.

So much blood.

I tried not to think about it as I went around to his side and slid his arm around my shoulder. He wasn't heavy to me in the slightest, but his body was cumbersome. I had to re-secure my sliding grip on his wrist three times before I dared jump the fifteen feet, pulling him with me.

We landed rough, sliding across the muddy ground in a pile of limbs. The storm raged over us, but Ash didn't wake.

"Goddamnit. Come on, you lazy oaf, wake the hell up—"

"Oh my god. Aaron. Aaron!" Another panicked voice

brought my cursing to a halt. I looked up at Amber's stricken face as she saw him and the deep crimson shade of his clothing.

"He's fine. Unconscious, but fine," I told her. Her hands shook as she got down and frantically searched for a wound.

"But there's so much blood!"

"Amber—"

"So much—"

I slapped her.

"Damnit, Amber, he's fine! I'm his signasti. Wouldn't I know? Anastasia slit his throat, but I fixed it. Okay? So I need you to calm down." I spoke in a calm, self-assured voice, even though I was anything but. The truth is that I was worried, but I didn't have time to perseverate. He was alive, and for now that would have to do.

Amber lifted a hand to her cheek, her lips parting in surprise. It took a full three seconds for the dazed and confused look to wear off and she saw the scene for what it was.

"We need to move him," she started slowly.

"Yes," I nodded. "But I need to be here fighting. Anastasia is still around here somewhere, and I did not just stick my neck out for her to slip between my fingers. Can you get him to the elevator on your own?"

"Go. I will take care of him. You're needed out there." She didn't waste another second speaking with me as she turned her full attention to Ash. I knew he was alright. I felt it. But I wanted to be with him and I couldn't. There was nothing I could say or do now.

I pulled myself up, breathing in the blood and stench of death.

All around me people were fighting.

Where they had come from, I didn't know, but they were clearly here.

What I did notice was that not even one was a Vampire. Made or Born.

My eyes swept the street, searching for signs of Anastasia.

I found Johanna holding her own against three larger males, Oliver and Liam had teamed up while Scarlett appeared to be using this as a chance to take out her anger on those she viewed as traitors. I couldn't say I blamed her when I was searching for where in god's name Lucas had gone.

Of course, it was right at that moment that I saw it.

Fire. Hellfire, to be specific, coming from the other end of the market.

I took off sprinting and didn't look back.

CHAPTER 40

OBSIDIAN FLAMES SWIRLED BEFORE ME. A TEMPEST OF DEATH. OF ruin.

I could not control the flames of hell, nor could I find a way through them to the other side. A nasty combination of rain and ice hailed around us, but the cyclone before me stayed untouched, acting as a wall of flame that separated me from my sister.

No one could put those flames out except for Alexandra.

No one but me could talk her demon down.

I ran at the wall of fire hoping for one desperate moment that I was wrong. Just as I began to feel any heat, the fire brought me to an abrupt stop. I rebounded, falling on my ass.

No. This can't be happening. It can't be—

What was I doing? Sitting here, panicking like this was the end of the line. I was a matter manipulator, goddamnit. *Anything* was possible. Isn't that what I keep saying?

There was a way into the cyclone and I was going to find it.

Trying to break through that wall would be useless. I couldn't even see on the other side, and with Alexandra's powers interfering with my own, ground entry wasn't going to be an option.

Which only left the top.

Where the winds were the worst and the fire fanned in wide sweeps.

It was also a solid hundred feet high off the ground. Higher than I could easily jump.

But not so high that I couldn't lift myself.

Heat pounded at my head as I began to sweat through my clothes. I couldn't burn, but that fire was hotter than anything here on earth. This was going to be one hell of a stunt if I could pull it off.

I widened my feet in a solid stance, closing my eyes. Darkness and death awaited me there, but it wasn't my mind that I was taking a trip through. I reached for the power inside me, the energy that whorled beneath my skin. It zapped through, pulling the air tight.

At its most primal level, I could build and destroy. Create and recreate.

At a fundamental level in how I learned control, it all started with one thing.

Moving an object from one place to another.

This wasn't so different, right?

Right now was not the time to be questioning myself. I didn't need the Selena that was working through her shit. I needed the Selena that never gave a shit. The one that fought down demons and Vampires without blinking an eye. The one that collapsed a building in her rage and grief.

The one that created an earthquake that spread hundreds of miles.

I needed a way to be both her and the girl I've been.

To be neither of them, and simultaneously both.

I needed to be...whole.

I could not be the girl I was three months ago any more than I could be the girl I was three days ago, or the girl I would be tomorrow. All I could be is what I was now. In this moment.

And right now, it was time for the world to know that the matter manipulators had returned.

That *I* had returned. That I was fighting. That I would not give up.

I would not bow. I would not accept failure.

Success was the only option.

And with that thought, I launched myself into the air. The winds Blair generated became my booster as I swept them up under my body, sending me higher. The air thinned as I shot well above the cyclone, reaching my pinnacle directly above the swirling vortex of fire and ash.

I hovered midair at the apical of my leap, staring down into the hellscape that awaited me. From this angle, it looked like the gaping mouth of a giant beast waiting to swallow the world whole. I could not make out the bottom, but I also did not feel fear. For my sister, for my vengeance, for my Ash—down the rabbit hole I would go.

Gravity caught up with me, whereas at the height of my jump it had been a vacuum, now I was sucked into the wormhole.

Fire licked at my exposed hands, eating at the edges of my clothes. A roaring filled my ears with the shouts and screams of those both inside the cyclone and the flames themselves. The scent of burning flesh and fur and cloth made me close my mouth and hold my breath against the ashes that sprayed the air.

I bit my tongue as the ground rushed in. Faster and faster, bracing my legs for the impact that was to come. I extended my feet, softening my knees, and at the very first touch of ground beneath my feet, I let my momentum carry me downward.

Strands of purple and black energy exploded outward as I landed, kneeling in the dirt, a single fist planted in the baked mud. The ground trembled upon my impact, collapsing inward before the force rolled out in a tidal wave of dirt and concrete.

A veil of dust and debris billowed in the sharp breeze as the rain and ice and fire began to die away. I swept a hand out and the cloud of filth sank to the ground where it settled in the mud.

In front of me, the terrain slanted, climbing until it tapered at the top. I frowned, rising off my knee to turn in a circle.

Suddenly, the slant made sense when I realized it wasn't an odd change in terrain, but that I stood at the bottom of a crater. One that my impact had created.

I turned in circles. Looking for any sign of my sister among the bodies that littered the ground.

But her fiery red hair wasn't one of them. I swallowed hard, unable to assume the worst.

Because if I did, if I let myself think that something could have possibly happened to her...it wasn't an option.

"Alexandra!" I yelled, my voice growing hoarse on the

third shout. I turned in circles, searching far and wide for either her or Anastasia, but neither of them were anywhere to be found. However, someone else was.

"You," I spat, leaping from the crater to flat ground.

I stalked toward Lucas, prepared to deliver the wrath of a god.

"Selena," Tori warned. There was an edge to her voice as she stepped in front of her brother. I didn't even think twice about pushing her aside.

"You lying piece of shit," I snarled. "Where are they?"

"Where is who?" Lucas asked, grinning like a damn fool. He readjusted his suit coat and presented me with a million-dollar smile.

Like a dog kicked one too many times, I snapped back.

Faster than he or anyone could react, I wrapped my hand around his neck and squeezed, drawing a tight, audible gasp. I pulled him down, making him fall to his knees before me.

"Where is Anastasia? Where'd she take Alexandra? Where is Lily being held?" I shouted in his face, not paying enough attention to how hard I squeezed. Lucas's eyes started to turn red around the pupils as he attempted to pull my hand from his neck.

"Let go of him," Tori ordered. I didn't twitch a muscle.

"Not until he tells me what I want to know."

I squeezed tighter, willing Lucas to talk. Willing him to fix this broken desperation in my chest that made me want to scratch and claw and scream.

"You're killing him!" she screamed. Small, pale hands tried to pry us apart, but Tori was no match for a demon.

And me—I was no match for my rage.

"If he dies, then I'll be seeing him in hell," I replied.

A bright red flush crept up his cheeks, quickly replaced by a darker purple. I shook him once, squeezing tighter. Liquid condensed in the corners of his eyes, spilling over, down his cheeks, dropping onto my hand.

I could do it. Right here and now.

Crush his windpipe. Hold him down as he choked to death by my touch.

My touch that he craved *so* much, he got Lily killed. He tried to get Ash killed. And now Alexandra was missing.

He deserved this—he deserved to die—

"*Don't do it.*" The voice surpassed all shields, permeating every crevice of my mind, making his presence known.

Ash.

"*Don't do it, Selena. He's not worth it.*"

"She got away, Ash!" I rasped, breathing hard. "Anastasia got away. Alexandra is missing. We don't know where Lily is. It's his fault. He deserves this—"

"*If you kill him, you'll regret it.*"

And there it was. The truth. Cold and hard like a bitter pill. I didn't want to swallow it, but here's the thing about facts. When all that other shit fell to the wayside, the truth would remain. It would endure.

"I hate him," I whispered vehemently, but my grip loosened a notch.

"*Love and hate are two sides of the same coin.*"

I took a shallow, unsteady breath, trying to prepare myself for what I was going to do next when his lips moved.

"No...ake...Ale..."

I narrowed my eyes in confusion, trying to make out

what he was saying. His eyes locked on something just behind me before rolling back in his head. I repeated it over in my mind. Blinking rapidly when it clicked. "Not... take...Alexandra."

I dropped Lucas and spun where I stood.

The black market looked like something truly out of hell.

Tents had been burned. Blood ran in the streets. The dead littered the ground. The skies calmed down to release a light misting. The cyclone of hellfire had died out entirely leaving only small patches here and there that continued to burn, but those were fading too. Slowly, but surely.

I searched the hellscape we created for a shock of bright red hair.

A light in the darkness.

But no such hair existed.

Behind me were Tori and Lucas.

Coming down the street, Oliver was helping a hobbling Johanna while Scarlett carried Liam.

Amber and Ash were nowhere in sight, but if he could pass my shields and speak to me, I knew they were okay.

To my left, the market had been decimated. Whether it had been my earth shattering, crater-creating impact—or the storm Blair created—I wasn't sure.

But standing on top of ten-foot-tall pile of ruined booths and splintered wood were Alec and Blair. They were ripping debris and garbage up by the handful, desperately trying to get to something—someone—when a hand shot through the hole they'd created.

My heart thrummed, hopeful but so scared to hope.

A second hand appeared and Blair leaned over to grasp them both.

Pulling up a girl with flaming...*black* hair.

She released her and the other girl lifted her chin, searching the remains of the devastated market. She twisted her hands together, a familiar nervous gesture. I doubt she even noticed the way she picked at her hair, even though it was on fire and kind of hard to ignore.

Her eyes met mine and I had to think this wasn't a complete and total failure.

One of her eyes was the same chocolate brown it'd always been.

The other was midnight black.

Alexandra and her demon had merged.

My little sister was safe and sound, even from herself.

I just wished I could say the same about the other one.

CHAPTER 41

I SAT AT THE END OF THE COUCH WITH ASH'S HEAD IN MY LAP. THE light coming from the fireplace reflected shadows across his face, still pale from the blood loss.

I suppose I should have been counting my blessings that I was able to save him, but after what went down tonight...I shook my head, running my fingers through his hair.

Someone squeezed my shoulder gently and I looked up. Blair stood beside me, leaning against the couch. Her grey eyes were shadowed, as if she was still fighting with the beast that lurked within.

"What happened out there tonight?" I asked her, still unable to believe it all myself. "We had them. Anastasia was in the market. How did she get away?"

Blair shook her head, sighing deeply.

"It's not that simple." She shifted away from the couch and went to the double French doors that overlooked the grounds. Not that much could be seen with the skies as dark and ominous as they were, hiding what little light the moon gave off.

"Not that simple," I breathed. My hands clenched into fists. "My sister is still missing. Ash almost died tonight. Meanwhile, Lucas is downstairs still breathing and you want to tell me it's not that simple?" I demanded, a wave of hysteria and madness entering my tone. It had nothing to do with being crazy, and everything to do with the impossible cards I'd been dealt.

"We were ambushed," Alexandra cut in. She sat leaning against the side of the fireplace, resting her flaming hair against the marble exterior. She hadn't figured out how to extinguish them, but it didn't seem to burn anything it touched.

Still, it was better to be cautious before she sent the whole mansion up in flames.

"Ambushed?"

"Yes, but it's not what you think. After the group split, we waited in the alley like we were supposed to. Everything was going according to plan. You and Aaron left. As soon as the screaming started, Jo and her group followed. Tam had Xellos open the portal to start getting people out..." She hesitated, her eyebrows drawing together. "The elevator opened behind us and the next thing I knew, we had a dozen Born Vampires in the alleyway. If it weren't for Alec *already* hiding us, we would have been slaughtered before we could act."

I blinked. "That's not possible. I *saw* the High Council's reaction when Gregory Kamarov showed up. There's no way they would have tried to save her."

Alexandra's eyebrows went up as she shrugged semi-sarcastically. "Well then, I don't know what to tell you because that's sure as hell what it looked like," she snapped.

"Even if they did," I started, taking a deep breath to try and keep my temper, "we were trained to hunt Vampires. A dozen Born against you, Blair, Tori, and Alec shouldn't have been a problem."

Alexandra shrugged again, looking away sharply.

There was something she wasn't telling me.

I opened my mouth to call her on it when another voice piped up.

"It was my fault." Tori raised her head away from her tucked knees, tears glistening in her eyes.

"What?"

True to my promise with myself, I couldn't find it in me to be terribly sympathetic given my night, but I didn't rip her apart immediately.

"I saw Lucas with her and thought I could do some-thin'," she said as her voice trembled. "I ran out into the street after him and the Born saw. Alec came after me. Then him and Lucas started fightin' and Blair got involved. She almost killed Lucas because he almost killed Alec, and next thing I knew, everythin' was on fire and Anastasia was gone."

Silence. Or as much silence as there could be with my blood roaring in my ears.

She blew everything for that lying piece-of-shit that had my sister murdered.

I couldn't even respond because the only possible thing I could come up with either involved throwing her out the

window or telling her how much of an idiot she was—
when neither action would help us now.

For better or for worse, I just had to deal.

"So, basically what I'm hearing is that the Born took Anastasia, but no one bothered with Lucas." I figured repeating the facts to make sure I had this right was the safest thing to do at the moment, for both me and her. Tori nodded, sharing a broken look with my sister that I was positive I wasn't meant to see. If I was being frank, her being Alexandra's rock was one of the only reasons I wasn't tearing into her right then.

"Speaking of, what are we going to do with him?" Amber interrupted. She sat on the other end of the couch with Ash's feet strewn across her lap. Dried blood saturated most of her shirt and stained her entire right arm and half her face. She was tougher than I gave her credit for.

"Question him," I answered like it was obvious. Amber pursed her lips.

"If you do the questioning, he might 'accidentally' end up dead. You sure you want that on your conscience?" Amber asked, cocking an eyebrow.

"She won't be doing the questioning," Johanna answered. "I will."

Under normal circumstances, I might have chaffed at her assumption, but in this case, we did have a better person for the job. As Amber said, me doing it could be... problematic. Tori or Alec wouldn't be well-suited either. We needed a neutral party. Or at least as neutral as a party could reasonably be.

"I think that would be best," Blair said. She shifted side to side uneasily, looking out into the night.

"I agree," I said, shifting to stand up. I lifted Ash's head and stuffed a pillow under it, moving to stand beside Blair. "I don't think I can be in the same room as him right now. After he and Anastasia tried to kill Ash..." I didn't let myself finish that sentence. I'd already lost too much. Tonight had been a massive failure, and that was a bit of an under-statement.

People hadn't just *almost* died. People *did* die. And for what?

For my crazy, insane plan that no one thought would work, but almost did.

I had failed because I'd underestimated Tori's love for her brother, the same love that drove me to these lengths. And now here we were, stuck between a rock and a hard place with fewer options and a climbing body count.

When was it going to stop? When were we going to say enough is enough?

I didn't have an answer for that. To kill Anastasia was to overthrow the Supernatural government. It would plunge the paranormal world into a dark time if there was not someone ready and waiting to step up.

But for that to even come to pass, we had to get close to her and settle this business with the Vampires.

I ran a hand down my face and pinched the bridge of my nose, inhaling slowly.

"So where do we go from here?" I asked them. It was the next obvious question. Accept our losses. Acknowledge why we failed and what we were going to do next.

Except that was the one question no one, not even Johanna or Oliver, seemed to have an answer for.

"Selena, I don't think we can—"

"Don't," I snapped, whirling on Alexandra. "Don't for one second tell me there's nothing we can do. There is *always* something that can be done. We hit a nerve with her and she responded. We were on the right path. There has to be something we can do."

She knocked her head back against the marble siding and closed her eyes. Her chest rose and fell, but she didn't respond.

"Under different circumstances, all the families of the Council have the right to call an accord," Alec said. He stood at the back of the common room slumped against the wall. I couldn't blame him for being exhausted. We all were, but some things couldn't wait for sleep. "But without someone to enforce it—whether it be a group or a single person—there's no one to force Anastasia to abide by it."

"We also have no idea what kind of deal she's made with the Born," Johanna added. She reclined back into Oliver's shoulder, her injured foot propped up on the edge of the black leather couch. "If the Vampires are helping her, it's going to take a miracle to fix this because she *is* the law."

Sitting on the floor in front of them, Scarlett sat stiff as a rod with Liam sprawled out in her lap, unconscious. He suffered a blow to the head by one of Anastasia's goons and sported a nice goose egg but was otherwise fine.

"I just wish we knew why all of this was happening. It doesn't make any fucking sense why she's going after Selena like this. Why she had Lily turned. Why *anything*," Amber grumbled.

"Anastasia only cares about her power..." I started.

"Exactly. So why does she bother with you? It's not like

you're a threat," Amber griped and waved a hand in my direction. "I mean, you are, but you know what I mean."

It's not like you're a threat...

My hand twitched towards the zipper of my jacket.

Where Elizabeth's envelope sat snug against my chest.

What's inside that folder changes everything.

Isn't that what she said?

Jo said we were going to need a miracle. Maybe this was it.

Maybe all hope wasn't lost.

I tugged my zipper down, pulling out the envelope.

There was no writing on the outside. No indication of what I would find. Only a few crinkles and a dark red stain near the bottom edge. It was as untouched as I could possibly hope for.

Elizabeth had told me to open it alone and I hesitated, looking to the people around me.

Their faces were just as grim as mine. Blood coated their hands. Mud splattered their clothes. They didn't have to stand by me through all of this, and I certainly didn't deserve it, but they did. They chose to.

My fingers shook as I bent the aluminum clasp and slipped the seal off of it. The paper made a crackling sound as I parted the opening and reached inside.

"What's that?" Blair said, scooting closer beside me. I pulled out the pieces of paper. There were images printed on them and black Sharpie writing. The words were written in a sloppy scrawl, like someone was in a hurry.

I knew instantly who these pictures belonged to.

"That's my mom's handwriting," Blair breathed. "Where did you get these?" She reached for one of the pictures in my hand, stepping away so she could trail her fingertips over them lightly. Her muscles tensed, but her face remained blank.

"Elizabeth came to me in the market before Lucas and Anastasia showed up. She gave me this folder and told me that it was evidence..." I swallowed hard against the crippling disappointment. "But these are just pictures."

Pictures with paranoid writing. A bedtime lullaby I'd heard a hundred times. A message that I had already received. Answers that I already had, not that they knew that, and I couldn't tell them.

Why was it that every time I thought I found something, a new piece of the puzzle, all I found was another dead-end with a body count?

I schooled my face handing off the rest of the photos to Alexandra. I didn't want to look at them. They were reminders from another time. Where I'd been weak and lost everything.

They took me to a place of memories that weren't real and dreams that couldn't have been planted, and a place inside myself where I didn't know what was right or wrong.

I got down on my knees and brushed the hair out of Ash's face. His eyelids twitched, slowly opening. "Hi there," he breathed. It was more of a rasp, but given that he was alive and talking at all, I'd take it.

"Hi," I said, smiling sadly.

"Did I miss anything good?"

I know he meant it jokingly to try and break the tension. All I could do was press my lips together in an awkward kind of answer.

"Nothing you don't already know," I replied. He looked at me without pity, reaching out to squeeze my hand.

"We'll get her back."

But would it be too late?

I could see that question in his eyes too, although neither of us said it.

"Selena," Johanna asked. There was a curious tone to her voice. An implied frown. I glanced over my shoulder to see her holding one of the pictures. "Who are these pictures of?"

My shoulders tensed but I answered her anyway. "My parents, why?"

She stared at it another minute before she answered.

"I thought you looked familiar."

Huh?

"What are you talking about, Jo?" I pulled away from Ash, moving to stand beside her. She held the one picture that had all of us together. My parents. My sisters. Alive and whole. We couldn't have been older than three or four. Our poofy dresses and bright smiles, so young and innocent.

Johanna stared at the picture, still as statue, before turning to look at me.

She knew something.

"Because," she paused to flip the picture around and point at my father. He looked so different here than any of the memories I held. "This man is Erik Fortescue."

I blinked. My lips parted, and I blinked again.

Was she implying—no, not implying—she was *saying*—

"Your father was Anastasia's uncle, which makes you..."

She let her voice trail off, cocking an eyebrow, waiting for me to say it.

Waiting for me to declare myself a Fortescue, the name that I hated most on this earth. Oh, how the world was cruel, but even so, if it were true...

"That's why Anastasia wants me dead," I mused as those pieces slid together in my mind. "If I'm a Fortescue—and to her knowledge, the only one alive that could challenge her place as Head of the Supernatural Council—then she wants me eliminated before that becomes an option."

My heart kicked into overdrive attempting to keep up with how fast my mind was going. Blair swore softly under her breath.

Elizabeth was right. This changed everything.

If I was a Fortescue, I had a leg to stand on with the Council. I could challenge her for the right to rule—I could do what the current heirs could not.

"But wait," Alexandra said, "if our father *was* Erik Fortescue—a man I have never heard of—then wouldn't I have at least heard his name when we were in a Supernatural school?"

Oliver shook his head.

"He died over a decade ago, and when a member of the ruling family dies, there's a power shift," he explained. "Anastasia was declared heir. Shortly after, she banished anyone from ever talking about it. This is standard for the Fortescues."

Scarlett and the others nodded, but they weren't completely correct.

"He didn't die over a decade ago," I said. "It'll be seven years this coming February."

Alexandra didn't comment one way or the other. She was too absorbed in laying out the photos. Arranging and rearranging them on the floor in front of her, like she could draw a picture that would tell us what we weren't seeing.

"If he didn't die, then someone faked his death," Ash said, getting to his feet. He swayed as he did and I was there to catch him.

"Anastasia?" Amber asked, like it was obvious.

"No," I disagreed. "It's not her style. If she was going to fake it, she would have killed us all, but it wasn't until Daizlei that things started happening..." My voice trailed off, not wanting to say where this plausible train of thought went.

Things had gotten strange ever since that dinner, where she commented on how much we looked alike. A trick, she had called it. More like blood—but a Fortescue? Did I really believe that? It seemed as outlandish as the idea that I was part demon, and that *was* true, so how crazy could it really be?

"My mother knew you were alive," Blair murmured. "That all of you were, and she wouldn't take you until you were older. We weren't to speak of you. Do you think—"

"She was in on it."

All eyes turned to Alexandra who sat staring at the pictures that told a story. She held her hand out and nodded to the picture in my hand. I passed it over, coming to stand behind her as she read the message that I hadn't seen.

The message I had mistaken.

"Girl of fate. Daughter I made. He was here. We could

not stay. Soul in pain. Come back one day. Mother of time. Don't delay. You must take revenge this way."

A cold chill entered my limbs. No, this wasn't quite the same wording as my childhood lullaby. Not when you put the pieces together.

When read here and now, with what I knew...

It wasn't just a warning of what was coming. It was a hint at what already happened. These photos started from the time we were young, well beyond the time when we all had supposedly died.

And the last one. The very last one...it wasn't a picture of my mother or father at all.

But of the old lady in the market with eyes that changed color.

The Crone.

You must take revenge this way.

It was a command scrawled beneath her yellow smile.

"What does this even mean?" Blair swept her hand out towards the pile of photographs, her frown deepening the longer she stared.

"I think," Alexandra said slowly, "it means our parents faked the death of our entire family and buried the evidence so that we would live long enough to stand a chance."

She was close. So close, but not quite right. I opened my mouth and again, no sound would come out. Valda's curse had become mine. Her burden and mine to bear.

This message had been worded so carefully. So close to that childhood rhyme and yet, inexplicably different. This wasn't just a warning to go after Anastasia. This was a command to the Mother telling her what she must do.

Oh yes, my parents bought us time—but the real question here was for what?

My gut roiled again, nausea hitting me with a sudden onslaught at the horror of what I suspected. I choked it down and said nothing.

"Perhaps," Johanna agreed. "But why would they feel they needed to hide you in the first place? What were you trying to stand a chance against?"

Ash came to stand beside me, placing his hand on my lower back, offering what little support he could. If only he knew...if only I could say...

"Thirteen years ago, Selena manifested. Wouldn't you hide your daughter if she was the first matter manipulator in a millennium?" Alexandra said, staring at Jo with one black eye and one brown. "Selena was powerful enough to throw me through a wall at five years old. How powerful was Anastasia? Because if she's willing to sacrifice thousands of lives for power now, what would a single five-year-old have been?"

Oh, Alexandra. You're not wrong. You just don't have the full picture. I clenched my fist, letting my fingernails bite into the soft pad of my palm. We were all covered in so much guck that the tiny droplets of blood that formed went unnoticed.

"This is all bloody well, but why they didn't isn't as important as can we prove it? Can we *prove* that they are indeed Fortescues? And"—Scarlett paused to look at me head on—"will you do what you need to do to put an end to all of this? Will you take up your name and force that lying cow to either face you or die a coward's death?"

Silence.

Would I do it?

Could I?

I turned to Violet, hoping for guidance, but she had no answer for me. It seemed that this decision I had to come to on my own.

I leaned back, pinching the bridge of my nose while I inhaled deeply.

Could I do it? Could I be who they needed me to be? Could I take up a mantle I wanted nothing to do with—a name I despised above all else—to be the rallying face for this war?

To win this war. To survive. To ensure Lily survives—I would do anything.

I had my answer.

"Scarlett, I'll do whatever you need me to do. Wear whatever name you need to me wear. At the end of the day, we're all fighting for the same thing. If that means my name is Selena Fortescue, then so be it."

Scarlett's anger was just and well-founded. I didn't blame her for asking me the hard questions. I'd never wanted to rule anything. I still didn't. Politics and government weren't what I was cut out for, but the same could be said about the thousands of Supernaturals that had been turned into Made over the last six months.

People everywhere were suffering and dying in the Fortescue name.

Families ripped apart. Half breeds considered lesser.

The world was an ugly broken place.

But if two warring families that caused a thousand years of darkness could come together, if I could be born, if a matter manipulator could walk the earth again...

Well, anything was possible.

And just like that, I, Selena Fortescue, became the face of a rebellion that would not just overthrow centuries upon centuries of oppression, but would rattle the very stars our ancients looked down from.

And I could have sworn that in that moment I heard a laugh, dark and lovely.

As if the Goddess of darkness herself was waiting for her chosen heir to do just that.

CHAPTER 42

Vengeance is a virtue. At least to some.

I was not expecting the surprise that awaited me when Victor had me summoned to the very chamber his Council had tried to bar me from. This time there were no such attempts.

The Made did not dare even look at me as they opened the door, silently letting me pass. I obediently strode to Victor's side, pleased by silence from the rest of the Council. It only took a single sweep of my eyes to see that Nikita was absent.

But my glee was short-lived as I saw the woman they had chained to the floor of the amphitheater.

"Flower, I believe you and my betrothed have met," Victor asserted. He rested the flat palm of his hand on my lower back and this time I did not mistake the affection.

"Anastasia," I breathed. My surprise only lasted for a full second at most. In a place like this, you cannot afford surprises. Nor can you afford to be thrown by them.

"Yes, she is the one that gave you to me as a wedding gift. Isn't that kind, flower?" he prompted, always testing me. Always asking more. Still, I gave him the answer he wanted to hear.

"Very. I am lucky to have you as my master," I replied.

We'd never openly acknowledged that I knew, but it seemed to please him that I came to this on my own. His smile sharpened, showing a hint of the predator he was.

"And I am lucky to have you as mine," he purred. I did not reply. "But you see, flower. She lied to me. She told me that in return for my people and our support, she would sire heirs and unite the Supernaturals and the Vampires. As it should rightfully be, don't you think?"

I had no choice but to agree, and frankly, being where I was now on the totem pole, I didn't really give a damn who united with who. Victor gave me a modicum of freedom and it was more than any of the others would have afforded me. I'd feed his ego as long as he liked.

"Certainly, master. Should you wish it," I replied. He continued stroking my back with calculated touches meant to enthrall me.

"Oh, Lily, how you please me. If only my betrothed were half as tolerable as you, I might not have to do this."

Ah, and there it was. The caveat I had been waiting for. I did not ask what. He wouldn't want it. If Victor wanted me to know something he would tell me, and it was my job to know that and not inundate him with stupid questions.

"You see, Anastasia is infertile, flower, and not only is she infertile, but she kept this information from me. She led me to believe that we would have powerful children together, when indeed, she could not give me children at all. Now I came upon this information on my own, but waited for her to come to me and attempt to make amends. Do you know what she did instead?"

I swallowed once but did not delay in responding. "Did she attempt to hide it and go back on your arrangement?" He smiled, somewhat amused.

"She did. She also neglected to tell me she isn't the only living Fortescue. That's a punishable offense, don't you think, flower?"

The hairs of my arms stood on end at the tone of his voice. Victor tucked a stray lock of black hair behind my ear before slowly guiding me down the levels of the amphitheater.

"Yes. Punishable indeed," I agreed. My darkness collided in my chest, wanting free, wanting to punish the girl who gave me this life. I suspected it wouldn't have to wait long, but I didn't dare let it loose.

Not yet. It was still too soon.

"I'm so happy you think so. Despite all of that, it is not what brought this about. Would you like to guess at what brought this about, my dear?" He licked his bottom lip, hungry for violence that he would have me bring.

"No, sir. There are any number of deplorable things she could have done. It would take far too long to guess which one has brought about her reckoning. I would not wish to waste your time even guessing." A sliver of unrequited rage slipped through and he chuckled in delight.

"You are the most pleasing creature I have ever owned, Lily. Leagues above all others." He brushed his fingers around the curve of my hip, but only for a second. "My betrothed broke her vow and publicly declared war on all Vampires, including you and me. She attempted to take the life of Gregory Kamarov, and when she failed, she fled the scene. I simply cannot allow a weak being like that to stand at my side. What would it say to our people?"

We stepped off the final level and onto the flat bottom. My

fingers twitched to end her, but I would not act until the command was given. Not for all the revenge in the world.

Vengeance is a virtue, and with patience, it would be mine.

"That you put a barren Supernatural coward above our people when she is without use," I replied. He liked that phrase. Without use. It was so very standoffish. A slap to the face.

"That it would, flower, you are right again. But our kind do not believe in a breaking of contracts. She is my betrothed, but she is not worthy. What would you have me do were you in my position?"

Oh, sweet, sweet, vengeance.

It would be mine.

"I would have her executed to send both a statement to the Vampires about where your loyalties lie and the Supernaturals about what you will not tolerate." My voice rang clear and true in the dead silence of the Council chambers. Not a single person made a sound.

"If only you weren't Made," he murmured. I don't even think he realized the way he brushed his thumb across my cheek. In this world, I existed for him. No Born would question a master having relations with their Made, so long as they weren't official.

Except perhaps, me. That was a thought for another time.

"I would like to give you a present, Lily, for pleasing me as you do," he continued. His breath smelled of peppermint and tasted of violence. I leaned forward a fraction, waiting for those words I knew I would hear. "Anastasia is yours to do with as you wish. I only ask that she does not leave this room ever again."

I nodded my head, concealing my smile.

"Thank you, sir," I whispered. Victor and I had been playing this game long enough that I knew what he wanted to hear, and he pretended that he did not goad it. Or maybe he really didn't

see the way he led me hand in hand towards his blood-filled world.

He nudged me forward by the small of my back and I did not hesitate to approach the chained woman. Her ankles wore large metal cuffs that trapped her to the floor.

She didn't stir as I advanced, perhaps already accepting of her inevitable death. I could not tell, and frankly, I did not care.

I reached out, placing my fingers under her chin to force her head up. The eyes that met me were not the blue of my nightmares, but the black of my soul.

The darkness snapped like an angry dog, breaking free from its hold in me and tunneling into Anastasia. She did not scream or cry as my victims often did.

No, she smiled as I searched through her essence, drawing it into me, feeding from it.

And in that final moment, I could have sworn I encountered a murky essence that tasted old...and her smile was of relief. Without realizing what I'd done, her energy began to fade and that ancient mass that slept inside of her turned to me, meeting my darkness like an old friend as it slipped inside my skin.

I shuddered for a moment as the invasive energy spread through me. As quickly as it had started did it settle and all that remained was a closeness with something that was not wholly me.

"Hello, Lily," it whispered in my mind. I blinked.

"What are you?" I asked silently, not afraid, but curious. I've stared into the dark so long now that voices and shadows were not unwelcome.

"Someone that has waited a long time to find a soul so well matched. We are going to do beautiful and terrifying things, my

dear." His presence was cold as it clung to my own, but I did not try to force it away. I couldn't if I tried.

I dropped my hand from the husk that remained of Anastasia. It echoed as it hit the marble floor. Bones and dust.

Anastasia Fortescue was no more.

SUNLIGHT STREAMED through the window of the common room as I jerked awake. Ash's strong arms were still wrapped around me where we had been sleeping on the couch. My body trembled and shook, quaking with such fear that it was only his exhaustion that had to have kept him from waking beside me.

Anastasia was dead. Lily had killed her. Reaping the vengeance that she so sought.

And in doing so, she damned herself to this curse.

Cirian had not died with Anastasia, but had gone to the next living Fortescue that could carry him.

And in the morning light of a new day, I wept silently for the sister whose soul died too.

Acknowledgments

Never have I had a book that tore me up so much to write. Every day was like pulling teeth to sit down at the computer and smash out this story. Despite that though, I couldn't get it out of my head. I would lie awake for hours at night thinking about it. I would wake up exhausted but unable to stay away from work for long because I felt this kind of compulsive need to get it out. In many ways, this is the most draining book I have ever written. I couldn't look at it for over a month afterward. But—I also think, it's probably the book that is closest to my heart. The journey Selena went on was an incredible rollercoaster from this author's point of view, and I hope that you, dear reader, feel the same. I poured everything I had into this book and I hope it shows. Thank you for supporting me and waiting for the story to come. I hope that as much as some of you may be cursing my name right now, you are excited to see where Selena's journey goes as she prepares for the fight of her life.

To Courtney, Carrie, and Analisa: you guys are my tribe and without your continuous support I think this book would not have gone the way it did. There were times that I wasn't sure how I was going to get through it. You guys are always there though, not just for the high days, but the low as well. I love you guys to pieces. Thank you.

Lastly, to Matt: I truly don't think I could have done this one without you. For the things you've taught me over the years and the love you've shown me. It sounds really corny to say, but I don't think I could write it if I didn't know or understand it. Thank you for being in my life and showing me what acceptance looks like.

Printed in the USA
CPSIA information can be obtained
at www.ICGtesting.com
CBHW020848220624
10493CB00023B/81